HANNAH'S CHOICE

*H*ANNAH'S CHOICE

A NOVEL

Jan Drexler

Revell

a division of Baker Publishing Group
Grand Rapids, Michigan

© 2016 by Jan Drexler

Published by Revell
a division of Baker Publishing Group
P.O. Box 6287, Grand Rapids, MI 49516-6287
www.revellbooks.com

Printed in the United States of America

Library of Congress Cataloging-in-Publication Data
Drexler, Jan.
    Hannah's choice : a novel / Jan Drexler.
        pages ; cm. — (Journey to pleasant prairie ; #1)
    ISBN 978-0-8007-2656-0 (pbk.)
    I. Title.
PS3604.R496H36 2016
813'.6—dc23   2015030806

Scripture used in this book, whether quoted or paraphrased by the characters, is taken from the King James Version of the Bible.

This book is a work of fiction. Names, characters, places, and incidents are the product of the author's imagination or are used fictitiously. Any resemblance to actual events, locales, or persons, living or dead, is coincidental.

Author is represented by WordServe Literary Group.

16 17 18 19 20 21 22   7 6 5 4 3 2

To my dear husband.
The best friend a woman could ever have.

Soli Deo Gloria

1

Conestoga Creek, Lancaster County
October 1842

Hannah Yoder stamped her feet against the October evening chill seeping through her shoes. Darkness already reigned under the towering trees along Conestoga Creek, although the evening sky had shone pale blue as she walked along the path at the edge of the oat field minutes ago. The north wind gusted, sweeping bare fingers of branches back and forth against scudding clouds.

Where was Adam? She had been surprised to see his signal after supper, when *Mamm* had asked her to check on the meat in the smokehouse. She had been surprised to see the bit of cloth hanging on the blackberry bushes so late in the day. They had used the signal since they were children, ever since Adam had discovered that they both liked spying birds' nests in the woods.

She shivered a little. The cloth on the brambles had been blue instead of the yellow Adam always used. It could be a mistake. Perhaps one of her brothers had caught his shirt on the brambles instead.

A breeze fluttered dry leaves still clinging to the underbrush around her. She would wait a few minutes more, and then go back into the house. When a branch cracked behind her at the edge of the grove, Hannah lifted the edge of her shawl over her head, tucking a loose tendril of hair under her *kapp*, and slipped behind a tree. Let him think she was late. It would serve him right to worry about her for a change. He had been so serious lately. What was it about turning twenty that made him forget the fun they had always had? Would she be the same in two years?

Like a hunting owl, a figure flitted through the trees to her right. Hannah stilled her shivering body, waiting for Adam's appearance, but the figure halted behind the clump of young swamp willows at the edge of the clearing. So, he was waiting to frighten her when she arrived. Hannah smiled. She'd circle around behind and surprise him instead.

As she gathered the edges of her cloak to pick her way through the underbrush, she heard a giggle from her left. Liesbet? Hannah waited. She didn't want her younger sister spying on her conversation with Adam.

The wind tore fitful clouds away from the harvest moon, illuminating the clearing as Liesbet stepped into the light.

"Where are you?" Liesbet peered into the dark underbrush. "Come now, I know you're here."

Hannah clenched her hands. Liesbet was like a pesky gnat at times, always following her when she wanted to be alone. She was ready to step out from behind the tree to confront her when Liesbet spoke again, in English instead of *Deitsch*.

"George, stop playing games with me. You're going to scare me."

Hannah froze. Who was George?

Suddenly a man leaped from the trees behind Liesbet and caught her around the waist. She turned with a little shriek and fell into his arms.

"George, you did it again. I know you're going to be the death of me one day."

Hannah covered her mouth to keep a gasp from escaping. The man who had been hiding among the willows wasn't Adam.

"Ah, lass, you're so much fun to scare, but you know 'tis only me, not some ghoulie prowling around the woods here."

Liesbet giggled and snuggled closer to George. As he turned into the moonlight, Hannah could see him clearly, from his blue corded trousers to the snug-fitting cap perched on top of his head. His cocky grin reminded her of a fox carrying off a chicken from the henhouse. Certainly not an Amish man, or even Mennonite or Dunkard. She had never seen him before, but Liesbet had, for sure. She ducked farther behind her tree before either one of them could spot her.

"Give us a kiss, lass. The boys and I are only here for the one night. We're heading on to Philadelphia tomorrow."

Hannah could hear the pout in Liesbet's voice. "You're going away again? You never spend any time with me."

"Aye, and my sweet Lizzie, whenever I ask you to come along, you always play the little girlie who stays at home."

"It wouldn't be proper for me to tag along with you and your friends."

George's low laugh sent chills through Hannah. "No, lass,

not proper at all." Then his voice took on its teasing tone again. "Admit it, you're just too young."

"I'm nearly sixteen!"

"Aye, like I said, you're just too young."

They grew quiet, and then Hannah heard a groan from George. She risked a glimpse around the tree. Liesbet was pressed up to him, her hands clinging to his shoulders while she kissed him. As Hannah watched, the man pulled Liesbet closer, one hand reaching up to pull off her kapp and letting her blond curls tumble to her shoulders. He buried his fingers in her hair, continuing the kiss until she struggled to pull out of his grasp. She stepped just beyond his reach and gave him a coy look.

Liesbet, what are you doing?

"Do you still think I'm too young?"

"Lizzie, you're enough to drive a man to distraction."

Hannah heard a warning in George's voice, but Liesbet turned her back on him and walked to the edge of the clearing. She was playing games with the man, but the look on his face in the moonlight was hungry. Predatory. Hannah shivered again.

"When will you get back?"

"In a week or so, you can bet on that, and then I'll be around for another of your kisses."

Liesbet turned to look at him, her face a careful pout. "Why can't you stay here? I don't like it when you're gone so much."

"I have to go, Lizzie, but you know I can't stay away from you too long."

There was another pause as Liesbet turned her back on the man. Hannah would have smiled if Liesbet's game wasn't so dangerous. It wasn't often she didn't get her way.

George snaked out a hand to catch her elbow and pull her close. "Lizzie, lass, give me another kiss. The lads are waiting for me."

After another lingering kiss, George released Liesbet and turned her around, giving her a solid swat on the behind before he took off along the creek bank, whistling as he went.

Hannah watched Liesbet as she stood in the clearing, bouncing on her toes, humming the same tune George had been whistling, her pretend pout gone.

Stepping out from behind her tree, Hannah tugged her shawl off her head. "Liesbet, what are you doing?"

Liesbet jumped, and then turned on her sister. "You were spying on me?"

"It's a good thing I saw you. Who is that man and what are you doing with him?"

Liesbet hugged herself and smiled at Hannah. "He's my beau."

"Your beau? You mean he's courting you?"

"Of course he is. You were the one spying on us. Didn't you see him kiss me?"

"Just because a man takes a kiss doesn't mean he has courting on his mind."

Liesbet waved her hand in the air to brush Hannah's concerns away. "You're just jealous because you're not the only one with a secret beau. I know how you and Adam meet out here in the woods and your silly signal flag on the bushes." Her voice gloated.

Hannah felt the blood drain from her face. "Adam's not so secret, and he's not my beau. We've known each other all our lives."

"*Ne*, Adam's not secret, but *Daed* doesn't know he's asked you to marry him."

Hannah caught her lower lip between her teeth to keep herself from retorting to Liesbet's accusation. *Ja*, Adam had spoken of marriage, but it was just a game they played. He wasn't serious.

Liesbet's smile set Hannah's teeth on edge. "And I know I saw him kiss you the other day."

Hannah felt her face heat up. Adam had stolen a kiss, one that had made her heart pound, but one kiss didn't mean anything, did it?

"Surely you can't compare that to what I just saw between you and that . . ."

"His name is George McIvey, and I'm going to marry him."

"Liesbet, you can't!"

"I am, and you can't stop me. If you say anything to Daed, I'll tell him all about how you and Adam have been sneaking around." Liesbet lifted her chin as she faced Hannah. "I'll tell Mamm too."

"Liesbet, not Mamm. You'll set her off on one of her spells," Hannah protested, but Liesbet had won the argument. There was nothing she could do to stop her sister except give in to her demands, the way she had for the last nine years. Liesbet still played the delicate invalid, even though Hannah suspected she had outgrown the effects of the diphtheria long ago.

And she couldn't have Liesbet spreading tales about their neighbor. It didn't matter that Hannah was eighteen and well into courting age. Adam wasn't Amish.

"Then you keep my secret, and I'll keep yours," Liesbet said.

Hannah hesitated. Liesbet smiled the way she always did when she knew she was getting her way, and her eyes glinted in the moonlight.

"But what if that man is dangerous? Can he be trusted? How long have you known him?"

A frown crossed Liesbet's face, and then the moon disappeared behind another cloud and the clearing was shadowed once more. Hannah could barely see her sister's silhouette against the darker trees behind her.

When Liesbet spoke, her voice was unsure. "I've known him long enough, and he's never been anything but kind to me."

"He isn't one of us. He isn't Amish."

"He isn't a backward Dutchman, you mean." Liesbet's voice was bitter, her uncertainty vanishing as quickly as it came.

Hannah gasped. "You better not let Daed hear you talk like that."

"Don't worry, I won't. But you can bet I won't be marrying any stick-in-the-mud farmer, either."

Hannah took a step toward her sister. "But, Liesbet, you'll break Mamm's heart . . . Promise me you won't see him anymore."

Liesbet shrugged, the movement only a rustle in the dark. "Whatever you want." She turned and ran back toward the house, a shadow in the night.

Left alone in the clearing, Hannah wavered. Following Liesbet would be a waste with her sister's harsh words ringing between them.

The wind blew another swirl of leaves along the floor of the clearing, propelling Hannah's feet to action. Could she confide in Johanna? *Ne*, as much as she loved her best friend, she was too aware of Johanna's loose tongue. Prone to gossip, that's what she was, and this secret wouldn't bear gossip.

Hannah followed the path along the creek bank toward the Metzlers' farm, the path she had traveled often on a sunny afternoon, but never in the dark of night. Adam would know what to do. He would know if Liesbet was in danger from this George McIvey.

Skirting the family cemetery, Hannah glanced at the graves of her little sisters and brother, the small mounds covered with scattered leaves. Mamm would be out here tomorrow, clearing them off again.

The path led her down to a runlet that drained water from the fields into Conestoga Creek. She jumped over the mud at the bottom and struggled through the loose leaves up the other side. The neighbor's farm, Adam's family's farm, was just ahead. The wind had blown the last of the lingering clouds away and the farm buildings stood silent in the evening, the stone corners sharp and clear in the moonlight.

Hannah paused at the edge of the creek bank where the trail led away from the trees toward the white frame house. Lanterns glowed in the windows, but should she dare knock on the door? It wasn't late, even though the evening sky was covered in stars, but if she disturbed the family now, there would be questions.

As she watched, the barn door opened and Adam stood silhouetted against the lighted interior. He closed the door and disappeared into the shadows on the other side of the barn, away from the house. He must be feeding the cattle his father had put in the pen there, waiting for butchering day.

Hannah hurried around the back of the barn. For sure,

there he was, throwing hay into the pen. She circled the split-rail fence and came toward him just as he landed the pitchfork into the haystack one more time. The breeze pulled at his black coat, hanging unbuttoned and loose on his tall frame, but his broad-brimmed hat stayed securely on his head.

He saw her coming and rested the fork's tines on the ground. "Isn't it a bit late for you to be taking a stroll?"

His face was shadowed from the moonlight, but Hannah could hear the concern in his voice.

"Adam, I need to talk to you."

Adam stuck the pitchfork into the hay and came toward her, taking her hands when he reached her. They were rough and calloused. A farmer's hands, cold in the night air.

"Is there something wrong? Is that why you brave a dark, windy night to find me?"

Hannah took a deep breath, resisting the urge to step into his strong embrace. How many times had he banished her fears through the years? But this was different.

"Liesbet told one of those teamsters about our signal and they've been using it to meet. I saw the cloth and thought it was from you. I found them together in the clearing behind the barn. I'm afraid for her."

Adam leaned against the fence rail and pulled her toward him. Moonlight threw shadows, turning his familiar face into a landscape of sharp angles. The cattle in the pen snuffled as they tossed through the scattered hay with their noses.

"Tell me about it."

As Hannah told him about the conversation in the clearing, his hands tensed and his handsome face grew hard.

"And I don't know if she's only playing with this man or not," Hannah finished. "You know how Liesbet can be."

Adam sighed. "*Ja*, I know how she can be. Does your father know anything about this?"

"That's just the problem. Liesbet said she'd tell Mamm we were courting if I told Daed about George."

"Why is it a problem if she told your mother we were courting?"

Hannah pulled her hands away from his and tucked them into her shawl. "Because we aren't, and Mamm wouldn't like it if we were."

Adam stood straight, his hands on her shoulders. "You think she wouldn't like it because I'm Mennonite and you're Amish."

"*Ja*. You know that's important to her, and to Daed too. I don't know what Mamm would do if she thought they were losing me to the Mennonites."

Adam grinned. "That's not a bad thing, is it? Our churches are so similar, there's no reason to keep us separate."

"But there is, Adam." Hannah stepped away from him. "You know there is. But if Mamm thought she was losing both Liesbet and me . . . What can I do? Liesbet says she's going to marry this man."

"Liesbet has always been like one of these leaves, blowing in the wind. Do you really think she's going to follow this path very long?"

Hannah shuddered, thinking of the way George had pulled Liesbet close as she had kissed him.

"What if she's already followed it too far? What if he takes her away before she decides she wants something different?"

"Do you think that might happen?"

Hannah nodded. Adam would know how to fix this mess. She had always relied on him to help.

"There's little we can do, but I'll try to keep a watch. Maybe I can stop him before he tries to visit her again."

"He said he was going to be away for a while. He told Liesbet he was on his way to Philadelphia."

"So the time to watch will be when he comes back. I'll keep my eyes open for any strangers around." Adam reached out and lifted her chin. "Don't worry, Hannah. Everything will be all right."

Would it be all right? Would Liesbet come to her senses?

"Come now, I'll walk you home. Maybe we'll catch a glimpse of that owl that lives in your barn."

Hannah let Adam lead her on the path back home, casting glances up into the tree branches as they went. She had never seen an owl in Daed's barn, but she watched for one just the same. It was better than dwelling on Liesbet.

The north wind had grown stronger during the night, blowing through the tops of the trees above the road, sending red and yellow leaves swirling down to the forest floor below in the early morning light. Here and there through the woods on either side of the road, butternuts and acorns peppered to the ground among the crisp leaves. Fat squirrels rooting among the litter ignored Daed's wagon, intent on gathering as much of the bounty as they could before the swirling leaves turned to snowflakes.

Hannah pulled her shawl more tightly around her shoulders and ran to catch up with the old Conestoga wagon lumbering along the road ahead. Looking past the horses, she could see the open country dotted with houses and farms that surrounded Lancaster. Daed wouldn't want her to fall behind this close to town. As the road emerged from the woods, it widened so that Hannah could walk next to him as he kept pace with Beppli, the left wheel horse.

"It should be a good Market Day, *ja*?" Hannah's voice puffed from trying to keep up with Daed's pace.

"*Ja*, for sure. Since it's the last of the year, we should have plenty of customers." Daed clicked his tongue at the horses, but Beppli and Blitz were well used to this route and the weight of the wagon. They flicked their ears, but kept on their plodding way. "I'm glad you were able to come along to help sell your Mamm's goods. The women customers would rather deal with you than with me, I think."

"I didn't want you to make the trip alone. I don't know why Liesbet didn't want to come."

"She's still a little girl in many ways." Daed sighed and rubbed the back of his neck.

"She's nearly sixteen. When I was her age—"

"You were never her age, Hannah." He flicked a fly away from Beppli's ears with his whip. "You've always been wise beyond your years."

Hannah glanced at him, but he kept his eyes on the horses now that they were nearing the houses on the outskirts of the town. Wise? She didn't feel wise. If she was wise, she wouldn't be so up and down, so confused about what her life was to be. A wise woman knew her place in life and was content. Hannah felt more like the creek on a spring day with snow melt churning the cloudy brown water into a mass of eddies and ripples.

They passed houses lining the road, closely spaced with only a small patch behind them for a garden. Town folk, who depended on the farmers bringing goods into Lancaster on Market Day.

Hannah's pace quickened when she caught sight of the roof of the Central Market Square. Soon Daed would be haggling with the Philadelphia buyers for his furniture, and she would be greeting the local housewives looking for garden produce. She had packed the last of the tomatoes for this trip, barrels of apples, and plenty of squash and corn. Mamm had also sent several lengths of her soft wool cloth. Daed's Leicester sheep were known for their long, soft fleece, and Mamm wove yards of extra cloth every year to sell at the Autumn Market Day.

And she would spend the entire day free from Liesbet's smug face. Liesbet had made sure she knew the tale of Adam courting her would reach Mamm's ears if Hannah let anything slip out about George. She would paint a grim picture, true or not. She was always quick to stretch the facts to fit her story in order to make things go her way.

Daed turned the team down the street leading to the Market Square, past a tavern where a group of teamsters stood on the corner. They were dressed the same way that George had been and spoke with the same lilting accents. One of them gestured toward the wagon with his tankard as they passed and bent to say something to his friends. Hannah didn't hear what was said, but the derisive laughter told her well enough that it had been another crude joke about the Amish. She turned her face away from them.

"Hurry up." Daed pulled the team to a halt in their usual place and climbed into the wagon. "We must get unloaded. We're late this morning."

Hannah took the kitchen chair Daed handed her to the edge of their space and set it down. They unloaded the rest of the furniture quickly, neighboring vendors giving a hand with the heavy pieces.

Daed brought her a long board to set across a couple of empty barrels, and she laid out the heavy squashes and pumpkins, then put some of the apples from a barrel into a basket so they could be inspected easily.

A woman came up just as Hannah laid Mamm's finely woven lengths of wool out for display. She lifted the edge of the walnut-brown piece and fingered it.

"You're the Yoders from up Conestoga Creek, aren't you?" She smiled at Hannah, her hair curled like fat sausages on either side of her face. "I bought a length of wool from you last year, and I've had so many compliments on the dress I made with it. I hoped you would bring more this year."

"Mamm tried a new blue dye receipt this year."

Hannah unwrapped three more lengths from the bundle, and while the woman fingered each one, Hannah noticed some men were gathering around Daed's furniture. It looked like they were going to have a busy morning.

"This blue is lovely, as well as the green."

As Hannah waited for the woman to make up her mind, another woman paused to examine the late-season tomatoes. *Ja*, it was going to be a busy morning.

By noon the furniture was gone, loaded onto a freight wagon heading toward the railroad station and then on to Philadelphia. The wool cloth and produce had been sold, as well as three bundles of wool fleece.

Hannah had watched the coins drop into Daed's pouch, hoping that somehow there might be enough to buy some bread from the bakery. One time, long ago, he had brought home a loaf of soft yeast bread from the Lancaster bakery, and she had never forgotten it. The bread they baked at home had a much coarser texture. Fanny had loved the Lancaster bread so much, Hannah had given half of her piece to her sister. Was there soft bread like that in the Blessed Land?

But that was before. Daed hadn't bought bread from the bakery since.

Hannah stamped one foot and then the other, trying to keep them warm while she waited for the next customer.

She could divide her life into before and after. The time before the little ones died was wrapped in shadows, like clouds over a sunny day. Once in a while the clouds pulled back to reveal a glimpse of that time, when she, Liesbet, and Fanny were inseparable, sisters forever. But today and every day were after. The hard, empty days of after.

As the sun started its downward journey, the crowds dispersed. Market Day was over.

"I'm going to get the horses, Hannah. You wait here, *ja*?"

Hannah watched the other families packing their wagons with leftover goods. Daed had already loaded the cotton cloth he had bought into the wagon, with paper packets of cinnamon and pepper he had purchased tucked safely into the folds. Children ran between the wagons while their mothers said goodbye to friends they might not see until next Market Day, in the spring.

A strain of music drifted over the chattering voices, pulling Hannah's attention to the tavern on the far corner. The teamsters were gathered around a table, singing a bawdy drinking song. One of the men played a fiddle, while another trilled an accompaniment on a pennywhistle. Hannah found herself humming along with the rollicking tune before she stopped herself.

Glancing around to see if anyone had noticed her, Hannah looked back at the teamsters. Her curiosity turned to suspicion when she heard a familiar voice rise above the rest. *Ja*, that was George McIvey, for sure. Didn't he tell Liesbet he was leaving for Philadelphia early this morning?

A girl from the tavern brought a handful of tankards to

the table, and as Hannah watched, George McIvey grabbed her around the waist and pulled her down on his lap, grinning at his friends. He gave her a loud kiss, and then let her go with a swat to her behind, just as he had with Liesbet the night before.

Hannah looked away from the scene. How a decent person could act that way in public . . . but of course, he wasn't a decent person. How had Liesbet gotten herself mixed up with someone like that? If she knew what Hannah had seen, she wouldn't be so smitten with the man.

When Daed came back from the livery with the horses, Hannah helped him hitch the team to the wagon. The well-trained team stood quietly while he fastened the traces and buckled the harnesses. After the full load coming to town, they would have a light load to haul home.

Hannah glanced at George McIvey again as the group launched into another song, and Daed noticed the direction of her gaze.

"Pay no attention to them, Hannah. Those fellows are here one day and gone the next, and good riddance."

"I've never seen them before, have you?"

He didn't give the teamsters a glance, but finished hitching the horses. "They've been through here before. They stopped by the farm a few weeks ago, wanting to haul goods to Philadelphia for me."

He chirruped to the horses, starting them on the journey home, nodding to acquaintances as they made their way out of the Market Square and onto the road.

Hannah hurried to catch up to him. "They've been to our farm?" Is that where Liesbet met this George?

"*Ja,* but I didn't like what they offered. They thought they were doing me a favor, buying the goods cheap and saving me the trip to the Lancaster Market, but I wouldn't do business with men like that."

"Why not? It would save a lot of time to have someone else haul the goods, wouldn't it?"

"*Ja*, but what would I do with the time, then?" He scowled at her. "Do you think your daed would be happy sitting on the front porch rocker while someone else did his work?"

Hannah shook her head at the thought. She had never seen him sit still unless it was the Sabbath.

"Besides, those men aren't like us. 'Be not unequally yoked' is what the Good Book says, and I'll live by that. I won't enter a partnership of any kind with men like those."

Hannah dropped back as they left town and the road narrowed to a track. What would Daed think if he knew of Liesbet and George McIvey? But from what she had seen outside the tavern, the man wasn't interested in Liesbet anymore. Perhaps now Liesbet would forget her girlish fantasies about the man and grow up into a woman more suited for a proper Amish husband.

As Daed drove the team to the barn, eight-year-old Margareta ran out of the house, followed by six-year-old Peter.

"Hannah, did you bring us anything?" Margli shouted and jumped around her.

"I have something for all three of you," Hannah said. She pulled the packet she bought from a neighboring vendor out of her pocket. "Where's William?"

"He's coming," Peter said, "but we can't wait for him. What did you bring us?"

By the time she unwrapped three pieces of horehound candy from her paper packet, two-year-old William had caught up with the others. Hannah sighed at his bare bottom and soiled shirt. Mamm must be having one of her spells again. She looked around for Liesbet. Her sister hadn't said anything about Adam or George McIvey, had she?

Hannah gave Margli a hug, her precious little sister. "Have you had your supper yet?"

"*Ne*, we've been waiting for you. Mamm put beans on this morning, and Liesbet and I have been watching them."

"Where is Mamm, then?"

Margli shrugged, candy filling her mouth.

Perhaps she should have stayed home instead of going to the market with Daed. But then, who would have helped him sell the goods?

Hannah went into the kitchen. The pot of beans simmered at the edge of the fire, just as Margli said. She'd start a pan of cornbread baking, and then clean William up. Keeping her baby brother in clean pants was one thing Margli hadn't learned to do yet, and Liesbet hated the task.

Happy shrieks of playing children drifted in the door as Hannah sifted cornmeal into a bowl. At least the little ones brought some joy to the house. Even Mamm smiled when she watched them play. Somehow, maybe it helped her forget before. The three littlest ones, coming along so soon after losing Hansli, Fanny, and the baby, should have been a healing balm, but Mamm still spent hours in the cemetery, as if she forgot she had other children.

Daed came in as Hannah put the cornbread in the oven. "Your mamm?"

"I haven't seen her."

"*Ja*, then I'll go find her. It's getting cool as the sun goes down, and she'll get a chill."

Hannah watched him go, his shoulders stooped. Mamm should be getting better, but this time of year, when the ground was damp and cold and night came on swiftly, was the worst of all.

Why did Mamm keep going to the cemetery? When Hannah passed by, it held no appeal for her. It was just a grove of trees with the graves of a hundred years of Yoders . . . and three small stones marking the place where Daed buried the little ones nine years ago.

After checking the cornbread in the oven, Hannah stirred the beans. Wild onions and bits of salt pork mingled with the cooked beans, sending an aroma that made Hannah's stomach growl. It had been too many hours since her hasty lunch of cornbread.

Margli ran into the house, followed by the little boys. Hannah could see Liesbet through the open door, walking along the sheepfold fence, bouncing a stick on the top rail as she came toward the house.

"Is supper almost ready?" Margli asked.

"As soon as the bread is done, and that will be just a few more minutes. You and Liesbet get the plates and forks, and I'll get William dressed."

Hannah pulled William's soiled shirt over his head and washed his face with a rag dipped in warm water. He squirmed under her attentions, but she held him tightly with one hand. "Come now, you must let me get the worst of this off before supper, and then clean clothes."

Peter tried to slip past her, but she caught him just as she gave William's cheeks one last swipe. "You too, Peter. You look like you've been playing in a hog wallow. Get yourself out to the bench and wash up."

Peter screwed up his face. "Not the hog wallow. William and I were building a house in the woods. We had to move rocks out of the way to make the floor smooth."

"And who was helping Jacob with the chores while you were playing?"

"He told us he could work faster alone and sent us off. He gave us the idea to build the house."

Hannah attacked the dirt in William's ears. At nineteen, Jacob was usually patient with his little brothers, but when he had work to do, he'd send them off somewhere instead of teaching them to help him the way Daed did.

Hannah stood up with William's naked body in her arms. "Go on out to the washing bench, like I said, and don't neglect your neck. And call Jacob to come in too. Supper's nearly ready."

William snuggled against her as she carried him into the bedroom behind the central fireplace. Mamm and Daed's room was always warm in the cold months, and as the youngest, William still slept in the cradle at the foot of their bed.

"Shall we put a clean shirt on you now?" Hannah asked William as she set him on the big bed and reached for some clean clothes.

"*Ne,*" he said as he stood up on the rustling mattress. "Go with Peter."

"Peter will be back." Hannah put a clean diaper on him and slipped the shift over his blond head. He was nearly old enough to wear pants, but not until he learned to use the chamber pot every time.

William put one little hand on each of her cheeks and

forced her to look at him, his face serious. Hannah held his
face between her own hands, ready for his favorite game.

"Who loves William?" she said, and kissed his nose.

"Hannah." William giggled.

"Who else loves William?"

"Daed, Mamm, Liesbet, Jacob, Margli, and Peter." The
little boy said each name louder and faster than the last,
shouting Peter's name at the end of the list.

"And now are you ready for supper?"

"*Ja*. Eat."

Hannah helped him down from the bed and followed him
back to the main room. Jacob and Peter had come in, Liesbet
had lit the lamp against the evening darkness, and Margli
was placing the last of the forks around the long table.

As Jacob took his place at the table, Hannah leaned close
to him. "Are they coming?"

"*Ja*." Jacob nodded, his brown hair and eyes making him
look like a younger version of Daed. "I saw them just beyond
the barn as I came in."

"And Mamm?"

"She seemed all right. I don't think she was crying this
time."

Hannah turned to the fireplace and lifted the oven lid.
The bread was perfectly browned. She pulled it out and set
it on the table just as the door opened and Daed came into
the house, followed by Mamm. She didn't look at the family, but stumbled her way to the chair next to the fireplace
and sat in it, still wrapped in her shawl, staring into the fire.

"Annalise, you must eat." Daed knelt at Mamm's side
and held her hand, but she didn't respond. He stood, his
shoulders hunched as he watched her.

"Daed," Hannah said, "come to the table. Supper is getting cold."

As the others took their places around the table, Daed sighed and took his chair at the end. He bowed his head and started praying the Lord's Prayer, using the High German from the Good Book. The children dutifully joined in, reciting the memorized words.

Hannah watched Mamm as they prayed, her eyes stinging as the firelight glistened in the tears making their slow way down her mother's worn face.

I'm sorry, Mamm. So sorry . . .

3

Annalise swayed, rocking her babies as the flames danced, gazing into the fiery center of the logs. One blue tongue flowed along a log like water, dipping down to the ashes and then retreating. It turned yellow, disappeared, and flamed again. She followed the pulsing heat back into the center of the fire, where orange and red coals shimmered. Warmth and light.

The children needed warmth, but the fire's heat would never reach them under the cold, dark ground. She clutched empty arms to her breast, always empty. Christian had pulled her away from them again. She could hear them crying for her, out in the darkness. Their mournful cries seemed to come to her from the fireplace itself, as if they were trying to come home.

A log shifted in the fire, sending sparks up the chimney. She held one hand out to the heat. Darkness wavered in her mind, unsure. Warmth seeped into her fingers, chasing away the chill, the pain. Darkness fluttered and other sounds filtered into her mind. A voice talking quietly, forks scraping plates, Christian's loud "ahem" to bring the family to the prayer at the end of the meal.

"Memmi?"

A child's voice pulled her mind from the fire. Hansli? Was Hansli calling to her again?

"Memmi?"

The voice demanded her attention. A small hand patted her leg. William. Not Hansli. William.

"*Ja, liebchen.*" Her voice came from somewhere outside herself, begging an entrance into her consciousness.

Her baby climbed into her lap and she wrapped him in her shawl, holding him close until he pushed away.

"Hot. Too hot," he said, and then turned to face her, straddling her lap.

He patted her cheek with one sticky hand, forcing her to focus her eyes on his. Her dear little William.

"Memmi want some bread?"

He held up his other hand, fisted around a mushed chunk of cornbread. Honey glistened on his fingers.

"*Ne*, William. It's your bread."

A smile found its way to her mouth as she watched William transfer the bread from one hand to the other and lick his sticky fingers.

Annalise raised her hand to brush his hair back from his forehead. White blond and straight, just like her Hansli's had been. The other two boys had their father's brown curls, but Hansli and William were blond.

William took another bite of cornbread, his eyes solemn. As he chewed, he lifted one sticky hand to her cheek and rubbed it.

"Memmi sad."

He rubbed his eye and then yawned. The last bit of corn-bread was forgotten as he leaned against her breast and relaxed.

Annalise dropped her head down onto his, breathing in his little-boy smell of dried sweat and dirt. No longer a baby.

Plates scraping against each other drew her attention to the table where Liesbet and Margareta were cleaning up. Hannah stirred the sourdough, feeding it for tomorrow's breakfast. Supper was over. Another day gone.

Hannah pulled the teakettle from the fire and glanced at her. Her daughter's face was tight, anxious. Like Christian's. They both worried about her, as they should. If it wasn't for Hannah, she would still have her babies.

Ne, she knew better, didn't she? The Lord gave and the Lord hath taken away. Blessed be the name of the Lord. God had done this thing, not Hannah.

But God had used Hannah, like Satan used the serpent in the garden. She had brought death to their home.

Hannah set the kettle on the trivet and came to her.

"William, don't bother Mamm tonight."

"*Ne*, Hannah, it's all right. Let him stay with me." Annalise pushed Hannah's hands away as her daughter reached for the baby.

She rubbed William's bare leg. He was warm enough. He was strong and healthy. If he fell sick, he might survive. She passed her hand over his forehead and caressed his cheek. No fever. He was safe tonight.

Today had been a bad day. Christian would say she had one of her spells. Was that what one would say when the waves of sadness became so unbearable she could only find relief in the grove of trees?

When had she gone there? Christian had left in the early morning with Hannah . . . the children had eaten . . . then she had gone to brush the fallen leaves off the graves . . . the cold graves. She couldn't bear to leave, not until Christian had come for her. She had been so cold. The ground under the trees was so cold.

Pull your mind away. Look elsewhere.

William sat up and finished his bread, licking the fingers on each hand.

"Now you need to wash your hands." Annalise smiled at her youngest son. Her baby.

"*Ne.* No wash. Clean." He held his hands up for her to see.

"They're still sticky, though." Hannah said, at her side with a wet rag to wash William's hands. "Shall I put him to bed for you?"

"*Ne, ne,* I'll do it." Annalise took the cloth from Hannah, finished William's hands, and started wiping the honey and crumbs from his face. She would keep her baby safe.

Hannah finished redding up the kitchen while Mamm put William to bed. She made sure to do everything the way she had been taught. The pot laid just so to dry near the fire, but not too close. The wooden table scrubbed, the floor swept, the sourdough sponge set for the morning. She hung the dishcloths near the fire to dry just as Daed, Jacob, and Peter came in from doing the chores.

"Tomorrow is going to be a fine day." Daed sat down at the table to remove his boots. "I'm taking the boys to the woods to gather hickory nuts. We could use your help, Hannah."

Glancing toward the closed door beside the fireplace, Hannah shook her head. "I think I had better stay here tomorrow in case Mamm needs me. Liesbet could go with you, though."

He looked up at the stairway, where Liesbet and Margli sat, waiting for evening prayers. "What do you think, Liesbet? You too, Margli? We'll make a day of it." He gestured toward the closed door. "Maybe your mamm will want to come too. And William." He scratched at his beard, his eyes becoming unfocused and distant. "When I was a boy, our whole family would go to the woods on an autumn day to gather the nuts. We looked forward to that day every year."

"Mamm won't want to come." Peter sat next to Daed, his coat still on and covered with straw. He yawned and let Hannah remove his coat. "She never wants to do things like that."

Daed tousled Peter's hair. "Perhaps one day she will, though, ja?"

Hannah took Peter's jacket into the entryway and hung it on its peg. Poor Peter. She remembered before, when Mamm would have enjoyed nutting in the woods with the family, but Peter only knew her after.

The conversation from the kitchen continued as Daed waited for the family to gather for the evening reading and prayers. She had time for a quick trip to the privy. Slipping out the door, Hannah followed the well-worn path around the house. The full moon rode above the trees and silver clouds flew across the sky. The air was crisp, like an autumn evening should be. Was it only last night that she had seen Liesbet with that George McIvey?

Hannah thought of Adam. Ever since he had attended the

camp meetings last summer, he had taken trips to Lancaster and beyond. "Meeting with friends," he had told her. She sighed. She liked the man he was becoming, but she missed the carefree boy who had helped her escape from the trials of home during the hard years after the little ones' deaths. He had seemed to know when Mamm was at her worst—when Hannah was the target for her anger and grief—and their signal of the bit of cloth on the branch was her salvation. He would take her into the woods and show her the things he had found: birds' nests, a badger's den, the first ripe strawberries. Whatever he thought might please her. He was the big brother who understood her as Jacob never did. After a few hours with Adam, she felt strong enough to return home and face Mamm again.

Hannah paused on the path, watching the moon. Adam still liked her, even now when she was grown up and didn't need to run to him for comfort. He and his family were always happy to see her, always willing to welcome her into their home for a meal or a visit. What would it have been like to be born into the Metzler family instead of her own? Always like before, and never after?

She looked in the kitchen window as she walked back to the house. Mamm was seated across from Daed at the table, and the others were gathered around. They were waiting for her. She hurried in and took her place beside Liesbet. Daed had the Scriptures open to the book of Psalms.

Slipping into her seat, Hannah smiled her apology as he started reading. She let the words roll over her, the familiar phrases covering her soul like a balm. The day's worries fled. Even Mamm sat on her bench, her face quiet and calm, listening to his voice.

Hannah looked from one face to the next around the table. Only Liesbet fidgeted, stifling a yawn. The others, from Jacob down to Peter, sat with their eyes focused on Daed, listening. This was the only thing left from before. As long as they had this house, this farm, this family table, maybe she could bring her family back to before.

∞

Annalise paused on the back porch, drawing a shuddering breath before making the journey across the barnyard. Chickens scratched in the dirt outside their run, cackling in the sunshine.

The wind changed during the night, as it often did in the autumn, and the air was warmer, without the searing bite of yesterday. A gust blew a shower of red and orange leaves down and swirled them between the chicken coop and the barn. Annalise let her gaze move from the chicken coop to the garden, and then to the smokehouse. Everywhere she looked there was work to be done. That burden never lifted.

If she could only count on the girls to help, but Hannah was always running off somewhere when she was needed at home. Christian could have gone to Lancaster alone yesterday, but Hannah had insisted on going with him.

Annalise pushed thoughts of yesterday aside and started toward the barn. Christian would be done with the milking, and she needed the milk in the house before breakfast. She picked her way around the droppings from the chickens, keeping her eyes down. She wouldn't look toward the rise beyond the barn, with the grove of trees nestled on the other side. Her babies would have to wait until after the morning chores were done.

Christian looked up from his milking as she entered the

open barn door, his frown deepening when he saw her. "Are you feeling better this morning?"

He held her gaze until she nodded. How could she answer him?

Christian turned back to the cow. Annalise waited behind him, watching as he stripped the last of the milk from Lottie's udder. Even at almost forty years old, his muscles were strong and able to work tirelessly through the day. When she was having a good day, when he wasn't worried about her, he still looked like the young man who courted her patiently all those years ago.

Annalise stood back as Christian rose from the milking stool with a full bucket of frothy milk.

"These spells of yours . . ." Christian looked past her, out the barn door as he spoke. "You're better, *ne*? They come less frequently?"

Annalise nodded, willing herself to agree with him, but how could she tell him of the depth of the darkness that had overcome her yesterday? The thought of winter coming had driven her to the grove of trees that sheltered those three graves—another season of relentless cold and darkness.

She forced her thoughts back to Christian. He mustn't think she was weak, unable to do her work. "It's a beautiful morning now, isn't it? A good day for working outside."

"*Ja*, and a perfect day for gathering hickory nuts in the woods. I'm taking Jacob and Peter with me."

"You'll be home for dinner?"

"*Ne*, we'll take it with us and eat in the woods."

He would be gone all day. Again. Annalise reached to take the milk pail from him, but he held the handle until she looked up at him.

"You could come with us. Bring William and the girls. Put together a cold dinner and we'll make a day of it." His eyes softened as he spoke, making him almost look like the young man she had married.

A wisp pulled at her, tugging her mind to thoughts of the sunny woods, leaves dancing in the breeze. She could see Christian and Jacob tossing forkfuls of leaves and nuts into the back of the wagon while she helped William find the big leafy squirrels' nests in the tops of the trees . . .

"Ne, you know I can't take a whole day off to go play in the woods. There is too much work to finish before winter."

Christian looked away, and then back at her, his expression tight. "We'll go another day then, ja? I'll wait for you, Annalise."

Her hand shook as she took the milk pail from his yielding hand. "Breakfast is nearly ready. You'll be in soon?"

"Ja, soon." He held her gaze in his own until she turned away.

As Annalise crossed the yard on the way back to the house, she couldn't keep from looking toward the family cemetery, nestled in its grove of ash trees. The leaves, still clinging to the branches, glowed yellow gold as they danced in the breezy sunshine, but shadows lay among the small stones marking the graves. Even in the sunshine, those stones never warmed. She hefted the milk pail to her other hand and hurried into the house.

Hannah had breakfast ready to lay on the table, but Liesbet and Margareta were nowhere to be seen. Annalise went to help Hannah with the heavy pot of Indian mush, holding the pot out of the fire while Hannah dished a scoopful into each of the bowls.

"Where is Liesbet this morning?"

"She got up when I did, but I haven't seen her since I came downstairs. I think she's helping Margli get dressed."

William sat on his stool, spoon in hand. Hannah set his bowl of mush before him and William reached for it.

"Hannah, what are you thinking?" Annalise snatched the bowl away from William. "He'll burn himself."

Annalise gave William a piece of cold cornbread to keep him from crying while Hannah finished placing the rest of the bowls on the table. She said nothing. No apology. Liesbet would never have done such a thing.

But Liesbet was still such a young girl, and not as strong as Hannah. She would grow into a fine woman someday, as long as she stayed healthy.

"Mamm, everything's ready."

The sound of her daughter's voice brought her back to the tasks at hand. While Hannah went to the door to ring the bell for the boys and Christian, Annalise gave William a cup of milk, her mind still on Liesbet. She didn't need to borrow trouble. Liesbet was stronger this year. Perhaps she wouldn't get sick again this winter.

At the sound of the bell, Liesbet came down the steps from the second floor, Margareta at her heels.

"Good morning, *liebchen*." Annalise gave Liesbet a quick hug and the girls slid into their places at the table. "I needed your help getting breakfast ready. Where have you been?"

"Liesbet was helping me comb my hair." Margareta turned on the bench to show Annalise the fancy looped braids in place of her usual neatly twisted hair under her kapp.

Christian came in the door, frowning at the girls. "Liesbet, you know those braids are too worldly for us. Our Margli should look like a proper Amish girl. Both of you go upstairs and don't come down again until Margli is presentable."

Annalise almost missed Liesbet's whispered comment, "Plain, you mean," as she pushed herself away from the table and pounded up the stairs, but at least she had sense enough to keep Christian from hearing her. Margareta followed.

Christian sat heavily in his chair. "Annalise, you shouldn't encourage them."

"*Ja*, Christian. I don't know where Liesbet gets her ideas, but the girls were just playing. No harm has come from it."

"No harm? When our daughters think wearing their hair like an outsider is fun?"

Hannah poured Christian's tea for him, and then took her place at the table as Peter and Jacob came in. Christian pointed at their eldest daughter with his spoon before stirring honey into his tea.

"You wouldn't see Hannah trying new things with her hair, would you? She's a true Amish girl. She knows to keep herself modest and pure."

Annalise bit back her retort. Christian always held Hannah up as a model of respectability, comparing the two girls. Didn't he see what harm he was doing to poor Liesbet?

The rest of breakfast passed in silence, Liesbet and Margareta joining them again just as Christian finished. They had to wait while he read the morning prayer, and then ate after he left with the boys.

After breakfast Annalise put Liesbet to work churning butter while Hannah and Margareta finished up the housework. It was time for a final check on the meat in the smokehouse.

Annalise made her way past the old cabin covered in bright red Virginia Creeper. The little smokehouse stood behind the cabin, wispy gray tendrils seeping through the log walls. For days Peter and Jacob had kept the fire smoldering with green hickory chips, filling the yard with a faint smoky odor.

Smoke billowed out as she opened the door, bringing tears to her eyes. She reached inside to feel the strips of venison hanging from the rafters and walls. *Ja*, they were well dried and ready to store in the attic. The fire could burn down while she left the door open to clear out the smoke, and then she and the girls could wrap the meat in the old linen cloths she had used year after year. The hooks along the limestone walls of the attic were empty and waiting for the bounty, and the smokehouse would be ready for the next butchering day.

As she stepped out of the smokehouse, she saw Adam Metzler coming up the road. The young man had a habit of showing up just in time to help with some chore, but not at mealtime. It was a good habit for a neighbor to have.

"*Hallo*, Adam. What brings you here today?"

Adam grinned as he lifted a complaining rooster by its feet.

"Ma sent this over for you. She heard you lost your rooster to a fox, and this one is always picking fights with our older bird."

"*Ja, denki*, Adam. Your mother is always so thoughtful." The Metzlers had always been good neighbors, even though they were Mennonite.

"I'll make a pen for him by your chicken house until he feels at home here." He looked around the yard. "Is Hannah busy? I thought she'd like to help me."

Annalise hesitated. Adam and Hannah had been inseparable as youngsters, but as Hannah grew older, she had tried to keep the girl busy at home. There was no reason for her to get too friendly with a boy like Adam. It wasn't good to encourage friendship with an outsider.

"If Peter were here, I know he'd want to help, but Hannah and Margareta can both help you. They should be done with their morning work by now."

As they walked together toward the big stone house, Hannah appeared on the porch with rag rugs under her arm. She didn't look their direction, but shook the rugs one at a time, turning so the breeze would carry the dust away from her.

Annalise glanced at Adam's face as he fell silent and slowed his steps. He was staring at Hannah with a look that made her heart lurch. Friendship was no longer a question. The boy she had watched grow up was gone. He was a man in love—with a woman he could never marry.

4

Hannah gave the rag rug a final shake, watching the breeze take the dust away over the meadow. Turning to the next rug, she saw Adam talking with Mamm near the smokehouse. When he saw her, he gave a wave with one hand. A rooster squawked and struggled as it hung upside down in his other hand.

Giving the last rug a quick shake, she folded it onto the pile with the others. Mamm was frowning as she watched Adam walk toward Hannah. What had he done to make her so unhappy? Hannah put the rugs on the chair just inside the door, ready to replace after the floor dried from the mopping she gave it earlier, and then stepped back to the edge of the porch just as Adam reached the bottom step.

"Good morning." His easy grin made her stomach flutter.

She smiled back at him, in spite of the awareness of Mamm's watchful frown. "What are you doing with that poor rooster?"

Adam lifted the bird up and looked him in the eye. The

rooster fell silent, then squawked and tried to reach Adam with his open beak. His wings beat so hard that feathers flew. "It's a present from my ma to yours."

"He's certainly welcome. The barnyard hasn't been the same since we lost Rory."

"Come with me to the chicken yard and help get him settled in."

"*Ja*, sure." Hannah glanced toward the smokehouse, but Mamm was no longer in sight. She stepped off the porch to join him as they walked across to the fenced yard. The gate was open to let the chickens feed for the day, and the curious hens gathered around Adam as he approached with the rooster.

"I'll get a crate from the barn to put him in while we fix a pen for him." She pushed one aggressive hen out of the way with her foot.

Adam lifted the rooster out of reach of the chickens. "That's a good idea. If we let him loose now, these hens are likely to peck him to death."

With the rooster safely enclosed, Adam went to work fencing off a corner of the chicken yard. Hannah watched as he set a post in the ground, and then lined up scrap boards to make a secure fence. His hands, strong and sure, made the task look easy.

"He'll only need to be in there for a couple weeks, *ja*?"

"That's right." Adam paused to straighten his back before tackling another board. "He's used to being around other hens, so it shouldn't take him long to want to be around yours. They just need to accept him."

Hannah glanced at the crate where the rooster sat huddled on the ground as the chickens surrounded him. They cackled and pecked at the wooden box, ready to drive the intruder away.

"Right now they look like they could eat him."

Adam laughed. "And by the time you put them together, they'll be glad to take him for their husband. He won't be a stranger any longer."

He went back to his hammering. Did he mean more than chickens? From the look on her face, Mamm would be glad to send Adam on his way. Perhaps that was why he kept coming around. He hoped Mamm and Daed would get used to him and accept him as part of the family.

"I wanted to ask you something." Adam hammered the last slat into place. He turned to Hannah, glancing at the house and barn before stepping close to her.

Hannah backed away until she was pressed against the fence.

"There's a camp meeting next week . . ."

"In the autumn? I thought you only went to those in the summer."

"Joseph Mast is holding one in his barn. The preacher is coming this way on his circuit and wants to hold the meeting." He took her hand in his. "Would you go with me? My life hasn't been the same since I attended the meetings last summer, and I want you to hear what the preacher says."

Hannah looked away from him. "What do your parents say about you going to these meetings?"

"They don't go with me, but they don't forbid me from attending. Pa says it's a better way for me to spend time than some other things I could be doing."

Hannah looked at his hand grasping hers. She had heard of the fiery preachers who stirred their audience into a frenzy of emotion, holding hundreds of listeners spellbound. Adam claimed it had changed his life, but was it of God, as he assured her?

"I don't think Daed would let me go."

Adam sighed, letting go of her hand. "I didn't think he would, but you could still ask him."

"It isn't just Daed . . . I'm not sure I want to go."

Hannah looked up to see Adam staring at her. "You don't want to? Why not? It's the best thing that's ever happened to me, and I want you to see it."

How could she explain this feeling she had inside when he spoke of the camp meetings? It was as if a hand was restraining her, keeping her from considering the thought of attending.

"When you went last summer, you were changed."

Adam nodded. "*Ja*, that's just it. I was changed, and for the better."

She looked into his eyes, willing him to understand. "I don't want to change, Adam. I know I'm following God's will the way I am right now. I don't need a preacher to tell me differently."

Adam stepped back and rubbed his chin with his hand. "It's your unyielding Amish faith, isn't it? It won't let any other ideas touch you."

Hannah bit her lip. "You make it sound like I'm turning a blind eye to anything different, and it isn't that way. I'm just careful about which new things I let affect me. I don't know if the things they speak of at these camp meetings are trustworthy or not."

Adam looked away from her, into the woods beyond the house. His jaw worked as if he was trying to control his temper. "I don't want to argue with you about this, Hannah." His voice was low. Controlled. "I wanted you to know this part of my life." He turned to her again. "I want you to be part of it. You know how I feel about you."

"We're friends, Adam. As your friend, I would ask you to remain true to your faith and not go seeking this . . . this exciting new religion."

"We're more than just friends, aren't we?" He looked deep into her eyes, searching for the answer she couldn't give him. How could she know when friendship turned into something more? He took her hand in his. "And these camp meetings help me to be truer to my faith than I ever have been before. Now I feel like I know the real Jesus and can claim him as my Lord. I was never able to understand that before."

Hannah shook her head and he backed away from her. "This isn't the way I was raised. This isn't what my ancestors died for."

"What did they die for, then? To be Amish, or to be Christian? Your ancestors and mine faced the same persecution, and it was because they needed to worship God in the way they knew was right, not the way the government said they should. They persevered through those terrible times because God called them to follow him. But over the years, we've lost their fire and determination. I feel that again at the camp meetings. God has called me to action, to a purpose, and I want you to share that. Please come with me."

"*Ne*, I can't." Hannah kept her eyes down. She couldn't face him now. Would he end their friendship over this?

He sighed and turned to the crate where the rooster crouched, pressing himself against the ground in an attempt to hide from the mob of hens. "I'll wait, Hannah. Maybe you'll change your mind and will go with me the next time the preacher comes around."

"I wouldn't count on that."

Adam grinned up at her as he opened the crate and grabbed the unhappy bird. "You never know what God might do to change your mind between now and then." He dropped the rooster into his temporary pen.

Christian paused, his hand on the orchard gate. Adam Metzler was visiting again, talking with Hannah near the chicken coop.

As a ewe butted his leg, he opened the gate to let the flock in to graze on the orchard grass. It was time to let the sheepfold grass recover before winter came, and the sheep relished the windfall apples they found among the trees in their new pasture, but they balked at the gate, none of the ewes wanting to be the first to explore new territory. One of the half-grown lambs pushed past its elders and jumped into the orchard, and that was all it took for the rest of the flock to follow.

Fastening the gate behind them, Christian looked toward the chicken coop again. What was Adam doing here? He and Hannah had been friends for years, but surely that friendship had cooled, the way it did when children grew older.

As he watched, Adam grasped Hannah's hand, but she pulled back. It looked as if he was asking her something, but Hannah wasn't agreeing. Good for her. She knew how to keep her distance from a Mennonite boy.

But did she? It was hard to see from this distance, but it didn't seem as if Adam was disappointed.

Christian watched until Adam left, heading down the creek path toward his farm. The same creek path Hannah often took when she headed out into the woods to be alone. She didn't follow, but went back to the house. Was there something more to this than childish friendship?

With Adam and Hannah both out of sight, Christian headed toward the barn and his next chore, passing the pigpen just as Jacob poured a pail of slop into the pig's trough. Jacob and Peter had spent a day last week rounding up their two pigs from the woods where they had spent the summer rooting for their food on the forest floor. Now the swine were being fattened up on kitchen slops and windfall apples in preparation for butchering day.

Jacob shook the slop pail, trying to get the last of yesterday's apple peels out, and his hand got a little too close to one pig's snout.

"Hi! Watch it there!" Jacob slapped the half-wild pig's nose away as the creature nipped at him.

"He thought he'd have a bite of your arm for breakfast." Christian held in a chuckle as Jacob glared at him.

"When are we going to butcher these devils?"

"I hope next month. I need to talk to Elias and see which day would suit him." As the only Amish left along Conestoga Creek, he and Elias Hertzler depended on each other to work together.

"And the Metzlers? I know they have a couple steers to butcher. We could share the meat."

Christian watched the hogs shove each other in their eagerness to devour the slop. Butcher with the Metzlers? It would make sense. The three farms lay one next to the other along the south side of the creek, with the Yoders in the middle.

They had worked together in past years, but lately . . . Christian scratched his beard. Had he let his family get a little too familiar with the Mennonites? The moment he had witnessed between Adam and Hannah seemed to point that way.

"Why the Metzlers? I think we'll have enough to do for one day with our two pigs and the Hertzlers."

Jacob shrugged. "We've included them before, haven't we?"

Christian broke off a long stem of dry grass, winnowing the seeds between his fingers. *Ja*, he had enjoyed the help of both neighbors in these tasks, but ever since the Amish districts had been redrawn last year, placing the Yoders and Hertzlers at the edge of the Pequea church district, Samuel Metzler seemed to think the two families should join the Mennonite church down the road. Christian balked under the pressure.

"*Ja*, we have, but perhaps not this year."

"It's because of the Eshelmanns, isn't it, and how they left to join the Brethren? You think one of us might marry a Mennonite and pull the family away from the church."

Christian rolled his shoulders. Sometimes it felt as if the world was pressing down, pushing him to take his family down the path toward ease and destruction.

"You don't think that could happen, Jacob?"

"Why would it? Even if I thought I might want to marry Hilda Metzler, she could come to the Amish church with us."

"It's human nature to follow the easy path. You may want your wife to become Amish, but it can be a demanding life for those not used to it. She would always be looking back to the church of her youth, with its wide path."

Jacob was silent, watching the pigs lick the wooden trough dry. "Is it wrong to want an easier life?"

Christian's heart twisted. *Ach*, that he would hear those words out of his own son's mouth!

"God calls us to follow the narrow path, to keep ourselves pure and spotless, separate from the world. Remember Christ himself said, 'Strait is the gate, and narrow is the way, which leadeth unto life, and few there be that find it.' Ours may seem like a difficult way, but it's the way to life."

When Jacob looked at him, Christian was glad to see no sign of hardness in his features. The boy wasn't being rebellious in his questions, but truly wanted to know.

"So, are the Eshelmanns and the Metzlers heading to destruction? If a person isn't a member of the Amish church, does that mean they're lost forever?"

"*Ne*, son. We cannot judge another man's heart or know God's plan for another. But we are responsible for ourselves, to live as God calls us."

Jacob didn't answer but turned back to watch the pigs digging and rooting in the dirt of their pen. Was he convinced of the truth?

Christian went into the barn and his next chore, but the weight on his shoulders threatened to crush him. The church's call was so clear—they were to separate themselves from the world—but with so many distractions surrounding them, how could he hope to keep his children steady in the faith?

That afternoon, Hannah and Liesbet stood at the edge of the garden. The first hard frost a few nights ago had killed off the remaining summer vegetables, and somewhere in the tangle of dried vines and plants were the last of the squash and pumpkins.

"Why didn't Mamm take care of this job before the frost?" Liesbet dropped her basket to the ground.

"You may as well ask why we didn't take care of it earlier." Hannah set her basket next to Liesbet's and began pulling dead bean vines from the soft ground.

Liesbet gave a halfhearted pull on a tomato plant. "I hate cleaning the garden in the autumn."

Hannah kept working. If she ignored Liesbet's complaining, perhaps she'd stop sooner.

"Admit it, Hannah. You hate it too."

Hannah moved her basket away from Liesbet, farther into the garden. When she glanced back, she saw that her sister hadn't done any more than pull up the one tomato stalk.

"Come on, Liesbet. If you don't work faster, this will take us all afternoon."

"Where do we put the dead plants?"

"On the pile over there. You know that."

Liesbet sat where she was and pulled up another tomato stalk. Hannah turned her back on her and kept pulling handfuls of tangled beans, squash, and cornstalks. When her hands were full, she threw them on the pile at the edge of the garden and then came back for another load. She glanced at Liesbet. She hadn't moved.

Hannah pulled the next cornstalk up with one hand, twisting it so that the bean and squash vines came up with it. If Liesbet would do her share of the work, life would be a lot easier. But if Hannah complained to Mamm or Daed, they would both tell her not to worry, like they always did. Ever since the diphtheria, Mamm never made her work. If she ever saw a spoiled child, it was Liesbet.

The next cornstalk stubbornly held its place, even though

Hannah twisted and pulled. She bent down with a stick to loosen the dirt around the roots.

Of course, Liesbet was still weak. She grew tired quickly, even playing games. Hannah had recovered from the diphtheria quickly, but Liesbet hadn't. For months she had stayed in Mamm and Daed's room, too weak to even get out of bed. The cough hadn't completely disappeared until several years later. Liesbet almost died, Hannah reminded herself, but that didn't give her an excuse not to try to help with the family chores. Hannah glanced at her sister again. More than once she wondered if Liesbet was actually healthy, but continued pretending to be sickly just to get out of working.

The cornstalk finally came up. Hannah threw it on top of the pile and moved to the next one.

"Hannah!"

She turned to look at Liesbet, standing among the tomato plants.

"I heard something under there. Is it a rat?"

"I don't know. It might be, but it won't hurt you. Just make a lot of noise and you'll scare it away."

"But, Hannah, what if it's a snake?" Liesbet's voice rose into a shriek.

Hannah sighed. They would never get this job done if Liesbet let herself be spooked by every noise. But she really was afraid of snakes, and what if it was a copperhead?

"Hold still, I'll be right there." Hannah picked up her stick and made her way to Liesbet's side, listening for furtive movement under the dried stalks and leaves. "Where did you hear it?"

Liesbet pointed to a spot a few feet from where she was standing. Hannah poked around with her stick. Liesbet shrieked when there was a movement, and then a cottontail rabbit ran from under the protective cover and toward the barn.

Laughing, Hannah pointed at it. "See? It's just a fat rabbit. He's probably been living off our garden all summer."

"I don't care." Liesbet was almost in tears. She threw the tomato stalks down on the ground. "I've had enough of this. I'm not going to do it anymore." She turned and ran to the house.

"Liesbet!" Hannah called, but her sister didn't turn. "Liesbet! Mamm wanted us to finish this today!"

The kitchen door slammed and Hannah was left alone with the chores. Again. Mamm wouldn't send Liesbet back to finish the job. Hannah bent down to pick up the tangled vines Liesbet had dropped and went back to the rows of corn and squash.

And if today was like other days, Hannah would end up doing Liesbet's chores in the house as well.

Little acorn squashes lay hidden among the vines. Hannah put them in her basket, and then went back to pulling cornstalks. She had planted this garden last spring, and here she was pulling it up. The corn, beans, and squash had done well, planted together in rows of hills. Johanna's family planted them in separate rows, and Johanna said it was easier to harvest them that way, but Hannah liked to have the beans use the cornstalks to climb on instead of having to put up poles for them. Besides, the corn needed less watering with the squash plants covering the ground around their roots and keeping the soil cool and moist all summer long.

The kitchen door creaked open and Hannah glanced up. Was Liesbet coming back to help? *Ne*, it was Mamm, on her way to the cemetery again. Hannah watched until she disappeared from view over the hill. She felt the tightness between her eyes and reached up to smooth the creases away. She needn't worry about Mamm on such a warm, sunny afternoon. Her spells came when the days were cold and dark.

Hannah shook off the shiver that gripped her and pulled on another cornstalk. She stopped and looked toward the small rise of ground concealing the quiet grove of trees. Mamm should be getting better. The spells should be gone by now. Giving in to the grief only seemed to make it harder for her to let go of the little ones.

Biting her lip, Hannah fought to keep her mind on her work. She found another squash and threw it in the basket with the others. She knew why Mamm wasn't getting better. Long ago, when Hannah had recovered, but the graves were still fresh, she had heard her say it. She could hear Mamm's voice now, strained and hoarse. "You brought death into our house." She had said those words over and over that winter. That long, black winter.

Hannah had been nine years old, old enough to understand. If she hadn't gotten sick, the others wouldn't have caught the diphtheria from her. If she had been stronger, she could have helped care for the little ones. If she hadn't fallen asleep . . .

If she had only gotten out of bed to help, Fanny wouldn't have died.

Hannah pulled at the cornstalk, willing it to leave the ground. Tears blinded her eyes and she kicked at the stalk but hit a rotten Hubbard squash instead. She stomped on the squash, smashing it to bits. She turned to the dry, twisted tomato vines. They pulled up easily, ripping from the soft

5

The fine weather lasted through the week. On Monday, Hannah asked Mamm if she could spend the afternoon with Johanna, and after the apple butter was taken off the fire to cool, she had finally agreed. Hannah nearly ran all the way to the Hertzlers' farm before Mamm could change her mind.

Johanna's stepmother, Magdalena, greeted Hannah from the front door, their newest baby, Veronica, in her arms.

"It's so good to see you, Hannah. How is your mother?"

"She's well, *denki*." Hannah loved Johanna's young stepmother as much as her friend did, although Mamm had been slow to warm up to her. Johanna's mother had been her cousin and best friend. The thought that Johanna's father, Elias, could marry a woman nearly half his age had made Barbara's death in childbirth even harder for Mamm to accept.

"Is Johanna here? Mamm said I could spend the afternoon."

"She'll love to have your company. She's on the back porch, stringing beans."

Hannah passed through the garden on the way to the back of the house. Magdalena had planted roses along this side of the house, and late blooms still clung to the canes, showing bright red against the yellow of the limestone wall.

Johanna squealed when she saw Hannah come around the corner of the house, dropping the bowl of beans on the floor as she ran to give her a hug.

"I was hoping you'd be able to come for a visit soon, but I didn't think it would be today."

"I thought I should come while the weather holds. We aren't likely to have sunshine for much longer."

"Come help me with the beans. We can talk, and you can tell me all the news." Johanna bent to gather the beans that had fallen to the porch floor.

Hannah took a seat on the rush bottom chair across from her friend and took the needle and stout cord Johanna handed her. She could hear Johanna's sister, twelve-year-old Susannah, through the kitchen door, playing with the little ones.

"Why do you think there might be news?" Hannah gathered a handful of leathery, dried green beans and poked her needle through the end of the first one.

"Oh, I only thought you could tell me how Liesbet is doing, or Jacob . . ." Johanna added another bean to her long string.

"What about Liesbet?" Hannah's fingers trembled. Had news of Liesbet's antics reached their neighbors?

"Well, not Liesbet so much . . ."

Hannah took in Johanna's red face as she bent over her task. Not Liesbet? Johanna wanted to hear about Jacob?

"I thought you were interested in Henry Miller."

Johanna leaned over her bowl of beans. "Henry Miller is a stuck-up pig."

Giggles drifting through the open kitchen door made Johanna turn that way with a frown, and she scooted her chair closer, lowering her voice to a whisper.

"He's been visiting Mary Kurtz. She says he comes to talk to her daed on Saturday evenings, but I've seen him looking at her during meeting."

"So you're giving up on Henry?"

"Why wait for someone who can't make up his mind when there are other boys around?"

"Especially one who lives just down the road, *ja*?"

Johanna laughed. "*Ja*. So are you going to tell me?"

"Tell you what?"

"Is Jacob sweet on anyone?"

"Not that I know of. But you know Jacob, he never tells me anything."

Johanna stopped stringing beans and sighed. "Wouldn't it be wonderful?"

"What would be wonderful?" Hannah took another handful of beans from the bowl on Johanna's lap.

"If we were sisters-in-law, of course."

Hannah halted her needle. "You want to marry Jacob?" Silent Jacob married to her talkative friend?

"Why not?"

Hannah smiled. "Why not? I'd rather have you for a sister-in-law than anyone else."

Johanna smiled back. She had finished her string of beans and measured out another length of thread.

"Did the men from Somerset come to talk to your daed?"

"What men?"

"It was Yost Bontrager and Eli Schrock. They came by yesterday and had supper with us. They talked for hours about a new settlement out west somewhere."

"*Ne*, I don't think so. Why did they come here? Is your daed thinking about going west?"

"I hope not," Johanna said. "But they spoke about the small community we have here, and how small their communities are becoming with so many people going on from Somerset County to Ohio."

Hannah sighed, thinking of all the families that had sold their farms along Conestoga Creek and moved west or to Canada where the land was cheaper.

"I wish there were more Amish families here, but I can't imagine Daed selling our farm."

"I didn't think mine would consider it either, until I heard him talking last night." Johanna lifted another handful of beans out of the bowl she had set between them. "But I know he is afraid one of us will jump the fence and go to the Mennonites or Brethren like the Eshelmanns did last spring."

Hannah started at the mention of the name. Clarence Eshelmann, the oldest son, had married a Dunkard girl a year ago, and by spring the entire family had left the Amish church. Since they were under the *bann*, no one was supposed to talk about them. Her hand shook as she speared the end of a bean with her needle.

"And they're not the only family that has done that," Johanna went on. "The Troyers, the Schmidts, the Zimmermanns—"

"*Ja, ja, ja,*" Hannah interrupted her. "Daed says the families who left us to join the Brethren or the Mennonites have lost the faith. They've chosen an easier way, but is that a reason for us to move away?"

Johanna sighed. "Daed seems to think so. He was telling Mamm that a larger Amish community would be better for us. Keep us pure."

Hannah bent her head to her work, her thoughts swirling. *Ja*, it would be good to take Liesbet away from men like George McIvey, but would Daed consider a move like this?

Shaking her head, Hannah pushed the thought away. "*Ne*, Daed would never leave the Conestoga. Our family has been here for generations. Our roots are here, our home is here. He wouldn't consider it."

"I didn't think my daed would either." Johanna pushed the beans she had just strung to the end of her thread. "Our family settled this area the same time as yours, but he says there are more important things than land."

As Hannah picked the last handful of beans from the bowl, her mind flitted to the three small graves in the cemetery. Mamm might never recover from her grief if she was forced to leave them behind.

"But, Johanna, what about your mother? Would your daed move west, leaving her grave here?"

Johanna lifted the hem of her apron and wiped her eyes. "I know. Sometimes I think he couldn't leave all the memories behind, but then I remember she really isn't there. She's in the Blessed Land, where there is no sickness, pain, or death. Whether we live here or somewhere else, we will always carry her memory with us."

Hannah poked her needle through the end of the last bean. What memories would she take with her of the three little ones who lay in those small graves? When she let herself remember them, all she could hear was Fanny's raspy voice, asking her to bring some water. Why didn't she force herself out of her feverish bed to do that one small thing for her sister? What if that one swallow of water could have saved her? But no, Hannah had succumbed to sleep, and when she woke, Fanny was gone.

The leathery bean crumpled in her fingers, the needle a bright point swimming in a blurred sea. She lifted her apron hem to her eyes. She could never leave Fanny. She could never leave the creek, the woods and fields. This is where her heart belonged.

When Hannah returned home, a strange wagon was in the yard. Mamm was bustling in the kitchen and the smell of frying mutton filled the house.

"Hannah, you're finally home. We have company for supper."

She glanced into the sitting room as she hung her cloak on the hook. Daed was sitting with two men, deep in conversation. *Ja*, it was Yost Bontrager and Eli Schrock, the same men who had visited the Hertzlers last night.

"Where's Liesbet?"

"She's occupying the little ones upstairs. William has been fussy all afternoon. If you can stir the beans, I'll get the corn pone out of the oven."

Hannah helped finish the dinner preparations, all the time straining to hear the conversation in the next room. Were they talking about the west? What was Daed saying?

When they were all seated around the table and prayers had been said, Eli Schrock picked up their conversation again.

"The land in Indiana is fertile and plentiful. There's plenty of farmland, some of it quite inexpensive."

Jacob looked from one man's face to the other, his eyes bright with interest. "I hear the land in Iowa is flat, with no trees, but plenty of water."

"*Ja*, well, you can't believe everything you hear." Yost Bontrager broke off a piece of corn pone. "I've been to Iowa and seen the land for myself. And *ja*, there's plenty of water and not as many trees as here in the east, but one has to wonder how good the land is where no trees will grow. Indiana has vast groves of huge trees, much like we have here in Pennsylvania. You know where there are good trees, there is fertile soil."

"What kind of Amish community is there?" Daed asked as if he were interested. As if he were considering such a move.

"Four families moved there from Somerset County last year. Preacher Joseph Miller and Deacon Sep Borntrager started the church, along with the Daniel Millers and the Christian Borntragers. We're both moving our families in the spring, and we're recruiting more to join us."

"Our desire," said Eli Schrock, leaning toward Daed with his sharp nose nodding in his direction, "is to start a community dedicated to the glory of God, with the discipline and direction of the church."

Yost Bontrager joined in. "There is room there for many families, and room to live in harmony with other people."

"So there are Mennonites there?"

Yost's beard bobbed as he nodded. "Brethren too. But each group is settling in their own communities, not mingled together as they are here."

Eli pointed at Daed with his knife. "The most important thing for me is that it's peaceful there. None of the talk of war and dissension you hear this close to Maryland and the other slave states, and no risk of abolitionists trying to talk a man into breaking the law by harboring runaway slaves."

As the men's conversation turned to news from the families who had moved to Somerset County from Conestoga, Hannah happened to glance at Mamm. Her face was pale in the lamplight and her mouth was pinched in that strained, drawn look she had when one of her spells was coming on. She would never agree to the move.

Hannah could hear the men's voices rise and fall long into the night. Mamm had excused herself as soon as supper was over, retreating to her bedroom and closing the door, while Hannah took charge of redding up the kitchen.

She had worked as quietly as she could but caught only snippets of the conversation—mostly comments about rainfall, the amount of timber, and how chill fever could be a problem for settlers in the low-lying areas. By the time the clock struck nine, she had the younger children upstairs and in their beds.

Liesbet fell asleep right away, snoring softly in the bed next to her, while Margli talked softly to her doll until she finally gave one final yawn and settled into sleep. Hannah lay still so she wouldn't disturb her sisters, but she longed to creep to the top of the stairway and hear what the men were saying.

Instead she went over the evening's conversation in her mind. Daed had shown such interest in the new settlement, but he couldn't be thinking of joining in on the trip west. From what the men had said, Indiana was the frontier. The forests would be thick and untamed, and there may be dangerous wild animals. And surely Daed hadn't forgotten about the recent Indian wars.

It would be much better to stay here where the hard work of clearing the land was already done. And where they were close to the market, and neighbors, and family. *Ja*, it was much better for them to stay here, where they belonged.

Soon after the clock struck ten, Hannah heard the men settle down for the night, the visitors on pallets on the parlor floor. When all was quiet, she began to drift off to sleep.

She wasn't quite asleep when the clock struck eleven, and then another noise drifted to her ears. The kitchen door opened with its distinct creak.

Certain she would see one of the visitors making his way to the outhouse, Hannah went to the window. A figure ran toward the woods, a white nightdress blowing in the wind.

Hannah took the extra quilt from the foot of the bed and crept down the stairs. If Mamm was having another one of her spells, she wouldn't feel the cold through her flannel nightdress until she was chilled through. Even then she might not come into the house to get warm.

Throwing her cloak around her shoulders and taking Mamm's from the hook, Hannah slipped out the door and followed the path to the family cemetery. The grass was wet and cold on her bare feet, and her toes ached by the time she reached the short picket fence surrounding the graves.

The waning moon rode low in the sky and gave little light to help Hannah pick her way among the family markers, but she knew where she would find Mamm.

Trees in the corner of the plot cast a shadow over the little graves, and there she was, huddled in the darkness. Hannah fastened her mother's cloak around her, and then wrapped her in the quilt. Mamm shivered, but didn't seem to notice Hannah's presence.

"Won't you come back to bed? It's cold out here."

"I can't leave them." Mamm's voice sounded hollow, as if she was far away. "I can't leave my babies."

Hannah's eyes smarted in the cool breeze. If only she could go back nine years. If only she could have saved the little ones.

Mamm's fingers twined themselves in the long grass, as if she could pull the dead bodies out of the grave that way. She paid no more attention to Hannah, but lay with her face pressed to the ground.

As though listening for their voices.

A prickling finger ran along Hannah's spine and she stood, backing away. At times like these, her mother was somewhere in another world. Hannah hated the way she let her grief consume her.

"Mamm, forgive me, please."

There was no answer. Hannah could have been speaking to the wind.

Once more, Hannah knelt next to the prostrate form, tugging at one arm.

"You must come back to the house."

Mamm roused and turned toward Hannah, hair flying and her face distorted. "Ne, ne. Leave me alone. Leave me alone!" Then she collapsed on the ground again, shoulders shaking as she sobbed.

Hannah rose and backed away until she reached the low fence, then ran for the house. Daed would know what to do.

C hristian roused at the shaking of his shoulder.

"Daed, come quickly."

"Hannah?"

"*Ja*, it's Mamm. She's down at the cemetery and won't come back."

He came fully awake. His bed was cold and empty. How long had Annalise been gone? "I'll be right there."

Hannah left the room and Christian stepped into his trousers, tucking his nightshirt in. He passed Hannah in the kitchen. The faint starlight from the window showed her waiting for him.

"Do you need me to come?"

He heard the tears in her voice. His dear Hannah. "*Ne*, you go back to bed."

Putting on his boots by the back door, he heard her light footsteps going up the stairs. He grabbed his coat and hat and stepped outside, casting a glance upward to judge the time from the stars. Sometime after midnight.

Christian paused at the edge of the porch, taking the time to button his coat against the frosty night air. The temperature plummeted quickly on clear nights like this.

"*Gott in Himmel . . .*" He shook his head. He couldn't pray to God for help when his prayers of the last nine years had gone unheeded. Did such a God even have time to look on his poor Annalise and ease her grief?

Forcing his feet to take the path to the cemetery, Christian sighed his acceptance of the burden God had placed on their family. So many years had passed, their house filled with children once more, and yet God saw fit to leave Annalise in this valley of grief.

He could almost forget her sadness in the spring and summer, when the long, warm days chased Annalise's spells away, but with the shortening of the days they returned without fail.

Reaching the edge of the cemetery, Christian stepped over the low stone wall. Annalise lay on Fanny's grave, her hand lying on Hansli's next to it. He could see her shoulders shuddering with deep sobs, her voice muffled in the grass.

Frustration rose like bile in his throat, sending waves of pain through his body. If he could pull the little ones out of their graves, he would. But they were gone. Gone, except for Annalise's unending grief.

"How long, Lord?" Christian dropped to his knees beside his wife. "How long must she suffer?"

There was no answer.

Christian laid his hand on the quilt covering Annalise's back, moving to grasp her shoulder. She shrugged him off, but he only grasped her tighter, pulling her up, turning her shoulders to cradle her in his arms. She struggled, and then surrendered, sobbing.

"Annalise." Christian spoke as he would to a frightened horse. "Annalise, you must stop this."

Annalise didn't respond, but her sobs grew quieter. Christian cast about, looking for something that might distract her from this grief that consumed her. He saw only limestone grave markers and drifts of leaves between them. How could she think of anything else when the sight of these graves reminded her of her loss?

If only he could keep her from seeing them, then perhaps she would be able to get beyond this consuming sadness.

But the only way to do that would be to move their family somewhere else. He shook his head, chasing away the thought like a summer fly. He couldn't leave this farm. It had been entrusted to him. So many generations of his family had lived here, he couldn't be the one to break so completely from the past. Christian let his gaze move beyond the cemetery to the dark shadows of the trees lining Conestoga Creek. He had played along those banks as a boy, just as his father had, and his grandfather. The clear water flowed in his blood.

He looked down at Annalise's face, her crying now over, her eyes closed, but not in the relaxed peace of sleep. Could he leave this farm for her? He would do anything to regain the close bonds they had enjoyed before the Lord took their three little ones.

Annalise's eyes fluttered, then opened and looked into his. They were clear and awake, not glazed the way they were when she was trapped by her spells.

"Are you better now?" Christian smoothed her hair, loosened

from the long braid she wore while sleeping. "Can we go back to the house?"

Her fingers clenched at his arm. "You wouldn't leave them, would you?"

"What do you mean?"

"I saw the look in your eyes when the men talked of moving west. I saw the eagerness on Jacob's face. You're considering it, aren't you?"

Christian swallowed. He had to admit that he had been interested in the news that Yost and Eli had brought. He had often looked at the western horizon, wondering what might lie beyond Lancaster City and the Susquehanna River. Annalise must have seen a longing as he listened to his friends.

"What if we did move west, Annalise. What would you think?"

"How could we leave these little ones behind?" Annalise sat up, pulling the quilt around her. One hand strayed toward the headstone with Fanny's name. "I can't leave them, Christian." Her voice dropped to a whisper. "I can't."

Hannah prepared breakfast the next morning. Corn mush with maple syrup. Christian missed the plate of crispy bacon, but they hadn't butchered the hogs yet. It would be another few weeks before they'd have pork again.

Yost and Eli ate their fill before they left.

"Will you be visiting any more of the families around here, then?" Christian asked as Yost gave his plate to Hannah to be filled again.

"I think you're the last of the Amish families in this area. We visited a few families up near Ephrata, and you folks here along the Conestoga." Eli pushed his plate away and blew on the cup of coffee Hannah had refilled for him. "We'll be heading back toward Somerset. It's time to attend to our own chores."

"When will you be leaving for Indiana?"

"As soon as the roads are passable in the spring. That way we should be able to find land and purchase it by mid-summer."

Christian turned his coffee cup, then picked it up and took a sip. He looked over the rim at his bedroom door. Annalise hadn't stirred yet this morning. "What will you do with your land here?"

"Mine is sold already," Eli said. He gestured toward Yost with his thumb. "He and his brother own their land together. His brother's staying in Somerset, so he's selling his share to him."

Christian glanced at the bedroom door again. Still closed. "What do your wives and families think?"

Eli grunted. "My wife says she doesn't want to move again, but she'll go along with it when the time comes. She only sees what she's leaving behind, but I've seen what our future is." He took another sip of coffee. "Our children are already being influenced by the progressives around us in Somerset County, even if she doesn't see it." He looked Christian in the eye, his expression serious. "Surely you've heard the same discussions here—talk of meetinghouses and doing away with the shunning. Some of the brethren have even taken public office." He shook his head, looking around the table at the children gathered there and then back to Christian. "I'm making this move to save my family. Sometimes the daed has to make the hard decisions, *ja*?"

Christian nodded his agreement, catching Hannah's eye as he did. Her face was troubled. She was afraid he was considering such a move.

"Do you think moving such a distance will solve the problem?"

Yost finished his meal, pushing his dish away as he pulled his cup of coffee toward himself. "I can't say for sure if it will or not, but I do know we have to do something. The Good Book tells us we are to be separate from the world, but how can we, when we live in the world?" He took a sip of his coffee, and then gestured toward the kitchen door, open to let the morning light in. "The world surrounds us here, in the settled east, but to the west . . ." His eyes brightened with his enthusiasm. "In the west, Brother Christian, there is such space, such freedom to live as God has called us. Land—fertile land—in abundance."

Christian smiled at the man's speech. "You make it sound like the Promised Land, Brother Yost."

Yost smiled back and finished his cup of tea. "Maybe it is. Maybe it is."

Christian looked from Jacob's eager face to Hannah's worried one. Her eyes held the question he couldn't answer. Would he consider such a move?

7

Christian checked the angle of the sun. Midafternoon and the farm was quiet. There would be no better time to talk to Annalise about moving west.

He paused in the mudroom to remove his boots. A regular thumping told him he would find her at her loom—her usual place between dinner and supper. He padded his way to the room off the parlor. It was an addition made years ago, with windows in all three walls to give plenty of light. The loom filled the space, with just enough room to walk around it. Christian slipped inside the doorway and leaned against the wall as Annalise finished her pattern. The loom glowed in the sunny room, the wooden uprights and crossbars golden with the patina that only comes from years of loving hands. Daed had made this loom for Mamma early in their marriage after they had bought the first of their flock of sheep from a farmer in Maryland. The loom would have to travel west with them if Annalise agreed to go. The sheep also. Farm equipment, household goods, food for the journey . . .

Pushing away the swirling details, Christian watched Annalise make a final pass with the shuttle and lay it on top of the woven threads. She turned on her bench to face him.

"Is there something wrong?"

"*Ne*, nothing wrong." Christian ran his fingers through his beard. "I just wanted to talk to you."

Annalise started to turn back to her weaving. Christian sat on the bench next to her and stilled her hands with his.

"We need to talk about moving west."

She wouldn't look him in the eye. "I have so much to do, Christian. Hannah has disappeared again, and I don't even know where Liesbet has gone off to."

But she let him pull her hand into the crook of his elbow. He leaned over and kissed the top of her kapp. His Annalise. Would moving west be the change she needed to stop this melancholy and bring her back to him?

"Tell me what you think."

She fiddled with a thread hanging from the edge of the loom. "So, you've made up your mind?"

"*Ne*, not for sure. I need you to tell me how you feel."

Her silence spoke for her.

"You don't want to go."

"Of course not. This is our home, Christian. How many generations has our family lived here? This is our heritage to pass on to our children. How can we leave it and go to a new wilderness where we would start with nothing?"

Christian glanced at her face. She was calm, with no sign of having to struggle against the demons today. He took a deep breath. Would she fight against his decision?

"I'm afraid for our children, Annalise. I'm afraid we'll lose them to the world."

She turned to him. "You've noticed it too?"

"Liesbet's rebellion. Hannah's interest in the Mennonite boy. And Jacob doesn't seem to think there's anything wrong with marrying outside the faith." Christian gripped Annalise's hand that still rested in the crook of his arm. "And where will the others go in a few years? I don't know." His shoulders ached with the weight of worry over his children. "Perhaps we've lost them already."

"But what can we do, other than pray?"

"We can take them from here, where they've been surrounded by influences from the outside. Look at our neighbors—only the Hertzlers are still Amish. What happened to the Eshelmanns could happen to anyone—and they aren't the only family we know who have either left the faith or been divided."

Annalise was silent. Her gaze went beyond the loom and baskets of dyed wool to the view out the east window. Toward the family cemetery. Her eyes slowly widened as she became lost in her thoughts, and he knew where those thoughts were leading her.

"They're safe."

Annalise startled and looked back at him. "What?"

"The little ones . . . they're safe in the arms of our Lord. They aren't our responsibility any longer, but the ones left to us are."

Her gaze went to the cemetery again and tears trickled down her cheeks. "I can't bear it, Christian. Every time I look out there, I see their cold bodies under the ground . . ."

Christian folded her into his arms and let her cry against his chest, seeing the memory that haunted her. That cold November day when he dug the graves and laid his little children to rest. The fear of that day, when they were so close to losing Liesbet and Hannah also . . . and poor Jacob, who somehow escaped the fever, digging alongside him in the bitter wind.

"But they aren't there. You know they aren't. Their souls rest with our Lord. Would we wish any different for them?"

"*Ja, ja,* I would, Christian. I would wish they had lived and enjoyed full lives."

"And go against the will of God?"

"I wish the will of God had been different." She relaxed into his arms, her tears subsiding.

"Annalise, sometimes I wish the same." He kissed her forehead and she looked up into his eyes. "But God knows best, *ja?*"

She sighed. A deep, shuddering breath of surrender. "*Ja.* God knows best."

Through the open door, voices drifted on the autumn breeze. Jacob and the younger children were coming home after an afternoon of fishing in the creek. They sounded happy. Content. Alive. Innocent. Untouched by the world. He stiffened with the urgency that swept over him. He must act, and soon.

"We must consider going west, Annalise, for the children we have left to us."

He waited for more tears, but when she spoke, her voice was calm. "*Ja,* Christian." She sat up, looking out the windows at the sheepfold, the old cabin, the barn. "We will pray and think. I would miss this house and this farm. And our friends."

"The Hertzlers are considering going also."

She smiled at him then. A true smile. "That would be good." She looked out the window once more. "I wonder . . ."

"What?"

"Was this how our ancestors felt when they left their homes in Switzerland?"

"They were driven out, fearful for their lives."

"And for their children. They wanted their children to grow up in the faith."

"*Ja.*" Christian felt a thread spanning the generations to the time of their forefathers. Were they really any different today?

Annalise stood and went to the west window. She rested her hand on the window frame, looking out toward the lowering sun. Christian walked up behind her and surrounded her with his arms, resting his chin on her head, his eyes on the line where the trees met the pale blue sky. Somewhere, out beyond the Susquehanna River and the endless ridges of the mountains that formed the edge of his world, was the west. Indiana. What would they find out there? They could hope for good farmland, good neighbors, and godly mates for their children. The future was spread before him like the clouds turning pink with the sun's glow.

"But if we go or not," Annalise said, her voice a whisper, "a part of my heart would always lie here."

Christian lowered his head to kiss the top of her kapp. If they moved west, would she be able to leave those graves that captured her thoughts and ruled their lives?

Jacob had already started the milking when Christian reached the barn. He took up the pitchfork to start mucking Beppli's stall.

After a few minutes of working in silence, Jacob cleared his throat.

"*Ja,* son?"

"I've been thinking about what Yost and Eli said last night, about Indiana."

"*Ja?*"

"I want to go. Even if it means leaving you and Mamm, I want to go west."

Christian smiled at the conviction in Jacob's voice. "You won't need to leave us quite yet, Jacob."

Streams of milk filled the pail.

"You can't keep me from leaving. I'm nearly of age."

"You misunderstand me, son. Your mamm and I are thinking of going."

Jacob jumped up so quickly he nearly upset the milk pail. "Really? When do we leave?"

Christian stopped pitching clean straw into the stall long enough to look over his shoulder at Jacob's eager face. "It hasn't been decided for sure, not yet. And if we do go, it wouldn't be until spring, so you have time to sit down and finish your milking."

"But we need to make plans. Do you know the way there? What will we take with us?"

"*Ja, ja, ja,* there are many questions to answer and many plans to make." Christian moved on to Blitz's stall. "I heard the Hertzlers are thinking of going also. The trip would be easier if we travel with another family."

"And then there are the others from Somerset. We might have a big group."

"*Ja,* we might."

"Will Hannah be coming too?"

"Why wouldn't she?"

Jacob was silent as he continued his milking. "Adam Metzler is sweet on her," he finally said.

"I thought he might be. But Hannah is still my daughter, and she would come west with us."

"What if Adam wants to marry her instead?"

A cold finger ran along Christian's spine. This was what he had been afraid of. "Do you think Hannah would marry outside the faith?"

Jacob finished his milking and picked up his pail to take to the house, pausing as he went past Christian. "I don't know if she would, but I think Adam might ask her in order to keep her here with him."

As Jacob continued on to the house, Christian finished spreading the clean straw. How far had this gone between Adam and Hannah? Were they no longer just childhood friends?

He stuck the pitchfork into the pile of straw next to the horses' stalls and spied Hannah hurrying toward the house. She had come from the direction of the Hertzlers', not the Metzlers'. She must have spent the afternoon with Johanna.

Christian paused at the door of the barn, his eyes drawn to the cemetery in the grove of trees. Nine years ago his life had been full, complete. Then in one terrible day his heart had been ripped in two as his little children succumbed to the fever. Hannah had been spared, although she had been so ill, and Jacob hadn't even been touched. Christian leaned against the barn door as he relived that night when Fanny had died, next to Hannah in the bed. Hannah hadn't woken as he took Fanny's cooling body from the room so Annalise could prepare her for burial, the fever finally gone.

Fanny had been the third to die. Catherine, barely four months old, had gone first, and then his little Hansli. His brave little Hansli, only five years old. His nose prickled as he remembered the boy's mischievous grin. What kind of young man would he have become by now?

He had wanted to bury all the children together, and so delayed digging the graves, waiting for Liesbet. His Liesbetli. Her breathing had been so shallow, her damp blond curls tumbled on the pillow as if carelessly tossed there. He and Annalise didn't leave her bedside through that long, long night.

Christian forced his thoughts out of the gray fog. Liesbet hadn't died. God had spared them that grief at least, although Annalise still looked concerned every time Liesbet coughed. She had been sickly for years afterward, but this summer she seemed to be stronger.

Christian turned his thoughts toward supper, the evening, and his children, and started toward the house. A furtive figure came from the woods on the other side of the clearing. He peered into the dusky evening. Liesbet? Her apron was twisted and her kapp was off. She pulled at her apron to straighten it as she hurried toward the house. Movement at the edge of the woods caught his eye. The figure stepped into the clearing—just one step—but Christian had seen enough. The tilted cap and cocky posture gave him away. It was one of those teamsters, watching his Liesbetli as if he had a claim on her.

A flash of heat surged through Christian and he saw himself rushing across the yard to confront the scoundrel. He would pound his fist into those leering eyes over and over . . .

Christian flexed his hands, relaxing his fists. He whooshed out a heavy breath. The man at the edge of the clearing disappeared into the trees, gone, but the temptation toward destruction remained. He shook his head, trying to clear it.

Years of discipline, study, preaching . . . and yet, at the first opportunity, the desire for violence reared its head.

He must think. He must handle this problem with a cool head and a tender heart. His Liesbetli! He could pray she didn't know this man was watching her . . . but the way her clothes were mussed . . . her missing kapp . . .

Pushing down the rage once more, Christian continued toward the house. Whatever he said, however he reacted, he couldn't do anything that would risk sending Liesbet into this fellow's arms.

From the shelter of the porch, Liesbet looked through the window. *Wonderful-gut.* Only Mamm and Hannah were in the kitchen. She wasn't late for supper.

She pulled her kapp from the waistband of her skirt and held it up in the light. George had pulled it off her head and thrown it on the ground as soon as he had seen her, and it had stayed there until she finally convinced him she had to get home. It had been stepped on, kicked, and sat on, and the poor thing looked terrible. Could she even salvage it? *Ne,* it was too torn and dirty. She'd just have to tell Mamm she lost it again.

Stuffing the kapp back in her waistband, Liesbet straightened her apron and dusted off her skirts. That George! She glanced back toward the edge of the trees, but he had gone. The memory of his kisses hadn't, though. She felt her cheeks, her palms cool against the heated skin. His kisses were like a summer rain—starting gentle and ending like a thunderstorm. She had managed to keep his hands under control, although toward the end she hadn't wanted to. What would it be like to let him kiss her as much as he liked? What if someday she let him . . . She shook her head. *Ne*, she would never let him go that far.

But once they were married, wouldn't it be fun?

She ran her fingers through her hair, pulling out the biggest leaves, and then twisted it into a bun as well as she could. Her hairpins were gone, but she could use some of Hannah's. She would just have to get upstairs before she was asked to help with supper.

As she slipped through the back door, Mamm never looked up from the pot she was stirring. Hannah raised her eyebrows.

"Liesbet!" Mamm said. "I wondered where you were. I need you to find Margareta and then both of you come and help with supper." She turned to the dry sink as Liesbet edged toward the stairs. "Hannah was out until a few minutes ago, and you disappeared right after dinner . . ."

Mamm's voice faded as Liesbet ran up the steps. That was easy, although Hannah would make sure their mother noticed her missing kapp. Mamm would take her side, though. She always did.

She found Hannah's extra kapp and the hairpins and quickly twisted her hair up. Now to find Margli and go down to the kitchen, and no one would even think she had been with her beau all afternoon.

By the time supper was on the table and the family gathered around, Liesbet breathed with relief. She had fooled Mamm, but Hannah wasn't going to let it go. She'd probably scold her once they got to bed, talking in hard whispers so she wouldn't wake Margli.

Daed was the one who made her squirm. He kept glancing her way with hard eyes, like he had seen her with George.

All through the meal Jacob kept asking questions about Indiana, and Liesbet stopped listening. She had no interest in Indiana.

She cut her potato into bites. When she and George were married, she would cut his potato up before she served it to him. And they would always have salt to season it, pepper too, perhaps. George's job would pay him so well she would be able to buy pepper at the market in the city every week—

"Liesbet? Where were you this afternoon?"

She jumped at Daed's voice, sharp in the sudden silence. Jacob shoveled food into his mouth, while Hannah watched her. The little ones kept their eyes on their plates.

"I . . . I was out in the woods." She took another bite of potato, buying time to come up with a believable story. "I thought I knew where there were some late blackberries, but I got lost and never did find them."

Daed watched her and she met his gaze. The best way to tell a story was to pretend it was true.

"You were alone?"

"*Ja*, Daed, of course. Hannah wasn't here, so I had to go alone."

She caught Hannah's frown. Her sister didn't like the attention going to her. She had probably been with that old stuck-in-the-dirt farmer, Adam.

Liesbet gave Daed a smile and took another bite of her potato. He kept watching her, as if he didn't believe her. But as long as he hadn't seen George, he couldn't know anything.

8

Hannah's stomach churned and she pushed her plate away. Ever since Liesbet had come home with her kapp missing and hair mussed, Hannah bit back words every time she looked at her sister.

How could she think Mamm and Daed wouldn't notice what was going on? Liesbet made all of her decisions as if she thought no one would be affected by them except herself. But it was her wayward behavior that would convince Daed to move the family west, if anything did.

Once supper was over, Daed moved to the side of his chair for the kneeling prayer and the family followed him. Hannah helped William settle next to her and folded his hands together. Daed's prayer was unusually long tonight, praying for each of them as he normally did, but also praying for God's leading in the decision of whether to move west or not.

He wouldn't consider that. He couldn't. Hannah said a silent prayer of her own.

Margli and the boys went to bed as soon as dishes were washed, while Mamm went into the weaving room. The moon wouldn't be bright enough for her to work at her loom tonight, but Hannah had often seen her spinning long into the night, a single candle the only light she needed.

As soon as Daed and Jacob headed to their beds, Hannah grabbed Liesbet before she could follow. "I need to talk to you."

Liesbet pulled her arm out of Hannah's grasp. "You don't need to say anything. I can see everything you're thinking in your oh-so-holy face."

"Girls?" Mamm's voice came from the weaving room. "Do you need something?"

"*Ne*, Mamm." Hannah grabbed Liesbet's arm again and pulled her to the door. "We're just going to the privy before bed."

"I will not—"

"You will." Hannah hissed the words as quietly as she could. She didn't want Mamm to hear what she had to say.

She kept a hold on Liesbet's arm until they were next to the orchard fence. The sheep were white shadows under the apple trees. One bleated at them as Liesbet wrenched her arm out of Hannah's grasp.

"All right. What do you want to say?"

"You were with George this afternoon, weren't you?"

Liesbet crossed her arms over her stomach and shivered. "Does that have anything to do with you?"

"You know it does. It would kill Mamm and Daed if they thought you had taken up with an outsider. You have to stop seeing him. Forget about him."

"I don't want to."

"He's not good for you, Liesbet. He isn't the kind of man—"

Liesbet turned on her. "What do you know about the kind of man he is? If you knew the kind of life he's had, you wouldn't be so quick to judge him."

"It doesn't matter what kind of life he's had. What matters is that he isn't one of us. He's not the man you should be encouraging."

"And Adam is?"

"Leave Adam out of this. We're talking about you and George."

"All right then." Liesbet shifted her chin up and turned away from Hannah. "George loves me, and he needs me. Nothing you say will make any difference."

"He needs you? What about your family?"

Liesbet turned to her again, her eyes icy cold in the starlight. "George is my family. He's the one I've chosen, and you aren't going to change my mind."

She ran into the house. Hannah started to follow, but why? There was nothing she could say that would change Liesbet's mind. She didn't seem to care about anyone except herself.

What drew her to George? Hannah couldn't think of anything about the man that was appealing.

Adam, on the other hand, was very appealing. If only he were Amish . . .

Christian shifted in bed, waiting to hear both Hannah's and Liesbet's footsteps going up to bed. When the door slammed and steps pounded up to the second floor, he relaxed. At least Liesbet was inside, safe. Hannah should be following her soon.

He had never thought raising girls would be so taxing.

Hannah was usually obedient and respectful, but this friendship with the Mennonite boy was a problem. She would stop seeing him if he asked her to. On the other hand, she was a grown woman, baptized into the faith. She was ready to set up housekeeping and start her own family. He couldn't believe she would allow Adam to entice her away, but there was still that friendship between them. It was too close, too entrenched.

He sighed, turning over again. Liesbet, however . . . Annalise had spoiled her, and he had allowed it. If he tried to put restrictions on her now, it would be like trying to snub a stubborn horse. She would pull back, fight against the restraints, exhausting both herself and him. And in the end, the conflict would only serve to drive her further from the faith.

Brother Eli had said that sometimes the daed had to make the hard decisions.

Ja, well, this decision was the hardest he would ever make.

The bedroom was dark, but he didn't need light to know every plank on the wall, every knothole in the ceiling, the view from the window, or which floorboard creaked when he put his weight on it. He had grown up in this house, just like his father had, and just like he had always thought his sons would. His grandfather had hewn the timbers that supported the ceiling. His father had cleared the pasture for the sheepfold. Their bodies, along with uncles, cousins, aunts, and—he swallowed hard—his own children filled the family cemetery.

Moving away from this farm and the creek would be like ripping his heart in two. But if God called, he must follow.

He heard the creak of the door opening. Hannah was in for the night. Both daughters safe for the moment. He could hardly hear her footsteps as she went up the stairs to her bed.

He would like to discuss this with Annalise. There was a time when they had planned everything together, working as partners the way it should be. So much they lost when the little ones died. He sometimes feared their marriage might die too.

Christian rose from the bed, the ropes creaking in protest as he shifted his weight to the edge and then stood. He waited, but his movements hadn't awakened William. He pulled his trousers on and went out to the kitchen in stocking feet. He could hear the whisper of the wheel in the weaving room where Annalise sat, spinning thread for the winter weaving.

Light from a single candle filled the room, bright after the dark bedroom. Annalise sat profiled against the window, the candle throwing her shadow against the dark glass. He stood in the doorway, leaning against the doorframe. She was still as beautiful as the day they had met. Beautiful in her plain clothes, her gentle ways, even in her grief that never seemed to end.

"Annalise."

She jumped at the sound of his voice.

"It's me. I want to talk to you."

"*Ja*, come in, then." He could hear the smile in her voice.

The wheel kept spinning as he took a seat on the weaving bench. Candlelight glimmered on the edge of the polished wheel and Annalise's face wavered and moved as the spokes spun between them.

"What we talked about this afternoon, about going west
. . . Have you given it more thought?"

"*Ja*. It's all I've been thinking of, especially tonight. When
I spin, my thoughts take off on their own, and tonight they've
taken me across the mountains to the west."

"I haven't heard you talk like that in a long time."

"How?"

"Thoughtful. Poetic. Peaceful." Christian hated to break
this mood, but he had to know. "And what did your thoughts
tell you when they took you over those mountains?"

The wheel slowed, and then stopped. Annalise's face appeared, whole and still on the other side of the spokes. "I
think we should go, Christian."

His heart clenched, and then eased. "What has changed
your mind?"

"I'm afraid of losing our children. I've seen how Adam
Metzler's face lights up when he looks at Hannah, and it's
only a matter of time before Liesbet catches someone's
eye."

He nodded. He couldn't tell her about the man he saw in
the woods, not until he was sure there was a threat.

"And the others," he said, "how will we find husbands
and wives for them when we live so far from other Amish?"

"I thought to myself, *There are the Hertzlers, but if they
go west without us . . .*"

"*Ja, ja*. I agree."

Annalise started the wheel spinning again. "I don't want
to leave."

"I don't either, but I think we should."

She returned his gaze through the spinning wheel and
pulled her lower lip in between her teeth. After more than

twenty years of marriage, he knew that was a sign she wasn't sure about what she was going to say.

"All right." She nodded, her confidence returning. "*Ja*, we'll go."

Christian rose and stepped around the wheel and baskets of fleece. Leaning over, he hugged her shoulders and kissed the top of her head. "We'll leave at the end of the winter. In time to get to Somerset County to meet Brother Yost and Brother Eli."

He blew out the candle, and then stood, pulling her up with him. "It's time to go to bed."

She followed him to the door, but then stopped, looking at the spinning wheel and the loom, standing in the starlit room.

"Don't worry." He patted her hand as he pulled it into the crook of his elbow. "I'll make a wagon big enough to take them with us."

Annalise reached up, as shy as a girl, and kissed him on the cheek.

9

Hannah hurried through her morning chores. Mamm was busy in the weaving room, and the fine weather held.

"Liesbet, let's take the children to the walnut grove this morning."

Her sister looked up from sweeping the kitchen floor. "Don't you think we have enough walnuts? There's a whole bin full of them in the shed."

Liesbet seemed determined to argue with everything Hannah said.

"We can always use more. Mamm ran out last fall when she was making dye, so I'm sure a few more buckets full will be welcome."

Liesbet gave an exaggerated sigh. "*Ja*, I suppose we can take the children out." She went back to her sweeping with a sideways look at Hannah. "You never know what we might find in the woods, right? The walnut grove is near the Metzler farm, isn't it?"

Hannah decided to ignore her. "I'll get the children ready while you finish the sweeping. We'll be back in time to fix dinner if we go right away."

Margli and William were in the chicken pen.

"You two know better than to bother the chickens." Hannah caught the back of William's shift and pulled him out. Margli followed, her hair full of downy chicken feathers.

"William wanted to pet the new chicks, but the hen kept pecking at him."

William held up a bruised hand for Hannah to inspect.

"Never mind. We're going to the woods to find walnuts. Do you know where Peter is?"

Margli shrugged.

"Then let's go find some sacks to put the walnuts in. Maybe Peter is in the barn."

By the time Hannah had rounded up all three children and empty sacks for everyone, the morning was half over. Peter led the way down the road to the walnut grove across from the Metzler farm where the children kicked their feet through the thick, crispy leaves to find the round walnuts underneath.

"William, you help me, *ja*? Find the nuts." Hannah swept leaves aside with her foot and pointed out the blackish green balls to her brother. Their hands would be stained from gathering them, but they could use every one they found.

Peter worked alone, trying to fill his sack before anyone else. Liesbet and Margli drifted off in another direction, but remained within easy calling distance.

William enjoyed the game, pouncing on each nut he found and throwing it into Hannah's open sack. As they circled a dense patch of raspberry canes, Hannah had the sudden, prickling feeling of being watched. She glanced around, but saw no one. Even Liesbet and the others were out of sight, although she could still hear their voices and the rustling leaves.

Standing still, she peered into the open undergrowth in the walnut grove. During the spring and summer, it would be impossible to see any distance through the green shrubs, but this time of year the thin branches were bare and the only barriers were the black trunks of the trees.

Slowly she turned to look into the raspberry brambles behind her. The stand was at least ten feet across, making a large mound in a sunny spot of the woods where a couple walnut trees had been cut down years ago.

Animals could hide in there, especially rabbits, and sometimes deer. She bent closer to the brambles, trying to distinguish shapes in the shadowy recesses. One shadow looked like a face . . . and then the face blinked its eyes.

Hannah jumped back, stifling a scream. The face rose out of the brambles and became a man. Dark skin scratched and muddy, with his clothes ragged and giving barely enough cover to keep warm. His face pleaded with her, his hand outstretched.

"Please, miss." His whisper was guttural, harsh. "Don't say anything. Please, miss."

William stood next to Hannah, his finger stuck in his mouth, staring at the dark man. An escaped slave. He must be. "Who are you?"

The man looked around wildly, his eyes red-rimmed and scared. "I can't tell you, miss."

Hannah reached out to pull William closer to her, ready to pick him up and run if the man made any move toward them. "Why were you hiding in the bushes like that?"

"Mister Adam, he tell me wait here. He say it safe."

Adam? What did he have to do with this man?

A stray breeze swirled through the branches overhead, sending brown leaves cascading down on them. The man shifted from one foot to another. He was bigger than any man Hannah had ever seen, his arms corded with muscles. At the sound of Liesbet's voice in the distance, he started shrinking back into the bushes, sending a wild glance toward Hannah.

"If Adam said you would be safe here, then you will."

The man relaxed as Hannah spoke. "You be a friend, miss?"

"What?"

"Mister Adam, he say there be other friends here, helping folks like me." The man's voice was low, urgent. "I know there be a group coming up the road, and they be needing a place to stay."

Hannah had heard about escaped slaves making their way through Lancaster County, always fearful of being captured, even in Pennsylvania where slavery was illegal. Was Adam involved in this dangerous business? "Does Adam know about this other group?"

"No, miss, I didn't have time to tell him. I was with them until yesterday afternoon when the bounty hunters got close, but I didn't dare stay with them. The dogs were after my scent, not theirs."

Hannah backed away. It wasn't her place to get involved in this. These escaped slaves were in a wretched position, but they were breaking the law. She had been taught to obey the law unless it went against God's express command.

"Please, miss. Can you find Mister Adam? Tell him about the others."

Hannah shook her head. "I can't get involved . . ."

"Miss, they're just women and children. They ain't strong like me. They get tired and hungry."

Hannah glanced down at William. He had lost interest in the stranger and had sat on the ground to play with a couple walnuts from the bag. If she were traveling alone, frightened and hungry in a strange place with William to care for, how would she find food for him, and a place to sleep?

"I'll find Adam and tell him." Hannah could hear Liesbet and the others coming closer to the raspberry bushes. "You stay hidden. Don't let the others see you."

The man nodded and sank back into the shadows under the brambles.

"Come, William. Let's finish filling our sack and find the others. It's nearly noon and time to get dinner ready."

Mamm was in the kitchen when they got back to the house. She stood by the window that faced in the direction of the cemetery and barely turned to acknowledge the children as they came into the house.

"Mamm?" Hannah looked to Liesbet for help, but her sister only slipped past her and up the stairway. "Mamm? We got some more walnuts. I'll fix dinner, *ja*?"

Mamm shook herself a little, as if she were waking from a deep sleep. She smiled at Hannah.

"*Ja*, you can fix dinner. The little ones will be hungry."

Hannah's stomach clenched. Which little ones did she mean? Mamm's mind often confused the past and the present. One winter she had wandered around the house day after day, looking for the baby. Finally Hannah played along with her, telling her baby Catherine was sleeping in her cradle, or that Liesbet was caring for her. Only then would Mamm become calm.

Daed had stroked his beard. "I think God can forgive this little lie." And then he had gone back out to the barn, as helpless as Hannah.

Now Mamm glanced out the window again. "It will be cold again tonight." She took Hannah's hand. "*Denki*. You are a good daughter to take the little ones out while the good weather holds." Hannah looked into her eyes. She smiled at the calm she saw there—no sign of madness.

"I'll make some rivel soup for dinner, and we can have the rest of the corn pone from breakfast."

Mamm nodded and went into the weaving room. Hannah walked over to the window where she had been standing. From here, the sunshine looked warmer than it really was. She could see the corner of the cemetery where the children were buried. If Daed took them west, perhaps Mamm could leave the past behind.

To the left of the cemetery, Hannah could see the little grove of blackberry brambles where Adam usually left his signal for her. It would be like Adam to help escaped slaves. He was outspoken against slavery, especially after he attended those camp meetings last summer. He came back full of fire, as if he had seen a different world while he was gone. His enthusiasm had tempered somewhat since then, but not the look in his eyes when he spoke about the abolition of slavery, or what he had read in the Scriptures, or about the work God was doing in his life. All strange ideas to Hannah, but she listened, even though she didn't understand. That was Adam. On fire for every new idea that came his way. It was a good thing he wasn't Amish. He would never submit easily to the *Ordnung*.

But this man in the walnut grove—how deeply was Adam involved? She had never seen escaped slaves around Conestoga Creek, although many freemen lived and worked in Lancaster.

A whirlwind swept through the clearing between the house and the barn, catching dried leaves as it went and spinning them into the air before releasing them to shower down on the grass again. Hannah shivered, even in the warm kitchen. She wondered about the group of women and children the man had told her about. Where would they sleep tonight? Who would feed them?

As soon as dinner was over, she would go to Adam and tell him. She had promised that man she would do it. And she would, but that would be the end of her involvement.

Hannah ignored the look Liesbet gave her as she slipped out the door into the cool afternoon air. Think what she might, Liesbet was wrong. Nothing was going on between her and Adam.

Pausing at the edge of the Metzlers' clearing, she debated where he might be. Just like the last time she had sought Adam, going to the house would bring all kinds of questions. Questions she wasn't ready to answer.

The big barn doors were open and she saw Adam's daed there, but no Adam. Had he gone to the walnut grove already? Had she missed him?

Then the door of the smokehouse opened, but just a crack. Just enough for someone inside to peer out. That's where Adam was.

Careful to keep out of sight of both the house windows and the barn door, Hannah got to the smokehouse door just as it opened wide and Adam came out with a large bundle in his hand.

"Adam, wait."

He froze, looking past and around her. "What are you doing here? Are you alone?"

"*Ja*." Hannah's heart was thumping harder than her short run across the bare garden allowed. All doubt was gone. Adam's bundle contained food. He was helping an escaped slave. "I had to see you. I met a man in the walnut grove this morning."

Adam looked quickly around, grabbed her arm, and pulled her back into the smokehouse with him. Stripes of sunlight seeped through the loosely fitting door, crisscrossing his face with bars of dark and light.

He pulled her close with one hand still grasping her arm. "What do you mean?"

"We were there this morning, gathering walnuts, and there was a man. He said you had told him to hide in the brambles."

Adam swallowed. "Did anyone else see him?"

"Only William. Liesbet and the others were on the other side of the grove. He wanted me to tell you there are others, and he's worried about them."

Adam released her. "Others?"

"He said there were women and children, and that they had been together until the dogs got close."

Adam shifted from one foot to the other. If they weren't in such a confined space, he would have been pacing the length of the room.

"You can't tell anyone about him, right? You have to forget you even saw him."

Hannah poked the front of his shirt with her finger. "He is an escaped slave, isn't he?" He shifted his gaze away from her. "I know what you're up to, Adam Metzler, and it's a dangerous business."

"Of course it is." He didn't deny it like she had hoped he would. "But these people—don't you see? If they're captured and taken back, they might as well have drowned in the river."

"But they would be alive and safe, wouldn't they?"

"The slave owners won't welcome them back with open arms. A man like Tom would be beaten within an inch of his life before he was put back to work."

"But it's against the law, Adam." She turned from him, trying to resist his plea. "We shouldn't even be involved in this. We keep to ourselves."

"Maybe you were taught that way, Hannah, but I know better. Helping these people is exactly what I'm supposed to be doing."

Hannah didn't answer. Couldn't answer. Her thoughts whirled in her mind. Of course she should help someone in need . . . but what about the law? What about submitting to the authorities God had placed over them?

In the distance a dog barked. The bark turned into a howl. Dogs on the hunt.

"Those dogs are getting close, Hannah. I have to go. Tom needs me to show him the way to the next station."

"Station?"

Adam nodded. "Like a railroad station." Then he gave her a sudden smile and reached up to pass his thumb along her cheek. "I hope someday you'll understand why I have to do this."

Without another word, Adam opened the smokehouse door, looked carefully around, and then slipped out.

10

The distant baying told Adam the dogs had picked up Tom's trail, but they were a good ways off. If he hurried, Tom would still have enough time to escape. Adam glanced behind him as he entered the woods. Hannah watched him from the smokehouse door, but made no move to follow. It was best she stayed out of it for now.

Tom had heard the dogs and hovered near the opening in the brambles. His huge body sagged with relief when he saw Adam.

"Them dogs—they caught my scent." Tom's voice was hoarse with panic.

"They aren't close yet." Adam pulled a loaf of bread out of his bundle and handed it to Tom. "You need to eat and keep your strength up. I have a boat down at the creek, and we'll take that as far as the outskirts of Lancaster. Once we're on the water, the dogs won't be able to get your scent."

Tom nodded and dug into the bread. He ate as if he hadn't had a meal in a week.

"Did the miss find you? She tell you about the others?"

"Yes, she did. Who are they?"

"My sister, another woman, and their children. I told them to come this way, and what sign to look for, but I couldn't stay with them. Them dogs, they looking for me. I hoped they'd leave the little ones be if I went on alone."

Women and children alone in these woods? "How many, and where are they?"

"Two women and six young. The boy's pretty old—old enough to help—but the others . . . ," Tom shook his head, shoving the rest of the bread back into the bundle, ". . . the others are just babies. Just babies. I left them hunkered down under some fallen trees, about two miles from where I saw your sign."

Adam nodded as his mind raced. He knew the place Tom described. But if he went with Tom to Lancaster, made sure he reached the next leg of the journey, those women would be left to fend for themselves. If they found his signal, would they even recognize it? He needed someone who knew the woods, who could find them and bring them to the farm. But there was no one else he could trust. Tom would have to go on alone.

"Are you ready?"

Tom nodded, his muscles corded like wound springs.

Adam retraced his steps out of the walnut grove and along the road, Tom following. He skirted the farm—if Tom was right and the dogs were on his trail, he didn't want to lead them straight to the only real safe place for miles. He and Tom jogged along the road, then doubled back and headed for the creek downstream from the Hertzler place. He had hidden his flat-bottom boat in some bushes along the stream near a rocky outcropping.

"Can you go on alone? Do you know how to handle a bateau?"

Tom looked at the little boat. "I sure can. I've used one many times."

"Good. Just follow the creek. With the oxbows and winding, you'll be on it for a good ten miles before you get near the town. After a couple hours, start looking for a stone house on the right-hand side of the creek. There's a gate along the creek—iron, with a dove in the center."

Tom nodded. "I look for a dove on the right hand."

"That's right. If everything is safe, there will be a quilt hanging in the yard." Adam rubbed the back of his neck. At the distant baying of a hound, sweat broke out on his forehead. "If the quilt isn't there, don't stop. Just keep going down the creek until you can find a place to hide."

"You ain't coming?"

Adam shook his head. "I'm going to try to find the rest of your family. I'll bring them to the Penningtons' farm, where you should be. It's five miles by the road, so don't expect us before dark. Keep your eyes and ears open."

Tom climbed into the boat, and then with a shove, Adam sent him down the stream.

Adam watched until the escaped slave disappeared around the bend. "God be with you, Tom."

As soon as the boat was out of sight, Adam erased all signs that anyone had been on the stone shingle along the creek. Keeping on the trail that followed the water, Adam avoided the road. If there were slave hunters on Tom's trail, Adam didn't want to meet them.

He jogged as quickly as he could. If he could find the women Tom had told him about, how would he get them to trust him?

Hannah.

Of course. If he could convince Hannah to help him, they'd trust her more easily since she was a woman.

Instead of going home, Adam went through the woods to the Yoder farm. He hadn't told Pa about his connection with the abolitionist group yet and wasn't sure how he'd take it. Perhaps he could persuade him to join in, himself, given enough time. But there wasn't enough time now, with slave hunters in the area and eight women and children needing shelter and safety.

He found Hannah piling dead leaves around the blueberry bushes at the edge of the garden. She left the chore and came to where he waited at the edge of the woods.

"Is everything all right?"

"Tom is on his way to safety, but I need your help." He looked toward the house and barn, but didn't see anyone. "Come with me."

He grabbed her hand and she followed him, just as if they were off on one of their childhood adventures. When they reached home, he could hear Pa and twelve-year-old Charles training the young oxen in the pen on the other side of the barn. He led Hannah into the smokehouse and closed the door.

"What is going on? Why do you need my help?"

Adam went to the barrel of supplies he kept there, out of sight of his family . . . at least until butchering time. He'd have to find a new hiding place by then. "Tom told me where to find the others . . . the women and children he was with. They need help getting to the next station."

Hannah backed away from him. "Adam, I can't get involved. I can't help you break the law."

"Hannah, we can't leave them out there, cold and lost."

103

The smokehouse was shadowed and dim, but he didn't need light to see her face. He knew her every expression, and right now she would be looking at him with doubt in her eyes, suspicion casting a slight frown on her forehead.

He picked up the bag filled with a loaf of bread, some carrots, and bits of smoked ham wrapped in a cloth. It wasn't much, but it could help bring strength to weary bodies.

"I need you." He stepped close to her, but she looked away. "They need you. If they see a strange man, they'll never come out of hiding. But a woman . . ."

Hannah raised her eyes to him. She understood. "We can't leave them in the woods, can we?"

"*Ne*, and we can't let them be found by the slave catchers, either."

"All right." She nodded. "I'll help you look for them."

"*Denki*, Hannah."

He opened the door, taking a cautious look out, and then he and Hannah both slipped out and through the woods to the road.

Hannah hurried to catch up to him as the hounds bayed again, closer than they had been.

"Why do you do this, Adam?"

"When I went to the camp meetings last summer, there was a speaker there from the Philadelphia Abolition Society. Once I heard that man speak, I knew I had to help."

"But why, Adam? Why you?"

"I don't know." Adam stopped in the road and faced Hannah. "Why do we do anything? God calls us. I heard that man speak and it was as if God was using his voice to tell me what he wanted me to do with my life. These people need help, and I'm right here where they need me."

The barking came closer, and then ahead of them, Adam saw the dogs. Three of them were lunging at the end of long leashes. Behind them were two men. One on foot held the dogs' leashes, and the other rode a tall black horse. As soon as he caught sight of Adam and Hannah, he spurred his horse toward them.

"Afternoon." He smiled at Adam, his teeth stained yellow-brown from tobacco. He turned to Hannah and tipped his hat. "Miss."

Hannah moved closer to Adam as he nodded a greeting to the man.

"Y'all be some of them Quaker folk?"

"No, we're not."

The man nodded. "Good. I've had my craw full of them abolitionist do-gooders." He spit brown tobacco juice at his horse's feet. "We're after some escaped property." He fished a handbill out of his coat pocket and held it up. "A big buck named Tom." He gestured toward Hannah as he stuffed the paper back in his pocket. "He's a dangerous one, he is. Wouldn't want the women folk to be near him, if you know what I mean."

Bile rose in Adam's throat. He had never been so tempted to smash another man's face. "I'm sure I have no idea where he is." Not a lie. He hadn't seen Tom since the man disappeared around the bend in the creek.

The man rose in his stirrups and took in the woods on both sides of the road. "Well, the dogs have tracked him here, so we know he's not too far." He spit another wad into the dust. "You keep an eye out for him, you hear? You help us find him, and we'll share the reward with you." He nodded. "That's right. Your share would be a whole dollar. So you let us know if you get wind of him."

He winked at Hannah, and then followed the man and his straining dogs into the walnut grove.

Hannah took Adam's arm. "They'll find his hiding place, won't they?"

"*Ja*, but Tom isn't there anymore." They listened to the dogs' barking fade into the underbrush. "I hope they lose his trail at the creek."

"What . . . what would they do to that escaped slave if they found him?"

Adam grasped Hannah's hand where it lay on his arm. It was soft and yielding. "Did you see the whip he had tied to his saddle?"

Hannah gasped. "He wouldn't use it on a man, would he?"

"*Ja*." Adam nodded. "That and much worse. These bounty hunters treat the black men like animals. The only thing that keeps them from killing the poor wretches is the reward they'll get for returning them to their owners down south."

"That's terrible." Hannah's voice whispered in the stillness left by the boisterous slave hunter, and her hand trembled against his sleeve.

"So do you see why I need to help these people? They have no one else."

She nodded. "But we have to hurry. I can't be away from home too long."

"Hannah." Adam waited until she turned her eyes on him. His Hannah. "*Denki*. You coming along today . . . it means a lot to me."

She turned and started down the road again. He followed her, praying they would find those women and children before the bounty hunters gave up looking for Tom and turned back.

Hannah wanted to wipe the memory of the bounty hunter's leering face out of her mind. Men like George McIvey were one thing, but this man was evil.

She hurried to keep up with Adam. He walked quickly but paused often, peering into the underbrush on either side of the road.

"Where do you think we'll find them?"

"Somewhere east of Wenger's Mill." Adam stopped, leaning on his knees. "Tom said he had been with them until yesterday afternoon when he left them to pull the dogs off their trail. He came this way, but it's hard telling which way they might have gone. The worst is that Tom was the only one of the group who knew the signs to look for. Without him, these people can get lost in no time."

They walked on for another mile or so before Hannah heard something.

"Adam." She caught at his sleeve. "Listen."

Adam heard it too. A child's cry. He turned off the road toward the sound, but Hannah could see nothing.

"Call to them, Hannah. They'll trust you sooner than they will me. Say 'I'm a friend of a friend.'"

Hannah looked around them at the sparse underbrush. She was sure the sound had come from this spot.

"Hello?" She glanced toward Adam and he nodded his encouragement. "Hello? I'm a friend of a friend. We're here to help you."

She waited, and then called again. "We're here to help you. I'm a friend of a friend."

There was rustling on the other side of a pile of fallen

trees, and then a head slowly rose above the broken limbs. "A friend of a friend, y'all say?"

Adam's breath went out in a whoosh as Hannah stepped forward. The woman was young, barely older than Hannah herself.

"That's right. We're here to help you. We have food and we'll take you to safety."

The young woman's head disappeared and all Hannah could hear was a whispered argument. A baby's cry rose and was quickly hushed.

Hannah and Adam stepped closer to the fallen trees, and soon two women emerged from their hiding place, each one carrying a baby. A boy about eight years old followed, and then more children, the youngest barely bigger than William.

"We have food for you." Hannah took the sack from Adam and held it out to the women. The older one hung back, but the first one stepped forward to take the sack. The children clustered around as she opened it and handed out chunks of bread and ham to them.

"How you find us?" The older woman spoke, her voice rough. Her hands shook as she reached out to hold the boy close to her.

Adam stepped forward. "Tom found me this morning. He asked me to find you to help you on your way."

At his words both women looked at each other.

"Where he be? He safe?"

Hannah couldn't watch as the older woman spoke. Her face bore old scars that disfigured her cheeks.

"He was fine, the last I saw him. I gave him a boat to go down the creek to the next safe house."

"The dogs . . ." The younger woman looked up from feeding the children. "How will he escape the dogs?"

"Once he was on the water, they wouldn't be able to follow his scent. He had several miles to go, so I hope they've lost him. The important thing is to get all of you to safety before the bounty hunters come back this way."

Hannah watched the children eating the bread and ham as if they hadn't had a meal in days. What horrors would compel these women to bring young ones on such a dangerous journey?

"My name is Adam, and this is my friend, Hannah. We'll take you to a safe hiding place for tonight, the same house where Tom is."

The two women looked at each other, and then the older one nodded. Their decision made, the younger woman straightened her shoulders and faced Adam.

"I'm called Tessa, and this is Sally May. She be Tom's sister, and these be his nephew and nieces."

"All right," Adam said, "we need to go. I'll lead, and Hannah, you bring up the rear. We have to move quickly and quietly." He stooped to let the smallest boy climb onto his back and started off.

Hannah fell into line beside Tessa. "Do you want me to carry the baby for a while?"

Tessa gave her a grateful look as she handed the bundle to Hannah. The baby didn't stir as Hannah moved the dirty blanket covering his face to look at the perfect rosebud lips and black lashes curled against his cheeks. His mouth moved in sucking motions. He couldn't have been more than a couple months old.

As Tessa took the hand of the smallest girl, Hannah kept pace with her. "How many of the children are yours?"

"Just baby Mose and Lily here." Tessa nodded ahead of them. "The others are Sally May's young'uns. They're all she has left."

"What do you mean?"

Tessa looked at her, and then glanced away. "I already done said too much. Sally May'll have my tongue."

"Why would you risk your lives and the lives of your children to make a journey like this?"

Tessa stopped walking and faced her. "You want to know?" Her voice dropped to a whisper. "It's freedom. I want freedom for my babies, and this the only way to get it." She reached her hand out to touch the baby's curled fist as it rested on his chest. "What future my babies got in slavery? Nothing. Nothing but work for the master. What if Mose wants to learn to read? What if my Lily wants to marry a man she loves? It don't matter to the master. They got to do what he says." She shook her head. "I want more for my babies. I want them to be free."

As Hannah and Tessa hurried to catch up with the others, Hannah looked down into the baby's face. His dark brown skin was as soft as any baby with white cheeks. His mother felt the same fierce love for him as any Amish mother. Were the abolitionists right? She had never considered the question, but looking at Mose she was convinced that no man had a right to own another.

11

Hannah held her hand against the stitch in her side as she hurried onto the porch. She rinsed her hot face in the cool water at the washing bench. She had gone along the creek trail with Adam, Tessa, and Sally May as far as she dared, but she couldn't be late for supper. She had handed baby Mose to Tessa, but her arms ached to take the sweet burden back.

She plunged her hands into the cold water again. What would happen to them? Would they reach the safety of Canada before the slave hunters found them? She might never know.

"Hannah, is that you?"

"*Ja*, Mamm," Hannah called back.

"I need your help with supper."

Hannah dried her hands and face on her apron as she went into the kitchen. The damp apron would soon dry in the hot room.

"I'm sorry I'm late. I lost track of the time."

"Don't worry about it. You're here now. I need you to start frying the fish while I finish the potatoes."

Hannah nearly dropped the pan of fish fillets Mamm handed her. No reprimand? No questioning where she had been? *Ne*, nothing. Mamm just turned to the pot of potatoes boiling over the fire.

The fish were fresh and already cleaned. Jacob must have been fishing today. Hannah dredged them through a bowl of buttermilk and then a plate of cornmeal. She put an egg-sized lump of lard in the spider skillet and waited for it to melt.

"Where is Liesbet?" Mamm pulled an apple cobbler from the oven as she asked.

"I haven't seen her since before dinner." Hannah caught William as he ran by and checked his underclothes. Still dry. He was doing better at finding the outhouse during the day.

"She wasn't with you?"

"*Ne*." Hannah placed three fillets in the skillet. They popped and sputtered in the hot grease, the aroma making her stomach growl in anticipation.

Mamm lifted the lid of a kettle hanging at the edge of the fire. Hannah breathed in deeply. The tangy combination of vinegar, sugar, and cabbage was heavenly. *Rote Kraut*, red cabbage, her favorite.

"She's been going off by herself more lately. Do you know what she might be doing?"

Hannah shrugged. She should tell Mamm about George, but she didn't want to upset her. "The weather has been so pleasant lately, perhaps she went fishing."

Mamm turned to look at her. "Liesbet? Fishing? I doubt that." She turned back to the *Rote Kraut*. "But perhaps she went for a walk in the woods."

"I wish she wouldn't." Hannah could imagine the scene Liesbet would have made if she had seen Adam and Hannah with the escaped slaves. Liesbet wouldn't have been able to keep something like that a secret, and then how would Hannah explain what she was doing?

"Why would you say that? Maybe she's meeting a beau." Mamm's voice had a teasing note.

Hannah turned to her, really looking at her for the first time that afternoon. Her eyes were bright, her face calm. Something had changed.

"What if she was?" Hannah wiped one sweaty hand on her apron. "What if Liesbet was meeting a beau you wouldn't approve of?"

Mamm put the lid back on the pot of cabbage and stirred the fire with the poker. "You know Liesbet would never do that. She knows what we expect of her."

A noise at the door made both of them look up. Liesbet stopped in the doorway, her skirts littered with dry leaves and her kapp clutched in her hand.

"Why, Liesbet, where have you been?" Mamm went to brush leaves out of her hair.

Liesbet didn't look at her mother, but sent a quick glance and a sly smile at Hannah. A cold knot formed in Hannah's stomach.

"I . . . I lost track of time."

"You look like you've been sleeping in a pile of leaves."

"*Ja.*" Liesbet gave Mamm an apologetic smile. "I sat down for a rest in the sunshine, and I guess I fell asleep. I'm sorry I'm late."

"Never mind." Mamm turned from her, waving her spoon in the air as she turned back to replace the lid on the pot.

"Straighten your hair and put your kapp back on, and then bring in the children. It's time for supper."

Liesbet ran up the stairs, not looking at Mamm or Hannah. Hannah watched her as she went. She had seen Liesbet try to hide her guilt before, and had seen her lie to Mamm before, but today she looked satisfied, as if she was the cat who finally caught the bird she was after.

Supper was on the table when Daed and Jacob came in. Liesbet had found the little ones, and Hannah made sure their hands and faces were clean. Once they were all sitting at the table, Daed cleared his throat.

"I have an announcement to make."

Hannah looked from him to Mamm. She wasn't smiling, but her face was calm. Whatever the announcement was, the two of them were in agreement. Jacob, on the other hand, sat in his seat with his chest puffed out. He knew what it was too.

"In the spring we'll be heading west, to Indiana. Eli and Yost's visit a few days ago gave me the final confirmation about something that's been weighing on my mind." He took Mamm's hand and looked at each of the children's faces, lingering on Hannah's, until she dropped her eyes. "It will be a new life for us, and one that will be good for our family."

Liesbet made a gasp as if she were choking and left her seat, her shoes clattering on the stairs as she ran to her room and slammed the door.

Daed and Mamm exchanged looks.

"Liesbet will come to accept the idea," Daed said. He smiled at the younger children. "What about you, Peter? It will be an adventure, *ja*?"

Peter wiggled in his seat. "*Ja*, an adventure. Will we see Indians?"

Daed grinned at him. "I don't know, but I wouldn't be surprised." He looked at Hannah. "What about you? Are you ready for an adventure in the west?"

"I . . . I don't know. What does Mamm think?"

All eyes turned to Mamm as she smiled at Daed. "I think a change will be good for us. Even though I'll miss our house and farm." She turned to Hannah. "The Hertzlers are thinking of going too. Won't that be good?"

Hannah's mind whirled. Leave the Conestoga? Leave their farm, their church, their friends? And what about Adam? Would she ever see him again?

Mamm and Daed were watching her, waiting for her answer. She put on a smile. "It will be good to have Johanna with us."

Her stomach churned. How could Mamm think of leaving their home?

"We have a lot to do before spring." Daed took another serving of corn pudding. "We'll need to build a larger wagon to take enough supplies for the trip, plus the household goods we'll want to take."

Hannah glanced up the stairway as Daed talked. There was only one reason she could think of for Liesbet being so upset at the news. George McIvey. He was a no-good scoundrel, from what she had seen of him.

After supper Hannah followed Margli up the stairs, tired after all that had happened today. She braided her little sister's hair and tucked her into bed. Liesbet's side of the bed the two of them shared was a soft mound. It wasn't like Liesbet to go to bed so early.

Hannah changed into her nightdress and brushed out her own hair. It was waist long, and thick, and if she didn't brush it out every night, it would tangle into a thick mess. Braiding it and tying the end with a bit of yarn, she glanced over at Margli. She was asleep already, her slight snoring loud in the quiet room.

Hannah blew out the candle and lifted the covers of her bed carefully, not wanting to wake Liesbet. The bed was cold. It should have warmed up by now. She turned to snuggle closer to her sister . . . but something wasn't right. Hannah sat up and pulled the covers back. The lump she thought was a sleeping Liesbet was only a wadded-up quilt.

The pieces fell in place, like a latch closing. Liesbet's disheveled look when she came home for supper. The satisfied smile. The way she disappeared after Daed's announcement. Mamm had been afraid she was coming down with a cold, but Hannah knew better. It had to be George.

She would want to tell him of Daed's decision—but what did she expect George to do? Come with them?

Hannah sat up in bed. *Ne*, not come with them. Liesbet had said she was going to marry him . . . She must have gone to find him—but where?

Wide awake, Hannah dressed again, binding her braid up so it would fit under her kapp. When she had come to bed, Jacob had been sitting with Mamm and Daed at the table, discussing the new wagon, from what she could catch of the conversation. If they knew Liesbet was missing, it would only worry them. She would start looking for them at the clearing. If she found Liesbet quickly, she could have her back in bed without anyone ever knowing she had been gone.

She stole to her bedroom door and opened it a crack,

listening to the murmur of their voices. In less than the fifteen minutes between one strike of the clock chimes and the next, she heard Mamm and Daed go into their bedroom, and Jacob came up the stairs to the boys' bedroom. She waited until he closed the door and then hurried down the steps as quietly as she could. She pulled her shawl off the hook and threw it over her head, running across the yard to the path she had followed so many times.

As she reached the clearing, she slowed, listening for voices, but all was quiet. She stepped into the open area. There was no moon, and the faint starlight didn't penetrate far into the woods. She stayed long enough to satisfy herself that the clearing was empty. Where else would Liesbet go?

She followed the creek trail toward the Hertzlers' farm, jumping at every noise. Who or what else was in these woods tonight? Bounty hunters? Pumas? The path led her closer to the creek, and then away from it, going in the general direction, but not following the creek's winding path exactly. When she reached the Hertzler farm, all was quiet and dark. Liesbet hadn't stopped here, if she had even come this way.

Perhaps she had taken the road instead of the creek trail. Hannah skirted the clearing around the farm buildings, holding her breath lest Shep bark an alarm. But the dog recognized her and greeted her by nosing her hand with his soft muzzle. She gave him a pat and went on to the road, leaving the curious collie watching her.

The road was a ribbon of silver in the cold moonlight, stretching empty in both directions. Hannah shivered in her shawl. She was getting farther and farther from home. What if Margli woke and called for her? Mamm and Daed would find both her and Liesbet missing and that would alarm them.

She chewed her lip, looking up and down the road. If she went home now, she would never know where Liesbet had gone.

She sighed in frustration and pulled her shawl closer around her shoulders. It was just like Liesbet to cause trouble.

Turning away from home she started down the road. As she went around a bend, she saw movement ahead of her. Ducking into the shadows behind a tree, she waited. It couldn't be Liesbet—it was a man. He walked as if he were weary, stumbling a little in the darkness. As he came closer, Hannah's heart slowed back to normal. It was Adam. She stepped out from behind her tree.

"Adam!"

He started at her voice, and then recognized her. "Hannah? What are you doing out here? I sent you home hours ago." He hurried up to her and grasped her arms.

"I'm looking for Liesbet. She's gone and I have no idea where she might be."

"Why are you alone? Where are your pa and Jacob?"

"I didn't want to worry the others. If Mamm knew Liesbet was missing, it might send her into one of her spells. You know how anxious she gets where Liesbet is concerned."

Adam pulled her close, warming her with his embrace. "I'll see you home, and then I'll go look for her."

Hannah pushed him away with her hand against his chest. "You'll do no such thing, Adam Metzler. You're exhausted. Did you make it all the way to Lancaster?"

"*Ja.* They're all safe."

"And the slave hunters? Did you run into them again?"

Adam shook his head. "I haven't seen any sign of them. I hope they've lost all track of Tom."

Hannah tried to peer into the dark woods around her. "It

doesn't look like Liesbet came this way. I thought she might have gotten it into her head to go to Lancaster, but you would have seen her on the road."

"Why do you think she'd go that far? What's going on?"

"At supper tonight Daed told us we'll be moving west in the spring." Adam's hands clenched her arms. "Liesbet got upset and left the table. She made it look like she had gone to bed, but she wasn't anywhere in the house."

"You're moving west? Where?"

Hannah shook her head. She couldn't think about Daed's news right now. "We can talk about that later. I have to find Liesbet."

"Do you think she might have gone to find that teamster you told me about?"

"I tried to tell her he was no good for her, but she wouldn't listen to me. But if she did go to find him, where would she look?"

"There's been a camp of them just off Snake Hill Road, near Wenger's Mill. Maybe he's with them."

"That isn't too far past your farm, is it?"

"Only a few miles. I'll walk you home, and then I'll go and see if Liesbet is there."

"I'm going with you."

"It's no place for a young woman, Hannah."

"Then Liesbet shouldn't be there, either."

Adam paused. He would relent. Adam always saw her side of things. "All right."

Hannah started down the road.

"But you do exactly what I tell you." Adam trotted to catch up with her. "And if Liesbet is there, we get her and go straight home, right?"

"Of course." Hannah let Adam take the lead. When she had left the house to find Liesbet, she thought she'd find her with George in the clearing. But if Liesbet had gone to the teamsters' camp, she could be in more trouble than she had bargained for.

12

Liesbet pulled off her kapp as soon as she was out of sight of the house and hid it under a bush. George didn't like her kapp. He said it reminded him of old ladies and starched collars, and he didn't want any of it.

She slowed when she reached the clearing near the creek. It was here that she had met him this afternoon, and he had taken her to his secret hideaway in the woods. She paused, hugging herself. The way he had kissed her, murmured endearments in her ear, she knew he loved her. He had wanted to do more than kiss her, but she had held her ground. Hannah might think she was a foolish girl, but she knew what she was doing. She had George right where she wanted him—anxious to marry her. He must be, as insistent and pressing as his kisses were.

Of course they would get married, just as she wanted. He had said he wanted her to meet him again tomorrow, before he and his friends left on another trip to Philadelphia, and the thought made her shiver with anticipation.

And wouldn't he be surprised when she came to him to-night? Once he heard about how Daed was planning to take her away, he'd let her come with him to Philadelphia, and they could be married there. George would do anything to keep her with him.

Liesbet turned to the creek trail and started toward Wenger's Mill, where George had said his camp was. It was a long walk, but he would be happy to see her. The creek moved slowly here past the Metzlers' farm, and the only sound she heard was a late frog plopping into the water. A dog barked in the distance. Liesbet almost tripped over a root and slowed her pace. It would do no good to arrive with a muddy skirt.

Hannah would never have a muddy skirt. She thought she did everything perfectly, and Mamm did too. Hannah's kapp was never crooked, her hair always neatly twisted. Her dresses always fit, her apron was never wrinkled. She could cook and sew, and Mamm never looked at her with the same worried look she used for Liesbet.

Lifting her skirt to step over a fallen tree, she caught the hem on a broken branch. Liesbet pulled it free and heard a rip. She picked up the hem to examine the tear. Hannah would never tear her skirt.

But never mind. Liesbet dropped the torn hem and hurried on her way. Hannah didn't have a handsome beau like George, either.

She hadn't gone more than a mile past the Metzlers' farm when she had to stop and rest. Last year's shoes pinched her feet, and she was out of breath. She always got out of breath easily. Mamm said it was because of the diphtheria, but Liesbet knew better. She tired easily because she was delicate. A real lady.

A real lady. Liesbet's breathing slowed as she let her mind dwell on her future. George was no farmer. They'd have a house in town. George had told her all about life in town. They would have a maid to do the cleaning and cooking, and their house would be beautiful, with furniture purchased in Philadelphia. Or better, the house would be in Philadelphia. They would live in the city. George would work at a fine job, and she would entertain her friends. He would be so proud of her and their fine home.

Liesbet looked around at the dark woods. If she wanted to get to Philadelphia, she would have to find George first.

She heard the camp before she saw it. She had been afraid she might be too late, that George would be asleep before she reached him, but she didn't need to worry. No one could sleep through this singing and shouting.

Stopping at the edge of the woods, Liesbet watched the firelit circle of tents and baggage. In the center were a couple dozen men, drinking from bottles. Most were clad only in dirty red undershirts and breeches. They sat on logs or on the ground. A couple of them were dancing a jig as one played on a fiddle.

Finally she saw George, sitting on a log away from the fire, apart from the others. Liesbet slipped around the edge of the firelight and came up behind him.

George jumped when she laid a hand on his shoulder.

"Lass, what're you doing here?" As he spoke, his voice a low, urgent growl, he stood and pulled her away from the firelight.

"I've come to go with you to Philadelphia, like you said."

George didn't say anything until he had pulled her into the trees, well away from the fire and his carousing friends.

"You mean you want to come with us now?" He rubbed his face and looked back toward the camp. "You can't, Lizzie. It wouldn't be safe for you."

"What do you mean? You're here to protect me, aren't you?"

"It just isn't safe . . ."

He was being stubborn. Liesbet stepped closer to him, putting her arms around his neck and pressing against him. She could make him see things her way. "You always said you wanted me to come with you." She pouted, even though he couldn't see her face in the dark.

George pulled her arms down and held her hands. "I was just playing with you, Lizzie. This is no place for a girl. You go on home and I'll see you when I get back from this trip."

"But, George, I don't want to go home. Daed is moving the family west, but I don't want to go. I want to stay with you."

One of the men in the camp was looking toward them. "Hey, George! What are you doin' out there? Do we need to come and get you?"

George pushed at Liesbet, away from the fire and the men. "Go now, Lizzie. Get out of here. You don't want these men to find you here."

"But—"

"Go. Just go."

She turned to walk away, but looked back once. George made a shooing motion, stepping back toward the fire. "Go on."

He didn't want her. He was sending her away. Liesbet stumbled over a root and fell onto her hands and knees, but George didn't come to her aid. He turned away from her and jogged back to the fire, joining the man who had called to him, slapping him on the back.

Liesbet rose to her feet, brushing the dirt off her palms. Well, too bad for him. If he wanted to treat her that way, then he'd see what would happen the next time he came calling. The next time . . . Liesbet covered her face with her hands. But he loved her, didn't he? Why would he do this?

She stood in the dark, watching George lead the next song. The men crowded around him, drinking from their bottles and laughing at the bawdy words of the song. They were all drunk. She smiled. Now she knew why George had sent her away. As drunk as these men were, they wouldn't listen to George when he told them she was his girl. He sent her away to protect her.

She twisted a curl of hair on one finger. She rose on her toes and back down again, in rhythm to the song, humming along softly. He was protecting her. Once he came back from this trip, she'd convince him to quit this job and these fellows. They were going to be married, and he needed to find a job that would keep him at home with her.

She turned back to the road and started for home. With any luck, she'd be back in her bed long before dawn and before she was missed.

Hannah heard the teamsters' camp before they saw it. Strains of music filtered along the road and deep voices sang in the night air, a low sound at this distance.

Adam cautioned her to silence with a finger to his lips as they approached the camp. A large fire in the center lit the scattered tents and the faces of the men who sat or stood around it. Hannah sucked in her breath at the sight of the slave hunters she and Adam had seen earlier in the day. The biggest of the pair upended a jug and passed it on to his friend before laughing at something one of the teamsters said.

Adam pulled her close to whisper in her ear. "There must be twenty or so of them. Do you see the man you're looking for?"

Hannah looked at the faces around the circle. As far as she could see, George McIvey wasn't there. She started to shake her head, but then a movement across the circle, at the edge of the firelight, caught her eye. She clutched at Adam's arm and pointed. It was Liesbet, talking to George. She had found him. They were too late.

As they watched, George led Liesbet out of the light, into the darkness beyond. Adam took Hannah's hand and led her around the camp to where Liesbet had disappeared. Hannah kept her eyes on the men around the fire, and saw George join them, but without Liesbet.

Adam stopped and his hand clenched around hers—a silent signal. She looked ahead and saw what he had seen. Liesbet was walking toward them, barely out of the light of the fire, watching George with the other men. When she saw them, she frowned.

"What are you two doing here?"

Adam grabbed her arm and pulled both of them into the darkness away from the camp. "Shush, Liesbet. Do you want those men to find you here?"

"You don't need to worry about them. George would protect me."

"Against that many? I don't think so, Liesbet."

Hannah took Liesbet's arm. "What are you doing out

here? We need to get home and back in bed before anyone knows we're gone."

Liesbet twisted her arm away from Hannah. "You didn't need to follow me. I know my way around."

She turned and walked away from them, toward the road. Hannah looked at Adam, but he was watching behind them.

"Is there something wrong? Did one of them see us?"

"I don't think so, but I have to wonder what those slave hunters are doing here."

"They probably wanted some company for the night."

"I hope that's all it is, and that they aren't trying to recruit some of those toughs to work for them. It's hard enough avoiding them."

"Come on, Adam. I need to get Liesbet home."

Adam stayed with Hannah and Liesbet all the way to their door.

"*Denki*, Adam." Hannah whispered the words as she took his hand and pressed it briefly.

He nodded, the starlight making his face into craggy shadows. "You'll be all right, then?"

Liesbet brushed past Hannah and into the house. She had been silent all the way home.

"*Ja*. We'll be fine. I'll make sure Liesbet gets to bed and stays there this time."

Adam smiled, tired and soft. He reached up with one finger to caress her chin. "I'll talk to you soon."

Hannah nodded and went in the house as he turned to go home. She hung her cloak and bonnet on the hook just as the clock was striking two. Liesbet had already gone up the stairs and was in bed. Hannah undressed and slipped in bed, her back to her sister, and waited for sleep to come.

Liesbet turned once, and then again, making the rush mattress bounce on the ropes. Then Hannah heard a sniff, and another one.

She turned over and rose up on one elbow. "Liesbet, are you crying?"

"*Ne*." She sniffed again.

"Whatever induced you to go looking for George tonight? Don't you know how dangerous that is?"

"Why should I tell you? You'll just go to Mamm and Daed, and then I'll be in trouble again."

Hannah touched Liesbet's shoulder. "You can trust me, I won't tell. Unless you're doing something that can harm you."

Liesbet gave a short laugh. "*Ja*, you won't tell." She turned over in the bed, facing Hannah in the dark. "You'll go tell Mamm first thing in the morning, and then I'll be in trouble. You were out tonight too."

"Looking for you! I was worried about you."

Liesbet was silent for a minute. "You don't need to worry about me."

"What were you doing tonight? Why were you looking for George?"

"Why should I tell you? Why should you care?"

"He's not the man for you. He doesn't care about you."

"You don't know anything about it."

"I saw him the day Daed and I went to Lancaster. I saw him with another woman. If you had seen how he was with her, you'd know he isn't true to you."

Liesbet sat up in the bed. "You're wrong. He loves me." Margli stirred and Liesbet dropped her voice back to a whisper. "He's going to marry me."

"Has he told you he loves you? Has he proposed?"

Hannah waited for Liesbet's answer, but her sister was silent.

"I didn't think so. You need to forget about him, Liesbet."

"I can't. I love him."

Hannah lay back down on her pillow and turned over. "You need to forget about him before you do something foolish."

"Foolish? Like what?"

How much did Liesbet know about what went on between men and women? Hannah turned back toward Liesbet. "Like letting him do more than give you a kiss. You can't trust him to . . . restrain himself."

"What if I didn't want him to restrain himself?"

Hannah sat up. "Liesbet, you haven't . . . You wouldn't . . ."

Liesbet gave a little laugh. "Don't worry about me. I know what I'm doing."

"Liesbet, tell me what you've done."

She settled back down on the bed. "I'm only teasing you, Hannah. You're always so serious about everything. George loves me, you'll see. Now go to sleep." She stifled a yawn.

Hannah lay back down next to Liesbet, but sleep didn't come. She listened to Liesbet's breathing slow and deepen, matching Margli's whiffling breaths. It was too shameful to contemplate, that her own sister thought she was in love with an outsider. And Liesbet was rebellious enough, Hannah could believe that she just might go as far as to leave the family and go away with him.

What would such a thing do to Mamm? Death had torn the family apart already, but at least they had hope that they would see the little ones again. If Liesbet continued down this road, it would be her spiritual death they would mourn. That separation would last forever.

13

Hannah pinned sheets to the clothesline on Monday morning. The wind whipped at the corners as she lifted the heavy cloth, but at least the skies were clear. The bedding would dry before noon.

Liesbet hadn't mentioned George McIvey at all the last few days. Hannah had caught her staring toward the clearing near the creek several times, but Liesbet hadn't gone out there at all. Hannah bit down on the clothes peg she held between her teeth. All that meant was that Liesbet didn't expect the outsider to be there. He was probably on another trip to Philadelphia.

The rattle of a wagon coming down the lane from the road made Hannah freeze. She peered around the sheets. The wagon was unfamiliar, but it was a farm wagon, not a freight wagon. The two men were Amish. The driver, the older man, looked to be about ten years older than Daed, with a long, full, gray beard. He pulled his team of horses up next to the barn and wrapped the reins around the brake.

Hannah looked from him to the younger man. He had turned on the high seat to look at her. When he saw that she had noticed him, he smiled and lifted his hand in a small wave. Hannah ducked behind the sheets.

Daed came out of the barn, and Hannah took advantage of the distraction to run inside the house.

"Mamm?" Hannah looked in the kitchen, but it was empty. The trap door to the cellar stood open, and Hannah looked down into the earthen hole. A lamp shone in the dark, and Mamm appeared at the bottom of the ladder.

"Hannah, hand me that crock of pickles on the table." She came two steps up the ladder and reached for the crock as Hannah handed it down to her.

"There's company outside."

Mamm turned and put the crock on the wide shelf cut into the earth and lined with whitewashed boards. "Is it the Hertzlers? We haven't had a good visit in a long time."

"Ne, it's two men. They're Amish, but I've never seen them before."

Mamm looked up at Hannah. "Two men?" She picked up the lamp next to her feet and blew it out before climbing the ladder. Hannah took the lamp from her and then helped close the trap door.

"We had better cook a fine dinner, then. They must be bringing news of some kind, and your daed will want to talk." She straightened her kapp as she thought out loud. "The *Schnitz und Knepp* will have to do for the main course, but we'll fix some biscuits and pie to go with it."

"There are still some apples on the trees."

"*Ja, ja, ja.* That will be good. You go pick the apples." Mamm continued to talk as she got out her bread board and the jar of sourdough starter from the back of the counter. "We'll do a cobbler instead of a pie, I think. That will stretch farther."

Hannah turned to go out to get the apples, and Mamm called after her. "If you see Liesbet, tell her to look after the young ones awhile longer."

"*Ja*, Mamm."

As Hannah passed the sheepfold on the way to the orchard, she glanced toward the barn. Both men stood outside the barn door with Daed and Jacob. None of them looked her way. Windfall apples were scattered everywhere under the trees, good for making cider or feeding the animals, but not for company cobbler. There weren't many apples left on the bare branches, but enough. She gathered up her apron to hold the apples as she picked them.

She had finished picking all the apples she could reach from one tree when she heard someone behind her.

"Liesbet, Mamm wants you to—" Hannah had turned as she spoke, but Liesbet wasn't behind her. It was the young man from the wagon.

"I wondered if you needed some help. I can reach the taller branches."

His accent was strange, but he spoke *Deitsch*, the Pennsylvania Dutch, just like all the Amish. His cheeks turned pink when she didn't answer right away, and he pointed to the apples clinging to the branches above her head.

"*Ach, ja*." Hannah felt her face turn as pink as his. She had never seen eyes quite the color of his. They were blue, but when he tilted his head down to look at her, they turned gray. He smiled again—a slow, gentle smile that made his eyes crinkle. Light brown hair curled around his ears.

He stepped around her and climbed up into the fork of the tree, reaching from that higher perch to pick the apples and toss them down to her. He worked without a word, but smiled at her as he jumped down from one tree and climbed the next, every motion effortless. He continued until Hannah's apron was full.

"I have enough now," Hannah said as he climbed down from the last tree. "*Denki* . . ."

"Josef." He leaned against the tree, gazing at her. "Josef Bender." He walked with her as she turned toward the house. "And you are Hannah, your *vater* said."

"*Ja*, I am Hannah." Her mind raced. If this young man stayed to dinner, perhaps Liesbet would take a liking to him and forget about George McIvey. "Have you met the rest of the family yet? My sister Liesbet?"

"*Nein*, I have not met any but you and your *bruder*, Jacob, and your *vater*."

That accent again, but a pleasant voice. They had reached the porch and Hannah went up the steps.

"You must stay to dinner, you and your daed."

"Not *mein* daed. My friend." He stood, continuing to look at her until she began to wish she had a free hand to check her kapp. "We will be friends, Hannah Yoder, *ja*?"

He stepped up on the porch to open the door for her.

"*Ja*." Hannah slipped inside the door. "*Ja*, we can be friends."

"Josef."

She felt her cheeks heating again and tried to turn her eyes away from his face. She swallowed and nodded. "Josef."

He let the door close behind her and turned toward the barn. Hannah took the apples to the table and set them, two by two, into the waiting bowl.

Josef Bender. What a strange man he was. Hannah held her bottom lip between her teeth to keep from smiling at the memory of his eyes on her. Liesbet should fall in love with this one. That would solve all their problems.

Josef looked around the farm as he waited for Daniel to finish his conversation with Christian Yoder. The barn was old and small compared to some he had seen on their journey here, but was in good repair. The quiet sheep in the fold and the sleek horses in the pasture showed the kind of farmer Christian was. Daniel would do well to go west with this man.

The young man, Jacob, joined him as he leaned against the fence.

"It's good to meet other Amish," he said, picking a brown stalk of grass and rubbing the seed head between his fingers. "You're from up Ephrata way?"

"*Ja.*" Josef picked his own grass and fiddled with the brown leaf clinging to the stalk. "Daniel's farm is northeast of the city about three miles."

Jacob was silent for a few minutes as he let the grass seeds fall between his fingers. "You're not his son?"

"*Ne.* I work for Daniel on his farm. When I came from Germany six years ago, he agreed to pay my passage if I worked for him. We had set the term for seven years, but if he goes west, I guess I'll be done sooner."

"You're a redemptioner, then."

"Daniel redeemed me, *ja?* I owe him more than the money he paid. He's like a *vater* to me. When I arrived from Rheinland-Pfalz, he welcomed me like a son."

Jacob looked at him, measuring. "You must have been very young when you came here. Were you alone?"

Josef nodded. "It's a long story."

"I'd like to hear it sometime."

Josef looked at the younger man. Some men treated him little better than a slave when they learned he was a redemptioner, working off the cost of his passage across the ocean, but Jacob's face was friendly. He was only curious.

"*Ja*, I will tell you sometime."

A bell rang from the house and Jacob dropped his blade of grass. "Dinnertime. I'll show you where you can wash up."

Jacob let the older men lead the way, with the two of them falling in behind. Josef wished they would walk faster. Hannah was in the house, and he couldn't wait to see her again.

From his first glimpse of her behind the clothesline when Daniel had driven in, Josef hadn't thought of anything else. He had never seen such a beautiful girl before, and she had seemed to accept his offer of friendship.

After washing up on the porch, the men filed into the kitchen and took their places around the big table. Josef tried to sit next to Hannah but had to be satisfied sitting across from her and next to her younger sister. Liesbet was pretty enough, with blond curls under her kapp, but her face looked tired and worn. Unusual for one so young.

Christian sat at the head of the table and led the prayer of blessing for the meal. Josef kept his eyes on Hannah as he waited for his plate to be filled with the *Schnitz und Knepp*. A basket of sourdough biscuits was passed and the ever-present pickles. He had his choice of pickled cauliflower, beans, cucumbers, and Brussels sprouts. If he closed his eyes, he could pretend he was eating at his *mutti*'s table once more.

Once Christian had filled all the plates, he turned to Daniel, sitting at his right. "You said you wanted to talk business over the meal. What brings you all this way?"

Daniel took a bite of the *Schnitz* as the family waited for him to speak. Josef almost smiled at this. Daniel knew how to keep his listeners anticipating.

"I heard you might be going west in the spring."

"*Ja*," Christian said, nodding. "We have decided to move to Indiana."

Beside Josef, Liesbet stiffened. He looked at her, but she only looked at her plate. He glanced at Hannah and caught her looking at him. She blushed and turned her face away, listening to the men.

"Nearly ten years ago, my three children all went west. They settled in Ohio. My wife and I, we thought we could make do at home without them, especially since we have Josef here to help out." He nodded toward Josef.

The whole family turned to look at him, and he was glad when Christian spoke again, turning their attention away from him.

"But now you want to join them?"

"*Ja*. My wife, she misses the children. We received a letter. There are grandchildren now, and the sons are doing well with big, prosperous farms. They want us to sell our farm and move to Ohio."

"You think we can travel together?"

"That's what I hoped." Daniel nodded toward Josef again. "A group traveling together is always safer."

Christian nodded his head and sat back with a biscuit in his hand. "That's true. It would be safer. There would be three families, if our neighbors agreed to join us."

Daniel smiled. "That would be fine, then." He nodded, satisfied. "Three families. *Ja.*"

Christian turned to Josef. "And you'll be coming too?"

Daniel waved his hand in the air. "Josef hasn't decided yet. I say he should come with us, but he says he'd rather be settled."

"*Ja*, I would like to be settled in my own home, with my own land." Josef made his decision as he spoke. His own home and land wouldn't be worth much without a partner, a wife, alongside. "But that land will be less expensive in the west, *ja*?" He risked a glance at Hannah. She met his eyes, and then looked down at her meal. "I would like to go with you to Indiana, if I may."

Christian nodded his agreement. "Another young man on the journey will lighten everyone's load, I think. This is a good thing."

The older man held Josef's gaze for a long minute, and then looked at his daughter. So, he hadn't missed Josef's interest and he approved. Good.

Josef finished the last bites of his meal just as Hannah brought a hot apple cobbler to the table. *Ja*, it would be good to have a partner like Hannah.

Dinner was redd up quickly after the men went back out to the barn. Hannah put a dish of sauerkraut and sausage in the oven for supper while Mamm took William into the bedroom for his nap. Hannah had just put more wood on the slow fire when she came back into the kitchen.

"I'm going to lie down with him, I think."

She looked tired.

"Is everything all right?"

"*Ja*, but I didn't sleep well last night." Mamm reached back to untie her apron as she talked. "There is so much to think about with this move west, and it's happening so fast."

"Daed doesn't let the grass grow once he makes a decision, does he?"

Mamm smiled, looking out the window toward the barn. "*Ne*, he doesn't." She folded her apron and draped it over one arm. "It may take a while for him to get to that decision, but when he does, he's sure about it." She started toward the bedroom behind the stairway, and then turned back. "Liesbet went upstairs to rest, also. Will you keep an eye on Peter and Margareta?"

"*Ja*, for sure. We'll get the next bag of fleece from the barn and start the carding."

Mamm nodded and went into the room while Hannah reached for her shawl. Hannah found Margli quickly enough, sitting in the lilac bushes with her pet hen on her lap. She let her play while she went into the barn. The men were inspecting Daed's old, green Conestoga wagon and didn't notice Hannah as she mounted the ladder to the loft that was just inside the door. Sure enough, there was Peter, lying on his stomach, looking down through the chute above the horse's mangers. When he saw her, he made a shushing motion and then waved her over. She lay down on her stomach next to him and found she had a good view of the tops of the men's hats.

"It's been a good wagon, all right, one of the last ones my daed and I built together." Daed patted the high rear wheel as he spoke. "But it's just too small to move our family that distance. I've started sorting the wood, and I'm ready to start building a larger one. Jacob can help me and learn the skills my daed taught me."

Daniel nodded his head, his broad-brimmed hat rocking up and down. "And this wagon? What will you do with it?"

Daed hesitated, and then slowly ran his hand down one wheel spoke. "I'll need to sell it, I guess. I hate to give it up, but we'll have no way to take it with us."

The older man jutted his thumb toward Josef. "If this one is going to Indiana with you, why doesn't he drive it? He doesn't have much of his own tools and furnishings to take with him, but he could haul our goods as far as Ohio."

Daed turned to Josef. "A good idea. What do you think?"

Josef nodded. "*Ja*, it would be a good thing. But are there enough horses to pull so many wagons?"

"Horses, or oxen." Daed scratched his beard. "My cousin John has a team of mules he might sell too. The big wagon will need a team of four. Six would be better."

The men walked out the back door of the barn to where Beppli and Blitz were pastured.

"Did you hear that, Hannah?" Peter's face was flushed as he sat up on the loft floor. "Daed's making a new wagon, and we're getting new horses."

"Or oxen, or even mules." Hannah stood up, brushing the hay from her skirt.

A voice sounded from behind her. "Which ones would you prefer?"

Josef? He was standing at the top of the ladder.

"I saw you come up here earlier." He smiled at her, and then spoke to Peter. "So, you were listening to the men talk. Which would you prefer to pull the big wagon your *vater* is planning to make?"

"Horses. Horses are better than oxen." Peter stood with his legs spread wide, facing Josef.

"But mules do a better day's work."

"*Ja*," Peter said, drawing out the word. He would never say any animal was better than his beloved horses. "Maybe mules would be all right. But not oxen. Their noses are too slimy."

Josef laughed as he nodded his head in agreement. "You're right. I vote we don't get oxen, but the final decision is up to your *vater*." He turned to Hannah, the laughter still showing in his eyes. "And what do you think, Hannah?"

"I think I need to fetch the bundle of fleece I came up here for." She could stand here all day talking to this man, but work needed to be done.

"I'll get it for you."

Josef picked up a bundle from the pile in the corner of the loft and tossed it down the ladder. He stood back while Hannah went down after it, and then followed her.

Lifting the fleece up to his shoulder, he smiled at her again, his eyes blue in the sunny open doorway. "Where should I take it?"

"On the porch, in the sun. Margli and Peter are going to help me sort through it to get it ready for carding."

"I'll help you until Daniel is ready to go. Let the *kinder* play, *ja*?"

Hannah couldn't help but smile back at him. His accent put a charming turn on his words, and it was tempting to let him help her with her work just to listen to him talk. "Well, you can help for a few minutes."

"Daniel may take more than a few minutes." Josef's voice had a warning note as they walked toward the house. "He loves to tell stories, and he has a new audience with your *vater*."

Hannah glanced up at her bedroom window. If Liesbet got up from her rest in time, she could sit with them on the porch and get better acquainted with Josef.

Josef set the heavy bundle down with an easy motion, and she hurried to join him.

14

Josef settled himself on the edge of the porch next to Hannah with the bundle of fleece between them. She had brought a large basket from the house, and as she pulled bits of twigs and other debris from the washed wool, she dropped the fiber into the basket. He watched, fascinated, as her fingers searched through the wool, pulling the foreign pieces out and leaving only the soft fleece.

"Liesbet really is a nice girl," Hannah said again as she pulled more wool from the bundle. "She can be a little shy around strangers, though."

"Who?"

Hannah's fingers stopped and she looked at his face. "Liesbet. My sister. That's who we're talking about, isn't it?"

"I'd rather talk about you."

"Me?"

"There isn't anyone already interested in you, is there?"

She went back to sorting through the fleece on her lap,

her face bright red. "I'm sure it doesn't matter if there is or not. However, Liesbet is—"

Josef laid one hand over Hannah's, stopping her. "I didn't ask about Liesbet. I asked about you."

She raised her eyes to his, holding her lower lip between her teeth. She glanced past him, as if the answer to his question lay in the woods behind him, and then down at his hand still covering hers. "I . . . I guess you could say there is someone who is interested in me."

He pulled his hand back. Was he too late, already? "And you? Are you interested in him?"

When she hesitated, he knew he could dare to hope. "It isn't as easy as that. Adam and I are friends, and that's all we can be. He isn't Amish."

He pulled another handful of wool from the bundle. "I don't want to push in where I'm not wanted, but I also don't have time to be proper." He picked at the wool, letting his words sink in. "My redemption period is nearly finished, and I'm looking for a wife, Hannah Yoder. If you would consider it, I would like to court you." He glanced at her, but her gaze was still on the wool in her lap.

"I don't know." Her words were so quiet, he had to strain to hear them over the sounds of the farm. "You're going to Indiana."

"Aren't you going?"

"I . . . I suppose I am." Her hands stilled, her fingers tangled in the fibers.

He glanced at her again. She was lost in thought, staring at the fleece in her lap. What was it about this Adam that drew her? Was he the one who made her doubt that she would be going to Indiana with her family?

"Then you will see me again? You will let me call on you?"

"*Ja*." She nodded. "*Ja*, you may call on me. Mamm and Daed would like that."

Josef dared to touch her again, to rest his hand on her arm. "*Denki*, Hannah. I don't know when I'll be able to come, but I will."

A whistle from the barn was Daniel's signal that he was wanted. It was time to leave. Josef stood, his knees shaky. With only six more months to go until he was free from his debt, it was time to find someone to share his life with. The thought that Hannah might be that person was wonderful.

"I must go now, but I will see you again."

Hannah looked at him, giving him a quick smile. "*Ja*, Josef. I will be looking for you."

That smile. It was all Josef could do to keep from jumping into the air with a triumphant yell, but he settled for a return smile. He backed away from her, toward the barn, his smile turning into a grin.

"I'll be back soon, Hannah Yoder."

She ducked her head down, and he nearly ran to the barn. Hitching the horses to the old farm wagon was a breeze, and he was soon holding the team steady as Daniel climbed into the seat.

"I'll talk to my neighbor, Elias Hertzler, about the route we discussed," Christian Yoder was saying. "He had mentioned going to the south, following the rivers before turning north, but if we want to stop in Ohio, we'll have to go overland."

"*Ja*," Daniel said from his seat on the wagon. "Talk to him. The overland route is shorter, and with the right teams and wagons it won't be any more difficult. I'll come down here again in a few weeks, and we can make our plans."

Daniel lifted the reins and clicked to the horses. Josef returned Christian's wave, and then turned on his seat to look for Hannah. She had stood to watch them go and returned his wave.

As the wagon turned from the farm lane onto the road, Josef settled in for the ride with a sigh. Beside him, Daniel chuckled.

"You didn't waste any time, I see."

Josef felt his face grow warm. "*Ne*. I don't believe in wasting time."

"I've noticed that."

Daniel drove on, following the river road until it turned north toward Ephrata.

"You surprised me when you said you had decided to move west." Daniel eased the team to the side of the rutted road, but Josef still bounced on the hard wagon seat. "What made you change your mind?"

"Hearing you and Christian talking about it, I suppose. It sounds like an adventure."

"Weren't you the one who said you were done with adventure in your life? That you didn't want to move to Ohio with us, but wanted to settle here in Pennsylvania?"

"*Ja*." Josef swallowed hard. "*Ja*, I remember saying that."

Daniel chuckled again. "I suppose you had second thoughts when you met the Yoders." Josef made a move to protest, but Daniel held up a placating hand. "I don't blame you, boy. Not at all. Hannah seems like the kind of girl who would make a fine wife." He looked at Josef. "She is the one you have your eye on, right?"

Josef gave up his protest. "Was I that obvious?"

"*Ne*, you weren't obvious at all, except that you couldn't

keep your eyes off of her all through dinner." He chuckled again. "And I don't think I've ever seen you cleaning wool."

"It was the only way I could talk to her."

"So you did right."

Josef thought the subject was closed, but Daniel went on. "You plan to settle in Indiana? Not Ohio?"

"From what Christian was saying, land is less expensive in Indiana."

"*Ja*, less expensive, but also more wooded and harder to clear. Ohio has good, flat farmland, and there are already a lot of Amish living there. This settlement Christian talked of is too new. There are only a few families."

"But with room to grow. And I'd hate to be the one who takes Hannah from her family."

Daniel nodded his understanding. "You know how that is all too well."

As they covered the next few miles in silence, Josef went through the conversation with Hannah in his mind. She had said he could come courting, *ja*, but what else did she say? Her *mutti* and *vater* would like it. She never said she would like it.

He could make her like the idea, though. When his sister was being courted by Helmut, before he left home, Ulla never let Helmut see how much she loved him. But whenever he left after spending an afternoon with the family, she would drop into a chair with a silly smile on her face. *Mutti* would hum as she went about her chores, happy and satisfied. But at twelve years old, Josef had been mystified, until Helmut finally asked if they could set a date for the wedding. Then *Mutti* told Josef that all was well. Ulla had wisely waited until Helmut was willing to make a commitment to her before showing him her true feelings.

Josef hoped that was the route Hannah was taking and that she was as attracted to him as he was to her.

Josef loosened his hold on the edge of the wagon seat and stretched his cramped fingers, working the tension out of them. This Adam she had mentioned, the one who wasn't Amish, hovered in the back of his thoughts. If Hannah thought of him as only a friend, as she claimed, why was he still preying on Josef's mind?

He looked closely at the crossroads Daniel passed, memorizing the route. He would need to make this trip soon if he had any hope of claiming Hannah as his wife.

Hannah pulled at another twig stuck in the fleece. What had possessed her to say he could call on her? What had possessed her to watch Josef drive away, as if he meant anything to her?

The twig stuck in a woolly tangle, and Hannah broke it to take the two ends out from different directions. That knot in the fleece would be hard to tame with the carders too. Just like her life. Things were complicated enough with Adam and Liesbet pulling her two ways, and then this Josef shows up. Her life would be so much simpler if he would decide Liesbet was the right girl for him. That would take care of two problems at once.

She dug into the fleece to reach a burr just as Liesbet came out of the house. Hannah patted the seat Josef had just left.

"Here, Liesbet. Sit down and you can help with the wool."

Liesbet reached for a handful of wool as she slumped down on the bench. She yawned, picking at the wool. "I don't know why you like this chore, Hannah. It's almost as bad as washing the wool at shearing time."

"It isn't that I like it. It's something that needs to be done." Hannah reached for another handful. "The wool has to be sorted before we card it, and so I do it. If I only did what I wanted to do, I'd . . ." Hannah stopped herself before she could say she'd be like Liesbet. As aggravating as her sister's ways were, it wouldn't do to start an argument about them.

"Well, I don't like to do it."

Hannah glanced at Liesbet. The girl's hands were still and she was looking toward the trees between the farm and the Conestoga.

"You aren't still watching for that George fellow to come back, are you?" Hannah kept her voice low.

Liesbet turned toward her with a hiss. "He isn't 'that George fellow.' He's my beau. And *ja*, I'm waiting for him to come back. He should be here any day now."

"Why don't you look for someone more suited to you? Someone like Josef Bender?"

With a snort, Liesbet tugged at the fibers of wool in her hands. "Someone like Josef? What a stick-in-the-mud! Did you hear the way he talked? He's just another dumb farmer. Whoever marries him won't have anything more in life than tedious chores and crying babies."

"Chores aren't tedious unless you make them that way."

"Maybe for you, but I was born for better things." Liesbet tugged at a stick and then gave up, throwing her handful of fleece in the basket with the bundles Hannah had already cleaned.

"Nothing could be better than this life, Liesbet. Working

with our hands, living a simple life . . . that's what God has ordained for us. We serve him through our work."

Liesbet snorted again. "You may have fallen for that line, Hannah, but not me. This—" She waved her hand toward the barnyard. "This is hard, dirty, and tiring. It's boring, and I don't like it. I want excitement."

"And you think you'll get that with George?"

Liesbet smiled. "Of course. George isn't a backwards farmer. He's going places."

Hannah shook her head. "Liesbet . . ."

"Besides, I saw the way Josef looked at you. He barely spoke to me all through dinner, but he couldn't keep his eyes off you."

Hannah felt herself blushing. "He looked at everyone. He's friendly and wanted to get to know us."

Liesbet stood, brushing off her apron. "Not us, Hannah. You. He wants to get to know you, and you're welcome to him." She started down the steps to the yard, then paused and looked back. "I wonder what Adam would think about Josef? He wouldn't be so happy to meet him, would he?"

She disappeared around the corner of the house. Hannah picked up the handful of fleece her sister had dropped and finished removing the stuck twig.

Josef Bender spun in her thoughts. So different from Adam. He surely had no hesitation about making his wishes known!

She reached for another handful of fleece. Adam could be bold, but he took longer to get to his point. He had mentioned marriage once, but then nothing had changed. Hannah tugged at a burr. He was the same as he had been last year and the year before, except for the stolen kiss. He should know she would never break her baptismal vows to become

Mennonite, even for him. Unless he chose to become Amish and give up this idea of helping the escaped slaves, marriage to him was impossible.

Josef, on the other hand, was a different story all together. They had barely spoken to each other, and yet he seemed sure they would make a good marriage. They shared the same views on religion and picking apples, but that couldn't be all there was. All that meant is that they wouldn't argue, but a marriage had to be more than friendship.

Hannah picked at the wool in her hands, digging for another burr.

She didn't want to settle for that kind of marriage. Watching Mamm and Daed . . . a marriage without love could be miserable. Hannah forgot the wool, leaning her head against the wall, listening to the thump of Mamm's loom. Daed left the barn, and he and Jacob headed down the creek path toward the Hertzlers'. Her parents had loved each other once, she was sure of it. Before . . .

It wasn't only the little ones who died nine years ago.

But lately, she had seen Mamm pat Daed's shoulder as she passed by him. Once Daed had caught Mamm's hand and squeezed it when he thought no one was watching. Perhaps their love, though it once seemed dead, was growing again.

H annah had nearly finished cleaning the wool fleece when Mamm came out to the porch.

"Has your daed gone to the Hertzlers' already?"

"*Ja*, he left a little while ago."

"Would you mind taking something over there for me? I promised to share the packet of cinnamon with Magdalena, and I forgot to send it along."

Hannah brushed twigs and dust off her apron as she stood up. "Why don't I take Margli with me? She can play with Barbli while I visit with Johanna, *ja*?"

Mamm nodded, pulling her shawl close. "Don't be too long, though, and take Margli's shawl with you. The air is turning chilly this afternoon."

Hannah took the shawls and Mamm's packet of cinnamon. It took some convincing for Margli to leave Henni behind, but soon they were on their way.

"Can we take the creek path, Hannah?" Margli skipped beside her.

"For sure. We never know what we'll see along the creek, *ja*?"

Margli ran ahead while Hannah took her time, watching the swirling waters of the Conestoga. Indiana couldn't have creeks as beautiful as this one. Birdsong filled the air, and Hannah caught glimpses of cedar waxwings. They were gathered in the wild plum bushes along the other side of the creek, eating the little dried plums and fighting over the laden branches. Soon the flock would head south, and they wouldn't be back until spring.

Spring. If she went west with Mamm and Daed, she wouldn't be here in the spring. How could they think of leaving the Conestoga behind? They couldn't turn their backs on the farm and the creek. They couldn't abandon the graves in the cemetery. This was their home. And yet they still continued with their plans.

"Hannah! Hurry up!"

Margli waited for her where the path bent away from the creek and toward the Hertzlers' farm. She hurried to catch up, anxious to talk to Johanna.

Daed waved to her from the barn where he stood talking with Elias. Jacob stood with the men, chewing on a straw. He nodded at Hannah and Margli, and then turned his attention back to the conversation. He stood with his back to the house, ignoring Johanna, who sat on the porch swing with some sewing in her lap. She dropped it on the swing beside her and ran to meet Hannah.

"Hallo! So good to see you!"

"*Ja*, you too." Hannah gave her friend a hug. "Mamm sent some cinnamon."

"Is Barbli here?" Margli jumped up and down until Hannah put her hand on the girl's shoulder. "Can she play?"

Johanna reached out to pull the string of Margli's kapp. "For sure, she's here. Go in the kitchen. I think she's helping Mamm make a pie for supper."

"Take the cinnamon with you." Hannah gave Margli the packet and watched as she skipped to the kitchen door. Excited squeals from the kitchen made her laugh. "It sounds like Barbli is happy to see her."

"They're best friends, aren't they? Just like the two of us."

"*Ja.*" Hannah linked arms with Johanna. "Just like us."

"And maybe they'll be sisters someday. Barbli and Peter could get married . . ."

"Johanna! And now you'll have William marrying baby Veronica."

"Why not? Who knows what will happen in the future?" She took Hannah's hand and pulled her to the porch. "Come on and sit by me. I hoped you would come when I saw your daed and Jacob."

Hannah picked up Johanna's sewing from her side of the seat and handed it to her as she sat down. "It's been a busy day, and a busy week. I have so much to tell you."

"Your daed told us you are going to Indiana with us. Won't that be *wonderful-gut*? Our families traveling together?"

"That will give you plenty of time with Jacob, *ja*?"

Johanna made a face. "He hasn't looked at me once all afternoon. He's too busy talking to the men."

"That's Jacob. Once he gets his mind on something, he doesn't think about anything else."

"It seems he'd think about me."

"Don't pout. There's another young man going west."

Johanna raised her eyebrows. "Who?"

"His name is Josef Bender, from Ephrata—" Hannah

stopped. What would Johanna think of Josef? He had said he wanted to visit with Hannah, but would he change his mind once he met Johanna?

"And? Is he handsome? How old is he? Will he be settling on his own farm? What do you know about him?"

Johanna's questions came faster than Hannah could think. "Um, I'm not sure. We didn't talk very much."

"But he talked to you? What did he say?"

Hannah looked down at her fingers, twisting themselves together on her lap. It was one thing to talk about Johanna and Jacob, or Adam, but Josef . . . he was different. "He wants to come see me."

"You mean he wants to court you?" Johanna's eyes grew wide. "How long have you known him?"

"We met this morning."

Johanna fell over into her lap in a pretend faint. "And he's interested in you already?"

"Get up." Hannah pushed her friend back into her seat. "He's very nice, and yes, he's handsome." If she wasn't careful, she could dream about his blue eyes all day. Hannah pulled her mind back. "He's a redemptioner, but nearly at the end of his term. He'll be just starting out in Indiana."

Johanna picked up her sewing again. "And you'll be his wife, starting out with him."

"I didn't say I was marrying him."

"You said . . ." Johanna stared at her, the sewing forgotten again. "You mean you're thinking about not marrying him?"

Hannah ran her hand up and down the rope that suspended the swing from the porch ceiling. "I'm thinking about not going to Indiana."

"But you can't do that. You have to go."

"Why?"

"Because . . . well, because your family is going."

"*Ja . . .*" Hannah grasped the rope tightly. If she refused to go, wouldn't Daed change his mind? She watched him, standing in front of the barn, gesturing as he talked with Elias. *Ne*, he would only force her to go.

"Maybe I'll be married by then and stay here." She glanced at Johanna.

Her friend's eyes were filling with tears. "I couldn't bear to go and leave you behind."

"You'll have your family, and Jacob."

"But who would you marry?"

"Maybe Josef would agree to stay here if I asked him to. He could buy our farm, and then I wouldn't have to go anywhere."

"And if he didn't? What if he insisted on going west after all?"

Hannah shrugged. "Then I'll marry Adam."

"Adam?" Johanna leaned closer, dropping her voice to a whisper. "Has he asked you to marry him?"

Hannah smiled at her. "Several times."

Johanna squealed, but Hannah shushed her. "I've always told him no. You know I can't marry outside our faith."

"And what does he say to that?"

"He says I should become Mennonite."

"Would you do that? Would you leave our faith behind and join his?"

Hannah pushed at the porch floor with her foot, making the swing rock. "I might, if that was the only way I could stay here." She looked at Johanna. "I can't leave the Conestoga. It's my home. I'm afraid my heart would break in two if I had to leave."

Johanna sat silently while Hannah waited for her outburst. It didn't come. Johanna only sighed. "I was hoping we'd be friends forever."

"We'll still be friends."

"Not if you stay here." Johanna took her hand. "We'll grow apart. We'll write letters, but we'll still grow apart. Our husbands won't work together, our children won't be friends . . ." She sniffed. "Who will I confide in?"

Hannah squeezed her friend's hand. She had no answer.

Hannah woke early the next morning. Liesbet's snores were loud enough to wake the soundest sleeper, and as used to them as Hannah was, she usually slept through them. But this morning she woke with a start, and then sleep was gone.

She slid out of bed and knelt by the window, looking for some sign of dawn. The quarter moon rode high in the sky, and the eastern horizon was barely gray. Still too early to be up, but going back to sleep was out of the question. She dressed and put her hair up in the dark, and then slipped out of the bedroom and down the stairs.

All night long she had been thinking of this new idea that had come to her while she visited with Johanna. Marriage was her answer to staying in Pennsylvania, and the key to keeping the family here. Daed wouldn't want to move if she was married and settled on the Conestoga. But even if the family moved west, if she married, she would be able to stay.

She passed the sheepfold slowly. If one sheep woke, the whole flock would start baaing, but they stayed asleep. Taking the trail through the woods, she passed the clearing where she and Adam would meet and went on to her favorite spot.

A tree, half fallen, reached out over the water. She gathered her skirts and climbed up the slanted trunk until she came to the fork where a branch and the trunk formed a seat above the water. She settled in, closed her eyes, and listened.

No birds sang other than a chirp here and there. In the spring the trees were full of nesting birds, their songs competing with each other until it was nearly deafening in the pre-dawn light. This late in the season, after the frosts, the insects were all gone. The flocks of birds had gathered and headed south. Only the sound of gurgling water remained, and the whisper of the breeze through the brown oak leaves still clinging to their branches.

She would never have to leave this place if her plan worked out. When she was an old woman, she could still come here to the banks of the Conestoga and listen to the creek's song. Her children would know this timeless music, and her grandchildren too. This farm her ancestors had settled, her grandparents had built, her daed had cared for . . . she wouldn't need to abandon it.

Josef was the key. As an Amish man, he would have Daed's approval to marry her. He needed a home, she needed someone to marry. Perhaps she would even grow to love him, *ja*?

She stirred on her perch. The air above the creek was chilly and seeped through her clothes. She gazed down into the water, watching for the fish that hid along the boulders and sunken branches.

Dreams of marrying for love were girlish. She blinked, her eyes smarting. She was eighteen and grown up, past the age of dreams. Josef was handsome enough, and he seemed kind. The type of man who would stay true to his faith. The kind of man who would value the same things she did.

A sound cut through the creek noises. Whistling. Only Adam whistled like that. What was he doing on the creek trail this early?

Hannah climbed down from her tree and made her way to the trail, reaching it in time to intercept Adam. The sky had become lighter, and even beneath the bare branches of the woods, she could make out his form, walking toward home from down the creek.

"Where have you been so early in the morning?"

The whistling stopped and Adam paused and peered down the trail toward her. "Hannah?" He came closer. "I could ask you the same thing."

"I'm an early riser today, but you must have been earlier than me if you're making your way home already."

Adam looked up at the sky through the branches. "Well, I haven't been to bed yet."

"What have you been—?" Before she finished the sentence, Hannah knew. "You've been helping those refugees again, haven't you?"

Adam stepped closer. "*Ja*, I have." His voice was low, guarded. "I guided some people to Lancaster, to a friend's house."

Hannah crossed her arms over her stomach, a shiver going through her. "How many times are you going to do this?"

"As many as I need to. This is what God has laid on my heart, Hannah. I have to obey him."

She walked to a fallen log and brushed it off, making a seat for both of them. "Sit down for a bit. You must be tired."

He sat on the log with a groan. "Walking all night after working all day is exhausting."

"Is it worth it, Adam? You're doing so much."

"There's no such thing as too much in this work." Adam rubbed his face with both hands, and then turned to her. "I'm glad we ran into each other. I've been wanting to talk to you about your family going west."

Hannah didn't say anything.

"Is this true?"

She nodded. "Daed wants to move to Indiana to join a new settlement there."

"And you're going too?"

She shrugged. "I don't know yet. I don't want to. I wish there was a way to convince Daed not to go at all."

"What would it take?"

"I think he's going west because the Amish community here is so small. It will get bigger again . . . it's just that so many families have left in the last year. If Jacob married and settled close, and Liesbet and I did, our community would grow and get stronger."

"So you're ready to marry to keep your Daed here?"

Hannah nodded, slowly. "I think I am."

"But I'm not going to become Amish, Hannah."

She laughed. "I know you aren't."

"There's no one else you would marry, is there?"

"How do you know a handsome Amish man wouldn't come along someday and ask me to marry him?"

He snorted. "That's the kind of stuff that only happens in stories."

"Well, an Amish man did come by."

Adam took off his hat, running his fingers through his hair. "He didn't ask you to marry him, did he?" His voice sounded strained.

"Not yet."

Adam stared at her. The sky was turning pink and orange behind his head, but his face was shadowed. He turned away from her and stood, replacing his hat.

"You have to do what you think is right, Hannah. You know how I feel about you."

"Do I?"

"You must. How many times have I talked about marrying you? We could have a good life together, Hannah. You know I love you."

Hannah couldn't answer. He said he loved her, but if she needed him, really needed him, would he be able to choose between her and the escaped slaves he helped?

Adam gazed at Hannah. Her face glowed in the morning light, looking more beautiful with every passing moment. But it was getting late. "I need to get home to help with the milking."

"And then will you try to get some sleep?"

His dear Hannah, always thoughtful. "*Ja*, sure. I'll get some sleep."

He left her and followed the creek trail the rest of the way home. Was Hannah serious about a new young man she had met? There were no new Amish families in the area. She must have been trying to make him jealous. Maybe she thought he took her for granted.

There were things he would change, of course. She could be more willing to help him in his work—that would be a good start. She could become better friends with Hilda too. Once they were married, the two of them would be sisters. They should be as close as Hannah was with Johanna Hertzler.

Pa was in the barn already. Adam hurried to help with the chores. Stopping to talk to Hannah had made him late.

"Hallo, son. I wondered where you were. Off hunting this morning already?"

Adam climbed into the loft and grabbed a fork to pitch feed into the cows' troughs. "*Ne*, not hunting." It was time to tell him what he had been doing. Escorting escaped slaves was too much for him to do alone, and with winter coming he couldn't expect the people to hide in the woods. He needed Pa's help.

"I need to talk to you."

"About where you are off to all hours of the night?"

"*Ja.*"

"And where all the smoked hams have gone?"

Adam glanced at Pa's face. He wasn't angry. He stood leaning on Bessie's back, waiting for an answer.

"I meant to return them, somehow." He cleared his throat. "I've been helping people. Refugees. They come here and they're hungry. I give them some food and help them on their way."

"You're talking about escaped slaves, aren't you?"

Adam finished filling the feed troughs and climbed down the ladder, where he could talk face-to-face. "*Ja*, I've been helping escaped slaves."

"You've joined the abolitionists? The Quakers?"

Adam nodded. "They aren't all Quakers. There are a lot of us, all working together to help these people get safely to Canada where they can live in freedom."

Pa leaned down and washed Bessie's udder as she settled in to eat her feed. "When were you going to tell me, son?"

"I wanted to tell you before, but . . ."

"But you thought I wouldn't approve. That I would forbid you to do something so dangerous."

Adam nodded.

"You should have come to me." Pa put his hand on Adam's shoulder. "I've talked this over with your ma. We want to help. It's too big of a job for you to do alone, and how are you going to care for these people when winter comes? How will you shelter them? I've heard there are many more travelers in the winter than the summer."

Adam watched the enthusiasm light Pa's face. "When the rivers freeze, it's the easiest time for them to come across to the north. I was going to ask you if I could use the smokehouse to hide them in during the day."

Pa shook his head. "That would never do. The smokehouse is too obvious." He stepped across the barn floor to the wagon bay. "I've been thinking your ma needs a new root cellar."

"Root cellar?"

Pa winked. "That's what it is, if anyone asks. I've been reading about these things in the Philadelphia paper. The best way to hide the people is in secret rooms. I think if we dig a cellar right here—" he tapped on the floor with his foot— "we'll be able to hide the trap door under a layer of straw."

Adam grinned at him. "And then when it's time to take them on to Lancaster, we can hide them in a wagonload of corn shucks or something."

"Your ma is already putting up extra provisions for our company." He looked at Adam. "What do you think? Should we make this a task for our family to do together?"

Adam nodded. "I didn't know if you'd approve of what I was doing." He swallowed. "I was even afraid you might forbid me to do it, and then I'd have to go against your wishes."

"Why did you think that?"

"What I'm doing—it's against the law."

Pa squeezed his shoulder. "It's God's law we must obey, not man's. Where man has erred, the people of God must act according to his word."

Adam grasped Pa's hand in his own and shook it. "Here's to our partnership."

Pa grinned. "It's a good work we do together. We'll need to continue to keep it secret, though, even from the other church members."

Adam rubbed his day's growth of whiskers. "Hannah has helped me before. She knows I'm involved."

Pa nodded. "I'm not surprised that's so. But she doesn't need to know this part—not unless it's necessary. The fewer people who know about this, the better."

16

The day before Sabbath, the last week of November, was dry and sunny. After days of cold rain, the children burst out of the house as if they couldn't move fast enough, running through the soggy leaves covering the ground and shouting to each other in the clear air.

Annalise stood in the doorway, her head against the frame, watching William chase Peter from one end of the yard to the other, laughing. Her eyes strayed to the cemetery, hidden within the grove of walnut trees. For the first time in years, she could look that direction without the clenching stab to her heart. *Ach*, she missed her babies. There would forever be an empty hole in their family, but in the last several weeks her heart could lie peacefully, resting in the comfort God had given her through Christian. The little ones were safe, warm, happy. The graves held no fear for them.

William tripped and fell to his knees. He jumped up, laughing, and ran after Peter once more. What joy these children gave her! It was as if a veil had been lifted. She was no longer blind to the gifts God had given. She thought of Job, the man in the Good Book who had lost everything—all his children in one day. When God later gave him a new family, did he feel this fragile layer of joy covering tempestuous waves of grief like a balm of oil?

"Mamm?" Hannah called from the kitchen behind her. "Do you want me to put the apples in the pot?"

Annalise turned to go back to cooking dinner. "The ham has been boiling for at least an hour. Go ahead and add the apples." She lifted the lid of the pot for Hannah to pour the dried apples and water they had been soaking in all morning into the pot, and the sudden odor of smoked ham brought bile to her throat. Setting the lid on the worktable, Annalise backed away.

"Are you all right?" Hannah looked up from her chore, the fire hissing when drops of water splashed on the coals.

Annalise nodded, her eyes filling. "I'll be right back." She fled to the porch, leaning over the rail at the far end, away from where the children played. Her stomach heaved, but it was already empty. She hadn't been able to eat breakfast that morning.

She straightened, leaning on the porch rail with one hand, letting her right hand caress her upset stomach. Could it be? She went over the symptoms in her mind. She had been so sleepy, taking a nap with William in the afternoons, but she had thought that was because she had been up in the middle of the night to use the chamber pot . . . Annalise smiled as the symptoms fell into place. *Ja*, it could be. Another baby in the summer. She would wait to tell Christian until she was sure. Until then, for another few weeks at least, she would hold this precious secret.

Hearing footsteps behind her, Annalise took a deep breath and turned to face Hannah.

"Are you all right?"

Annalise nodded. "I'm fine. The air inside was suddenly too close. I'm sorry if I worried you."

Hannah looked into her face for a long minute. "If you're sure that's all it was . . ."

"I'm sure. Why don't we sit out here for a while to rest?"

Hannah sat next to her on the bench. "It's such a nice day."

"I hope it stays for tomorrow."

"Will we go to meeting tomorrow?"

"We'll see what your father says, but we most likely will. It's at John Yoder's, and that isn't as far to go as some are."

Hannah sat, watching the little ones play. Annalise glanced at her. The more she considered the move they would be making in the spring, the more she was convinced it was the right thing to do. Hannah was eighteen, old enough to be courting. But whom around here would she marry? That Josef Bender was a possibility. He seemed a likely enough young man. If he liked Hannah, and if Christian liked him, then perhaps Hannah would like him too.

Until then, they would need to keep her friendship with Adam Metzler just that—a friendship.

Hannah turned toward her. "May I ask you a question?"

"*Ja*, for sure."

Hannah looked down at her toes as she drew an imaginary circle on the wooden porch floor. "Your spells . . ." She looked into Annalise's eyes. "Do you think they might be gone?"

Annalise sighed. "I hope so. I feel so different, like a blanket has been lifted off my soul. I don't know how else to describe it."

"What happened? What caused the change?"

Annalise let her mind probe the black shadow at the edge of her mind as she thought of how to answer her daughter. It still lingered, but it no longer threatened. She could hope the lingering remains of those dark moments would fade with time.

"It was something your daed said, about the little ones. I couldn't let myself believe they weren't suffering, but he reminded me of where they are, and in whose arms they rest." She turned to Hannah and took her hand. "They no longer need me, but you do, and the others."

Hannah looked away, biting her bottom lip.

"What is wrong?"

Hannah rubbed at a tear running down her cheek. "I know I'm to blame . . . for Fanny." She turned to Annalise, tears falling. "You were right, when you blamed me for . . . for Fanny and Hansli and Catherine . . . It was my fault they got the diphtheria."

"*Ach, ne, ne.*" Annalise pulled her handkerchief out of her pocket to dry Hannah's tears, but Hannah took it from her and swiped at her own eyes.

"It is my fault. I was the first one who got sick, so I know I brought the sickness into the house. And Fanny . . . I couldn't get out of bed to get her the water she wanted. If I had, she'd still be alive. They might all be . . ."

Annalise pulled Hannah toward her with an arm around her shoulders. "Hush now, Hannah. It wasn't your fault. I was wrong when I said I blamed you. You were so ill, yourself. There was nothing you could have done to help Fanny."

Hannah pushed against her, refusing her comfort. "All she

asked for was a drink, but I couldn't move. All I remember was blackness, and when I woke, she was gone."

"Oh my *liebchen*. You were just a little girl, barely older than Margareta is now, and so ill."

Hannah shook her head. "I should have been able to save her. How can you ever forgive me?"

The last words were whispered so quietly, Annalise almost missed them. "Forgive you? For what? You did nothing wrong. I'm the one who needs to ask forgiveness from you."

Hannah turned her head away. A cloud passed over the sun, bringing a chill to the breeze.

"Hannah, did you hear me? You did nothing that needs forgiveness. Fanny . . ." Annalise paused. Could she say the words aloud? "Fanny and the others died. It was God's will. You and Liesbet nearly died also, but you didn't. You survived, and that was God's will also."

"What do you mean?" Hannah looked at her again. Her daughter's eyes were red with unshed tears.

"'The Lord gives and the Lord takes away.'" Annalise knew those words. She had said them to herself often over the last nine years, but she straightened in her seat and smiled at Hannah as she finished the verse. "'Blessed be the name of the Lord.' He gave us your life, and Jacob's, and Liesbet's." Annalise reached out to stroke Hannah's cheek. "You were meant to live, dear one, and you have been a blessing to me ever since, even if I haven't been able to show you."

"*Denki*, Mamm." Hannah sighed and turned away from her again, watching William kick through a pile of soggy leaves. "I'll try to remember what you said."

She got up from the bench and walked away, slowly at first, and then faster until she was running past the barn and into the woods. Annalise rubbed at a twinge in the small of her back, and then stood to head back into the house and the chores she had left unfinished. She looked toward the woods, but Hannah had disappeared into the trees.

All those years, wrapped up in her own grief, caught up in the depths of her pain, she hadn't seen how miserable her own daughter had been. What else had she missed in Hannah's life? Or in Liesbet's?

Hannah made her way toward the creek, heading for her favorite spot—the tree overhanging the quiet stream. She had to think about what Mamm had said. Could it be that she no longer blamed Hannah for the tragedy?

She reached the tree and climbed onto the low-slung branch, scooting along it until she reached the fork. Beneath her the water rippled over a submerged rock, and a few late water skaters rode the current, their feet barely denting the surface. The water was brown from decaying leaves, but soon it would be wreathed with ice at the edges. She knew her stream, knew all of its seasons and moods. Right now the faint gurgle lulled her senses, allowing her to contemplate Mamm's words.

Her littlest sister, Margli, was nearly the same age she had been when the diphtheria struck. If something like that happened again, even if Margli did something out of meanness or spite, she wouldn't hold her sister to blame. Such a little girl—how could she be held accountable for childish actions?

Hannah went back into her memory, pulling out the image of nine-year-old Hannah. She couldn't blame herself for being a child.

But Mamm had blamed her. In her grief and despair, she had lashed out at Hannah, blaming her for the tragedy and the deaths of the little ones.

Hannah leaned forward on the branch, lying along the thick length on her stomach, letting the swirling waters take her to a place in her mind she rarely let herself go. Back through years of Mamm's bitterness. She had tried to make up for what she had done, had tried to make things better, but when Mamm fell prey to one of her spells, nothing Hannah could say or do would bring her out of it.

If it hadn't been for Adam, for his patient listening, for his way of distracting her from the darkness at home, what would she have done? Adam had been there every time she needed him. He was a solid rock.

Hannah's eyes followed a swirling curve beneath the surface of the water. The curve turned into a tail, and then an entire fish, resting downstream from the submerged rock and moving just enough to stay in one place in the water's current. It was a trout, a real beauty, Adam would say. He had taught her how to slip her hand under a fish like that, to gently tickle its belly to keep it still, and then grab it. He had caught many fish that way, but Hannah didn't have the patience. She always moved the wrong way or too quickly, frightening the fish away.

Would Adam be jealous of an Amish man who wanted to court her? When she told him, earlier this week, it didn't seem as if he believed her.

If she had to make a choice of whom to marry . . . She closed her eyes and thought of Josef. Nice. Handsome. But a stranger. She really didn't know him at all.

And now Adam. As strong as an oak tree. She knew she

could lean on him in any storm. He would be a *wonderful-gut* husband . . . if he were Amish. Would he consider changing if that was the only way to marry her?

She sat up on the branch and scooted back to the grassy bank. There was one way to find out. She would tell him all about Josef Bender, and that he had asked to call on her, and see what he said. If he was serious about marrying her as he claimed, he would do something. He might even consider becoming Amish.

She made her way along the creek path. As she grew closer to the Metzler farm, she could hear the creak of the windlass, and when she emerged from the woods she saw Adam and his daed pulling hay from the big farm wagon up to the hay loft, using the windlass on the end of the barn. As she walked toward them, they got the last of the wagon load into the haymow, and Adam got onto the wagon to drive it out to the field again.

"Adam!" She picked up her skirts and ran toward him, waving to his daed as she went. Adam heard her and stopped the wagon. "Can I come along?"

Adam pulled the horses to a halt and helped her onto the wagon seat when she reached him.

"You want to come with me?" He laughed at her as he spoke. "You don't even know where I'm going."

"Back out to the fields to get another load of hay, *ja*?"

He winked at her and clucked to the horses. "You're right, but it's a bit of a drive. Elias Hertzler let Pa have some of the haystacks from his meadow, since they're heading west and won't be needing it."

Hannah smiled back at him, and then focused her gaze on the horses pulling the wagon. She only had a few minutes to tell him about Josef, but how to bring it up in the conversation?

"The Hertzlers are excited about going to Indiana, *ja?*"

"Elias sure sounds like he is. He's already sold his farm." Adam chirruped to the horses again.

"I hadn't heard about that. Who bought it?"

"I did."

Hannah looked at him. He was smiling. "You bought the Hertzlers' farm? Why?"

He shrugged, grinning now as he looked at her. "I thought we might want our own home when we marry."

"Adam, I never said I would marry you."

"I know you didn't, but you'll change your mind. Indiana is a long way from here, and I know you won't be able to leave me behind."

"So you've decided to turn Amish?"

"You were going to turn Mennonite."

"I never said I was."

"The wife needs to follow the husband's church, so to be my wife you'll become Mennonite."

His face was serious, but his eyes still held a twinkle. Did he really think she would give up her faith? Raise her children in the progressive ways of the Mennonites?

"Stop the wagon, Adam. I want to get down."

He pulled the horses to a halt, but stopped her with a hand on her arm. "Hannah, don't go." His eyes had lost their mocking look, and he moved his hand from her arm to around her shoulders. "We belong together, don't we? You belong here, along the Conestoga, with me. Can you even think of moving so far away?"

Hannah couldn't look at him. He was right. Could she

ever leave him and the Conestoga behind? But if she became Mennonite to marry Adam, she would lose her family. They would have to sever ties with her forever. But if he refused to become Amish, that would be the result.

How could he ask her to choose between him and her family?

Hot tears ran down her cheeks and she shook her head, pulling out of Adam's embrace.

"I can't think right now. I can't tell you what I should or shouldn't do. I . . . I just need to be alone. To think."

He let her climb down from the wagon. "While you're thinking, Hannah, remember that I love you. Never doubt that."

Saturday evenings were always busy, as Mamm worked hard to prepare for the Sabbath rest the next day, but tonight it was even more so since the services were at Uncle John's, only a few miles away. She had pledged to bring corn pone to help feed the community and kept the oven fired until long after supper, baking pan after pan.

Hannah gave the children their baths in the warm kitchen while Mamm stirred batter and filled the pans.

"It will be good to go to meeting tomorrow, *ja*?" Hannah checked Peter's ears after his bath. Boys had a way of missing the dirt in the folds.

"I don't think so." Peter wrenched his head out of her hold, so she grabbed his ear instead, scrubbing at it with a soapy cloth. "Ow! Hannah, that hurts."

"Then you should learn to clean your own ears. You're big enough." She turned his head around and tackled the other ear. "And tell me, why don't you want to go to meeting?"

"None of my friends are there anymore. Why don't we go to the Dunkard Church like the Eshelmanns?"

Mamm slid another pan of corn pone into the oven. "We go to meeting to worship God, not to play with our friends. Josiah Eshelmann isn't a good friend for you anyway since his family turned Dunkard." She went into the bedroom to finish putting William to bed.

"Why did the Eshelmanns turn Dunkard, Hannah?" He bent his head down so she could scrub the back of his neck.

"Clarence Eshelmann married a Dunkard girl, and his family followed him."

"Why did they have to follow? Josiah didn't marry any old Dunkard."

Hannah sighed. "I don't know, but I think they felt like they had to choose between keeping their family together outside the church, or be separated from Clarence."

"Why?"

"When Clarence married the Dunkard girl, the church had to put him under the *bann*. The church members must avoid him until he comes to repentance and back to the church. That meant his family had to shun him too, but instead they chose to leave the church."

"Would our family do that if you married Adam?"

Hannah finished scrubbing Peter's neck and handed him the washrag. "You know Daed would never leave the church. We are Amish, and we'll stay Amish." She tousled Peter's wet hair as she rose from kneeling next to the tub. "I won't marry Adam as long as he isn't Amish. It's too important for our family to be together."

Mamm came back to the kitchen to check the bread just as Liesbet slipped out the door.

"Liesbet? Where are you going?"

She poked her head back into the kitchen. "Just to the privy and to check on the hens. I want to make sure the gate is fastened."

Hannah filled the big kettle and pushed it over the fire to heat more water for the next bath. Liesbet never did anything with the chickens unless forced to. She must be using that as an excuse so Mamm wouldn't worry when she didn't come back right away. She went to the entryway and took her shawl from the hook.

"I'm going to help Liesbet with the chickens. We don't want a fox to get in the pen tonight."

Mamm, distracted by her baking, just nodded her head, and Hannah slipped out the door.

Just as she thought. There was no light from the privy, and the hens were settled and quiet. Liesbet was nowhere around. Hannah made her way around the barn and down the path to the clearing. She could hear their voices before she reached the spot where they met.

"But I have to get back. You know I can't stay long."

"Lass, you need to forget about your parents once in a while. They won't even notice you're gone."

"They will when it's time for evening prayers."

Hannah stopped on the path just outside the clearing. The waning moon hadn't yet risen and the two of them were shadows in darkness.

"Let me show you what evening prayers with me are like."

Liesbet giggled as the two shadows merged into one. Hannah started toward the clearing to interrupt them, but stopped. How would she confront a man like George McIvey?

He reminded her of the bounty hunter she and Adam had met—coarse, forward, and worldly.

She retraced her steps until she was several yards from the clearing, and then called as if she had been sent to look for her sister. "Liesbet! Where are you?"

After a few minutes, Liesbet emerged from the path into the farmyard where Hannah waited. She stopped, straightening her hair and replacing her kapp.

"Did Mamm send you out after me?"

"*Ne*. Your excuse to check on the chickens sounded false to me, so I came out to keep you out of trouble."

"You're not my mother, Hannah Yoder. And I'm a grown woman. I can do what I want."

"You're still an unmarried girl living under your father's roof. You owe him your respect and obedience."

Liesbet leaned toward her and hissed. "I owe him nothing."

Hannah's hand slapped Liesbet's face before the thought came into her head. She grabbed the offending hand and held it. "Liesbet. I'm so sorry."

Her sister's voice was ice cold. "You're not sorry. You've been wanting to do that for years, and now you've had your chance. But don't ever do it again."

Tears welled up at Liesbet's words. "What has happened to us? We used to be so close—you, Fanny, and I. Don't you remember how the three of us shared a bed because we couldn't bear to be parted from each other, even for a night?"

"I'll tell you what happened. Fanny died. She died, Hannah. And when she died, we all did." She whirled away and Hannah heard her sniff. "I'm not going to ever go through that again. I've found a new life, and I'm going to do what I want." She turned to face Hannah again. "You may think

you're pleasing God or something by being the good daughter, the helpful daughter. But you can't please a God who hates you, and I'm not going to waste time trying. I'm going to live for me, and the rest of you can move to Indiana or wherever. I don't care."

"But, Liesbet, think of Mamm. Of Daed. Think of what you will do to the family—"

"I told you. I don't care. They will get over me. In fact, they'll probably be glad I'm gone and they don't have to worry about me anymore."

Hannah's feet were freezing. She wrapped her shawl closer. How could Liesbet say such things? How could she think such things? "Come back to the house, Liesbet. Get some sleep. Perhaps you'll feel differently in the morning."

"I'll come back to the house, but only to keep peace until I marry George. I'm not going to change my mind Hannah. I'm going to marry him, no matter what you, or Mamm, or even Daed says. They can't keep me a prisoner."

Liesbet walked away, her steps stiff and hard across the frosty barnyard. Hannah followed slowly. There must be a way to keep her apart from George.

17

Hannah woke suddenly, the pounding of Daed's fist on the door of the boys' room ringing through the house. Beside her, Liesbet rolled to one side, pulling the covers over her ears.

Hannah tugged at the edge of the quilt. "Liesbet, come quickly. It's a meeting day."

Liesbet responded with a groan, but Hannah got up and lit the candle. She splashed her face with cold water, and then put on her best dress, covering it with her everyday apron until after breakfast.

She shook Liesbet's shoulder, and then sat on the edge of Margli's bed to wake her. "Come now, sleepyheads. It's time to make breakfast. We're going to Sabbath meeting today."

Margli stretched and yawned, but Liesbet snuggled farther under the covers. "It's still dark," she said. "Why do we have to get up this early?"

"You know why, Liesbet." Hannah smiled at Margli and pulled her sleeping kapp off her head. She crossed to the big bed again and tugged the covers out of Liesbet's hands, pulling them to the foot of the bed. "Mamm needs help with breakfast and William needs to be dressed. Hurry up!"

By the time Hannah left the room to go downstairs, Liesbet was awake enough to help Margli get dressed. Mamm stood over the fireplace, stirring the porridge that had simmered all night.

"Hannah, I'm so glad you're up. The girls?"

"They're coming. I'll go get the eggs and milk, and then I'll wake William."

"*Ja, ja, ja.*" Mamm nodded her head, but her attention was on wrapping the corn pone cakes she had baked last night, getting them ready for the long walk to the meeting.

Hannah took the egg basket and her shawl and opened the door to the frosty night air. The clock had said it was morning, but five o'clock still seemed like the middle of the night. The chickens clucked with sleepy voices as she went from nest to nest in the dark chicken coop, searching for the warm eggs under the hens. She spread feed on the floor of the coop, propped open the door to the pen, and let them sleep.

The next stop was the barn to fetch the milk. She could hear Daed's voice as she opened the door to the lantern-lit interior and slipped in.

"You mean you walked all night?"

Who was he talking to?

"*Ja.* It was not that far."

The accent was familiar. Hannah walked around the farm wagon. There was Josef Bender, pitching hay to the horses along with Daed while Jacob milked the cow. When Josef saw her, he put the pitchfork tines on the ground and acknowledged her with a little bow.

"*Gut morgen*, Hannah." The tones of his voice were soft as he spoke her name. Hannah blushed as Jacob looked from her to Josef with a silly grin on his face.

"Josef decided he wanted to go to meeting with us, so he walked here from Ephrata last night." Daed caught Hannah's gaze and gave her a quick nod. "A dedicated man, *ja*?"

"*Ja*, Daed." Hannah's answer was automatic, but her mind was racing. Josef had promised he'd see her soon, but she had never expected him to come all this way to go to Sabbath meeting with her.

Jacob finished milking and she took the pail from him. "I'll let Mamm know we'll have a guest for breakfast."

"Not a guest, Hannah." Daed slapped Josef's shoulder. "A member of the family."

Hannah left the barn as quickly as she could with a basket of eggs in one hand and the pail of frothy milk in the other. She hurried into the house. Liesbet and Margli looked at her as she burst into the kitchen. She took a deep breath to calm herself and set her burdens down on the table to buy some time.

"Hannah, you look like you were chased in here by King George's cavalry," Mamm said, turning from the fireplace. "What has you so flustered?"

"Not so flustered, Mamm, just in a hurry. Daed said to set an extra plate for breakfast. Josef Bender is here to go to meeting with us."

Liesbet let out a laugh, but Margli and Mamm stared at her.

"Josef Bender?" Mamm turned to stir the porridge before it could burn. "From Ephrata? Here this morning?"

"*Ja, ja, ja.*" Hannah hung her shawl on the peg in the

entry and then pushed past her sisters to the bedroom door under the steps. "He walked all night, I suppose. He's doing chores with Daed and the boys and will be in for breakfast with them." She pushed the door open before anyone could make a comment. "I'll get William up."

She left the door open to let light into the room from the kitchen. William was already half awake, roused by the voices in the rest of the house.

"*Gut morgen*, William." She reached to pick him up, but he pushed her hands away.

"Do it myself." He rolled over the high sides of the cot and stood for a minute. He pulled at his diaper. "Pot, Hannah. I use the pot."

"*Ja*, William, that's a good boy."

Hannah dressed him in clean clothes when he finished and went back into the kitchen with him. The men had come in from the barn and were seated around the table. Peter stared at a plate piled high with slices of cold corn pone while Liesbet and Margli bustled around the table, laying out cups and plates. Josef had been sitting next to Daed, but rose when Hannah started to lift William onto his stool.

"You will let me help you, *ja*?" He set the little boy on his seat.

"*Ja, denki*."

Hannah caught a glance pass between her parents as she went to help Mamm spoon the porridge into bowls. Her face grew hot, and it wasn't only from the heat of the fireplace. Josef was being too obvious. Anyone could see that he was here to visit her, and Daed had already adopted him as part of the family. She had no say in this matter. Was he thinking they would be married without so much as a minute alone together to get to know each other?

She sat next to Liesbet, waiting while Daed read the morning Scripture, but she didn't hear a word. What kind of man walked several miles, through the night, just to attend Sabbath meeting with a girl he barely knew? She stole a glance and saw that he was sitting with bowed head, listening to Daed read. Then he looked at her, and their eyes met for a brief second before she looked down at her folded hands, lying on her lap.

Adam wouldn't have done such a thing. He spent hours helping the runaway slaves and walked miles to attend one of his camp meetings, but would he ever sacrifice the time to attend a Sabbath meeting with her?

Breakfast was finished quickly, and the family stacked the dirty dishes into a dishpan as they finished. The walk to Sabbath meeting would be subdued, Josef knew, as the family contemplated the worship service to come, followed by fellowship with the rest of the community.

He fastened his coat while he waited for the others. The sun had not yet risen and the air was frosty, so shoes had to be worn and coats brought into the kitchen from the lean-to to warm. He watched Hannah with her little brothers and sister as she helped them get ready. Her soft brown hair, so light it was nearly blond, gleamed in the lamplight, framing her face. Her kapp covered most of her head modestly, as it should. She was wearing a black dress with a white apron, as all the women did, but on her the black had a holy feel rather than somber.

Once the children were ready, Hannah reached for her shawl. Josef helped her settle it around her shoulders, and she gave him a smile. How *wonderful-gut* it would be when he had the right to kiss those smiling lips!

Christian led the way, carrying little William. He motioned for Josef to join him at the front of the family line.

"Meeting is at my brother John's farm today. It's only two miles."

"Two miles? That's the farthest Daniel travels for Sabbath meeting."

"The community there isn't as widespread as ours. Families have left the Conestoga recently, so many that the district lines were redrawn last spring. Now our family and the Hertzlers are at the edge of the district that is mostly in the Cocalico area, down towards the Pequea Creek."

"What happened to the other families around you? Have they all moved west?"

"Two families moved to Somerset several years ago, and some more moved to Canada, where they heard land was cheaper. The worst, though, is that as those families moved out, outsiders moved in. Instead of Amish neighbors, we now have Dunkard or Mennonite. Quakers bought one of the farms, and Methodists another. We've lost more families to the influence of those new neighbors."

"When you and the Hertzlers move to Indiana, there won't be any Amish along the Conestoga?"

Christian shook his head. "Not until someone else moves in. I hope our farm will stay in the family. My nephew, John's oldest son, is interested in buying it—so it might stay Amish. And the Cocalico district is growing, so eventually there will be more Amish here, perhaps even a district again. But we can't wait that long." He looked over his shoulder at Jacob walking behind them. "There is too much at stake to remain where we are surrounded by outsiders."

Josef glanced back also, at Jacob, Hannah, and Liesbet following along behind them with Annalise and the younger children.

"*Ja*, my *mutti* felt the same way. Once my sister married, the two of them were settled. Then her thoughts turned to me."

"Was she afraid of losing you to the world?"

Josef nodded, his throat tight, thinking of *Mutti*'s face that last day. "The army had taken my *vater*, and he never came back. She knew they would come for me too."

Christian nodded. "I can understand. It's much better to never see you again, knowing you're safe in America, than have you lost somewhere in Europe. It was a great sacrifice she made."

Ahead of them, another group of Amish filled the road.

"It's the Hertzlers, Daed," Jacob said, catching up. "I'll go tell them to wait, and we'll walk with them."

"*Ja*, it will be good to journey together."

When they caught up to the Hertzlers, the women embraced. Josef took Elias's hand in greeting.

"It's good to meet you, Josef." Elias turned to walk beside Christian, while Josef fell back to walk next to Jacob.

"He came to attend Sabbath meeting with us," Christian said, winking at Elias.

As the older men walked on ahead, Jacob said, "Is that the only reason you came all the way from Ephrata last night? Just to attend Sabbath meeting with us?"

Josef glanced behind them. Liesbet walked close to them,

and behind her was Hannah arm in arm with the oldest Hertzler daughter. "Today is an off Sunday for our district, so I came to get to know your family better. If we're going west together, we should become friends, *ja*?"

Jacob glanced behind them too, and then leaned closer to Josef so his sister wouldn't hear. "It isn't the family you want to know better, is it? Hannah is the one you have your eye on."

Josef laughed. "Is there any better reason for me to be here?"

Jacob grinned, and they hurried to catch up with the older men.

Christian had said the meeting was at his brother's farm, the closest farm in their district other than the Hertzlers'. The John Yoder farm was larger than Christian's, closer to the size Josef was used to around Ephrata. Open fields surrounded the red barn and frame house, and the barnyard was well-kept. Josef still hadn't become accustomed to the difference in America, where the Amish farmers owned their land rather than working as tenants for the landowner. The work these farmers did benefited the farm and their families instead of sending most of the profit to the landowner.

The two families joined the rest of the community, gathered into the house that smelled of bean soup. The host family would have started cooking the noon meal yesterday afternoon, and now a big pot of soup simmered on the fire. The congregation took their places on benches in the big main room. Josef took off his coat as the room grew warmer and checked to see where Hannah was sitting. She caught his eye from her seat between her mother and Elias's daughter, and then turned away as one of the men started singing the first hymn.

Josef sang along with the familiar song. The slow, almost

chanting rhythm of voices singing in unison taking him back to Sabbath meetings at home. They had sung the same songs from the Ausbund there, in the same way. The heritage of his ancestors and the worship of the community blending into one. He looked over to the women's side again. Hannah was singing, her face quiet as she contemplated the words of the hymn.

Ja, she was the one he had been waiting for. The woman who would become his partner in life.

Since they had a shorter walk home today, Daed was in no hurry to leave the meeting. He and Elias stood with the other men outside under the cellar overhang of the barn, talking until midafternoon, gathered in a circle with their hands folded behind their black coats, identical hats nodding as each one had his say.

Beside Hannah, Johanna sighed. "We'll never start home if they keep talking out there."

The girls were sitting together on a bench beneath a window that gave them a view of the men.

"They'll tire of talking presently. Someone will remember milking time is coming and it's a long walk home."

Johanna grasped Hannah's arm. "I have a favor to ask."

"What is it?"

"Don't walk with me on the way home."

"What?"

"Walk with that Josef, or with Liesbet. Let me walk alone, and then maybe Jacob will feel sorry for me and walk with me."

Hannah shook her finger in Johanna's face. "You know that if Jacob wanted to walk with you, he would. You don't need to be scheming behind his back."

Johanna slouched on the bench. "But he doesn't do anything. When he's at our farm, he never even looks at the house. And you've seen him today, always talking with Josef Bender. You'd think Josef would want to be talking with you, not your brother."

"All right." Hannah laced her hands over one knee, using the leverage to support her back. It was sore from the morning's walk and then sitting on the backless benches during the three-hour meeting. "I have a feeling Josef will want to walk with me, anyway."

"Did he really walk all the way to your house from Ephrata last night, just to attend meeting with you this morning?"

Hannah felt her face getting red. "*Ja*, he did."

"So when is the wedding? You can tell me."

"I've hardly said two words to him all day. I just met him. I'm not thinking of marriage."

Johanna poked at her arm. "You can't tell me you're not thinking of marriage. Of course you don't know each other yet, but that will change. You'll get to know him, he'll get to know you, and before you know it, he'll be making plans for a spring wedding. Maybe even before we leave for Indiana."

Hannah looked out the window again. The circle of men was breaking up. She couldn't tell Johanna that if things worked out, her family wouldn't be going west at all. She wouldn't tell her until she was sure.

The women inside the house started gathering the children together for the walk home. Johanna went to help Magdalena with the baby, but Hannah stayed by the window. Josef fit in with the men. Every gesture, every nod of the head, was in unity with the other men. He belonged. Adam would never fit in so well. He would probably cause dissension as he shared his views on slavery and holding political office. But he would make himself fit in if he loved her, wouldn't he?

Johanna's plan for walking home worked. Hannah hung back and took a place behind Mamm and Magdalena, leaving Johanna alone just behind Jacob and Josef. But it wasn't Jacob who fell back to walk beside her, it was Josef. He talked to her briefly, and then when she motioned to the back of the group, he stepped aside to let the others pass until Hannah caught up to him. Meanwhile, Johanna hurried to catch up with Jacob.

"May I?" Josef made his little bow and indicated the spot next to her on the road.

"Of course you may." Hannah stepped aside to let him join her.

"Your friend seems to be anxious to talk to Jacob."

"She's sweet on him, and hopes he'll notice her."

"And you? Were you hoping someone would notice you?"

Hannah felt her cheeks burning. She was glad for the edges of the shawl that hid her face from his view.

"You don't have to worry." Josef lowered his voice as he spoke. "I noticed you."

She walked on in silence. She didn't know how to answer such a comment.

Josef slowed his pace and Hannah matched him, letting Peter go past them with Margli and Johanna's sister, Barbli. So he had found a friend after all, even though she was a girl.

She glanced at Josef. "You must be tired after walking all night, and now to meeting and back again."

"Not too tired."

"And you must walk home yet this evening?"

"*Ja*. Daniel expects me home in time to do the milking tomorrow."

She stopped in the road, waiting until he halted and faced her.

"Why did you do it? Why did you come all this way?"

Josef stepped closer to her. "I wanted to see you. I wanted to spend time with you and your family. I asked if I could call on you, remember?"

She nodded.

"This is the way for me to know you, to find out if we would make a good match."

"And? Have you decided?"

He smiled at her, crinkles forming at the corners of his blue eyes. "*Ja*, I have decided."

Hannah looked past him at the backs of her family disappearing around a bend in the road. She knew what he was going to say. She didn't need to ask him . . . but . . . She looked into his eyes again. His smile faded as he stepped even closer, reaching out with his hand to cup her cheek inside her hooded shawl. Her stomach flipped over and pressed all the air from her lungs. His hand was roughened from work, but warm and tender against her skin.

"You are all I have thought of since we first met. You are everything I have been looking for in a wife. Your *vater* is a *gut* man, and I have seen what a *gut* daughter you are." He brushed her cheekbone with his thumb. "I already know you are a good cook, and you like children. And you're beautiful."

"You know all that already, when we've just met and have barely spoken?"

He smiled again. "*Ja*. I want you to be my wife, Hannah Yoder, and I will do everything I can to convince you that you want it too."

18

By the time they returned to the Yoder farm late in the afternoon, Josef was even more sure of his decision.

It had been so hard not to kiss her as they had stood alone in the middle of the road, out of sight of her family, but he had restrained himself. They would have a future together, and he would be able to kiss her to his heart's content then. Now was the time to learn about each other. So he had taken her hand and they had run along through the drifts of fallen leaves until they had caught up with the others. She had laughed at him, breathless from running.

Josef closed his eyes as he waited for her to come out of the house—she had promised she wouldn't let him leave until she said goodbye—and brought back the image of her face, so pretty, so fresh as she laughed with him. He stored that picture away in his memory to bring out during the long winter nights ahead.

And then during the rest of the walk home they had talked of everything from their favorite pie to what color was the best for a man's shirt. He learned all about each of her siblings, her favorite places to visit in the woods near her house, and her favorite story from the *Martyr's Mirror*. They had reached her home much too soon for him.

The sound of the door latch brought his mind back to the present.

"*Ja*, Mamm, I won't be long." Hannah closed the door behind her, and Josef took her hand, threading it through his elbow.

"You'll walk me to the road?"

"*Ja*, for sure."

"And perhaps even a little farther?"

He couldn't see her smile around the edge of her shawl, but she ducked her head in a quick nod. Even now, after such a short time, he knew her face was turning a becoming pink in her embarrassment. He laid his hand over hers as it rested on his arm, and he started down the farm lane.

"I will come see you again, but I don't know when."

"I'm glad you came today, Josef." She turned her face toward him. *Ja*, she was blushing. "I'm glad we had time to talk and get to know each other better."

Josef walked slowly, wanting to make their time together last.

"I have a question for you." He pulled her to a stop when they reached the end of the lane, right at the edge of the road. She looked up at him, her face framed by the soft edges of her shawl. "Even after such a short time, do you think you . . . I mean, you know I want you for my wife. Do you want me for your husband?"

"There's one thing . . ."

"What?"

Her face took on a different look, one he hadn't seen before. Harder, more determined.

"I don't want to move to Indiana. I want to stay here, along the Conestoga."

"But the plans are all made. Your *vater* will be selling his farm." Josef paced away from her and back again. What was she thinking?

"Daed hasn't sold the farm yet. If he knew I was staying here, I think he'd change his mind about moving."

"Your *vater* isn't going to change his mind."

Hannah bit her lip, a little less sure. "If I refused to go, he'd want to stay here to keep our family together."

"He's going to go west, and so am I."

"Well, I'm not."

If she had been a mule, she would have sat right down in the dirt. His eyes locked with hers. Of all the stubborn, foolish women!

"You can't stay here by yourself. You'll come west because your *vater* and I say so."

Tears pooled in her eyes, and she dropped her gaze from his. He stepped closer, caressing her shoulder, but wanting to grab her into his arms and hold her until she came to her senses.

"Hannah, Hannah." Her name spilled from his mouth. He pulled her to him and hesitated. Tears glistened on her cheeks, but her face no longer had the stony look of just a moment ago. He leaned down, captured by her lips, red and trembling. Lowering his mouth to hers, he kissed her softly. Once, and then again. He pulled away, wanting to continue but satisfying himself with running his thumb across her lower lip.

"We will be married." He couldn't speak above a whisper. He couldn't break the spell of that moment. "I will come again, when I can. Watch for me, *ja*?"

She nodded.

He leaned down again to kiss her cheek, pressing his lips against the sweet softness of her skin, and then turned and strode down the road toward Ephrata. If he turned back, if he even glanced back, he would never be able to leave her.

Hannah watched Josef walk away, up the road past the Metzlers' farm, sliding behind a spruce tree just in case he looked back. He didn't.

She took a deep breath and let it out slowly. What was it about him? So . . . so pigheaded and stubborn one minute . . . but then kissing her the next. Kissing her . . . Adam's kiss hadn't felt anything like that. Nothing had ever felt like Josef's kiss.

Turning back toward the house, Hannah went over their conversation again in her mind. Before he kissed her, he had given her an ultimatum. It was one thing to say she would obey Daed, but obey Josef? He wasn't her husband. Not yet.

She tripped over a root sticking out of the ground and kicked it again in frustration.

If he was going to treat her like this, he would never be her husband.

"Because I said so." She mimicked Josef's accent as she repeated his words. The more she thought about them, the angrier she got. Who was he to think he had the right . . . ?

She stopped, grasping the top rail of the sheepfold fence. He barely knew her, and thought he would marry her. And he was right. From the first moment she had heard his voice this morning until he left her with his kiss still burning on her lips, the thought of marrying him had been the first thing on her mind.

Until he gave her the order to move to Indiana.

Ne, until she told him she wouldn't move.

Was the argument her fault? *Ja, ja, ja*. It was her own stubborn pride that had brought this about. But at the same time, it had shown her a side of Josef she hadn't known existed. As tender and gentle as he was, he still had an infuriating streak of dominance.

It was good to get that out in the open. Now she knew how he felt and he wouldn't fit into her plans to stay in Pennsylvania at all. She would need to find another way to make sure Daed changed his mind about going.

She turned back to look at the spot where Josef had left her. Tears prickled in her eyes. The memory of his embrace, the sweetness of his kisses, the rightness of it all . . . Why did they have to have that argument?

"Are you sure you want to take me?" Hilda looked up from fastening her shawl.

Adam turned his hat in his hand. He had been waiting all afternoon for his sister to get ready for this evening's young people's gathering, but she had to make sure her hair was right, and then something was wrong with her dress. Finally she had to borrow one of Ma's prayer coverings because her own wasn't white enough.

"It will be fun, and you know I'm not going to let you walk all the way by yourself."

"You know what would be even better?" Hilda waved to Ma and Pa as Adam followed her out the door. "If Hannah would come with us."

Adam fell in beside her as they walked down the lane toward the road. "I don't know if she'd come."

"How do you know? You've never asked her, have you?"

"She still thinks there's too much of a difference between her Amish church and our Mennonite one, even though I think she'd fit in fine."

They turned onto the road and Hilda nodded toward an Amish man walking toward them in the late-afternoon shadows. "Is that Jacob Yoder?"

"*Ne*, not Jacob."

"He's coming from the Yoders' farm, though."

Adam took another look as they drew closer. The man was young, and walked as if he was lost in thought. A sudden suspicion crept into his mind. This could be the man Hannah had told him about. The one who had asked to call on her.

"Good afternoon," he said as Hilda and Adam came close.

Adam stopped as the other man did. "Good afternoon. A fine day for a walk, *ja*?"

"*Ja*." He folded his right arm across his waist and bowed in Hilda's direction. "I am Josef Bender, a friend of the Yoders. You are their neighbors, *nicht wahr*?"

Josef Bender? He fit Hannah's description perfectly. Adam felt his jaw clench but put a smile on his face. "*Ja*, that's right. I am Adam Metzler, and this is my sister, Hilda."

Josef flashed a glance at him under his eyebrows before turning to Hilda again. Hannah had probably mentioned him, as well.

"How long have you known the Yoders?" Hilda smiled at

Josef, like all women probably did. The man was too hand-some for his own good.

"We met just a few weeks ago, but we will be traveling west together in the spring. We have gotten to know each other quite well." Another glance at Adam, this time with a quick lift of those eyebrows. Just how well had he gotten to know Hannah today? He must have spent all afternoon with her.

"Are you sure all of the Yoders are going west?"

Josef's jaw clenched, the muscle twitching, but his voice was as smooth as ever when he answered. "There's some question with one of the daughters, but *ja*, I think the family will stay together, don't you?"

Hilda forgotten, Adam stared at Josef. He couldn't be thinking Hannah would leave her home behind to go off to the western wilderness with him.

His sister tugged at his sleeve. "We're going to be late, Adam."

"*Ja*, Hilda." He nodded at Josef. "Good to meet you."

The other man gave his little bow again. "I'm sure we'll be seeing each other quite often between now and next spring."

Adam and Hilda continued down the road to the Franz farm, while Josef went the other direction, toward Ephrata.

"He seemed very nice." Hilda hurried along the road, forcing Adam to jog after her until he caught up. "Do you think he was calling on Liesbet?"

"*Ne*, he was calling on Hannah."

"Hannah?" Hilda turned to look at him and nearly tripped.

Adam took her arm. "You don't need to hurry so fast. Stephen Petersheim won't sit with any other girl but you."

Hilda slowed to his pace, but Adam didn't release her arm.

"Why would Josef Bender be calling on Hannah? Didn't she tell him she already had a beau?"

"That's the problem. As far I'm concerned, she has a beau. But in her mind, we aren't together until I become Amish."

"Or she becomes Mennonite." Hilda tilted her head to look at him again. "You aren't thinking of turning Amish, are you?"

"*Ne*, for sure not."

Josef Bender was Amish. He was just the kind of man Christian Yoder would be looking for in a son-in-law, and Hannah wouldn't have any arguments with him about meeting-houses or if the abolitionists were breaking the law or if a man should run for public office. Josef Bender was the kind of man Hannah would be expected to marry . . . but would she marry a man she didn't love?

Wednesday afternoon, in bright Indian summer sunshine, Hannah knocked at the apples still clinging to the highest branches in the orchard. Jacob had found a long cane fishing pole for her to use. The hook he attached to the end helped her grasp the branches. She finally hooked a branch and gave it a shake, sending apples showering to the ground.

Peter and William scrambled on the ground around the tree, making a game out of gathering the fallen fruit.

"Why are we bothering with these apples?" Peter dropped another handful into the basket.

"Because there might not be any apples yet in Indiana. Mamm wants to dry as many as she can to take along."

"Apples." William put an apple into the basket, squatting down to lay it with the others.

"*Denki*, William."

He grinned at her and went after another one.

Dried apples to take to Indiana. Jacob hunting every day for fresh meat so they would have extra dried and pickled meats to take to Indiana. Mamm weaving for hours every day to make cloth to take to Indiana. Daed sitting at the table every night figuring how to stow everything into the new wagon he was building to move to Indiana.

Hannah whacked at another branch. If she heard one more person talk about Indiana, she might scream. That Josef and his plans. He had probably already planned the cabin he was going to build for their first home.

In Indiana.

She moved to the next tree, hooked the center of the tree, and shook it, pelting all three of them with apples. William giggled while Peter howled.

"I'm sorry, Peter. I didn't mean for it to hit you."

Ja, it should have hit Josef. Or Daed. Perhaps it would knock some sense into them. Why did they think they had to uproot everyone and move west? There was no reason for it. They were doing fine right here.

Adam called from the orchard fence to get her attention. "Hannah!"

She waved. "Peter, you and William keep picking up apples. I'm going to talk to Adam for a few minutes."

Leaning her pole against the tree, she walked through the orchard to the fence. Adam's smile was like a warm caress, welcoming and open. He wouldn't force her to leave her home.

"*Hallo*, Adam." She climbed up the stile and sat on the top step, facing him.

He moved closer, peeked around her at the boys, and then took her hand. "I've missed you."

"It's only been a few days since you last saw me."

"But I still missed you." He lifted her chin with one finger so she had to look into his face. "The last time we spoke, you told me to give you time to think."

Hannah nodded.

"Tell me then, have you been thinking?"

Hannah's breath caught at the look in his eyes. He loved her.

Ja, he had said it . . . but what did it mean, to love another? Adam's eyes, soft brown above his gentle smile, those were eyes of love.

"I . . . I think I will consider what you said, Adam."

He leaned closer. "You'll become Mennonite? You'll marry me?"

"I can't become Mennonite." She would never promise that. "But I want to stay here, to live on the Conestoga and raise my children here."

Adam squeezed her hand. "Then you'll marry me?"

"You'll become Amish?"

Adam looked away. Hannah waited.

"I can't promise that."

Hannah nodded.

"But we have a beginning." He leaned down and kissed her cheek. "It's a beginning, Hannah."

19

December blew in with rain and plummeting temperatures. After the breezy warm day when Hannah and the boys picked the last apples, the next day's storm caught her by surprise.

Mamm called to her before she went out to care for the chickens in the morning. "Let Jacob feed the chickens this morning. He's already out, and there's no need for the rest of us to get wet and cold."

Hannah stared at her, but Mamm continued stirring the porridge while Margli and Liesbet set the table. She couldn't remember a time when Mamm had let her stay in during a storm.

"And Hannah, after breakfast, would you help me with the apples? Margareta and Liesbet can redd up the kitchen and watch William. We need to slice the apples and lay them in the attic so they can start drying."

"*Ja*, Mamm."

Hannah glanced at her mother's face as she turned from

the fire to help Margli pour syrup into the small pitcher. She looked peaceful. Even happy. The change that had started in Mamm weeks ago still continued, even on a blustery cold day like this one.

After breakfast, Hannah brought the baskets of apples in from the porch. The rain was turning to ice as the day progressed. Daed had said he expected ice before the snow came, and he was right. She set the baskets on the benches along the table, and then took her seat between two of them while Mamm sat on the other side of the table, between her own two baskets.

"Do you want the apples sliced straight through, or should we core them first?"

"What do you think?" Mamm said, getting the knives out.

"You . . . you're asking what I think is the best way?"

"You're old enough to know which way you prefer to do it."

Hannah couldn't answer. Mamm had never asked her opinion before. Finally Mamm looked at her, an apple in one hand and her knife in the other. "Well?"

"I think . . . Let's core them first. It will save work later."

"*Ja.*" Mamm nodded and started slicing her apple. "That's a good plan. We have time to do it now, and we might not then."

They worked in silence, listening to the little ones play in the attic. Hannah glanced at her mother a few times, but her face was peaceful, and she hummed quietly to herself as she worked.

"Mamm, is anything wrong?"

"*Ne*, why do you ask?"

Hannah shook her head. "I don't know . . . it's just that . . . you seem different."

Mamm smiled, as if she were keeping a secret. "I am different." She glanced at Hannah, then at her apple again. "I'm happy for you, for one thing. Josef is a fine young man, and he seems to be well suited for you."

Josef. Hannah didn't know what to think of him. Sometimes she would remember his kiss, and her knees would go weak, wanting to relive that moment again and again. But then other times, when she remembered his domineering attitude about moving west, she couldn't care if she never saw him again.

"Don't you like Josef?" Mamm glanced at her again.

"Of course I like him. He's nice."

"You never speak of him. When do you think we will see him again?"

Hannah felt her face growing hot. "I'm not sure. He didn't know when he could make the trip, but said he would try to come soon."

"So then, we'll leave it in God's hands."

When had Mamm ever been content to leave the future in God's hands? For half of Hannah's life, her mother had been fighting against God and the tragedy that had come to their family. But now she was content to wait on him?

Hannah peered at Mamm again. Her hands worked quickly, peeling each apple, cutting it in two, cutting out the core, and then slicing the rest into thin strips that would dry quickly. Content. She was content. That's what was different. Gone were the impatient gestures, the biting comments, the anxious look.

How could she be so much at ease when Daed was going to uproot their lives in the spring?

"Mamm?" Hannah bit her lower lip, choosing her words

carefully. "Daed and Jacob are looking forward to moving west, but what about you?"

Mamm's hands stilled, halfway through a slice. "You're worried about me?" She smiled. "Don't be. I'm in agreement with your daed and looking forward to being settled in our new home."

"But what about leaving our house, and the farm, and everything else? Even the trees these apples came from. All this is the legacy our ancestors prepared for us, isn't it? *Grossdawdi*'s hands smoothed the timbers in the ceiling and laid the stone for the fireplace. Everywhere we look we see the care and love they had for us. Can you just leave it all behind?"

Mamm nodded, her eyes bright with tears, but a smile on her face. "*Liebchen*, anything of this world is just straw that can be destroyed in a moment's time. Your daed and I want to preserve what is imperishable and much more important. Compared to you children and our faith, this . . . ," she gestured at the house around them, ". . . is nothing. We're making this move for you, much as our ancestors left their homes in Switzerland for their families."

Hannah turned her apple in her hand as Mamm went back to slicing hers. "I thought our ancestors left Switzerland because otherwise they might be imprisoned or killed."

"That was part of it. But when you are a parent, you never do anything or make any decision only for yourself. Everything you do is to help your children have a better life. Our ancestors left their homes not only to preserve their lives, but to save their children's lives, and to provide a home where they could live and worship God."

"So Daed is moving the family west to save us? From what?"

Mamm reached for another apple and started peeling it. "From being tempted by the ways of the world."

"You're afraid we will leave the faith?"

"You might, if the circumstances were right. What if you had never met Josef? I know how you and Adam Metzler are friends. Don't you think you might have been tempted to join the Mennonite church with him in order to marry?"

Hannah studied the apple in her hand. It was lopsided, and it would be difficult to make a straight cut. "I see. When your world isn't perfect, like this apple, you adjust. You make do so you can live the kind of life you want."

"Not the kind of life you want, Hannah." Mamm reached for Hannah's apple and sliced it along its crooked core perfectly to make two balanced halves. "You yield to the bends and crooks God places in your life until you turn out to be exactly the way he planned. Perfect and whole in Christ."

"But what about what I want?"

"Would you rather have the good life you have planned, or the perfect life God has planned?" Mamm cored and sliced another apple. "I've learned the hard way that when you fight against God, all you are left with is misery."

Hannah thought of all the years Mamm had suffered the grief of losing the little ones. Misery for sure.

"So that's why . . . that's why you've been so different lately?"

Mamm nodded. "I stopped fighting with God. Once I accepted Fanny's death, and Catherine and Hansli . . ." She stopped and wiped her eyes with her handkerchief. "Once I accepted that even that was God's will and his plan, then I was able to rest in that. No more worrying. No more darkness." She looked at Hannah, her eyes bright with tears, but peaceful. "He changed my life, Hannah. He gave me this peace. I don't know why I couldn't yield to him before, but I couldn't see my way out of the darkness. We've lost so much time, haven't we?"

Hannah reached across the table and grasped Mamm's hand. Her own throat was tight. "We can start from here, *ja*?"

Mamm held her hand with a firm grip. "*Ja*. We can start from here."

The last of the apples were spread on clean sheets and suspended from the attic ceiling before dinner.

Mamm stepped back to look at the piles of pumpkins and other squash, ropes of onions and bundles of herbs filling the attic. "We'll be well fed this winter and have plenty of provisions for the trip west, as well."

"It's a good feeling, isn't it?" Hannah picked up some gourds that had been scattered during the children's play and put them back in their piles along the north wall.

The freezing rain had stopped before too much ice accumulated, but Peter and Margli had still begged to go out to play. She could hear their shouts through the window and glanced out to watch them.

"Dinner will be ready in another hour." Mamm made her way to the ladder. "Can you make corn pone to go with the soup while I work on the weaving?"

"*Ja*, for sure." Hannah didn't see Liesbet with the younger children. Had she come back in the house while they played? "I'll be down in a few minutes." She turned to pick up a few more gourds.

Looking out the window again, Hannah smiled when

William plopped down on his bottom. Margli and Peter came to help him up, and then pulled him along the ice between them. She and Liesbet used to play like that with Fanny. Hannah leaned her head against the cold window frame, her breath fogging the glass pane. What a happy time that was; they had so much fun together. No one knew how fleeting that time would be.

If only things would never change! Life would be so sweet if this moment could be captured . . . if it could last forever. But these moments would fade into the background and become memories. Clouded memories, just like the attic window. Hannah wiped the fog away, and the view was clear once more.

Why wouldn't Daed change his mind and remain here on the Conestoga? The plan to keep her family from leaving, so simple and right a few weeks ago, fell apart in Hannah's mind. Daed wouldn't keep the family here if she married Adam, because he refused to consider becoming Amish. And Josef . . .

Hannah wiped the window again. Josef was determined to go west. The memory of his kiss made her stomach flip. Why did he have to be so demanding? Perhaps she should give up her plan and go west with Daed and Josef. See what happened in the future.

The sun found its way through the overcast clouds, a bit of light before the promised snow.

To go west would mean the family would stay together. Stay together and grow, if she married Josef . . .

Margli grasped both of William's hands in her own and spun him around, his feet flying off the ground. The future spun just as quickly, pulling Margli and the little ones out of their childhood and into their years of growing to adulthood. Why couldn't childhood last longer? Why couldn't they stay this innocent for a few more years?

Hannah glimpsed a movement at the edge of the woods. A dark figure . . . Liesbet? She was taking the path to the clearing in this weather.

Not stopping to think, Hannah rushed down the ladder and the stairs to the kitchen. Grabbing her shawl from the hook, she stopped to wrap it firmly around her shoulders. The back steps were covered with ice, and the barnyard stretched out in front of her as a slippery barrier, glistening dangerously in the weak sunlight.

"Hannah!" Peter shouted from the lane where he slid back and forth on the ice. "Come play with us. You can pull us on the sled."

She waved at him, not answering, but made her way toward the barn. She slid down the path between the chicken coop and the empty cornfield and went quickly through the grass to the edge of the woods, the ice-covered blades breaking under her feet. Once she was under the trees, she was away from the icy ground, although it was still slippery in places. The ice-wrapped branches crackled all around her, sending showers of shards down with every breeze. At least this hadn't been a severe storm, where the ice could cover the branches in a layer an inch thick and destroy whole trees with its weight.

Ahead of her, Hannah saw Liesbet's tracks on the path, quickly being covered by the light snow that was now falling. She went as fast as she dared, finally coming to the clearing where she found Liesbet standing alone.

"Liesbet?"

Her sister turned toward her. "What are you doing here? Following me again?" She wiped at her eyes with one hand.

"I saw you come into the woods . . . Are you crying?"

"What difference does it make to you?" Liesbet sniffed and looked into the woods around them.

"You're meeting that man again, aren't you?"

"He isn't just that man, Hannah. His name is George." She sniffed again. "But I guess I'm too late. He's left already." Liesbet's face was sad, holding none of the hard bitterness that so often reigned over her features.

"You don't think he expected you to meet him in the storm, do you?"

"He promised." Her face crumpled as her tears fell.

Hannah moved closer to Liesbet and wrapped her arms around her. Liesbet stiffened, but then relaxed in Hannah's embrace. It had been many months since Liesbet had allowed her to offer comfort.

"Don't you think it's time to forget about George? Find an Amish man who can truly care for you? One who will keep his promises?"

"*Ne*." Liesbet shook her head and pulled away. "You don't understand." Her face was set and she wiped the last tears away. "Nothing will ever take me from George. He's the only man I'll ever love."

"When the family moves west, you'll be coming too, *ja*? George will stay here, and you'll have to forget him. You'll find someone new in Indiana." Hannah smiled, willing Liesbet to agree. "I can see him now. Young, handsome, a hard worker . . ."

Liesbet backed away. "*Ne*, Hannah, *ne*. You don't understand anything. You don't know what it's like—" A sob escaped and Liesbet hugged her arms to herself. Hannah had never seen her look so miserable. "You don't know what it's like to be in love. Truly in love."

She pushed Hannah's outstretched arms away and ran back up the path toward the house. As stubborn as ever.

Hannah dashed her own tears away and started up the path, suddenly remembering the corn pone she had promised to make for dinner.

Liesbet and her parents. Adam and Josef. She was a rope in a tug of war, with Liesbet and Adam pulling one way and her family and Josef the other. She had to be strong so the rope wouldn't end up being pulled in two.

20

Hannah saw Adam's signal as she hung dish towels on the line after dinner the next Tuesday, the blue rag dancing in the chilly breeze.

All week she had skipped back and forth between Josef and Adam . . . but Adam's pull was the strongest, with his promise of a home along the Conestoga. Whenever the memory of Josef's kiss intruded, she pushed it away. If she could only convince Adam to become Amish.

Taking the rest of the clothes pegs into the entryway, Hannah put the basket on the shelf.

"Mamm?" She heard an answer from the weaving room and went to the doorway. Surrounded by skeins of finely spun wool, Mamm was in the middle of threading the big loom, a job that would keep her busy for hours.

"Can you spare me this afternoon?"

Distracted by a tangle, Mamm nodded her head. "Liesbet is here, *ja*? And Margareta? They can watch William when he wakes from his nap."

"*Denki.*" Hannah left before Mamm could ask where she was going.

She took her shawl from the peg near the door and pulled her shawl over her kapp. Adam would be waiting in the clearing. She ran down the path, dry after last week's storm, and worn to dirt after all these years of using it. A sudden thought slowed her feet, and she stopped where the path entered the trees lining the creek. Turning, she looked all around her, at the fallow barley field, the sheepfold next to the barn, the roof of the house peeping over the rise—all the familiar sights of home. If she went to Indiana, if she followed her family and Josef, she would never see these things again—these things so familiar they were as much home as the smell of Mamm's bread.

Continuing toward the clearing, she walked slowly, drinking in the aroma of the dead leaves, the farmyard odors, the decaying vegetation along the edge of the creek. This was home. She could never leave it.

Adam was pacing in the clearing, waiting for her.

"Come with me," he said, grabbing her hand, "I need your help."

He pulled her along a few feet before she planted her heels in the ground. "Wait, Adam, what are you doing?"

"There's a group of passengers trying to get to our farm, but they don't know the way. I need you to show them while I try to get the slave hunters off their trail."

She pulled her hand out of his grip and stood, arms folded. "You mean no one else can do this for you? I thought your daed was helping you."

"Pa can't help this time. He's gone to Mechanicsville, and Ma doesn't know how to bring them through away from the main roads. You've helped me before, Hannah. You know what to do."

Hannah wrapped her hands in her shawl. *Ja*, she had helped Adam before, but she couldn't shake the feeling that it was wrong.

"I don't know, Adam."

"Hannah, you know how desperate these people are."

"But it's against the law. The Good Book tells us to obey the civil authorities."

"But it also tells us that we are required to help our fellow man." Adam took off his hat, running his hands through his hair. Was he just as confused as she was? Or frustrated? "These people are escaping an unjust system, one that enslaves one group of humans to another, just because of the color of their skin. It's wrong, Hannah, and we can help fix that wrong."

"Isn't there another way? Must we disobey the law, compounding the wrong?" Hannah cast about in her mind for possible answers. "Couldn't you work to make slavery illegal in the south as it is here? Wouldn't that be the better way?"

"But it wouldn't fix the problem we have right now, right here in our own township. It takes time to change laws, and we don't have time." Adam rubbed at the back of his neck and glanced at the angle of the sun. "I need your help today, Hannah. Those people are in danger of being captured."

"And so are you, aren't you? What would happen to you if those slave hunters knew you were helping these refugees?"

Adam couldn't meet her eyes.

"You would be arrested, or beaten, or worse."

He nodded. "But I'm willing to take that chance. I knew the danger when I started this, but the rewards outweigh any danger. I know I'm doing God's will, Hannah, can't you see that?"

"But have you thought of the danger you put your family in? And me? When you ask for my help, you put me in danger too."

"I . . . I can protect you, Hannah. You know I will."

"You can't protect me if you're caught, though, can you?"

Adam turned from her, staring off into the trees. "I hadn't thought of that." He faced her again. "But I'm so sure that what I'm doing—what we're doing—is right. God has given us his protection so far, hasn't he? Don't you think he will continue?" He stepped closer. "We don't have time to debate this now. Those people are waiting for us to rescue them, and the bounty hunters are close. I need you now, Hannah. Think of those people who are in danger."

Hannah's thoughts wavered. She hated being put in this position. She had no choice.

"I'll help you, but this is the last time. Don't ask this of me again, Adam."

He grinned and pulled her to him in a hug. "We'll talk about that later."

Hannah followed Adam as he strode along the creek path, almost running to try to keep up. If Adam loved her like he claimed, he wouldn't put her in danger like this. And yet, he was right. If she didn't help, then these people were in danger of being caught. She shivered at the memory of the heavy whip the one slave hunter had carried, and the evil look in his eyes. If only she had never learned of this problem. Once knowing, she had to decide to take the responsibility to help or not. If she never knew . . . Why did Adam have to involve her?

Because he knew that once she knew there was a need, she couldn't refuse him. She couldn't leave strangers alone and in danger if she could help them.

Adam continued past his family's farm, past the bend in the creek where the boys had a swimming hole, past the Hertzlers' farm. Hannah could hear Johanna's voice calling to her sisters, but hurried on. Johanna didn't need to get involved in this.

Not too much farther and Adam led her down to the creek, at a place where a tree had fallen across a narrow place. The water gurgled and complained as it was forced to squeeze between boulders, but the log formed a bridge where there was no road. Adam climbed up onto the makeshift bridge and reached for Hannah's hand.

"You don't mean we need to cross the creek?"

"*Ja*, we do." Adam reached for her, his impatient grasp snagging her hand. "This is the only way across that's hidden from the road. You'll have to bring them back this way too."

Hannah let him pull her up next to him, and started across the expanse. When they reached the other side, Adam jumped down and then helped her climb to the ground. As well as she knew the woods near her farm, Hannah had never explored this side of the creek.

"Where do I need to take them?"

"To our barn. Hilda and Charles should be there to help you."

Deception, hiding from the slave hunters, breaking the law, and Adam's sister and young brother were in it as deep as she was. Hannah swallowed hard.

"Hannah, can you do this?"

Her eyes grew wet with hot tears. "Why do you ask me this now? I have to do it, don't I? I can't turn my back on these people who need help."

He smiled at her. "That's my Hannah. I knew I could count on you." He wiped at her wet cheek with his thumb. "This is a wonderful thing we're doing together. It's just a little farther to their hiding place."

He took her through the trees where there was no path. One time her shawl caught on a snag and Adam carefully extracted it for her, checking to make sure none of the fibers were left behind.

"You'll have to be careful as you lead them through here. We can't leave any mark of their route."

Hannah nodded.

Before many minutes, they topped a small rise and Hannah could see a group of people, their drab clothes blending into the dead leaves littering the floor of the dell where they rested. The shrubby undergrowth of the woods was bare, the thin branches giving no cover to the fugitives. Two of the women sat on the ground, one holding a sleeping baby. There was another woman and five men, along with two boys about Peter's age. Eight adults, two children, and a baby, and in plain view of anyone who happened to come by. The only way they could come this far was through God's Providence—it was impossible to think otherwise.

One of the men stepped forward as they approached and took Adam's hand.

"We were beginning to think you weren't coming back, but Ruby said to have faith."

"I had to find someone to help me." Adam stepped aside

and brought her forward. "Bill, this is Hannah. She knows the way to a safe place where you can rest until nightfall. She'll take you there while I try to keep the hunters off your trail."

"We heard them go by a while ago, on the road." The man pointed behind him, up the rise on the other side of the dell. "They'll be back though, you know they will."

Adam turned to Hannah. "Move as quickly and quietly as you can, and keep a sharp eye out. If you hear someone coming, find a place to hide. As far as I can tell, these slave hunters aren't using dogs, so that's a blessing." He grasped her shoulders. "Will you be all right?"

Hannah felt her face reddening as Adam held her in front of these people. "You take care not to get caught, yourself."

Adam nodded, and he squeezed her shoulders. "You had better get going."

He turned and left the dell, climbing up the far side. Hannah looked at the faces watching her, depending on her knowledge of the woods to keep them safe.

"Are you ready? We need to go to the creek, cross it, and then on to the safe place."

"We sure are, miss." Bill said. The others nodded, even the children's faces solemn and frightened.

Hoofbeats sounded from the top of the dell, the direction Adam had gone. The road must be very close, even though Hannah couldn't see anything. If they moved, if they tried to leave the dell on the other side, they would be spotted by whoever was up there. Hannah motioned for everyone to crouch down, as she did, and they all froze in place.

These people knew the dangers they were facing even more than she did. They were trapped just as surely as the mice who fell into Daed's lead-lined grain bin. If they moved, they'd be caught, but hiding here wasn't any better if those horsemen decided to leave the road in their search.

The hoofbeats stopped. Hannah heard the jingle of harness as a horse shook its head. Men's voices drifted into the dell, indistinct, but harsh. Then Adam's voice. They were questioning him—he would be caught—she would be found, along with these poor people. She looked around her at the tense faces, etched with exhaustion, every one of them watching the edge of the dell above them.

The horses moved on along the road. As soon as they were out of earshot, Hannah saw Adam's head and shoulder appear at the edge of the dell, waving a sign of all clear. She breathed a sigh of relief.

"Thank you, Jesus."

Hannah glanced at the woman who had spoken, the one called Ruby. Her eyes were closed and her hands clasped, raised toward heaven, and tears streamed down her face. Were her words a prayer? She had never heard someone speak to their Lord in that way.

"We need to be going." Hannah gathered her shawl in close and stood up. "Is everyone ready?"

The men and women rose slowly, the men keeping an eye on the top of the dell.

Bill came close to her, speaking low. "We must be careful as we top that rise there." He nodded toward the edge of the dell away from the road, the route they must take to reach the creek. "We all got to keep our heads down. We're too close to the road."

Hannah nodded and looked around at the other faces.

Trusting faces. Even the boys ready to do her bidding, to follow her to safety. Would God protect them as Adam said?

"You all heard Bill. We must be swift, but silent. Be careful not to leave a trail . . ." She stopped as they all nodded. Of course they knew these precautions. This had been their life ever since they had escaped from their slave masters. How far had they come? From Maryland? Farther south? Bill's accent was different from Tom's and the other escaped slaves she had met. She shook her head at the thought of the enormous task these people had undertaken, and with winter not far off.

As she led the way, the women followed her, Ruby in the lead. Next came the two boys, and then the men brought up the rear. She took them the same way Adam had brought her and nearly collapsed in relief when they reached the river.

The log bridge proved no obstacle for people who had crossed countless streams, and before the sun had dipped below the tops of the trees, they had reached the Metzler farm. The fields between the creek and the barn were empty, bare of crops and cover. How could she be sure it was safe to cross them?

"You wait here," she said to Bill. "I'll go to the house to make sure everything is as it should be."

Bill nodded, and the group sat down wherever they could find a spot between the shrubs and the trees.

Hannah started across the field, pretending that this visit to her neighbor was no different than any other. Adam had said his daed was in Mechanicsville, but Dora, his mother, should be at home, as well as his sister, Hilda, and Charles, the youngest son. But if there were visitors, or if the slave hunters were around, she needed to know.

Dora answered the door. "Hannah! Have you come for a visit?"

"*Ja.* I mean, if you aren't busy . . ."

Dora looked past her, toward the barn and fields. "I'm expecting some company, some of Adam's friends, but you're welcome."

Hannah hesitated. How much did Dora know of Adam's activities? And the way she was speaking, it sounded as if she didn't know of Hannah's role.

"I . . . I brought Adam's friends with me. I wanted to make sure of their welcome."

Dora took Hannah's hands in her own and smiled. "Adam said he knew someone who might help today. Don't worry. The way is safe, and Charles and Hilda have put the provisions in their place. They're out in the barn now and will give you all the help you need."

Hannah tried to smile back but couldn't. They weren't safely in hiding yet.

"*Ja, denki.* I'll take the visitors to the barn, then."

She ran back across the field, looking all around as she went. They might be safe from the slave hunters for now, but if Jacob or Liesbet saw her, she would have a lot of explaining to do.

As she beckoned to Bill, the group started across the field to meet her. She took them into the barn, where Hilda and Charles waited for them.

"Hannah! It's you!" Hilda embraced her in a quick hug, and then held her at arm's length. "But we were expecting Adam. Where is he?"

"He's trying to get the slave hunters off our trail, and he asked me to bring these people here."

As she spoke, Charles lifted a hidden trap door, revealing a root cellar underneath the barn floor. Ruby led the way down the ladder, and then reached for the baby. Hannah helped the other women onto the ladder, and then the boys.

"There are candles on the shelf," Hilda called down the ladder, "and plenty of food. Take as much as you need."

Bill hesitated before following the others down into the root cellar. "I don't mean to sound ungrateful, but it's safe down there?"

"Yes," Hilda assured him, smiling with the same confident smile Adam had. "My pa and brother made the root cellar solid, with plenty of good air. You'll only need to stay there until dark, and then Adam will take you on to the station in Lancaster."

Charles lowered the door, and the three of them scattered straw over the floor, hiding the entrance. As a last disguise, Charles pulled the family carriage forward to cover the space.

Hilda grasped Hannah's hand and pulled Charles toward her with her other arm. "We did it! They're safe and sound. No one will find them there."

"Ma said not to stay in the barn, though. If the hunters came by, they'd get suspicious." Charles squirmed out of Hilda's embrace and ran out the door.

"Just like any other twelve-year-old boy," Hilda said, "never still for a minute." She turned to Hannah, pulling her hand into the crook of her elbow. "Our visitors are having their dinner, so why don't you come to the house and have some coffee with me and Ma? We made molasses cookies this morning."

Hannah's stomach growled. It seemed like it had been hours since dinner. She followed Hilda into the house, determined not to go home until she was sure Adam was safe and the refugees were on their way to Lancaster. The big floor clock in the entryway struck three-thirty as she followed Hilda into the house. Surely Adam would be here before supper time, and then she could go home.

21

Adam paused to let a wagon pass by. As the main route between Lancaster and Philadelphia, the New Holland Pike was a busy road.

Once he had convinced the slave hunters he hadn't seen any sign of runaway slaves and given Hannah the all-clear signal, he encountered them two more times on the walk to Lancaster. Even though the early December air was cool, their horses were lathered and panting from the pace the men set as they galloped toward town and back, but the slave hunters—two he hadn't seen before—were determined to find their quarry. He stayed as close to them as he dared without making them suspicious, keeping track of their progress. As long as they kept to the road and were heading away from home, Adam was confident that Hannah was safe.

Once across the bridge over the Conestoga he stopped at the crossroads just outside Lancaster. He paused at a farm gate to get a drink from the pump. It wasn't unusual for farmers along this route to provide water for travelers, and today he was thankful. The December sun was pale, but bright, and walking in his woolen clothes warmed him up.

In the distance, he saw the slave hunters again, hurrying their horses down the road at a loping gallop. When they reached the pump and horse trough, they pulled up.

"This water for anyone, son?"

Adam nodded. They didn't seem to recognize him from the earlier questioning. The one in the red shirt pumped the horse trough full, and then cupped his hand to scoop water into his mouth. The horses drank, one of them crowding near Adam, between him and the men. He breathed in the salty odor of horse sweat and silently thanked God for the cover.

"We ain't seen hide nor hair of them runaways." The man's voice whined. It was the man at the pump—red shirt.

"We'll just keep looking. They got to be around here somewhere." The other man's voice was gravelly. He spit onto the ground at the horse's feet.

"They must-a gone to ground. They for sure ain't on this road."

"We ain't seen them, but they've got to be heading for Lancaster." The gravelly man leaned over the edge of the trough and sluiced water up onto his neck, letting it splash back into the trough. He shook his head then, even getting Adam wet with the drops from his long hair. "Thanks to that pipsqueak down by the river telling us about those Quakers, we know right where they're headed." He chuckled. "And once they get there and find their precious hidey-hole is gone, we've got them."

"Then why don't we just wait for them in Lancaster? We don't have to go all over creation hunting them down."

Gravelly-voice splashed in the water again, making the horses shy back. Adam glanced at him, memorizing his face, before the horse moved back in to continue his drink.

"'Cause they might get wind of what we did and hightail it for somewhere else. Them Quakers got hidey-holes all over this county. We got to keep a sharp eye."

The men mounted and took off, heading up Butter Road, away from Lancaster, without a glance at Adam.

It was all he could do to keep quiet while they were talking, but now Adam leaped to his feet. Were the Quakers he was talking about the Penningtons? What did those men mean, that the "hidey-hole" was gone? Adam's stomach turned as he trotted down the road, worry for the elderly couple who had devoted their lives to helping runaway slaves spurring him on. If they had been exposed, what had these men done to them?

He had two miles to go before reaching the secluded Quaker farm. The Penningtons lived in an oxbow of the creek on the southern edge of Lancaster, enduring the annual spring floods in return for the fertile fields the floods left behind. The entrance to their farm was overgrown, hidden from prying eyes. When Adam reached the farm lane, he stopped, breathing hard. Listening for anything unusual, he walked to the white frame house with cautious steps.

The door of the barn stood open, but as far as he could tell, the entrance to the hidden room was closed and covered, as usual. Perhaps this wasn't the Quaker farm the hunters had spoken of. He climbed the porch steps and knocked. For long minutes there was no answer, and then he heard footsteps, and the door opened.

Martha Pennington's face, tight with worry when she first

opened the door, relaxed into a welcoming smile when she saw Adam.

"Oh, Adam, dear boy, come in."

She moved back to let him into the short hall, and he stepped into the kitchen at the back of the little house. Jess Pennington sat at the kitchen table, a bandage around his head. Adam rushed toward him, taking the chair Martha kept against the wall for visitors and moving it next to his friend.

"What happened? Was it slave hunters?"

Jess patted Adam's knee. "Quiet thyself, young man. They have come and gone, and all is well." He took a sip of tea from the cup in front of him and peered at Adam. "But what of your cargo? Did thee not bring it?"

"The cargo is safe until dark. There are a couple new bounty hunters around, and we were pinned down. We couldn't make the trip here last night."

"It's just as well thee didn't." Martha put a cup and saucer in front of Adam and poured tea for him. "Some men came yesterday—"

"Hush thee, Martha. They did no harm."

"No harm! No harm? They took two of the best laying hens, and scared the rest so they won't lay for a week." Martha sat down with a sob. "And my poor Tilly-Cat." She pulled a handkerchief out of the waistband of her gray dress and dabbed at her eyes. "Thee knows that man ran her down on purpose."

"Were they the same men I saw? A skinny one with a red shirt, and a taller one with a gravelly voice?"

Jess nodded and took another sip of his tea. "They searched all through the outbuildings and the house. When they found the root cellar behind the hen house, they thought they had found . . . the place where we store the cargo."

Adam nodded and sipped his own tea. The old Quaker's calm acceptance of the violence he experienced was a quieting balm to his own soul.

"Those men are watching all the roads between Mechanicsville and Lancaster, and they know we were headed here."

"How?" Martha twisted her cup on its saucer. "How did they know to look here?"

Adam looked from Jess's bandage-covered white head to Martha's worried face. "I heard them say there was an informant, at the river crossing. It had to be at Peach Bottom. That's how they knew."

"Oh, Lord, how we need thee now," Martha said softly, holding her handkerchief over her eyes.

Jess slumped in his chair, this blow worse than the one on his head. "A traitor among us."

He sat quietly, his eyes closed and head bowed. Adam had learned to wait, giving his elderly friend time to pray and think. He took a swallow of his cooling tea. Silence, marred only by the ticking of a clock in another room, filled the small keeping room. He pondered this quality he had seen often with the Penningtons—to them the silence was a presence, not the absence of sound. He drained his cup.

"We must continue the work." Jess's voice broke the silence, and he raised his eyes to Martha's and then Adam's with a fire of resolution in them. "Our lives and property mean nothing if we have passengers who are in danger."

"Isn't it dangerous for all, though?" Adam could only imagine what would happen if he tried to bring Bill and the others here tonight.

Jess nodded. "It's dangerous, but what else can we do?"

"We can wait them out. The passengers are safe at our farm for now. We can keep them there for a few days, until these slave hunters give up and figure they've missed them."

"Thee has wisdom in thy young years, Adam." Jess nodded his agreement. "We will wait a few days and will keep thee in our prayers."

"And I'll keep watch until they're gone." Adam stood, resting his hand on Jess's shoulders to keep the elderly man from rising. "I'll see myself out. I must get going if I'm to get home before full darkness sets in."

Martha walked him to the front door and peered through the curtains before opening it for him. "Thee take care, young Adam. We don't want those hunters suspecting thee, also."

"I will. I'll see you in a few days."

Adam headed up the lane toward the main road. At the bend in the lane, he looked back. The elderly couple was watching him. He returned their wave and then turned toward home.

Adam stopped at Tennant's Mill, just downriver from the railway bridge, to purchase a sack of barley meal. He expected to run into the slave hunters, and the sack of meal would provide the reason for his trip into town. Returning empty-handed would arouse suspicions.

Glancing at the angle of the sun, he headed east on Butter Road, the direct route home. He hoped he wouldn't run into the hunters again, hoped they would have given up for the night. The sun would be gone by the time he reached the farm, but walking in the dark didn't bother him. The evening was still early, and if he hurried, he'd be home before supper.

Dusk was just filling in under the trees when he heard the horses approaching. Jingling harness, galloping hard. Those hunters were as hard on their animals as they were on their quarry.

"Hey, boy!"

Gravelly Voice called to him, and Adam debated. Stop, or go on? Going on would only make them angry. He stopped and turned toward the men, balancing the sack of meal on his shoulders. The men reined their horses in. Red Shirt looked about ready to drop from exhaustion, but Gravelly Voice leaned forward in his saddle, chomping furiously at a wad of tobacco.

"We're just running into you all over the place, ain't we?" He spit a dark stream into the bushes at the side of the road.

Adam took a step closer, peering up at the dark-haired man as if trying to remember. "*Ach, ja.*" He shifted from German to English. "I remember you. You stopped me earlier and asked if I had seen any runaway slaves."

"That's right." The man shifted his chaw to his other cheek. "What are you doing here? Didn't we see you on the other side of the creek last time?"

Adam nodded his head, as if he was eager to help the man remember the details. "*Ja,* that's right. I was on the New Holland Pike. I ate dinner with my *Oncle* Hans at noon, and then went to Lancaster to buy meal." He shifted his shoulders to indicate the fifty-pound sack he carried.

The man leaned back in his saddle, regarding Adam through narrowed eyes.

Red Shirt shifted. "Come on, Hiram. It'll be dark soon. Let's go get some supper in town."

Hiram shifted his gaze to Red Shirt, and then back to Adam. He spit brown juice into the dirt at Adam's feet. "I don't know. This boy's heading home. I'd be willing to bet someone's waiting supper on him. I could use a good, home-cooked meal about now."

Adam's stomach churned. To keep up the ruse of a simple farm boy, he'd have to invite them home for supper, but he couldn't risk that. He wouldn't be surprised if Ma had invited Bill, Ruby, and the rest of them into the house for their supper instead of bringing it to them in their safe hiding place.

"It . . . it's quite a ways to the farm. The family will have eaten everything by the time we get there. Ma's not expecting me tonight . . . but . . . I wanted to see . . . ." Adam cleared his throat. "Well, there's this girl." He looked at their faces. Hiram and Red Shirt looked at each other and guffawed.

"Maybe we should come with you to meet this girl, eh?" Hiram winked.

Adam felt his face heating and breathed slowly to beat down the anger.

Red Shirt guffawed again. "Looky there! He's blushing. She must be a pretty one."

Hiram pulled at the reins of his horse, turning back toward Lancaster. "Aw, come on. I'm too hungry to waste time with the farmer. Let's get supper. We've got a long night ahead of us."

As the hoofbeats faded, Adam let the heavy sack down and sat on it, his knees trembling. He took off his hat and ran his hands through his hair, soaked with perspiration. Close calls or not, he didn't want to live through that again.

The sun dipped closer to the horizon as he sat, throwing the road into dusky shadows. Adam shouldered his sack of meal again and continued on his way, listening for returning riders every step of the way.

Lamplight glowed from the kitchen windows as he approached the farmhouse, but before going in, he opened the barn door and examined the interior as a stranger would. No light shone anywhere. There was no sign someone might be here. He dropped the barley meal next to the door, and then lit the lantern. He paced from one side of the big barn floor to the other, looking for any clue, anything out of place. He could see nothing. Were they even here? Did Hannah make it home with them?

With a sudden clenching, he had to see for himself. He hung the lantern from its hook on a post and pushed the carriage out of the way. Shoving straw away with his feet, he found the hidden handle and pulled. The hole was dark and quiet, but Adam could smell the burned tallow from the doused candle.

"Bill? It's Adam. Are you all there? Is everyone all right?"

A scratch of a match, and light filled the cellar. Bill stood at the bottom of the ladder, a candle in his hand, the others behind him.

"Yes sir, we're all right. Is it time to go?"

"Not yet. Those slave hunters aren't giving up, and they know where the station is. You'll all have to wait here a couple more days. Do you think that will be all right?"

Bill looked at Ruby and the others. Ruby nodded her head once.

"I reckon so, Mister Adam. It'll be cramped, but nothing like sleeping in a swamp."

Adam nodded. "We'll try to find some safe way for you to spend time up here in the barn, or in the house, but I can't promise."

"That's all right. We're grateful for a warm, dry bed and plenty of food."

"Ma made sure you got your supper?"

"Oh, yes sir, she sure did. Your ma's one good cook."

Adam smiled. "I'll tell her you said so. I need to close the door now and set everything to rights. I'll check on you again later, all right?"

"That'll be fine." Bill nodded. "That'll be fine."

Adam closed the trap door and covered it again, pushing the carriage back into place. Putting the lantern back by the door, he blew it out and shouldered the meal sack once more. What would Ma say when she saw what he brought home? They'd have barley cakes for breakfast for weeks.

The sack made his footsteps heavy on the porch, and Pa swung the door open before he reached it.

"You're late, son. We were worried."

As Pa took the sack from his shoulders, Ma stepped forward to grab him in a hug. He looked over her shoulder. Hannah. Hannah was sitting at the table, her face blotchy in the lamplight, a twisted handkerchief in her hands.

She had waited for him, and it was the most beautiful thing he had ever seen.

Charles jumped up between him and Hannah. Adam let go of Ma to grab his brother's shoulders in a tight squeeze. "Where have you been, Adam? Hannah said there were slave hunters. Did they catch you? What happened?"

"*Ja*, there were slave hunters on the road." Adam sat down on the long bench next to Hannah. If he looked at her, he wouldn't be able to stop himself. He'd take her in his arms right there in front of Ma and everybody. "But they didn't know I had any connection with our passengers, so I was safe."

"Why were you gone so long, then?" Hannah pressed close to him as she asked her question, laying her hand on his sleeve.

"I overheard them say they had heard about the Penningtons and had destroyed the hiding place."

Ma gasped. "Are they all right?"

"They're fine, although Jess was bandaged up. Those slave hunters must be new at their job, though. They found the Penningtons' root cellar and thought they had destroyed the station when they wrecked it. And all day they rode up and down the roads, looking for our passengers, not knowing they would never use public roads." He looked at Pa. "They're out there tonight too. We'll need to keep the people here until they've left the area."

Pa nodded. "That sounds like a good idea. We'll just lay low."

Hannah rose from the bench. "I need to get home. Mamm and Daed will be worried about me, since it's already dark."

"I'll walk you home." Adam stood. His feet were sore from all the miles he had already walked today, but he couldn't let Hannah go off alone, not with those strangers around.

The moon had risen, casting a white light over the fields. As Adam closed the door behind them, he listened, but he couldn't hear any hoofbeats. He gave Hannah his arm and led her toward the road, the shortest way from his house to hers. He could feel the light press of Hannah's arm against his own. Could hear her breathing, could smell the lye soap her clothes had been washed with.

How could he think of anything else when Hannah was next to him?

She broke the silence. "I was worried about you."

"I hurried home as quickly as I could." He grasped her hand where it rested in the crook of his elbow. "I was worried about you too. Wondering if you had made it here safely. The only comfort I had was that if the slave hunters were still out there, that meant they hadn't found you."

They walked in silence, and then Hannah asked, "If we married, this is what our lives would be like, isn't it? A hiding place in our barn for runaway slaves, you out somewhere barely escaping from danger, and me at home, wondering if you've been caught or not."

Her words ended in a sob, and Adam turned, taking her in his arms. He waited until her crying stopped and she pulled away to wipe her nose on her handkerchief.

"I can't promise you there won't be more days like this one."

She shook her head. "I know they will only get worse. More groups of people needing your help, more slave hunters . . . smarter slave hunters."

"But we'll be working together. Think what that means, Hannah, to dedicate our lives to helping other people."

She sniffed, playing with the buttons on the front of his coat while he waited. She had to see the future he could see so plainly.

"I'll have to think about it, Adam. I . . . I know it would help people, but I just can't imagine what my life would be like, living that way."

"You know that if your family moves west, staying here with me will be the best thing for you."

They walked on until they reached the edge of the porch. Adam could hear her family inside the house. They were waiting for her. He turned her toward him and lifted her chin with one finger until she was looking into his eyes.

"You know what I want, Hannah. Say you'll be my wife. Say you'll stay here on the Conestoga with me."

In the light from the window, he could see her eyes filling with tears.

"I can't say that, Adam. I can't."

From the dark recesses near the barn door, a man cleared his throat. "I know why she can't say that."

He walked closer to the house. Josef Bender.

Adam put his arm around Hannah's shoulder, but she slipped away, standing between him and Josef.

"Good evening, Josef. I didn't know you were here."

He smiled at Hannah, but returned his hard gaze to Adam. "I can see that. *Guten Abend, Herr* Metzler. I think you are surprised to see me, also, *ja?*"

Hot anger rose suddenly, turning Adam's stomach. Jealousy, exhaustion, and worry all rolled into one hot, churning ball.

"What are you doing here, Bender?"

"I come to visit Hannah, and then I find her in another man's arms. I think I should be asking you the question of what you are doing."

Adam glanced at Hannah. She looked from him, to Josef, and back again. She wanted him to leave.

"Hannah was helping me this afternoon and spending time with my mother and sister. I was thanking her."

"By asking her to marry you?"

"Stop it." Hannah stepped closer to Josef. "You are both

acting like little boys. I have not said I would marry either one of you. You need to settle your differences, or I'll ask you both to leave."

Adam turned to Hannah, ignoring Josef Bender. "*Denki*, Hannah. You were a great help today."

"Don't ask me to do that again, Adam." She looked at him, her eyes pleading. "I . . . I can't go through that waiting and worrying again."

Beyond Hannah, Josef shuffled his feet, but Adam refused to include him in this conversation. He reached for Hannah's hand, leading her away from Josef. He bent his head close to hers. "If I promise to keep you safe . . ."

"All the promising in the world won't help if something goes terribly wrong."

Adam moved away. Nothing would go wrong. "I'll see you again, though?"

"*Ja*." She looked down at her feet. "We're friends, aren't we? Of course we'll see each other again."

Adam backed away, then turned and started for home. Leaving Hannah with that Josef Bender . . . it was harder than anything he had ever done. But he could tell, looking into her eyes, she wasn't his.

22

Hannah stood silently next to Josef as they listened to Adam's footsteps grow fainter.

"What brings you to the Conestoga this evening, Josef?" Hannah's voice was strained, and she cleared her throat.

"I came on an errand for Daniel and to see you." His voice was harsh. "But it looks like that was a wasted trip, perhaps."

"I told you, Adam is a friend."

"A friend who asks you to marry him is a bit more than a friend." Josef bit his words off in crisp chunks. "And what was it you helped him with? Was it so important that he would put you in danger?"

A lump rose in her throat. Adam's work was important, but she still resented his assumption that she would be as enthusiastic as he was. When it came to this mission of his, she seemed to fade into the background. She was only another tool for him to use to accomplish the task.

"It's nothing you need to worry about. This is between Adam and me."

"Hannah . . ." Josef's voice dropped to a whisper and he took her in his arms. She relaxed into his embrace, hungry for his strength and protection. "I didn't come all this way to quarrel with you." He partly released her, keeping one hand around her waist. With the other hand he tilted her chin up. In the dim light from the house, his face was tender, pleading.

She nodded. "You're right. We won't quarrel. Does the family know you're here?"

"*Ne.*" He stroked her cheek with his thumb. "I had just stabled the horse when I heard someone coming down the lane."

"Then we must go in. I know Daed will be pleased to see you."

Hannah's late return was forgotten when she walked into the house with Josef.

Daed rose from his seat to greet him with a hug. "Josef, it's so good to see you again. What brings you this far?"

"Daniel had some questions about our journey west, so he sent me to discuss them with you and Elias."

Mamm handed Josef a cup of tea. "And how long will you be able to stay with us?"

Josef caught Hannah's eye as they all seated themselves around the table. "Daniel doesn't expect me to return before Monday evening. I came early to spend the Sabbath with you, if that is all right."

Daed took the cup of tea Mamm gave him. "Tomorrow is a home Sabbath. We'll go to the Hertzlers' first thing on Monday."

"Did you walk from Ephrata again?" Jacob leaned forward.

"*Ne.* Daniel had me take the horse. Riding is much faster than walking and he wanted to be sure I'd get home on time."

After evening prayers, the conversation turned to the trip west, with Josef just as excited as Daed and Jacob. Hannah put William to bed, and then sent Margli and Peter to their beds as the evening got later. Liesbet followed them up to their room, yawning as she went.

When Hannah came back into the kitchen after saying good night to Margli, Josef was speaking.

"I hope to have enough money saved to buy a quarter section, if there's one available."

"A quarter section?" Jacob took a cookie from the plate Mamm had gotten out while Hannah was upstairs. "One hundred sixty acres is a lot of land to clear."

"But it will be worth it, as long as the prices stay low." Josef took a bite from his own cookie. "And I don't have to clear the entire section at once. I'll work on forty acres to start with, and I can always sell some of the land to another settler if I need to."

Daed nodded. "That sounds like a good plan. By the time you may need to sell, prices will probably be higher."

Josef smiled at Hannah as she took a place at the table and pushed the plate of cookies closer to her. "I hope we'll be able to find land near each other, Brother Christian, and near the Hertzlers, also."

"I hope there's still land available in the same area where the families settled last year. A strong community can start with only a few, can't it?"

"And what about you, Jacob? Will you be buying your own land, or go in with your *vater*?"

Jacob's eyes lit up. "I hadn't thought I would buy my own

land, but if it's not expensive, I could buy some acres next to Daed."

Hannah yawned as the men started discussing the type of trees they would find, and how likely it was to buy land with water available. Her day had been long and stressful, and morning was going to come very early.

"I must say good night," she said to Mamm. The men didn't notice as she slipped up the stairs.

Hannah went to bed, exhausted. But once she climbed into bed with Liesbet, sleep refused to come. Josef Bender was here, and he had come to see her. But he wouldn't consider staying along the Conestoga. From his conversation with Daed and Jacob, he had forgotten that was her plan. He had his heart set on moving west.

What was it about adventure and new frontiers that drew men so strongly?

Indiana wasn't a settled place, like home. There would be trees to clear, a house to build, a barn and other outbuildings to put up. Josef would need to clear stumps before a crop could be planted. And where would they find a cow and chickens? What would they eat once the supplies were all gone?

And there were other dangers. Illness, Indian attacks, lawless men, wild animals . . . And yet Daed expected to take his family there and have a good life? Josef thought the two of them could start their housekeeping in a place like that? What would happen when children came along?

But on the other hand, when Josef held her in his arms . . . The thought alone banished all those fears. She sank into the memory of his kiss, his strong arms, his comfortable embrace . . .

Liesbet shifted, bringing Hannah back to wakefulness. Her sister got out of the bed, putting on her shoes.

"Where are you going?" Hannah whispered so she wouldn't wake Margli.

Liesbet jumped. "I'm . . . I'm going out to the privy."

"In the dark?" Hannah turned over, anxious to get back to her thoughts of Josef. "Why don't you just use the chamber pot?"

"I'd rather go out to the privy than have to clean the pot in the morning."

"Whatever you choose. Just don't wake me up when you come back in."

She tried to bring back the memory of Josef's embrace, but as she descended into sleep, it was Adam's confident arms that filled her mind. He held her close, too close, his hand over her mouth as riders thundered by. She saw the whips tied to their saddles, the dark horses galloping. And then Adam left her, covered with hay, crouched in a wagon bed, trundling down a road. Ruby held her hand, but the other woman's eyes were closed as she repeated "Help us, Jesus," over and over.

The hay sank down onto them, covering Ruby, pushing between the two of them. She lost Ruby's hand just as a baby started crying. Hannah pushed at the hay, trying to find the baby. Someone had to help it, but no one else was there. She stood up in the wagon, pushing away the hay. Adam was driving. He could help her. But when she finally got past the hay, the driver turned to her, his face leering. It was the slave catcher—they were captured!

Hannah sat up in bed, still breathing hard. It was just a dream, wasn't it? Only a dream.

She turned to lie back down, and then she noticed. Liesbet hadn't returned.

Closing her eyes, she tried to will herself back to sleep, but a part of her listened for Liesbet's step in the hall. Finally, she rose and went downstairs. The house was quiet, the fires banked. Looking out the window toward the privy, she could see no light from the little building at the edge of the yard, no figure walking back to the house.

The clock struck the hour. One o'clock. Liesbet had been gone for more than two hours. Hannah wiggled her toes, trying to keep them warm. Had she gone off to meet with George again? Whatever she was doing, it was a stupid and thoughtless thing to wander off into the night, and on such a cold night too.

Then Liesbet appeared, making her way past the barn, coming from the direction of the path to the clearing. She looked safe enough. Hannah hurried up the stairs and into their bed. The last thing she wanted tonight was an argument with Liesbet.

Josef sought out Hannah after the noon dinner of cold meat and bread and found her sitting on the bench near the back door. The same bench where he had helped her clean the wool fleece the first day he met her.

"The weather is fine today, *ja*?" He sat near her, and then scooted a bit closer. She smiled at him, and then looked out toward the barn and the woods beyond.

"*Ja*, it is fine."

"A good day for a walk." He scooted a little closer on the bench. "Perhaps you would like to show me your farm. Take me to some of your favorite places."

"Why would you be interested in our farm when you'll be leaving soon?"

Josef rubbed his chin. The way she spoke, she still wasn't planning to go west with them.

He stood and reached for her hand. "When I was a boy at home, my *mutti* taught me to love all things of nature and this world, but to hold them lightly." He pulled Hannah's hand into the crook of his elbow and started walking toward the barn.

"Why did she do that?" Hannah's hand tightened on his arm, pulling herself close to him as they walked.

"*Mein vater* died when I was young. He was a soldier in a battle. We never knew who was fighting or why, we only knew he never came home. Someone brought us word that he had been killed." He followed Hannah's slight nudge and turned to go down a path that led past the barn. "*Mutti* knew that someday, the soldiers would come for me too. She prepared me early to leave home, teaching me not to hold too closely to things, but to grasp the knowledge of God with both hands and hold on tight." He grasped at the air in front of him, balling his hands into two fists, just as *Mutti* had shown him when he was a little boy. He could see her earnest face in his mind as he did so, and his throat grew tight.

"How old were you when you left?"

"I was fourteen years. The king of the state where we lived was gathering soldiers to fight against another king—the wars are endless—so *Mutti* found passage for me on a ship to America. The week before I left for the ship, I walked the land I had grown up on. I visited the woods, the streams, the fields. I even said goodbye to our beastly cow who always kicked over the milk bucket."

"How could you bear to leave? Not just the farm, but your family?"

The path led into the trees and Hannah released his arm, leading the way to a quiet clearing. "My sister was married the year before. Her husband was wealthy. A landowner. *Mutti* went to live with them, and I know she is well cared for."

"Do you ever hear from her?"

"*Ja*, we have exchanged letters. She is doing well and enjoying her life as the *grossmutti*. My sister, she has four *kinder* already."

Hannah went across the clearing to another path. She led the way to the creek bank where a fallen tree hung over the water. "You wanted to see my favorite places." She stepped onto the tree trunk and walked along its length until she was out over the water. She sat down where a branch forked from the trunk. Josef followed her and sat, his legs dangling over the water.

"This is my very special spot. I come here often to think and to pray."

Josef swung his feet, watching the water beneath them. In the shallows by the creek bank, a thin layer of ice spanned the distance between rocks, but in the center of the creek, brown water flowed slowly to the west. The place was secluded, the quiet broken only by the sound of the water and an occasional bird call.

"I can see why you like it." He watched a fish in the lee of a rock, moving just enough so it wouldn't be carried away downstream.

"You're the first person I've ever brought here. No one knows about this place."

"Even Adam Metzler?" He looked at her, and she met his gaze. Her face, framed by her kapp, was lovely. She smiled at him, and then turned back to the flowing water beneath her.

"Even Adam Metzler."

Her words brought a warm glow. Josef watched her profile as she dangled her feet above the flowing water, tossing bits of twigs and bark into the water.

"Do you ever feel like those twigs, flowing west toward the future?"

She turned to him. "*Ne*, Josef. Never. My future isn't in the west, it's here."

"But your family is going west. You can't stay here while they go . . . while I go."

"No matter how Daed and my brother talk, I don't think they'll make that trip in the end. Our lives are here. Our futures are here. Why would we want to leave?" She stood on the tree trunk and he scrambled to his feet.

"You are wrong, Hannah. Your *vater* is set on leaving this farm. All the arrangements have been made." He jumped to the ground and reached back to help Hannah.

"The arrangements can be changed. The farm hasn't been sold yet, or any of the animals."

Hannah started to walk along the creek, but Josef grabbed her hand. "What about me, Hannah? What about us?"

He pulled her closer to him and reached up to caress her cheek. She blushed and looked away.

"You . . . you could stay here. You could buy land here, along the Conestoga. You don't have to go to that unsettled frontier."

He pulled her chin around so that she looked into his eyes. "I'm going west, and I want you to go with me." Her lips were a pale pink bow. He pulled her closer. "I want you to be my wife, Hannah Yoder. I want us to have a family together, to make our own home. In Indiana, we'll have opportunities we would never have here." He leaned in and kissed those soft lips. "Say yes. Say you'll come with me."

"You don't understand." Her eyes filled. "You don't know what you're asking me to do."

"I'm asking you to trust me. To believe that I know what is best for you and our future."

She turned away from him, hiding her face from him. "I don't know you well enough. I don't know if I can trust you."

He took her hand again and started down the creek path, tucking her fingers into his elbow. "All I need is a chance."

She laced her fingers together, holding his arm. She walked silently beside him as he waited, pacing off the moments. Finally she squeezed his elbow. "*Ja*, I will give you a chance."

23

The Yoders' turn to have Sabbath meeting at their house was the next week, and Annalise welcomed the extra work. She was certain she was expecting, and it was all that occupied her mind. The last three times her heart had been filled with dread at the thought of bringing another child into the family, but not this time. This time she welcomed the new blessing. Even on a busy day like today, Annalise found herself lingering at her chores, her mind on the coming baby.

"Mamm, where do you want me to put these beans?" Liesbet struggled to carry the wooden bucket up from the cellar.

"Here, let me help with that." Annalise reached for the bucket and set it on the table.

Liesbet sank to the bench, exhausted, while Annalise closed the trap door.

"Help me sort them. We need all of them for tomorrow's dinner." Annalise poured the beans into her kneading trough and began to pick through them. She glanced at Liesbet. The girl's face was pale.

"Are you feeling all right, Liesbet?"

Liesbet started. "*Ja*, I'm fine. I'm just a little tired from carrying the bucket up the ladder."

"You haven't been eating very much lately. You need to keep your strength up."

Christian always said she spoiled Liesbet, but the girl had been more frail and tired more easily, ever since the diphtheria. It wasn't just that she took a long time to recover, but it was as if the illness had left her with lingering damage to her lungs or heart.

Liesbet stirred at the dry beans with her finger, pulling out a black one.

"I might be coming down with something." She sorted out a few more discolored beans from the bowl. "I've been so tired, and my stomach doesn't feel good."

"We'll make some ginger tea after we put the beans to soak. That should help you feel better." Annalise smiled as she sorted. Ginger tea would help her too.

After the beans were sorted, Hannah joined them at the table for a cup of tea. The little ones were playing in the attic, their voices drifting down the stairs.

"Do you think many will come all this way for meeting tomorrow?" Hannah stirred a bit of molasses into her cup.

Annalise sipped her tea. The thought of adding sweetener to it made her stomach even more queasy. "I don't know. The weather seems to be holding, but if it turns rainy, I'm sure some will stay home."

"Living at the edge of the district, the way we do, makes it hard for the older folks to come."

"I don't see why we don't just build a meetinghouse somewhere in the middle." Liesbet ran her finger along a seam in the tabletop. "That would make it easier for everyone, wouldn't it?"

"Don't let your daed hear you talking like that." Annalise put her cup down. "You know that isn't our way."

Liesbet shrugged. "Just because it isn't our way doesn't mean it's a bad idea. The Mennonites never have to travel as far as we do for meetings." She yawned. "I'm going upstairs to lie down for a while." She pushed up from the table. "Don't wake me for dinner . . . I'm not really hungry."

As Liesbet left, Annalise turned to Hannah. "Has Liesbet been sleeping well at night?"

Hannah didn't meet her eyes. "Why do you ask?"

"This is the second day in a row that she's taken a nap in the morning, and she doesn't have much of an appetite."

"She's gotten up to use the outhouse, but other than that, I think she's sleeping all right. She is probably just fighting a cold or something."

"*Ja*. That must be it." Annalise sipped her tea. Something was certainly bothering Liesbet.

"How much more do we need to do to be ready for the meeting tomorrow?"

"We'll start the beans soaking for the soup, and then these downstairs rooms need to be cleaned. Your daed is cleaning the barn, and Jacob is working on the henhouse. This afternoon we'll have the little ones pick up sticks in the barn yard and along the drive. . . ."

"It's an awful lot of work, isn't it?"

"*Ja*, but it's only twice a year, and the whole house is so clean when we're done." She took a sip of tea, but Hannah only turned her cup around in her hands.

"What's wrong, Hannah?"

"This will be our last time to have the meeting here. By our next turn, you'll be in Indiana."

Annalise stopped, her cup partway to her lips. "What do you mean, 'you'll be in Indiana'? You're coming with us."

Hannah shifted in her seat. "I haven't decided yet."

"If you stayed here, what would you do?"

"Adam has asked me to marry him. He's buying the Hertzlers' farm, and . . ." Hannah's words stopped. "I don't know what to do."

"I thought Josef was courting you?"

"*Ja*, but Adam is so determined. I can't decide between them."

"Isn't it easy? Adam is Mennonite. You know an unequal marriage will never work."

"He wants me to leave the Amish. To become Mennonite."

Annalise ignored the churning in her stomach. "You wouldn't consider that, would you?"

Hannah didn't answer right away. She looked out the window toward the creek, and then sighed. "I don't know, Mamm. If he would become Amish . . . but he won't even talk about it." She sipped at her tea. "But I think the only reason why I can't decide is that if I married him, I would be able to stay here. I don't want to leave our farm, and the Conestoga. I don't want to move west. But I don't want to become Mennonite, either. I guess I don't know what I want."

Annalise reached across the table and took Hannah's hand in her own. "I think I know what it is. You don't want to lose your home. All your life your home has been here, with your daed and me. Your home has been this house, this farm, the woods, and the creek. But whether you decide to marry Adam and stay here, or marry Josef and go west with us, your home is going to change. That's part of growing up."

"Is it gone forever, then?"

Annalise laughed at the same time as tears filled her eyes. "Ne, liebchen, it isn't gone forever. Wherever your husband is, that will be your home. Wherever your daed and I are, that will be home too. And we look forward to the home God is preparing for us in heaven. Home is where your heart is. Always remember that."

After worship was over on Sunday, Hannah and Johanna dished up steaming bowls of bean soup for members of the church. Since the weather had turned blustery and cold overnight, attendance was sparse. None of the elderly members of the church had made the journey to the Yoder farm, and mothers stayed home with babies and young children. As soon as dinner was finished, the ones who had come would start bundling up for the long walk home.

"I have something to tell you." Johanna handed a bowl of soup to John Yoder as she whispered the words to Hannah.

"Ja?"

"Ja. A secret."

The men had all taken their bowls of soup. As they ate, Hannah cut another pan of cornbread for the women and children.

"After everyone is served, we can take our dinner up to the attic. We can talk there and no one will disturb us."

A few minutes later, Hannah took her bowl and bread and led Johanna up the stairs to the third-floor attic. It was chilly up there, and Hannah was glad for the warm bowl of soup.

"What is the secret?" Hannah sat on a large pumpkin and balanced her piece of cornbread on her knee.

Johanna took the pumpkin next to hers, wiggling so much from excitement she almost spilled her soup.

"Jacob came by our place last night."

Hannah grinned, but hid it behind a bite of cornbread. "That's no secret. I saw which way he went after supper was over. He just went to talk to your daed about something."

"That's not why he came."

"He didn't talk to your daed?"

"Well, *ja*, he did. But he didn't need to, did he? Don't you think he came over just to see me?"

"Well, did he?"

"What?"

"See you."

Johanna sighed. "I was in the house the whole time. He came to the house and knocked, though. He must have known Daed was in the barn. I think coming to the house was just an excuse to talk to me."

"So what did he say?"

Johanna dipped her head. "Nothing." She stirred her soup. "Could it be that he's just shy?"

Hannah sipped a spoonful of broth. "You're still set on marrying my brother?"

Johanna looked at her, eyes serious. "*Ja*, for sure I am."

"Has he said anything to you about it?"

Johanna sighed. "*Ne*, but I know he likes me."

"Why?"

Johanna smiled at her. "Just the way he looks at me."

The way he looks at her? Hannah stirred the hot beans and broth in her bowl, remembering the way Josef looked at her, caressed her arm, lifted her chin to look into his face. His kiss. Could Jacob really be thinking of marriage the way Josef was? And Adam? At least Johanna and Jacob would be a good match, one both their daeds would approve of.

"What does Adam say about you moving west?"

Hannah shifted on her pumpkin. It was a little small for a seat and was becoming uncomfortable. "He doesn't want me to go."

"I don't think he would, especially if he saw the way Josef looks at you."

How much could she tell Johanna about Adam? She didn't want the whole community to know about his plans to marry her. "He hasn't been around here much. He's been busy."

"Busy with what?"

Hannah's fingers grew cold. She couldn't tell anyone about Adam's activities. Every time she had seen him lately, he had been either coming from or going to Lancaster. He hadn't asked for her help again, but she was involved, just the same. She knew what he was doing.

"You know how busy a farmer is in the fall. He and his daed butchered three steers last week, and that was a lot of work."

Johanna grabbed her arm so suddenly Hannah dropped her bread into her soup. "Do you think he might marry you to keep you from moving away?"

Hannah fished the crumbly cornbread out of her bowl with her spoon.

"Hannah, you're not answering my question."

Hannah nodded, taking a bite of soup. Johanna had come very close to the truth with her guesses. "*Ja*, I think he might ask me, if he thought I'd do it."

Johanna's voice rose in a squeal. "Well? Would you marry him?"

"Shhhh." Hannah cast a glance at the open attic door. "Don't tell anyone, please? And I don't know what I'd say."

"Do you love him?"

Hannah shrugged her shoulders. "He's Mennonite, an outsider. There's a lot more to consider than whether I love him or not."

Johanna chewed on her lower lip like she always did when she was thinking. "He could become Amish . . ."

"*Ne*, he wouldn't."

"How can you be sure?"

Hannah cast about in her mind. She was sure, but she didn't want to tell Johanna how they had discussed this very thing. "He doesn't really see how our faiths are different. He thinks differences like meeting in homes the way we do aren't important, but they are. There's a reason we don't have meetinghouses."

Johanna shrugged. "I never really thought about it."

"It's the reason our daeds are moving west. They want us to be free of distractions that would pull us away from our faith." Hannah paused. Adam was one of those distractions. Every hour she spent with him, he pulled her heart closer to his and further from the Amish faith.

"I don't know how you can even consider Adam when Josef is around." She stopped until Hannah looked at her. "He is still around, isn't he?"

"He comes to visit when he can, but that isn't very often. He spent Sabbath with us last week, but that's the only time I've seen him since he came to meeting with us last month."

"But he's Amish, so he should be the one you marry."

Hannah sighed and put her empty bowl on the floor. "If only it was that easy."

"Well, I don't worry about it. I know Jacob is Amish and will stay Amish." Johanna set her empty bowl next to Hannah's and laced her fingers over her knees. "Whoever he marries will have a strong, faithful, handsome husband."

"And you want to be the one to marry him."

"*Ja*, of course." Johanna grinned at her. "I'm just glad you're his sister. I'll be the only one to capture his attention on that whole trip west."

"Just don't be too sure of yourself. Daed is planning to stop in Somerset and in Ohio on the way. There are sure to be girls in those communities who could catch his eye."

Johanna picked a loose corn shuck from the floor and rolled it between her fingers. "Perhaps we'll be betrothed before then. Who knows?"

Hannah brushed at her apron as she stood to join the others downstairs. Who knew what the future held?

The next week was busy with butchering. Johanna's daed, Elias, brought his swine to the Yoder farm, and the men butchered six hogs.

While Liesbet and Johanna's younger sisters watched the little ones, Hannah helped Mamm and Johanna wash the sausage casings. Hannah refused to think about what they really were as she rinsed the slimy tubes. Magdalena minced scraps of meat into bits, ready to mix them with herbs to make sausage.

"Annalise, are you all right?" Magdalena put her knife

down and caught Mamm as she sank toward the floor. Hannah joined her to help Mamm to a bench.

Mamm glanced at the bowls of fat on the table waiting for rendering and turned away, her face white.

"What's wrong?" Hannah knelt by her side.

She waved her away. "It's nothing. You go on working. I just need some fresh air." Another hog's squeal sounded from the barnyard and she shook her head. "If I could find some fresh air."

Magdalena sat next to Mamm, wiping her hands on a towel. "I think I can guess what's wrong."

Hannah couldn't believe she was smiling when Mamm was so ill . . . unless it was . . . "Mamm? Are you expecting a baby?" Hannah whispered. If she was wrong, she didn't want rumors starting.

Mamm nodded. "*Ja*, in the summer. It will come after we get to Indiana."

"Does Daed know?"

"I told him as soon as I was certain. I'd hoped to keep it secret until at least Christmas, but I guess I can't any longer."

Hannah took Mamm's hand. "And are you all right? Everything is all right?"

Mamm gave her a hug. "*Ja*, Hannah. Everything is just fine."

"Why don't you go and rest while we finish up this part. You can join us again when you feel better." Magdalena patted Mamm's arm.

"I can't shirk my duty." She started to stand, but then swayed on her feet. "You're right. I'll go in and lie down for a few minutes."

As Magdalena helped Mamm into the bedroom, Hannah joined Johanna at the sink. They went back to their work.

"A new baby in the family?" Johanna whispered. "How fun will that be? Do you hope it's a boy or a girl?"

Hannah shook her head, still trying to believe the news. Mamm having another baby? She remembered how sad she had been before William was born, but she was so different now.

"I don't care which it is, as long as Mamm is happy." Hannah took another long tube and started turning it inside out. "But this explains why she's seemed so tired lately. I was afraid she was becoming ill."

Johanna turned another casing inside out. "What do you think Liesbet will say about it? She complained about taking care of the little ones today."

"Until Mamm told her it was either that or help us in the kitchen." Hannah rinsed the tube in a pail of clean water. "I don't know what she'll say. She's been acting so different lately, almost as if she was getting sick again."

"What do you mean?"

"She sleeps so late in the mornings I have to drag her out of bed, and she hardly eats anything. But mostly she acts like she used to when she was still getting over the diphtheria." Hannah couldn't tell Johanna about the times she had woken in the night to find Liesbet's side of the bed empty, but Liesbet was always back in her bed by morning.

"Well, if we were expecting another baby, I'd love it. I keep hoping that after I marry, Mamm and I will have babies at the same time. Wouldn't that be fun?"

Hannah laughed. Johanna had the funniest ideas. "You're right. That would be fun."

With six hogs to butcher, the work took the whole week. After the men had spent a day doing their part of killing, skinning, and gutting the animals, the women's work was just beginning. Liesbet chose to stay with the younger children, and Hannah didn't mind. If she had helped in the kitchen, she would have only complained endlessly. As it was, she and Johanna made the most of the time they had together. Mamm helped them cure the hams and shoulders while Magdalena took care of rendering the lard in the big pot over the fire in the yard.

"The farther I am away from the rendering pot, the better," Mamm said, but she still kept the smile on her face.

On Saturday, after Johanna and her family had gone home, Hannah was finishing the last batch of lard when she saw Adam. He came from the woods trail like he always did, but his strides were purposeful and he headed straight for Hannah.

"I heard something today."

No greeting, no small talk.

"What did you hear?"

"I met Elias Hertzler out in the woods, and he told me you're planning to go along when your families are moving out in the spring. He said it had been decided for weeks." Hannah turned to the fire. If she didn't keep an eye on the pot, the lard could burn. But Adam took her shoulders and faced her toward him. "Are you going?"

"I don't know." Hannah shook free from his grasp. "I can't let my family go without me, especially now."

"I thought it was settled. I hoped you were going to stay here and marry me."

Hannah stirred slowly. "I want to stay here, but is that a reason to marry you? We're friends, Adam, but I'm not sure our friendship will make a good marriage. You've been so busy with . . ." She glanced around to see if anyone could hear them. "You're always on your way somewhere. We haven't talked for weeks."

Adam took his hat off and rubbed at the back of his neck. "You're right." He put his hat back on and took the paddle from her. "But we can talk now. How soon is your pa leaving?"

"Daed says as soon as the winter weather starts turning to spring. He wants to get to Indiana in time to plant a crop."

"And you'll marry that foreigner, Bender, and go with them."

Hannah's tongue felt like it filled her mouth. Josef was so different from Adam, but was she only attracted to him because of that difference? Or was she beginning to love him? But more than that, she couldn't abandon Mamm when she would need her help on the journey.

Adam stirred the lard. They both watched it bubble over the low fire.

"I've asked if you would let me court you."

"And I told you, I can't marry outside my faith."

Adam looked at her. He glanced toward the barn, and then the house. "You could still become Mennonite."

"And you could still become Amish."

He stirred for a few silent minutes. "If I did, would you stay and marry me?"

Hannah's heart leaped. He would become Amish? For her? Her mind looked down the years ahead as Adam's wife, raising his children, growing old with him. As much as she loved Johanna, Adam had always been her closest friend. If he loved her enough to become Amish, could she learn to love him also? What would it be like to be joined with him for the rest of their lives?

And then the faces crowded into her mind—the dark faces of all the people who depended on Adam to help them find their way from Peach Bottom down on the Susquehanna River through the county to the safe house in Lancaster, where they could rest before continuing on their way to safety in Canada. If Adam became Amish, he would have to turn his back on them. Would he give up what he believed in for her?

Did she want him to?

"You need to count the cost, Adam."

He glanced at her, then back at the pot. "I can only see what I would gain."

"You're different than an Amish man. Ever since you went to those camp meetings last summer, you've changed."

Adam nodded. "You're right. I have changed. I wish you could understand what I experienced listening to those preachers." He swirled the paddle in the pot. "I can't sit back and let things like slavery continue in our country. I have to act."

"That's just what I mean. You talk like an *Englischer*, an outsider. If you became Amish, you would have to act as an Amish man, obedient to the civil laws, to the *Ordnung*, and to Christ."

Hannah took the paddle from Adam as the steaming lard started to pop and crackle. The job was nearly finished.

Adam stepped back from the fire and shook his head. "I can't obey the civil laws when they require me to do the opposite of what Christ says I should do. I have to be involved in the abolitionists' efforts to help the slaves."

"That's what I meant about counting the cost, Adam. You can't escort escaped slaves and be Amish. It just wouldn't work."

"Then you'll have to become Mennonite. You've already helped me with these people. You know how important this is."

He waited for her to answer, but Hannah couldn't speak. The sweetness of the baby she had carried that first day, the conviction in his mother's voice as she spoke of freedom for her children rang in her mind, Ruby's open thanks to Jesus for their escape from detection. *Ja*, she could agree that what Adam was doing was important. But was it more important than her faith and her family?

24

Liesbet shifted in her seat again. Winter evenings were so long, and she could never get this sock right. Hannah's knitting needles clicked together in rhythm with Mamm's as stockings seemed to flow from them. Liesbet's needles tangled in the yarn and knotted the loops together. She'd have to ask Mamm to turn the heel for her again.

She laid the bunchy mass of yarn in her lap and stretched her fingers. Daed's voice droned on, reading some story about a man burning at the stake while his wife looked on, weeping. How many times had she heard these stories? The people in them were long dead and fools on top of that. Going through all that pain when all they had to do to live was to say they'd bow to the wishes of the state church. That is what she would have done. She would never understand her ancestors.

Finally Daed reached the end of the story. Liesbet wrapped her knitting into a loose ball and stuck it in the basket.

"Where are you going, Liesbet?" Daed's voice stopped her as she tried to slip unnoticed through the door.

"I have to use the privy. I'll be right back."

"You can wait until after prayers."

Liesbet sighed as she took her place again, sitting rigid on the edge of the chair. Her need to go was urgent. The last couple weeks she had barely made it to the privy in time. It was just another sign that made her sure that a baby was coming. George's baby. She glanced sideways at Mamm. She had seen her go outside more often than usual too.

Daed started praying, reading from the Book of Prayers his father and grandfather had owned. All the prayers in this book were long and tedious. She'd rather have a silent prayer like they did at mealtimes. At least then she could let her mind wander for a few minutes.

It was nearly bedtime, and then she would see George. Her stomach jumped a little at this thought. It was time to tell him.

Her mind went to the house they would have. As soon as he knew about the baby, he'd insist that they should be married, and then he'd find a job in Philadelphia and then she'd be Madam McIvey, a fine lady. No more muddy trips to the privy on rainy nights. No more cooking over a fire with all the smoke and balancing pots over hot coals. She'd have a stove, like the one she saw in the store window in Lancaster. Shiny, black, and clean.

Daed's voice droned to an end, and Liesbet jumped from her seat. A quick trip to the privy and then into bed. If Hannah thought she was asleep, she'd keep Margli quiet and they'd both be asleep sooner.

Once under the covers, she kept her breathing soft and

deep as she listened to Hannah helping Margli into bed. She had to fight to keep awake as she waited for Hannah to undress and climb into their shared bed. Hannah turned back and forth, turned her pillow over and then lay still.

Liesbet rose from the bed as soon as Hannah's breathing grew deep and regular. She grabbed her clothes and crept to the hall and down the stairs.

George would be waiting for her. It had been a week since she had seen him, but he promised he'd be there tonight.

She didn't dare stop anywhere in the house, but went out to the barn through the frosty air. She dressed quickly and left through the rear door, heading for the creek.

She shivered under her shawl. It would snow any day now, Daed had said. Then how would she see George? The one time she had said it was too cold to come, he had been angry, but then just as quickly showed her he could keep her warm.

He waited in the clearing. She went to him and he pulled her to him without a word, kissing her. He could keep her warm on the coldest nights.

Liesbet pushed him away. She had to talk to him now . . . before . . .

"I need to tell you something."

George pulled her back. "Can't it wait? I've missed you so much this past week." He kissed her until she pulled away again.

"No, it has to be now." She stepped back and smoothed her dress.

George's voice sounded like a groan. "What is it?"

Now that the time had come, could she tell him? It was one thing to consider it as she did her chores, but quite another when he was standing right in front of her, waiting.

"I'm . . . there's going to be a baby." She whispered the words. She couldn't say them aloud.

George grabbed her and pulled her close. "You told me that last week when I was here. Your mother is having a baby. What is that to us?" He grabbed her braid and forced her face toward his. "Forget it and kiss me."

Liesbet shook her head. "No, you don't understand. I'm going to have a baby."

He let go and stepped away from her. "What do you mean?"

"Just what I said." Her voice strengthened. What would she do if he didn't believe her? "I'm going to have a baby."

"You're sure?"

"Of course I'm sure. I wouldn't have told you if I wasn't."

He took another step back. "Then you need to do something about it. Get rid of it."

Liesbet's hands, so warm when George was holding her, chilled in the cold air. "I . . . I can't do that. This is our baby."

George ran his hand over his face. "There must be some way . . ." He pointed a finger at her. "I'll take you to Philadelphia. There's a woman there who takes care of these things."

Liesbet's hand went to her stomach, her throat tight. How many times had she wished this thing would just go away? But she couldn't do what George wanted. "If I went with you, I'd never be able to come back home again."

"If you don't do what I say, how long do you think they'd let you stay at home with your belly getting bigger every day?"

George started pacing from one end of the clearing to the other. Liesbet felt hot tears running down her cheeks. This wasn't what she imagined at all. He was supposed to be happy about the baby. He was supposed to say they could get married, that he would take care of them. The bright future she had dreamed of turned into a dark, empty hole.

"I . . . I hoped we'd get married . . . that you'd like to be a father."

He grabbed her arms and shook her. "Do you think I want to be saddled with crying brats and a whining wife?"

Tears ran down Liesbet's cheeks. She wiped one cheek and then the other with quick movements. George let her go and backed away.

"Now don't you start crying, Lizzie. You know I can't bear it when you cry."

He paced the clearing once more. She sniffled and he glared at her. Was he angry, or was he going to give in? His face was shadowed in the dark clearing. When he didn't say anything, hope grew. She squeezed out a few more tears. She'd do anything to live out her dreams.

He stopped in front of her with a groan. "All right, lass. What do you want from me?"

Liesbet considered her answer. If she asked him for too much, he'd leave and she might never see him again. But she could be patient. He'd give in little by little.

"I only want our baby to have a mother and a father. I want you to . . . " She sniffled again. ". . . to marry me, and claim the baby so it won't have to live with any stain on its name." She took a deep breath, letting it catch in her throat.

"I don't have anyplace for you to live, and you can't go traipsing around the country with me and my mates."

"I'm sure you could find work in Philadelphia, and a place for us to live." Liesbet sniffed again for good measure.

George rubbed the back of his neck again. "Yeah, I might find work with my uncle . . ."

Liesbet threw her arms around George, giving him a kiss that made him pull her to him again.

"Enough of that, lass." He pushed her away, holding her at arm's length. "That's what got us into this predicament."

She kissed him again, relishing the power she held over him. "It doesn't matter now, though, does it?"

He gave in, kissing her as if he meant to devour her. "No," he said between kisses, "it doesn't matter anymore."

George watched Lizzie until she was safely in the house. He was a dead man, trapped by that girl's pretty face and soft body. Trapped as surely as his old dad in Ireland had been.

Da talked big when he was in the pub. About how he was on his way to being a champion prize fighter until he was trapped by a pretty face.

"Don't ever make my mistake," he'd say, poking at George's chest with his dirty finger. "Don't let yourself be trapped by a whiny girl who says she's in the family way." Then Da would take another drink from his tankard and pound it down on the counter. "She'll be the ruin of you. So keep clear, my boy, keep clear."

George never knew what to say to that. If Da hadn't fallen for that pretty face, he would never have been born. And Mum wasn't a whiny girl—she was just Mum.

But now, here he was with Lizzie telling him she was expecting a baby. Maybe Da was right. He should have just stayed clear.

When Lizzie disappeared into the house, he pulled his cap down firmly and started for the camp. It would snow soon, and then keeping his trysts with Lizzie secret would be impossible. There was no hiding his trail in the snow, and the boys would soon find out about her. Maybe she was right, and he should find another job, but by the saints, he would die if he had to work in some mill like Uncle Brian.

Of course, living in the camp he and the boys had made wouldn't be very pleasant once winter set in. A couple of them had taken up with girls in town, just to have a warm bed to sleep in when the cold wind blew. He envied them on nights like tonight.

He wouldn't mind keeping Lizzie with him at night, but where? How? And what would they do when the baby was born?

Profanity streamed from his mouth like a muttered prayer. If only he didn't like the girl. Another man would just leave, letting her take care of herself and the baby. He didn't have to stick around. Except he couldn't help thinking about Mum, and what she would say.

Mum had been a saint, no matter what Da said about her. She had put up with the beatings and the drinking and no money . . . and she had loved her children. She had cried when he left home, but he had turned his back and gone anyway. A woman's tears turned him to jelly.

And now Lizzie. If he left her to fend for herself, she'd cry. Her face would haunt him for the rest of his life, it would. Her pretty face and her tears.

If only there wasn't a baby, then they could just keep having fun the way they had been. But her face when he suggested getting rid of it told him she wouldn't put up with it. He was stuck with her and the baby, at least for now.

The wind picked up, finding the holes in George's coat. It

was turning into a bitter night, this one. Too cold for sleeping alone in a tent.

All right, maybe he would take Lizzie to the city. Not Philadelphia, but Lancaster. He could rent a room over the Blue River tavern and find a job. There might be a town job that wouldn't be too bad, and then he'd be warm for the winter, at least. Lizzie could work too. There was always room for another barmaid. With her face she'd do well making tips.

George changed direction and made for the road to Lancaster. He'd be there by morning and could sleep indoors tomorrow. And then go get Lizzie.

It wasn't perfect, but at least he'd be warm at night.

Liesbet hummed as she hung dish towels on the clothesline. Any time now George would come for her and take her away from this—she snapped a towel in the air and fastened it with a clothespin—this stupid, cold, boring life of slavery. She shouldn't have to work this hard, and in the cold too. Mamm should have had Hannah hang these towels.

The wind was a sharp knife today, slicing right to her bones, and it wasn't even winter yet. Mamm was making *Schnitz und Knepp* for dinner again. The only thing good about it was that it was hot and warmed a person from the inside.

She picked up the last towel, and as she straightened she saw George waving to her from the other side of the blackberry brambles.

Biting her lip, she glanced at the house. No one was outside, but she could be seen from the window. She had to take a chance. She had to see what George wanted.

Keeping the flapping towels between her and the house, Liesbet walked quickly to the old cabin, and then used it as a shield until she was well into the trees. Circling the house was easier when she got to the sheep pasture. The sheep browsed the space between the trees, keeping it clear of underbrush and she could go faster. Near the creek, though, the trees were larger and she resorted to following a deer trail until she came to the clearing.

George stood in the center, eyes on the treetops where a flock of crows were making a racket. She almost ran to him, but stopped herself. She mustn't appear too eager. She waited until he turned.

"I wasn't sure you'd see me."

"I nearly didn't."

He looked all around the clearing, peering through the trees.

"I'm not used to being here in the daylight. You're sure no one can see us?"

"No one will come this way today. Daed and Jacob are busy in the barn, and the others are all in the house." Liesbet shivered and George came closer, pulling her to him.

"I found a room for us."

"A room? Not a house?"

"A room was all I could find right now. I know you wanted a house, but we'll have to wait for spring to look for one."

Liesbet swallowed her disappointment. Spring was a long time, but at least they'd have a house before the baby came. "When will it be ready?"

"Now. If we start right away, we'll be there in time for supper."

"Now? What about . . ." She stopped, biting her lip. Isn't this what she had been longing for?

"There's no time to argue about it. Do you want to come or not?"

"I have clothes and things I want to bring."

George swore as he pulled his hat off and ran his fingers through his curly black hair. "Things you want to bring? Like what?"

"I have a quilt, and pillows, and a few things I've made. And then my other dress and my nightclothes."

He nodded. "All right, then. We can wait while you go back to get them. Can you get them out of the house today?"

Liesbet let her mind go over the possibilities. She could bundle everything in her quilt, but getting the bundle down the stairs while everyone was awake would be impossible.

"Not until tonight, when everyone is sleeping."

George let out another string of profanity. "We can't wait that long. Just bundle it all up and throw it out the window. Then no one will see you taking it."

"I guess I could do that while everyone is at dinner . . ."

"How long?"

"What?"

"How long until you're back here?"

"You're not going to help me?"

"If I tried to help, we might be seen. If your da sees me, he'll never let you go."

Liesbet nodded. If Daed knew what she was doing, she'd never be able to leave. She'd have to tell him about the wedding afterward.

"All right. I'll meet you here in about an hour. I'll go back to the house and say I'm ill, and they'll let me go to bed."

"Be quick about it, then." George stamped his feet to warm them. "I want to get out of here."

Liesbet hurried back to the house and opened the door. The kitchen was warm, heated by the large fireplace. Hannah looked up as she came in.

"You took a long time to hang up a few towels."

"I . . . I used the privy too."

"It's nearly time for dinner. You finish setting the table and I'll get the little ones ready."

"I need to go up and lay down." Liesbet started toward the stairs.

Mamm looked up from stirring the pot over the fire. "You're not feeling well?"

"*Ne*. I feel tired." She coughed a little. "The wind was so cold, and my chest hurts."

"Then you go right upstairs." Mamm's face had the familiar worried look on it. "I'll bring your dinner up to you."

"Don't bother." That would ruin everything. "I'm not very hungry. I'll have some broth when I get up."

"If you're sure . . ."

Mamm's voice faded as Liesbet hurried up the steps. They would think she was sleeping, and no one would disturb her for at least an hour, maybe two. By then, she and George would be halfway to Lancaster.

She opened the chest at the foot of the bed and sorted through the things inside. Hannah had more quilts than she did, and even some linen dish towels and the dress length of blue wool she had woven last summer. Hannah would need all those things if she married Adam Metzler or that funny Josef Bender. Stick-in-the-mud farmers, both of them.

Liesbet found the quilt *Grossmutti* had made for her years ago and spread it out on the bed. She put her pillow in the center, and then glanced at Hannah's pillow. Should she take both, so George would have one too? It would make things more homelike, wouldn't it? She piled Hannah's pillow on top of her own, and then took her nightdress and extra dress off the hooks on the wall, folding them loosely before adding them to the stack. Of course, she wouldn't be wearing plain clothes anymore, but she could make them over until George bought her more material.

Finally she put in her comb and pulled the corners of the quilt together. Opening the window, she looked for any sign someone was about. No one. She went to the bedroom door and eased it open a crack. Daed's voice carried up the stairs—something about the wagon he and Jacob were building. Now was the time for her to go, but she lingered, listening. Would she miss this? The family sitting together around the table? Once she left home, Daed wouldn't allow her back unless she came asking for their forgiveness.

She closed the door with a firm push. Forgiveness for what? For living her life the way she chose instead of how they wanted her to?

Taking the bulky bundle, she pushed it out the window, watching it drop onto the flower bed. She climbed out after it, finding the window frame below with the toes of her shoes and dropping onto the pile of quilt, pillows, and clothes.

Pulling the bundle together again, she started off across the yard to the barn, shivering. She had left her winter shawl on the hook in the lean-to off the kitchen, but she couldn't go back for it now.

At the edge of the barnyard, just before taking the path into the woods where George waited for her, she glanced back at the white frame house. Mamm would cry when they found she was gone, but they'd soon get used to it.

She turned her back on the house, anxious to see George again. Today was her wedding day, wasn't it? It was the beginning of her new life.

25

Liesbet was gone, leaving an empty gap at the table, in the bedroom, in Hannah's life. Even Margli grieved, crawling into Hannah's bed at night. Hannah would always wake and hold her close, as if she could keep her little, warm, and safe. Sisters slip away so quickly.

The first days after Liesbet left, Daed and Jacob had spent the daylight hours combing the woods, fields, and creek banks for some sign of her. And then on the fourth day, Adam had come to say he had seen Liesbet. She was living over a tavern in Lancaster.

Hannah watched Mamm closely. Would this news send her into her spells again? But although she would often seem to get lost in watching the fire in the fireplace, she would rouse herself and restart whatever task she had been doing.

On Tuesday, four weeks after Liesbet left, a storm threatened. Daed came in from the barn at midmorning.

"We brought the livestock in from the pastures." He blew on his coffee to cool it as Hannah sliced mutton off the bone from last night's roast.

"Even the sheep?" Mamm was breaking dried bread into crumbs to mix with the meat and some of her dried garden herbs.

"*Ja.* The signs have all pointed to a hard winter this year, and we're getting it. But we're prepared. No matter how much it snows, the animals are sheltered and have plenty of food."

Mamm's hands slowed in the mixing bowl.

"Mamm?"

She shook herself a bit and smiled at Hannah. A tired, strained smile. "I'm all right. I was just thinking . . ."

Hannah could read Mamm's thoughts. Liesbet, off living in the city without her winter cloak. She had always been prone to coughs and chills, but who would care for her now?

Daed finished his coffee and rose from the table, patting Mamm's shoulder as he shrugged his arms into his heavy coat. He stopped at the door. "We all think about her, Annalise."

Mamm gave him a smile, but tears stood in her eyes.

A familiar anger rose, but Hannah pushed it down. Liesbet might as well be under the *bann*, as far as Daed was concerned. As long as she chose to remain unrepentant, he would not forgive her. If she was older and a baptized member of the community, she would be shunned by the church, and even by her family. Hannah glanced at Mamm. The tears were rolling down her cheeks now, and she wiped at them with her sleeves, her hands covered in bread crumbs.

"I'll finish this if you want me to."

"*Ne.*" Mamm sniffed and smiled at Hannah. "I need to keep busy. If I stop to think . . ." Her eyes grew shadowed as she looked away from Hannah. "I don't want to let the darkness take over again."

Hannah's stomach turned. If she had only told Mamm and Daed about George McIvey sooner . . . Why couldn't she be a better daughter? She was the cause of Mamm's tears again.

"Mamm . . . I'm sorry." She turned the bone and leaned down to see where she could cut off more meat. Anything to avoid looking at her mother.

"You're sorry? For what?"

"I . . . I knew Liesbet meant to go away with a man. I knew she wanted to marry an outsider, but I didn't think she'd really do it."

Mamm's hands stopped and she stared at Hannah. Out of the corner of her eye, Hannah could see the sadness. "It isn't your fault."

"*Ja*, it is. Months ago I saw Liesbet with a man, but I told her not to see him again. I told her he wasn't for her." Hannah carefully minced a piece of mutton. "I hoped she would give him up."

Mamm went back to her mixing. "Your daed and I didn't have any idea she was serious about anyone, but Liesbet . . ." Her voice faltered. "I know I turned a blind eye to her afternoons spent in the woods. I thought the time resting in the sunshine would help her get better."

Hannah's heart sunk. If she had told Daed about George . . . would it have made any difference? Could any of them have stopped Liesbet?

Mamm cracked an egg into the bread crumbs and added the bowl of minced mutton Hannah had cut off the bone.

"We can only pray for her." She shook her head. "I just hope she's keeping herself warm, and that she'll come back to us." She glanced up, catching Hannah's gaze. "There's still hope for her, you know. She can come back."

"*Ja.*" Hannah put the mutton bone into the pot she had ready with vegetables and water. Someone needed to talk some sense into Liesbet. The silly girl was stubborn enough to stay away just to prove she was right, no matter what happened. After this storm, she'd get Adam to go into town with her. He'd take her to see Liesbet, and she could bring her sister home.

The first big storm of the winter lasted into the night, and then blew itself out, leaving a knee-deep cover of snow on the ground. By Friday, the warm sun had turned the snow into patches of melting drifts with soggy brown leaves between them.

With the excuse that she needed to trade some yarn with Adam's sister, Hilda, and telling Mamm she would be gone all day, Hannah left for the Metzlers' farm right after breakfast.

She found Adam in the barn, forking hay into a wagon.

"Adam." Hannah kept her voice to a whisper, in case Adam's father was around.

He looked up at her, glanced around, and then smiled. "What brings you here this morning?"

"I need your help." Hannah looked down at the floor where he was moving loose hay around with his feet. "What are you doing?"

"Never mind." He stopped fooling with the hay and walked over to Hannah. "What do you need help with?"

"I need to go into Lancaster today and be back by suppertime. Can you take me?"

Adam glanced at the stack of hay in the wagon. "I was planning a trip to Lancaster, myself, but I'm not sure it would be safe for you to come along."

"Why not?"

"I'm not going alone, and my cargo is risky."

Hannah looked at the wagon. "Hay is a risky cargo?"

Adam shook his head. "The cargo is under the hay."

Escaped slaves. Hannah clasped her trembling hands together. "I need to go to town. Let me come with you."

Shaking his head, Adam turned her toward the barn door. "No. I can't. It will be too dangerous."

"But I need to go to Lancaster." Hannah tried to dig her heels into the wooden floor as he pushed her toward the door.

Adam stopped trying to push her out of the barn. "You know what I have to do today, and you told me to never involve you again, remember?"

"Please, Adam."

"Why?"

"I need to find Liesbet. Try to get her to come home."

Adam sighed. "Do you think you can change her mind?"

"I have to try, for Mamm's sake."

"All right. We'll leave right away." He smiled at her. "I have to say, I'll enjoy having you along. And we'll do our best to look like an old, married Amish couple, *ja*?"

Hannah laughed at the comical face he made. She helped him hitch the team of horses to the wagon, and then he reached down and opened the trap door in the barn floor. If she hadn't known it was there, she never would have thought to look for it. The trap door had been made of planks of various sizes so that when it was closed it was nearly invisible, blending with the barn floor of the wagon bay. Two men came up a ladder at Adam's signal.

"This is Henry . . ." One of the men nodded to Hannah. "And this is John."

Adam pulled the hay aside, revealing a cavity framed with lumber. "It will be a little tight, but you'll only need to be in there for a couple hours."

The men crawled in and settled themselves. Adam replaced the hay, making sure it stacked naturally in the wagon.

Hannah climbed onto the seat of the wagon and Adam drove out into the yard and onto the road. As they passed the house, Adam's father waved to them from the door.

"I was surprised when I found out your whole family is involved in this," Hannah said as she waved back.

"They say they're proud of what I'm doing." Adam glanced at Hannah. "I know you still think it's something the Amish wouldn't be involved in."

"I know it's something we wouldn't do, but I'm not sure how wrong it is. It's so confusing, isn't it?"

Adam grinned at her. "Hannah, I think you might be turning more Mennonite every day. The next thing I'll hear you say is that your daed is building a meetinghouse."

"I don't think I'd ever go that far."

They rode in silence for a while. The road dried quickly where the sunlight peeped between the bare branches of the trees, and the air was warm for January.

"This is nice, isn't it?" Adam didn't look her way as he spoke, but kept his eyes on the road ahead.

"What is?"

"Riding together into town, just the two of us."

Hannah glanced back at the load of hay. If she hadn't seen Henry and John settle themselves in the hidden cavity, she would never be able to tell they were in the wagon with them. The men hadn't made a sound.

"We're not really alone, Adam."

"Oh, I know. But I try to forget about the extras. I don't want to risk giving them away if someone comes along."

"Do you think anyone else is on the road?" Hannah peered into the woods. The bare trees were thick enough in places to hide a man.

"It isn't very likely, this far from town. But as we get closer, we'll have to be careful. The Penningtons' farm has been raided before, and it may be watched. We have a signal worked out so I know if it's safe to stop there, or if I should go on to Columbia."

"When we get to town, you can leave me where you saw Liesbet, and I can look for her while you take your friends to their destination."

Adam shook his head. "I'm not going to leave you anywhere in Lancaster alone, especially the area where I saw Liesbet."

"Why not? Daed often leaves me on market days."

"He leaves you in the market with your goods, right? That's different than a girl alone on a street corner."

Hannah didn't answer, but remembered the teamsters who had jeered at her on her last trip to the city. Adam was right. It wasn't a place for a girl alone, especially an Amish girl.

While they were still outside of Lancaster, before they reached the edge of the woods, Adam stopped the wagon. He climbed down to adjust the load of hay.

"Henry? John? How are you doing in there?"

"We're just fine, Mister Adam. Just fine."

Hannah couldn't tell which man spoke. His voice, low and soft in its southern drawl, held a tremor of anticipation . . . or perhaps it was exhaustion. The more of these runaways she met, the more she was convinced slavery was wrong. But at the same time, it was the law, and they were to obey the civil authorities. But she couldn't say Adam was wrong—sometimes the civil law went against God's law, and God was the one they must obey. Daed often said he feared there would be war over the issue of slavery, but Hannah prayed not.

"We're getting close to Lancaster. Be sure you don't make a sound. Slave hunters are probably on patrol, but you have to be careful all the time. You never know who might want to turn you in for the reward."

"You've no need to worry about us. We'll be quiet as church mice."

Adam settled the hay back in its place. He walked around the wagon, and then went to the team, checking their harness as he walked by.

When he climbed back onto the seat, he gave Hannah a smile as he picked up the reins. "All right, little Amish wife of mine. Are you ready to deliver our cargo?"

Hannah laughed at his words, in spite of the serious look in his eyes. "*Ja,* for sure."

Adam clicked his tongue and the horses started out down the short slope to the open fields surrounding Lancaster, his face set, his smile gone. Hannah's stomach roiled. *Ja,* she was willing to help Adam in this venture in exchange for his help in finding Liesbet, but she wasn't risking her life the way he was.

She kept a silent prayer repeating in her head all the way to town. *Lord, if it be your will, let any slave hunters have blind eyes today.*

26

A dam kept the horses at a steady, slow pace, as if he was in no hurry at all. He turned off the main road at the edge of town, following the less traveled route that would bypass the center of the city. They hadn't traveled far on this road when he turned onto a road that was little more than a farm lane. They soon reached a river, and the lane turned to follow it.

"This is our own Conestoga Creek, Hannah."

The river was twice as wide as the lazy creek that meandered past their farms at home.

"What makes it so much bigger here?"

"A lot of other smaller creeks and runs empty into it as it makes its way toward the Susquehanna. You should see how big it is where it meets that river."

Hannah drew her shawl around her shoulders. She preferred her own little creek to this stranger.

They continued past three or four small farms sitting between the road and the river, all of them with well-kept houses and barns.

"Who lives here? These aren't Amish or Mennonite farms, are they?"

"No. The folks along the river here are Quakers. There aren't as many here as in Philadelphia, but there are a few."

The road bent to the right as the river curved in a long oxbow to the left. Hannah could see the river again ahead of them as it came back to meet the road. Adam turned the wagon into a farm lane nearly hidden by the trees that lined it.

"This is the Pennington farm. There was no signal, so I think it's safe to go on in." Adam took Hannah's hand. "If there's any trouble, don't speak English. Keep to your *Deitsch*, and I'll do the same."

Hannah gave Adam a smile she hoped was reassuring, but his taut face sent chills through her.

The tree-crowded farm lane opened into a barnyard, with a small white frame house placed along the oxbow of the river on the left, and a small barn on the right. An empty field stretched down to the loop of the river, setting the little farm on a peninsula, protected on three sides.

Adam pulled up in front of the house when an elderly man came out onto the porch to meet them.

"I have the hay you ordered, Mr. Pennington."

The man nodded and came toward the wagon as Adam jumped down.

"Did thee see anyone on the way?" His voice was quiet, guarded.

Adam shook his head. "No one."

Mr. Pennington changed to a normal tone. "We'll put your hay in the barn, and then thee can come into the house for some tea." He nodded at Hannah. "Thee can come in and have a word with Mrs. Pennington. I know Martha will appreciate the company."

Adam reached back to help Hannah from the wagon, and then climbed back into the seat to drive the short distance to the barn. "We'll be in shortly."

Hannah nodded. As often as she had been in and out of the Metzlers' home over the years, she had never stepped inside an *Englischer* home. She avoided contact with outsiders as much as possible, but here she was knocking on the door of a Quaker home. And as soon as Adam was finished with his business, they'd be searching in the city for Liesbet. More outsiders. She pushed down her rising irritation at her sister and smiled as a small woman in a plain gray dress opened the door.

"Come inside, dear. Thee must be chilled from the long drive."

"Thank you." Hannah stepped inside and followed Mrs. Pennington down a short corridor to the back of the house.

"We spend most of our time in the keeping room," the older woman said, indicating a chair for Hannah. "Since our children are grown and gone, this room meets all our needs."

Hannah took in everything as she looked around the room, from the pots of herbs growing in the window above the dry sink to the large fireplace at the end of the room. All was clean, neat, and spare. She could certainly feel at home in this simple room.

"I didn't know Adam was married." Mrs. Pennington poured some peppermint tea into a china teacup for Hannah and some for herself.

"Oh, we aren't married." Hannah warmed her fingers by

cupping them around the delicate china. "We were hoping to avoid any suspicion as we came into Lancaster with—"

"Thee has said enough," Mrs. Pennington interrupted. "Today, thee are a married couple. Tomorrow will attend to itself." She took a sip of her tea. "Thou art Mennonite, also?"

Hannah shook her head. "No. We're Amish."

"Amish?" Mrs. Pennington peered at Hannah over her glasses. "'Twould be a marvelous thing if the Amish joined us in our work."

"Oh, but I'm not working with Adam. I needed to come into town, and since he was coming I rode with him."

"In full knowledge of the work he's doing."

Hannah nodded. "*Ja*, I know of his work."

Mrs. Pennington smiled. "God works in mysterious ways to bring about his will. Thee will find the yoke easy."

"Oh no, you don't understand. I'm Amish. We don't involve ourselves in such things."

Hannah was spared further questioning by the men coming into the house through a back door.

"Thee settled our guests well?" Mrs. Pennington rose to get two more of the china cups and poured tea for the men.

"We did at that." Mr. Pennington eased himself into a chair at the table.

"Dinner will be ready soon." Mrs. Pennington turned to Adam. "Thee will be welcome to join us."

"No, thank you." Adam glanced at Hannah as he spoke. He knew how anxious she was to find Liesbet and get home. "We have errands to run in Lancaster and we want to get home before suppertime tonight. We don't want Hannah's parents to worry about her."

Finishing their tea, Hannah and Adam prepared to leave. Mr. Pennington walked them to the front door.

"Thee will need to remain mindful of interference until thee reach the main road."

"Have you seen any more slave hunters around?" Adam's question was breathed so quietly, Hannah hardly heard the words.

"No, but they are suspicious of any of the Friends, knowing our convictions." He laid his hand on Adam's broad shoulder. "The traitor in Peach Bottom has been found out and is no longer in a position to harm us. But that doesn't mean we relax our guard."

Adam nodded. "If anyone stops us, I'll tell them we delivered a load of hay to you. They may come by to check out the truth of my words."

Mr. Pennington smiled. "We'll be expecting them, and they'll find nothing but hay." He patted Adam's shoulder. "The Lord bless thee, and may he keep thee in his peace."

"And the same to you, my friend."

When Adam turned to help Hannah into the wagon seat, his eyes were misty. She waited until they had waved a goodbye and were on their way before asking, "Is anything wrong?"

Adam looked back at the secluded farmhouse and then grasped her hand. "The slave hunters are closing in, and they're violent men. I'm afraid for those two, but they won't stop what they're doing."

Hannah's mind went back to the peaceful keeping room and Mrs. Pennington's serene face. They were breaking the law, and they knew it, but they wouldn't stop as long as they believed they were following God's law. She glanced at Adam's face. He had the same determination.

Adam traced their route back to the main road, passing the quiet farms. Everything was quiet, with even the birds and animals silent. Adam looked around.

"Does it seem a little too quiet to you?" His voice was a whisper and he gathered the reins closer in his hands.

Two men stepped out of the tangled underbrush as they approached the main road. One of them grabbed the near horse's bridle while the other one came close to Adam.

"Well, just where you been, son?" He spit into the bushes at the side of the lane and shifted a wad of tobacco from one cheek to the other.

This wasn't the same slave hunter Hannah had seen in the woods in the autumn, but his voice had the same rough tone.

"My wife and I are on our way to Lancaster. We just delivered a load of hay to a farm back a ways." He nodded behind them. Hannah had to keep herself from staring at Adam. His English words were heavy with a German accent.

The man walked past Adam to peer into the wagon box. He spit into the shrubs again and came back.

"Hay, huh? Is that all you delivered to them?"

"*Ja*, one load of hay."

The man regarded both of them through heavy eyes. The one at the horses' heads took off his hat and wiped his forearm across his brow.

"C'mon, Jasper. They're just farmers."

Jasper didn't move except to spit one more time. "Yeah, just farmers, but them clothes look like Quaker clothes. You some of them slave-loving idiots, farmer?"

Hannah looked down at her knees and smoothed the edge of her shawl over her dress.

When Adam spoke, his voice was calm. "We're Amish, not Quaker."

"Huh. Amish?" Jasper looked at his friend and back at Adam. "You Amish are just as likely to help them runaways as the Quakers in my book."

Jasper looked over the edge of the wagon box. Hannah tried to pray, but couldn't. Adam was lying to these men, claiming they were both Amish. Lie upon lie.

"What farm did you deliver your hay to?" Jasper spit again, this time aiming at the near horse's hind foot.

"The Penningtons." As Jasper signaled to his friend to move back down the lane, Adam added, "They're an elderly couple. I'm sure they're not part of anything illegal."

"You're sure, huh?" Jasper grinned at his friend. "Y'all just wait here. We'll check out your story and be right back."

As soon as the men disappeared down the lane, Hannah said, "Let's go, Adam."

Adam lifted the reins in his hands, but hesitated, peering down the shadowed lane after the men.

"What if they find something? I should go back to help the Penningtons."

"If they find something, they'll know you lied to them." Hannah put her hand over her mouth. He had lied to them about delivering only a load of hay, and he had lied when he claimed to be Amish. Did lies always come this easily to him?

"But the Penningtons are defenseless. Who knows what those men might do to them?" Adam stood, trying to get a better view. "Besides," he slid back down onto his seat, "if we leave now, those men will be suspicious, thinking we have something to hide."

"How long will they be?"

"I don't know, but it shouldn't take too long to verify that I delivered the hay like I said I did."

"Won't they find—"

"Don't speak of it." Adam's voice was a hissing whisper.

Hannah waited, but her thoughts flitted between the gentle Penningtons and what she might find once they found Liesbet. Her stomach turned to think what Liesbet might have done to stay with that worthless George McIvey.

Finally Jasper and the other slave hunter came back down the lane.

"Y'all go on about your business." Jasper waved them on as he took up his position back in the underbrush, ignoring the wagon.

"Them bucks gotta be coming this way, don't they, Jasper?"

Hannah tried to keep from hearing the men's conversation as Adam urged the horses on. They spoke about the runaway slaves as if they were animals or cargo, not men.

Once they were well down the road, Adam turned to Hannah. "You did well back there. Those men didn't suspect a thing."

"I don't like this whole business, Adam." Hannah pulled her shawl closer around her shoulders.

"I admit it's dangerous, but we're doing God's work."

"Doing God's work shouldn't require you to lie."

Adam smiled, but his mouth was tight and grim. "Sometimes it does."

"It doesn't seem right."

"Didn't Rahab lie when she hid the Israelite spies?"

Hannah didn't have an answer.

The streets of Lancaster were muddy, with bits of dirty snow left here and there where traffic had left it undisturbed.

Hannah searched the busy walkways for a sign of her sister as Adam drove to the corner where he had last seen her. He turned off the main street and headed toward the railroad tracks and the rows of warehouses at the junction of the Pennsylvania and Lancaster Railroads.

When he reached a corner tavern, he pulled the horses to the hitching rail and stopped them.

"This is it." He nodded toward the step in front of the tavern. "She was standing there until she recognized me, and then ducked up those stairs there."

A wooden stairway clung to the outside of the building, leading to a second floor.

Loud voices rose from inside the tavern and then subsided. A seedy man clutching a thin butternut jacket around his middle opened the tavern door, releasing the reek of stale beer and brewing hops.

Hannah cringed. "You're sure this is the place?"

Adam nodded. "I don't know if she's still here, but I know she went in that door at the top of the staircase."

Hannah shuddered at the thought of climbing the rickety stairs.

"I'll go up, if you like."

Hannah looked around her. She didn't want to stay alone with the wagon. "We'll go together."

Adam got down and turned to grasp Hannah around the waist, lifting her down and over the muddy gutter in one swinging motion. He led the way up the stairs and knocked on the door.

When the door opened a couple inches, Hannah got a glimpse of Liesbet's face in the darkened room.

"Hannah? What are you doing here?" Her voice was a whisper.

"I've come to take you home. Mamm and Daed are worried about you."

Liesbet shook her head and started to close the door. "I can't, Hannah. Go home and leave me alone."

Adam stuck his foot over the threshold to keep the door from closing all the way.

"Why, Liesbet? You know they'll welcome you back home."

A mumbled curse sounded from inside the room. "Lizzy! Close that door."

Liesbet glanced over her shoulder, and then stepped out on the stair landing. Hannah couldn't keep a gasp from escaping when she saw her sister in full light. Her thin face was gray tinged, her hair unwashed and limp. Liesbet didn't look Hannah in the eye, but shuffled out far enough to close the door behind her. Adam stepped away from them, a couple steps down the stairs.

"What has happened, Liesbet? Are you ill?"

Liesbet shook her head, coughing a little. "*Ne*, Hannah. You need to go home. Leave me."

"You need to come home. You need some good food and a warm house. You need Mamm to take care of you." She took a step toward her sister and Liesbet's shawl fell open, revealing a swollen stomach.

Hannah froze. Liesbet turned back and grasped Hannah's hand with her own cold, rough one. "I can't come home. I'm married, and soon there will be a baby." She coughed again.

Liesbet was ill. Hannah recognized the shadowed eyes,

the hollow cough. She reached up a hand to Liesbet's cheek. *Ja*, and feverish too.

"You may be married, but you're sick. You need someone to take care of you."

Another curse sounded from behind the closed door, and the heavy footsteps came toward it. Liesbet cringed from the sound. The door was wrenched open and George McIvey filled it.

"What's going on out here?" Stench rose from his body, clothed only in a shirt and breeches.

"It's all right, George." Liesbet reached out a hand to block him from Hannah and Adam. "My sister just came for a visit, but she's leaving now."

George stared at Hannah, his eyes bleary. He grimaced. "More Amish." He stumbled back into the room and Liesbet closed the door behind him.

"You have to go."

"I can't leave you here."

"He isn't always like this. It's just . . . last night was a bad night. But he works hard, and supports us."

Adam made a sound behind Hannah that matched her thoughts.

"Come home with me, Liesbet."

"And leave my husband?"

Hannah glanced at Adam. What should she do?

"Come home until the baby is born. Just until summer."

Liesbet shook her head and turned the doorknob. "I can't, Hannah." She looked over her shoulder as another curse sounded from inside. "He isn't always like this. He does love me, I know he does." She slipped inside the door before Hannah could reach out for her. "Go home. I'm fine." She closed the door.

Hannah stood outside the door. The inside latch fell with a click.

"Hannah, come away."

Adam's voice penetrated the roaring in her head. She let him lead her down the stairway and up into the wagon seat. He untied the horses and headed them toward the center of town.

Hannah kept the tears in until they were past the town houses and heading back home, but then they fell silently until she sniffed and Adam looked her way. Without a word he pulled a handkerchief out of his pocket and handed it to her.

"I'm sorry, Hannah. I wouldn't have let you come if I had known how she was living."

"It's too late, isn't it?"

Adam drove in silence for a few minutes, and then put one arm around her, drawing her head to his shoulder.

"It's never too late for anyone, but they have to want to change. Unless Liesbet decides to come home, there isn't anything you can do."

Hannah let Adam's arms comfort her. The only stable, sure part of her world. With Liesbet gone forever, her family was torn asunder again. What would she tell Mamm and Daed?

27

"You have to tell them, Hannah. You can't keep this a secret."

Adam had driven the empty wagon to Hannah's house, arriving just as the sun disappeared below the edge of the surrounding forest, leaving bare tree branches looking like black lace against a fiery background.

"It will devastate them. It's one thing for Liesbet to be gone, to think she's making a life for herself in the *Englischer* world, but if they knew . . ."

"They need to know. Your pa will want to do something—bring her home somehow."

Hannah shook her head. "He won't unless she asks for forgiveness. She's already as good as dead to them. This would just cause them more pain."

"If Liesbet was our daughter, I'd want to know."

Adam's words, spoken softly, clenched at Hannah's heart. If she and Adam married, they would have children together—children he would love and protect. He would be a wonderful father.

"Do you want me to come inside with you? I could tell them, and perhaps it wouldn't be as hard for them to hear."

"*Ne*, they wouldn't want an outsider . . . someone from outside the family to be part of this." Hannah took a deep breath and let it out in a long sigh. Daed and Jacob were still working in the barn. Light spilled from the partly open door across the yard to the house. Mamm would be fixing supper, waiting for her return. It was getting late and she would be worried.

She turned to Adam. "*Denki*, Adam. I appreciate the ride into town and all your help."

Adam pulled her close and gave her a kiss on her cheek. "I will help you any time you need it, Hannah. You know that."

Hannah nodded, not trusting herself to speak. Adam had been a true friend today. She walked to the house as he drove away, dreading the questions she would need to answer as soon as she opened the door.

Jacob and Daed caught up with her as she stepped onto the porch.

"*Ach*, Hannah, are you just getting home now?" Daed sat on the bench to take his boots off before going in.

"I took longer than I thought. Adam brought me home in the wagon."

Jacob glanced at her as he rose from the bench, boots in his hands. "That was handy." He grinned at her and then held the door open as she walked in.

Hannah hung her cape and bonnet on the hooks in the entry while Daed and Jacob put their boots away. The kitchen smelled like home. Hannah stopped to take in the sight of the three little ones sitting at the table, Margli intent on cutting a pan of corn pone.

Mamm turned from the fireplace and saw Hannah. A relieved smile burst through as she dropped her spoon onto the table and came to give Hannah a hug. It was the first smile Hannah had seen since Liesbet had disappeared.

"I'm so glad you're home."

Hannah hugged her back, although she would rather cling to her and let her tears flow. "I'm sorry. I stayed out longer than I should have."

"Never mind now. Come sit down. Supper is ready."

Hannah helped finish putting the stew on the table along with the plates and bread. She waited for Daed to lead the blessing, and for the little ones to be fed. She waited until William and Peter had finished their stew. The longer she waited, the more her stomach twisted and turned.

"I have to tell you something."

Daed glanced at her, then at Mamm.

"*Ja*, daughter?" Daed took another bite of stew.

"I went to Lancaster today."

"Not to the Metzlers'?" Mamm looked at Daed, and then at the children. "Margli, take your brothers into the bedroom and play a quiet game. Hannah and I will clear up supper."

Once Margli had taken Peter and William into the other room and closed the door, Mamm nodded to Daed.

"Tell us about it." Daed pushed his plate away and brushed crumbs from his beard. Jacob took another piece of corn pone.

"I . . . I asked Adam to take me to town. I wanted to see Liesbet."

Mamm choked back a sob at Liesbet's name.

"Why would you do that?" Daed's brows nearly covered his eyes, they were lowered so far.

"I thought I could convince her to come home."

"She will come home when she's ready."

"*Ja*, but she's so thoughtless at times . . . . I thought if I told her how serious her actions were, she might come back."

"Did you see her? What did she say?" Mamm grabbed Hannah's hand and clung to it. What would her next words do to her?

"*Ja*, I saw her." Hannah stopped. She must go on. "She won't be coming home."

"Not at all? You're sure?" Daed looked as devastated as Mamm.

"*Ja*, I'm sure." Hannah swallowed. Hard. "She . . . she's married."

Daed stood and walked to the fireplace, his hand running through his hair, clutching at it. Mamm sat back, leaning heavily against her chair. Jacob stared at Hannah. She had never seen him so angry.

"She's married?" He spit the words out, his voice rising.

"How did this happen?" Mamm turned to Daed standing behind her. She clutched at his sleeve. "How did she meet a man who would do this to her? Someone who would take her away from her family without even approaching us, letting us meet him?"

"He is an *Englischer*." Jacob's words were hard, unyielding. "He knew Daed would never give him permission to marry Liesbet, so he stole her. We have to get her back before it's too late."

Silence followed Jacob's words. He turned to Hannah. "Unless it's too late already."

Hannah nodded. "Liesbet is expecting a little one."

Mamm leaned forward. "She told you this?"

297

"I could tell when I saw her."

Jacob heaved himself from his seat, the bench crashing to the floor as he strode out the door.

Mamm looked at Daed, then back at Hannah. "She's only been away a few weeks. If you can already tell . . . that means she knew when she left . . ."

Hannah nodded, squeezing her eyes closed on the tears that threatened. Neither Mamm nor Daed said anything.

Daed finally moved from the fireplace, his steps slow and heavy. He leaned his hand on Mamm's shoulder as he passed, on his way to the door, following Jacob's steps. He turned before leaving, his eyes meeting Mamm's.

"I blame myself for this. I should have acted sooner, when I first knew of Liesbet's ways. We will leave for Indiana in the spring as we planned. I will not risk losing another one of our children to the world."

As January turned to February, one snowstorm after another kept Hannah inside the house. She longed to visit Johanna, or even help Daed and Jacob with the wagon building in the barn, but Mamm grew increasingly tired as the weeks went on and her stomach grew rounder. She needed Hannah's help.

Every day it didn't storm, Hannah bundled up the children and took them outside to play for an hour, giving Mamm a chance to nap with William inside the quiet house. She taught Margli and Peter how to make snow angels and how to play ducks and geese by tromping down paths in the snow for the playing field. After their time outdoors, the children were content to play quietly in the house while she helped Mamm prepare supper.

One evening, as Daed read from the *Martyr's Mirror*, Hannah listened, absorbed in the stories. Each one was short, but gave an account of men and women who would not renounce their faith, even in the face of imprisonment and torture. Some accounts ended with miraculous deliverance from their persecution, others with the gradual weakening and death of the martyr.

Tonight Daed ended with the most heartbreaking story to listen to. It was the account of Hans Meyli and his wife, whose children were sent out to live with strangers when their parents were imprisoned. Hannah sat with her knitting in her lap, her hands still, as she stared at the fire. Had those children followed the faith of their parents, or were they lost forever? What a terrible choice it must have been for the mother, to either deny her faith or keep her children with her.

Even Peter sat quietly when Daed finished reading. William slept on the floor in front of the fire, snoring softly in the stillness.

Margli broke the silence. "Why did they do it, Daed?" She turned around and laid her hand on his knee, searching his firelit face. "Why didn't they just do what the evil men wanted them to do?"

"Because to do so would have been denying their Lord, who refused to deny them as he hung on the cross." Daed patted Margli's hand absently as he stared into the fire. "Can we do any less?"

"But we aren't being imprisoned or killed." Jacob leaned forward in his chair.

"*Ne*, but we are hemmed in on all sides, beset with temptations from strangers who would pull us from our family and way."

Then he turned to look at Hannah. "We must hold to our faith through any threat of persecution or temptation from the world."

Hannah met his eyes but couldn't bear the intense look he gave her. She dropped her gaze to the forgotten knitting in her lap and picked it up again. She realized that Daed's reading was for her. He was afraid they would lose her to Adam and his faith. She would be as dead to them as Liesbet if she married their neighbor and friend, because as faithful as he might be, he wasn't Amish.

Adam was a man of faith. He was strong, courageous, a willing worker, and would be a good provider. But he wasn't Amish. After he had attended the tent meetings last summer, Hannah wasn't even sure he could still be called Mennonite. His thinking was changed—full of ideas that he said followed Christ's teachings. Were his ideas from man, not God?

Hannah went back to pick up a stitch she had dropped in her knitting.

What did Adam believe? He had compassion and risked his life for the well-being of others. But where did his actions fit in with his beliefs?

A knock sounded at the door. Mamm and Daed exchanged glances, and then Daed went to the kitchen to answer it. Hannah followed him.

Wind pushed their visitor into the room, and he stood, unwrapping a woolen scarf from around his head.

"Josef Bender?" Daed shook his head in disbelief and helped him with his snowy coat and hat and then led him into the parlor. "We didn't expect to see you until spring."

"*Ja, ja, ja.*" Josef chaffed his hands in a brisk rub and took Daed's chair when it was offered.

He glanced at Hannah, his eyes reflecting the smile he gave her. It had been so long since she had seen him, and so much had happened, that she had nearly forgotten how warm his smiles were.

"I've reached the end of my redemption, and even though I had thought I would continue helping the Nafsingers prepare for their move to Ohio, Daniel suggested I come to see you. He said they had very little for me to do, but you might want an extra hand."

"He's right about that. It was a thoughtful thing for him to think of us." Daed winked at Hannah and her face burned. "How long can you stay?"

"I can stay as long as you need me, all the way until our departure next month, if it's all right with you."

Daed combed through his beard with his fingers and glanced at Mamm. She gave him a quick nod. "We'll be glad to have you."

"I'll fix myself a place in the barn, if that's all right."

"You'll do nothing of the kind." Mamm rose to her feet. "You're one of the family, not a hired hand. Peter and Jacob have room."

"*Denki*." Josef nodded at Mamm and Daed, and then looked at Jacob. "I hope you won't mind company."

Jacob grinned from his seat on the bench next to Hannah. "I welcome it. We can get to know each other better."

"*Ja*, we can." Josef's gaze slid over to Hannah. She bent her head to her knitting. To have Josef here, every day? A *wonderful-gut* thing, to be sure.

"Well then," Daed said, "let's get you settled. We won't need to leave so early in the morning for Sabbath meeting. Tomorrow we meet at the Hertzlers'." Daed picked up William, still sleepy, from the floor. "You know where the boys' room is, and Jacob can show you where to put your things."

Josef started to get up from his seat, but Daed pushed him back again with a hand on his shoulder. "But don't be in a hurry. After your journey today, I'm sure you'll want to rest. You young folks sit and visit for a while. We'll see you in the morning."

Silence filled the room after Mamm took the little ones out and up to bed. Soon she heard Mamm come back down the stairs and into her room. The door closed, leaving Hannah alone with Jacob and Josef.

She put her knitting away. "I had better be off to bed also."

Josef stood as she rose. "I wish you wouldn't."

Jacob looked from her to Josef and back again. He stretched and rose to his feet. "It's been a long day and I need my sleep. Good night." He winked at Hannah as he left the room, and she was alone with Josef.

"I've never known the folks to go to bed so early."

"Perhaps they wanted to leave us alone, so we could visit." Josef stepped closer to her.

"We could visit with them here, couldn't we?"

He lifted her hand to his lips and kissed it. "Not the way I'd like to. Some things just can't be discussed when little brothers and sisters are around."

His hand was still icy from his long walk. "You must be cold after coming all that way." She sat in Mamm's chair and he took Daed's.

"*Ja*, for sure. But once Daniel said I could go, I couldn't wait to get here. My only worry was that I'd arrive too late in the evening, and everyone would be in bed."

"What would you have done then?"

"The barn would have been comfortable enough, except I would have had to wait until morning to see you."

"Why the hurry?"

Josef leaned forward with his elbows on his knees. "The last time we talked, you said you needed to know me better. I want to spend as much time with you as I can."

"You are very confident, Josef Bender."

He smiled at her, squeezing her hand. "We belong together, Hannah Yoder, I'm sure. All I need to do is convince you."

28

Monday morning brought Hannah awake as soon as she heard Daed leave the house to do chores. She smiled as she stretched in her bed. Josef was here and wouldn't be going home. Every evening could end like the last two evenings, with pleasant conversation and a sweet kiss good night.

She relished the camaraderie that blended one day into the next. When she had considered marriage to Adam, she had thought of enjoying his protection, cooking his meals, and taking care of his home. But she had never thought of spending long hours with him the way she spent with Josef the last two days. Her conversations with Adam always turned to his work with the escaped slaves or to the camp meetings, and they ended up quarreling.

She and Josef hadn't quarreled at all since he had arrived. But they hadn't talked of her wish to stay along the Conestoga, either. How could he make her forget her greatest desire?

Rising, she lit the lamp and washed her face. She dressed quickly in the chilly room.

"Margli." She shook her sister's shoulder. "Margli, it's time to get up."

Hannah combed her hair while Margli stretched and yawned. "It can't be. It's still dark outside."

"That's because it's winter. Mamm needs the eggs for breakfast, so get up and get dressed. I'm going down to help in the kitchen."

She paused long enough to make sure Margli was getting up and then stepped into the hall, right into Josef.

"I'm sorry, I didn't see you there."

"It is dark. I didn't see you either."

Light filtering up the stairs from the kitchen showed Josef's silhouette against the white-washed walls. He had grasped her arms to steady her when she bumped into him and didn't release her, but pulled her closer. Was he going to kiss her? Did she want him to? He held her another moment, and then he took a step back, dropping his arms.

"I could get used to running into you in the passage."

"Isn't seeing me at meals enough?"

Hannah's eyes had adjusted to the dim light of the hallway, and she could see his eyes, dark and serious. "*Ne*, Hannah. It isn't nearly enough."

She smiled at him and went down the stairs to the kitchen.

At breakfast, Daed planned the day's work with Jacob and Josef.

"The wagon bed is nearly done, and I'd like to finish that today. But the horses need to be taken to the farrier."

Josef had finished eating and leaned on his forearms, sipping his tea. "You don't shoe them yourself?"

"I've never needed to learn. Hiram Studebaker, down the road toward Lancaster, is a fine farrier. I have a small forge, but I've never done my own horseshoeing." Daed looked at Josef. "Do you know how?"

"I know how to do it, but I haven't for a long time. I learned from my neighbor in Rheinland-Pfalz. Daniel's brother was a farrier, so he didn't need me to shoe his horses. I'm afraid I've forgotten a lot."

"But when we're in Indiana," Jacob said, finishing his eggs, "who knows how far we might need to travel to the nearest farrier? And how much he would charge?"

Daed smiled. "It sounds like you'll need to brush up on your skills, Josef, and we'll need to find an anvil and other equipment." He drained his cup. "Meanwhile, why don't you take the horses to Hiram this morning and talk to him about what you need. He could make some of the tools for you."

"That's a fine idea, except I have no money to buy the tools."

"Don't worry about the money. I'll pay for the tools in exchange for your services, *ja*? We'll need you to make repairs on the journey, and it will be a good business to start once we get to Indiana."

Hannah rose from the table to start clearing the table. Daed had everything planned out, and Josef was going right along with him. She glanced at Josef as she took his plate. His smile was contagious. If she wasn't careful, she'd be getting excited about the trip west too.

She took the dishes to the dry sink and pulled the pot of warm water from the fire. On a morning like this, moving west to new opportunities didn't seem like such a bad idea. If Josef was a farrier, then he would earn the cash he would need to start farming, or even barter his services for help on the farm. The future held bright promises with this new development.

She turned back to the table to get more dishes, and Liesbet's empty place caught her eye. How could they leave while Liesbet remained separated from the family? How could Daed look forward to this journey, knowing he was leaving Liesbet behind?

After breakfast, Josef went to the barn to look at the horses Christian wanted him to take to the farrier. They were draft horses, of a kind Josef had never seen in Rheinland-Pfalz. The farmers called them Conestogas, and they had been bred to pull the wagons that shared their name. Josef talked to each one in turn, getting to know the giant animals.

Christian stopped by the stalls as Josef checked the last horse.

"Well? What do you think?"

"You're right. I'll take them to the farrier's before dinner, if that's all right with you."

"*Ja, ja, ja.* The sooner started, the sooner finished." Christian patted him on the back and turned to go back to his wagon building. "You should take Hannah with you. She would enjoy the outing, and she can show you where the Studebakers' farm is."

Josef grinned at him. He had already thought to ask her.

He found her in the house, carding wool. She combed the fleece over and over, until a soft roll was ready for spinning.

"Your *vater* thought you might like to go with me to the farrier's."

She gave him a smile as she finished a roll of fleece. "I'd like that. We can stop by the Hertzlers' on the way home. I have some blue wool to trade with Johanna."

"What color does she have?" Josef helped her put the carding boards away.

"She made a beautiful green this summer. A different shade than I've ever seen."

Hannah went to the weaving room to tell Annalise where she was going, Josef watching every step. He had thought she was a pretty girl the first time he met her, but every day he enjoyed her beauty more and more. He would have to ask her to set the date for the wedding soon. But he had to be sure of her, to be sure she would agree to marrying him.

Christian had the horses ready. Four of the Conestoga horses stood tied to the fence outside the barn. The powerful animals followed quietly behind Josef and Hannah as he led them down the lane to the road.

"The Studebakers live on the next farm past the Hertzlers. It isn't far."

"You'll be warm enough for the walk?"

Hannah turned to him, her face rosy from the chilly air, but smiling. "I'm warm enough. It's a beautiful day, isn't it?"

Josef looked up at the blue sky showing between the bare, black branches rimmed with frost. The air was clear and cold. "It is a beautiful morning. We've had much snow this winter, but when it is packed on the roads, traveling is much easier."

"As long as it's cold enough to keep the roads frozen."

"*Ja.* Mud is not good for travel."

The conversation fell away. Josef searched his mind for something worthwhile to talk about. Something more important than the weather.

308

"If all goes well, we'll be leaving for Indiana in a month."

"Only a month?" Her voice was so quiet, he almost didn't hear her.

"Or even three weeks. It's important to get to Indiana in time to plant a crop." He glanced at her, but she had turned her face away. "I'm taking seeds for a garden. I have beans, squash, and corn. Are there any others I should be taking?"

"Greens are easy to grow. If you plant turnips, then you can eat the greens and then have the turnips for winter." Her words didn't match her quiet, detached voice.

Josef stopped in the road and waited until she looked at him. "What is wrong? Ever since I brought up the trip west, you have acted like you don't want to be with me."

She smiled, but it wasn't a natural smile. "I'm happy for you. The plans you're making for your home in Indiana sound wonderful."

"Those plans don't mean anything without you." She turned away from him and he caught her arm. "Hannah, I mean what I say. I don't understand why you wouldn't go with us, with your family. Don't you want your family to be together?"

"It isn't that simple." She turned back to him, took a step closer. He could put his arm around her if he dared. "Liesbet won't be going, so our family will be broken apart, either way."

"Why isn't Liesbet going?" Josef hadn't seen her since arriving Saturday evening, but since no one had said anything, he assumed she had been visiting friends.

"She . . . she's married. She will be staying here, and we'll never see her again." Hannah shook her head and stepped away from him. "I can't believe Daed will go and leave her behind. I keep waiting for him to change his mind, and then we won't move." Her voice dropped, muffled in her shawl as she buried her chin in its folds. "We won't have to leave home."

"Liesbet is married? She is so young." Josef remembered how sullen she was when he had first met her.

"She is. It wasn't the best . . . so don't you see? Perhaps we won't be going after all."

"Your *vater* hasn't stopped preparing. He's finishing the new wagon, *ja*? Nothing has been said to make me think he is having second thoughts." The horses pulled at their lead ropes, anxious to move on, but he ignored them. "If Liesbet has a new life with her new husband, they will come with us or they will stay, but it's up to them to make that decision. You need to come with us, Hannah. There would be nothing for you here if you didn't."

She didn't answer. He pulled her closer and lifted her chin so she had to look at him. "I am liking you more every time I see you. I dream of making a home with you, and making you happy. You will come, *ja*?"

Her eyes filled, but she didn't turn away. "My heart is torn."

"We belong together. You know we do. We would never disagree on how to live, or how to raise our children, or what church to belong to."

"You mean that Adam and I would."

He nodded. "You and Adam Metzler are friends, but you aren't the same. I see him look at you, but the woman he wants to marry isn't you. It's the Hannah he carries in his head. The one who would be different from what you are now." He rubbed his thumb along her cheek. His words made the tears in her eyes overflow. "I would marry you, just the way you are."

She didn't speak for a long time. He gathered her in and held her close to his chest, leaning his head on her bonnet. When she spoke, it was a whisper. "It would be so easy to marry you."

He pushed her back to look into her face. "Then you will? Are you saying yes?"

"I don't know what to do. Just when I think I see a clear path to the future, something happens to make the way muddy again. I don't want to marry because it's convenient."

"Convenient? What do you mean?"

"I don't want to marry someone who seems to fit too easily into my life and I into his. To marry someone because I've always known him, or because we both like to eat pie, or because we have something else in common."

"What is wrong with agreeing with your husband on things like that?"

"It isn't enough. I want to marry for love."

"Love? Love doesn't just happen. Love grows, *ja*?" She didn't answer. "You and I, we have many things we both like. Many goals that are the same. Our love will grow from those things."

Hannah wiped her hands across her cheeks. "How can we be sure that it will grow? What if it doesn't, and we end up not even liking each other?"

He pulled her close again and hugged her. "That's where we trust God. He is the one who will make our love grow."

Hannah thought about Josef's words all the way to the Studebakers' farm. To be close to him, to be held in his arms, set her heart to racing. She wasn't sure that was love. Perhaps Josef was right. Love needed time to grow.

Hiram Studebaker was the best farrier in the area, and Daed had used his services as long as Hannah could remember, even though he was a Dunkard. Josef made arrangements to come back for the horses later in the day, and then they left. Hannah wanted to visit Johanna and return home before dinnertime. She hated to leave Mamm with only the little ones for help for too long.

As they reached the road again, Hannah turned toward the Hertzlers' farm, but Josef stopped her.

"What is that in the road?" He pointed down the road in the opposite direction of home, where it made a bend before going on toward Lancaster. A bundle was on one side, as if a pile of blankets had fallen from someone's wagon.

The bundle moved, and then lay still again.

Josef started down the road. "Something is wrong. You wait here until I see what it is."

She followed a few steps but waited as he had asked. Was it someone hurt? Or was it a trap—some ruffian waiting to rob a passerby?

Josef reached the bundle, turning it over. "Hannah, hurry!" His voice was urgent, carrying over the distance. "It's Adam Metzler."

Hannah ran to where Josef knelt on the frozen ground, cradling Adam's head in his lap. "He's unconscious. You stay with him while I get help."

She froze, staring at the bloody cuts and bruises covering Adam's face. She dropped to her knees and took his head onto her own lap. He didn't wince or cry out . . . he lay in her arms as if he was dead.

"I will stay with him. But hurry! Go to the Studebakers' to borrow a wagon and team. We must take him to his parents."

Hiram Studebaker brought his team and wagon and helped lift Adam into the bed. Hannah rode, holding him, while Josef knelt on Adam's other side, trying to keep his body from shifting too much in the jolting wagon. The ride to the Metzlers' farm seemed endless.

Adam's daed came running out of the barn as they drove in. With one look into the wagon, he called for the rest of the family.

"We must get him inside. Ma will look after him." Even as he took control of the situation, Samuel Metzler's face was twisted with worry. He turned to Hannah. "You must come in too. He will want you with him."

She turned to Josef. His clothes were as bloody as hers—Adam's blood.

"Go with him." Josef nodded toward the house and the men taking Adam inside. "His *vater* is right. He will need you. I will tell your parents where you are."

He nodded again, urging her on. She turned toward the house, and then looked back at him once more. His face was calm. Determined. She followed Hiram and Samuel into the house, but her mind was on the man she left behind in the farmyard.

He was right. Love grew. She could feel the vines taking root as Josef turned away to leave her to do what she must for Adam.

29

Hannah pressed the cool, wet cloth against the gash on Adam's forehead once more. The bleeding had stopped from most of the cuts on his face, but this one continued to seep.

"Has he woken yet?" Dora brought in a fresh bowl of water and a clean rag and exchanged it with the one Hannah was using.

"Not yet, although he has stirred a couple times. I think he may feel the pain of us cleaning his wounds."

"We may need to stitch that one on his head. It's quite deep."

Hannah pressed the clean rag to the wound and held it there for a minute, but when she released the pressure and removed the cloth, the blood flowed as freely as before. "I think you're right."

She applied pressure again while Dora prepared the needle and thread. Adam didn't awaken during the stitching, and Dora was soon finished.

"I hate seeing him like this." She pushed damp hair off his forehead. "It's the way of mothers, to always think of their grown men as they were when they were little boys." She looked at Hannah and smiled. "That must seem strange to you, doesn't it?"

Hannah couldn't answer. She had never heard Mamm talk like Dora had . . . but whenever Mamm thought of Jacob as a little boy, she would also think of Hansli . . .

Samuel appeared in the doorway of Adam's room. "How is he?"

"He seems comfortable," Dora said, straightening the covers. "Hannah said he has stirred once or twice."

Samuel stepped farther into the room, just as Adam turned his head and groaned. "Son? Are you awake?"

Hannah moved the basin of water to the floor as Adam's arm jerked. He opened his eyes, focusing first on Samuel and Dora, and then turned. He smiled when he saw Hannah, but then winced.

"Don't try to do too much just yet." Dora laid her hand on his shoulder and he relaxed at her touch.

"How did I get home?" Adam's voice was raspy, but he reached for Hannah's hand as he spoke. "Where are the others?"

Samuel leaned over Adam. "There were no others. Can you tell us what happened, son? Do you know?"

Adam's hand squeezed Hannah's as he closed his eyes, a frown twisting his features.

"We were attacked by slave hunters." His face grimaced. "I'm afraid I . . . I lost them, Pa. The . . . the passengers. Toby and Jackson. The slave hunters jumped us. They must have been waiting, watching for us." He struggled to sit up, but Dora's hand on his shoulder held him down. A tear ran a slow track down his cheek. "I failed them. The last time I saw them, the slave hunters had them in chains, and all I could do was lie in the snow and watch them leave. And then everything went black."

Hannah would have left the room, slipping out quietly, but Adam's grip on her hand was too tight. Her heart wrenched. Those poor men. What were they facing now? And what would they face when the slave hunters returned them to their masters?

"It isn't your fault, Adam. Sometimes evil wins." Samuel's shoulders slumped.

"The Penningtons need to know what happened. They were expecting us, and they'll worry if we don't show up."

"I'll take word to them." Samuel squeezed his wife's shoulder. "I'll drive into Lancaster right now."

"You must rest, Adam." Dora stood and kissed her son's cheek. "We'll leave you alone now."

"Not Hannah." Adam's grip on her hand tightened. "I want Hannah to stay here."

Dora smiled at her as they left the room.

"Will your daed be all right, making the trip to the Penningtons'?"

Adam's thumb pressed into the back of her hand. "He should be. He doesn't have any passengers, and there's nothing to connect him with me." He let go of her hand and shifted in his bed, turning away from her. "The slave hunters have gotten what they were after. They're on their way south again." His voice was bitter.

"Your daed is right. It isn't your fault."

"But I am responsible. Those men trusted me, and now . . ."

He clenched his fist and hit the mattress with a thump. "And now I can't even go after them or try to help them."

Hannah took his hand, tried to open his fist and relax the muscles, but he pulled away from her. "Don't, Hannah. Don't try to make me feel better."

She rose from her seat. "I should go. You need your rest."

He took her hand and held it to his cheek. "I'm glad you were here. Did Ma or Pa ask you to come?"

"Josef and I were taking Daed's horses to the Studebakers for shoeing. Josef saw you on the road and we brought you here."

"Josef Bender."

"He's staying with us . . . helping Daed prepare for the move." She glanced at Adam's face. He was looking past her, toward the window. She knew his every expression, every look. He was angry, but not with her.

"*Ja*, well." Adam's eyes closed and he released her hand. "I think I'll sleep now."

Hannah backed away from his bed and to the door. He didn't move, not even as she opened the door and slipped out of the room. She hurried down the narrow stairway and waved to Dora on her way through the kitchen.

Before leaving the Metzler farm, she glanced back at the second-story window of Adam's room. He could have been killed. She could have lost him today.

Tears filled her eyes at this thought, but she held them back. She wouldn't cry until she was someplace where she could be alone. If only she could take the creek path, to go to her special place where the tree overhung the creek, but the snow was too deep. No one would go that way until spring.

When she reached home, she broke a path through the

deep snow to the smokehouse. It was empty and cold, but it was sheltered, and no one looking from the house would see her trail to the door. Once inside, she sat on an upended log and let the tears flow. Using her apron for a handkerchief, she buried her face in its skirt and sobbed.

What if Adam had died? What if she and Josef had found his cold, lifeless body on the road? They had talked of how dangerous his work was, but she had never really thought of what that meant. She had treated it like a game, trying to avoid the slave catchers. But it wasn't a game. It was deadly serious business. Why hadn't she tried harder to convince Adam to stop? She should have done more—even promised to marry him if he would give it up.

Her tears spent, she wiped her eyes and tried to smooth out the wrinkles in her damp apron.

But even if she had begged him to, he could not give up his work. She would never be able to marry Adam, not even to stay on her beloved Conestoga. His involvement with the Quakers and the abolitionists was more important to him than his home. Than his family. Than her.

Hannah sniffed, wiping her cheeks once more, just as the smokehouse door opened wide, blinding her with the sudden light.

"Are you all right?"

It was Josef. He had come for her.

"I needed some time to think."

"Will Adam be all right?" Josef came in and pulled another log over, sitting close enough to put his arm around her.

"I think so. Dora stitched up the worst of his cuts and cleaned the rest. He should be all right with a few days of rest."

"This wasn't a random attack by bandits, was it?"

Hannah shook her head. Adam's activities were a secret, but she wouldn't lie to Josef.

"When this happened, was he doing that same thing you told him you would no longer do?"

"*Ja.*"

Josef pulled her close. "I don't know what he was doing, and I don't think I want to, just as long as you aren't involved." Hannah leaned her head on his shoulder. "Promise me. Promise you'll never do the dangerous thing again."

Hannah hesitated. She didn't want to be involved, didn't want to be in danger or put anyone else in danger. If Adam came to her again, needing her help to rescue people from those slave hunters, she wasn't sure she could refuse him. And after what happened today, perhaps Adam would not be able to continue.

"I promise, unless the need is so great—"

"*Ne.* I don't care about the need. Nothing is worth putting you in that kind of danger." He tilted her chin up so he could look into her eyes. "Promise me, Hannah. I don't think I could live, knowing your life might be at risk." He ran his thumb along her bottom lip. "If Adam loved you, he wouldn't ask you to do this."

Hannah dropped her gaze. He was right. If Adam loved her, if he wanted to protect her, he would never have asked her to help him that first day.

Three days later, Adam was still confined to his bed. Sitting up made him dizzy, so he lay back on the pillows and had plenty of time to think.

Time to think about the slave catchers and what they had done. Time to think about Toby and Jackson and what they might be suffering because of him. Time to nurse his anger at the same time as he nursed his wounds.

He shifted in his bed. Didn't he have the right to be angry? Those men had attacked him, leaving him for dead, but it wasn't his injuries that bothered him as much as the fate of the two men who had depended on him. Trusted him with their lives.

And he had failed.

Failed.

That one word echoed through his mind, awake or asleep.

A soft knock at the door. He opened his eyes. "*Ja?*"

The door opened and Hilda's head poked into the room. "Do you need anything?"

"Just a new head. This one hurts so much I'm ready to cut it off." He rubbed his temple, the only thing he had found to ease the pain.

"You don't need to snap at me." Hilda came into the room and straightened his covers. "I know it hurts, but you must be patient."

"Patient? I'm tired of being patient." He clenched his fist and pounded the mattress. At the sudden motion, pain surged through his head, but he ignored it. "How can I be patient when the men who did this are getting farther away every hour? And Toby and Jackson—they have no time for patience."

"Pa told the Penningtons what happened. If anything can be done, I'm sure they're doing it."

Adam let his head fall back on the pillow. He was so tired, and he couldn't get anyone to understand the urgency of what needed to be done. The Penningtons? As much as he loved the elderly couple, they were Quakers. They wouldn't take any action to change what had happened. They would accept his failure as God's will and prepare for the next time.

Hilda moved to the table near his bed and poured a glass of water. She took a packet from her pocket and mixed a few grains of powder into the water.

"What is that?"

"Ma said to give you some laudanum if you were hurting. As surly as you're acting, I'd say your head hurts pretty badly."

"Don't give me that stuff. It will put me to sleep."

"And isn't that what you want? You need to rest so you can get better." She sat on the chair by his side, holding the glass. She was only trying to help.

"I'm sorry." He reached for the glass. "I don't know why I talk the way I do. I wouldn't blame you if you didn't come up here anymore."

She smiled. "I just want you to feel better. Drink the medicine and then sleep. I'll bring your supper up in a few hours."

As she left the room, Adam set the glass down on the table. The laudanum would dull the pain, but it would make everything else dull too, and he had to think. What was he to do next?

Hannah had been right. When he first started helping the runaway slaves find their way through Lancaster County, he hadn't thought too much about the consequences. He hadn't counted the cost—wasn't that the phrase she used? But he wouldn't have done things any different.

But what if she had been with him on Monday? His head

throbbed. If she had been with him then, if she had been hurt . . .

Adam closed his eyes, imagining the scene. He imagined hitting the slave catchers with his fists . . . taking their whips from them and letting the end of the lash curl around their knees the way they had with Toby . . . driving them off, broken and bloody . . .

He unclenched his fists, willing his hands to rest on the coverlet. That same image had come to him again and again as he lay here, as helpless in his bed as he had been on the snowy road. But it wasn't the Mennonite way to be violent. As long as he could remember he had been taught to back away from confrontation, to turn the other cheek. In his church, as well as for the Amish and the Dunkards, it was a virtue to be defenseless, going beyond avoiding vengeance to welcoming persecution as an outward sign of his commitment to following Christ.

All his nonresistance had gotten him was a busted head and sore body. He could live with that.

But what had his nonresistance gotten Toby and Jackson? Beatings, chains, and re-enslavement. They were worse off now than if they had never escaped in the first place. They would be fortunate to survive the trip back south, and he hated to think what would happen to them when their slave masters got a hold of them again.

Is this really what Christ meant when he told his followers to turn the other cheek? That by his obedience to the church, he would bring about the suffering and possible death of innocent people?

Could it be that what his church had taught him, what Pa and Ma had taught him, was wrong?

At the camp meetings, the preachers spoke against slavery, urging all Christians to work against it. They advocated the use of force, if necessary. Of deception. Of breaking the civil law to uphold God's law.

All this thinking made his head hurt. He reached for the glass of laudanum and stirred it slowly, letting the powder mix with the water, and then drank the bitter liquid in one gulp. He settled back on his pillows, waiting for the drug to take effect.

He looked out the window, toward Hannah's house. The farm was hidden behind a thick stand of trees, but he didn't need to see it. He rubbed his hands over his face, feeling the numbing drug take hold.

One thing he would never do again was to put Hannah in danger. Never within reach of the slave catchers.

More than a week after the attack on Adam, Hannah saw him walking up the lane to the house and met him on the porch. The February wind was cold and held the promise of snow in gusts that whistled around the corner of the house. She stepped off the porch to meet him.

"Hallo. It's good to see you up and about again."

Adam stopped a few feet away. "I need to talk to you." He shifted on his feet. "Is there somewhere we can talk without being overheard?"

Hannah wrapped her shawl tighter around her shoulders. "And somewhere out of the wind." She looked back at the house. It was warm, but Mamm was inside with the little ones and they would have no privacy. "Let's go to the barn."

As she hurried to get out of the wind, Adam caught up with her. "Aren't your pa and Jacob . . . and Josef in there?"

"*Ne*, they all went to the Hertzlers'. We'll be alone."

When they shut the door on the wind, the barn loomed around them in sudden silence. Hannah turned to face Adam. She hadn't seen him since the day she and Josef had found him lying in the road. His bruises had faded, but the cut on his head was still an angry red.

"How are you feeling?"

"I'm doing all right. The blow to my head was the worst part, and it stills aches a lot, but I can get around again."

"That's good."

"I . . . I came to tell you . . . I'm leaving the Conestoga."

"What do you mean?"

"I can't stay here any longer. I'm going to Philadelphia to join the larger abolitionist movement."

"But what about your family? Your farm? Aren't you buying the Hertzlers' farm?"

Adam paced to the door and then back, facing her. He took his hat off, turning it in his hands. "My family doesn't know yet. But I'm leaving the money to pay for the farm." He looked at her, a halfhearted grin twisting his mouth. "It would make a good dowry for Hilda, wouldn't it?" His grin faded as quickly as it had come. "I hope you will understand, but I have to withdraw my offer of marriage."

Hannah looked down at her fingers, rolling the edge of her shawl between them. "Are you sure this is what you want to do, Adam?"

He sighed and then leaned over to lay his hat on the wagon tongue. The new wagon. The one Daed had built for the move to Indiana.

Adam was leaving. Everything she had counted on was slipping away as fast as dried beans through her fingers. She couldn't keep him from leaving any more than she could keep Daed from going west. Her life was going to change. It was changing already. Tears pricked in her eyes. She was powerless to stop it.

"Hannah, look at me. Please."

She turned to face him again, and he stepped up to her, taking her in his arms. "I never wanted to hurt you. I never wanted to put you in danger. But I have to do the task God has laid before me. Do you understand?"

She nodded. "I understand. You must do this, but I'm afraid for you."

"Don't be."

"You have no surety that what happened last week won't happen again. And you're walking right into the middle of the hornet's nest." Adam released her and started to step away, but she stopped him. "You be careful, Adam Metzler."

He pulled her to himself in a sudden, quick embrace, and then just as quickly let her go. He took his hat and slipped out the door without looking back.

Hannah sank onto a keg sitting near the wagon. He was gone. She could hope he would change his mind, that he would never leave . . . but she knew better. Adam was a man who never took action on a whim. If he said he needed to go to Philadelphia, he would go.

She stared, unseeing, at the straw-littered floor, her stomach a hollow, sour pit. He was gone as quickly as the water flowing by in the creek, never to return.

30

Annalise sat at her loom, the rhythm of the flying shuttle and beater punctuated by the rattle of the harnesses shifting as she alternated them with her feet on the treadles.

With her hands busy, Annalise's thoughts were free to light on whatever subject was foremost in her mind, and today it was Liesbet. Christian had forbidden fellowship with her daughter, but he couldn't forbid the anguished thoughts that followed one another in a haphazard race.

Her baby, setting up housekeeping in the city, having a child with an outsider. Her Liesbetli, lost to them forever. The shuttle came to a halt as Annalise's thoughts pulled her gaze to the window facing Lancaster. The weaving room was on the opposite side of the house from the kitchen, and the view was only snowy woods. But on the other side of those woods were her Liesbetli . . . and her *Englischer* husband.

Annalise sighed and pulled the shuttle the rest of the way through the shed, brought the beater forward, and shifted the harnesses once more. She was weaving sturdy brown linsey-woolsey to make trousers for the men, with wool dyed walnut brown for the weft and linen threads for the warp. Yards of cloth to clothe her family, and the weaving had to be finished before the end of the month when the loom would be dismantled and packed into the big Conestoga wagon with the rest of their household goods.

Another inch of weaving done, and Annalise paused to roll the finished fabric under again, making it easier for her to reach the unwoven warp. The babe was growing larger and more active as the winter passed, and weaving became more difficult. She straightened up, pressing her fists into the small of her back. Did Liesbet feel the same heaviness? Did she feel her babe move and cherish the memories? Was she warm enough? Did she have enough food?

Seeing a movement at the door of the room, Annalise turned. Margli leaned against the doorframe, her finger in her mouth.

"*Hallo, liebchen.* Did you and Hannah finish the carding?"

"*Ne*, Mamm, but Hannah said I could get a drink."

Annalise smiled and patted the space next to her on the bench. Margli climbed up beside her and watched the shuttle flying back and forth.

"I think you went the wrong way. The water is in the kitchen."

Margli touched the tightly strung warp as Annalise paused to roll the finished cloth again.

"I know. But I like to watch you weave."

"You can watch me for a few minutes, but the last of the wool needs to be carded today so we can spin it into yarn." Annalise looked down at her daughter. Margli was staring at the big loom. "Do you want to try weaving?"

Margli nodded her head and Annalise shifted over so the little girl was seated on the center of the bench.

"Take the shuttle like this . . ." Annalise showed her how to push the shuttle along the shed. Margli stretched to reach far enough, and pushed the wooden shuttle most of the way through. Annalise took it from the other side and pulled it the rest of the way. "All right, now pull the beater bar down to snug the thread tight against the cloth."

Margli got up on her knees to reach the beater, and Annalise helped her bring it forward with the right pressure.

"I did it. I can weave too."

"You'll make a fine weaver when you're older." Annalise shifted the harnesses to alternate the warp. "All right, now you send the shuttle back the other way."

Margli made a few more passes with the shuttle, and then sat back down on the bench. "Will we take the loom with us to Indiana?"

"*Ja*, for sure we will. How would we make clothes for our family without the loom?"

"But where will we get wool?"

"Daed will take our sheep to Indiana."

Margli was silent, and Annalise glanced at her. She had stuck her finger back in her mouth.

"What are you thinking, daughter?"

"I don't want to move to Indiana."

"You'll learn to like it there. You'll make new friends, and Daed will build a new chicken coop. You'll see. Everything there will be like it is here."

"But Liesbet won't be there, and she won't know where to find us."

Annalise stopped the shuttle, closing her eyes. Margli had

spoken the thought that she had been pushing away for weeks. Liesbetli. If she ever wanted to come back to the family . . . how would she know where they settled? Indiana was a vast wilderness. Annalise straightened and sent the shuttle back through the shed. "God will watch over our Liesbetli. He'll help her find a way to come to us if she wants to."

But would she ever want to? Liesbet had turned her back on them all. She had chosen a worldly path, and one full of sin and danger. *Ach*, Liesbetli!

"You go back and help Hannah with the carding now." Annalise fought to keep her voice even. "She'll be wondering where you went."

"*Ja*, Mamm." Margli slid off the bench and ran back to the parlor, where Hannah had set the baskets of washed wool near the fire so the two girls would be warm while they worked.

Annalise sent the shuttle flying through the shed again, over and over, each pass pushing the dark shadow farther back into the recesses of her mind. The new baby stirred once, and then settled into the rhythmic motion as Annalise swayed back and forth with the weaving.

Her spells had retreated—Annalise hadn't fallen prey to that paralyzing darkness since before the snows came—but the threat still hung within those lingering shadows. The baby helped. Annalise paused to rub the round ball that was once her waist. A mother couldn't forget her baby, and the anticipation of this new child was sweet.

"Mamm?" Hannah's voice drifted to her from the kitchen. "We have visitors."

Annalise left the shuttle on the loom and hurried to the kitchen. Magdalena Hertzler greeted her with a kiss, still wrapped in her snowy shawl.

"Magdalena, what a wonderful surprise!" Annalise reached out to take baby Veronica from Magdalena's arms while Hannah and Margli helped the other girls take off their shawls.

"Elias wanted to bring some things over for Christian this afternoon, and he suggested we all come along. It's been ages since we've had a good visit."

"*Ja*, for sure it has." She looked for Hannah, already deep in a conversation with Johanna. "I think we have some cookies, and I'll heat up some water for tea. It's certainly a cold day."

"*Ne*, now you sit down with Veronica and I'll make the tea." Magdalena moved the kettle closer to the fire.

"And we'll take the children up to the attic to play," Hannah said, wrapping some cookies in a cloth. The children ran up the stairs, following Margli to the big, open attic.

"Between our two families, we have enough children to start our own school, I think." Magdalena took two mugs from the shelf and measured tea into the teapot. After only a few years of marriage, Magdalena was just as much at home in Annalise's kitchen as Barbara had been.

Annalise jiggled baby Veronica in her arms, thinking of her best friend, gone six years now. Magdalena, Elias's new wife, was nearly young enough to be her daughter, but Annalise had grown to love her nearly as much as she had loved Barbara.

"When we get to Indiana, we may have to start a school."

Magdalena poured hot water into the teapot and closed the lid. She held her lower lip in her teeth and looked at Annalise.

"Does it ever worry you?" she said, sitting on the bench across from Annalise.

Annalise tucked the blanket around the sleeping baby and looked at her friend. "You mean moving to Indiana?"

"*Ja.* It's a long way to travel, and we have no idea what we'll find along the way." Magdalena glanced toward the stairway where the children's voices drifted down from the attic. She leaned closer to Annalise. "There are Indians still living there and wild animals. It isn't safely settled like we are here. And then there's the journey. I know Christian and Elias have planned all they can, but what if . . ."

"What if?" Annalise smiled and reached for Magdalena's hand across the table. "There will always be 'what if,' no matter if we travel halfway across the country or if we never leave home."

"But so many things can happen on the trail . . ." Magdalena stopped, her eyes filled with tears. "Silly me." She sniffed and reached for a handkerchief. "I know God will provide and watch out for us—" she blew her nose and gave Annalise a shaky smile—"but I just can't stop thinking about it."

The fears Annalise had been keeping at bay crowded into her mind. Turning her thoughts elsewhere wouldn't work this time. Magdalena needed reassurance. Annalise needed to have enough confidence for both of them. "We both know terrible things happen." Magdalena nodded at Annalise's words. "Both our families have lost loved ones, but we're still here. Think of our ancestors and the troubles they endured. They found their strength in God's presence, and we will find nothing less."

"I can't help thinking of when Elias lost Barbara—what a tragic time that was for his girls. They were still missing her terribly when he married me, and there wasn't much I could do to help them since I was so young, myself."

Annalise averted her eyes, pretending Veronica's blanket needed straightening. Barbara's death, so soon after the death of her own little ones, was a terrible time, and she still missed her.

"You were just what Elias and his family needed, Magdalena. A mother for the girls, and you gave Elias his two sons and sweet baby Veronica. You brought happiness back to your family." Annalise fell silent, turning her own words over in her mind. She had been too wrapped in her own grief to look for what happiness God brought to her own family . . . but she had Peter, Margli, William . . . and now this new little one. God had given her so much, even though her losses had been so great.

"But what if . . . what if something happened to one of us? Or one of the children?" Magdalena covered her mouth. "What if something happened to Elias or Christian?"

Annalise covered Magdalena's hand with her own. "We are not to live in fear. *Ja*, terrible things could happen but so can *wonderful-gut* things. What is that verse in the Psalms? 'My help cometh from the Lord, which made heaven and earth . . . he that keepeth thee will not slumber.' God will not leave us alone and without help. We can trust in his care."

Magdalena smiled, even though tears still stood in her eyes. "Where would I be without you, dear Annalise? I'm so glad we're traveling together. I'll need your wisdom and confidence every step of the way."

Annalise gave her friend's hand a squeeze. She had never thought of herself as a wise woman, but with God's help, they could both be strong for their families on this journey.

After breakfast on Friday, Hannah was helping redd up the kitchen when Mamm beckoned for her to follow her to the weaving room.

"Margli," Hannah said, handing her sister the broom. "Finish the sweeping, and then can you play with William?"

"Can we go outside?"

"*Ja*, but be sure to wear your warmest clothes." Hannah paused in the doorway to the weaving room. "And Margli? Keep William away from the chickens."

From her slumped shoulders, Hannah could tell the chicken coop was exactly where she had planned to take William. "We'll play in the orchard."

Hannah went into the weaving room where Mamm waited, sitting on the bench.

"Shut the door." When the door was closed, Mamm said, "I've been worried about Liesbet. The weather has been so cold, and I don't know if she has enough food." Tears stood in her eyes. "And I want to tell her that we're leaving. I want to say goodbye."

"I know." Hannah sat on the weaving bench next to her. "But what can we do? Daed won't go visit her."

"You did before."

Hannah shifted on her seat. "*Ja*, but Daed was right. I shouldn't have."

"Daed doesn't have to know."

Hannah stared at Mamm. If her face hadn't been so serious, Hannah might have laughed. "You wouldn't lie to him."

"But I don't need to tell him everything, either." She laid her hand on Hannah's arm. "I won't lie to your daed. Rachel Troyer has been ill, and it would be a Christian and neighborly thing to do to take her a pot of soup. Christian can't object to that, even if she is Mennonite. And we may stop in for a visit at the Hertzlers' on the way home. If we go into Lancaster in between, then we do."

"But won't Margli or William say something?"

"We'll go, just us two. Margli can watch William. Rachel Troyer's illness may be catching, and we wouldn't want to risk their health."

"I thought she had rheumatism?"

"Your daed doesn't need to know that."

Then Hannah couldn't hold back a giggle, and Mamm joined in. "It will be fun, won't it? Just the two of us going visiting? Now, let's get a couple pails of soup ready, and I've made some clothes for Liesbet, and some things for . . . for her baby."

Hannah's own throat felt full as her voice caught. This was Mamm's first grandchild, and she might never hold it.

"*Ja*, let's do it."

Once Daed heard of their plans, he insisted that they take the wagon and a team of horses. "I know how you women get to talking, and I don't want you walking home late." Other than that, he had no reservations about the planned visits. "You go and have fun. Jacob and I will take care of things here."

"What about Josef?" Hannah hadn't seen him since breakfast.

"He went into town to take care of a few things for us, and he wanted to go to Ephrata for a visit while the weather was calm. I asked him to discuss some details of the move with Daniel. He'll be home tomorrow."

They set off, Mamm driving the team. Hannah was always surprised at how well she drove. She rarely had an opportunity to do it.

The Troyers lived a few miles down Butter Road, between home and Lancaster. Hannah shuddered as they passed the place where she and Josef had found Adam. She still hated to think about that day.

Rachel Troyer was happy to see them and invited them in for coffee.

"*Ach, ne,* but *denki,*" Mamm said as Hannah carried the pail of soup into the house and set it on Rachel's gleaming stove. "We're going into Lancaster to run another errand, and then I want to stop at the Hertzlers' this afternoon."

They were soon back in the wagon and on their way to town. Mamm slowed the horses to a walk as they approached the city. The road outside of Lancaster had been covered with snow, packed and rutted, but the streets in town were full of mud. Hannah pointed out the way to the tavern where she had last seen Liesbet, living in the room above.

When Mamm pulled the team to a stop outside the tavern, she sat, staring at the building. Shouts filled the air all around them, and horses, wagons, and ox carts were churning the mud to thick sludge. Hannah took her hand. She knew what she was thinking—Liesbet had turned her back on their quiet, peaceful home to live here.

"If you want, I'll go up and see if she is at home."

Mamm shook her head. "*Ne,* we'll go together."

Hannah picked up the remaining pail of soup while Mamm gathered her bundles. Hannah found a rock to step on between the wagon and the boardwalk, and neither of them soiled their high shoes too badly. Mamm's eyes were wide as she took in the tavern and the rough workers gathered outside.

"Come this way." Hannah tugged at her arm and they

went to the side of the building where the steep steps led to the second story. The door at the top stood open.

Hannah led the way up the steps and she knocked on the doorframe.

"What is it?" It was a man's voice. George's voice.

"It's Liesbet's sister and mother. Is she here?"

"Mamm?" Liesbet appeared at the open door. Her blouse barely stretched to cover her swollen stomach, and her hair was dirty and hung on either side of her face. But her eyes, as blue as ever, shone with tears when she saw them. "Mamm, I never thought I would see you again! Come in, come in."

She stood aside as they walked in. Hannah took in the dirty room, George sitting in the one chair shoving his feet in his boots, and a couch in the corner, covered with a rumpled quilt, but Mamm only took Liesbet in her arms, having no thought of anything or anyone else.

"*Ach, mein liebchen, mein* Liesbetli." She murmured the words over and over.

George pushed past them and out the door without a word.

"We brought you some soup," Hannah said, when Mamm released Liesbet.

"Mamm's soup?" Liesbet breathed in the hearty aroma. "You can put it on the table there."

Hannah pushed some papers out of the way and set the pail down. Liesbet looked more ill than the last time she had seen her. Her once pretty face was swollen, distorting her features, and her skin was tinged with a yellowish gray.

"Liesbet, how . . ." Mamm looked around them at the crowded room, and then back at her daughter. "Are you all right?"

"Of course I am." She sat on the chair, motioning for them to sit on the couch. "George is looking for a new job. In the spring we'll go to Philadelphia or Pittsburgh where it will be easier for him." She spoke quickly but didn't look into their eyes as she talked. "And we're to have a baby, Mamm. Did you know that?"

"Hannah told me." Mamm's voice was quiet, a contrast to Liesbet's brittle prattle. "We brought you some things. Some clothes . . ." Her words faltered as she looked at Liesbet's clothes.

The blouse was pink, and her skirt a shade of red. Nothing else would have shown the change in Liesbet more than the disgust on her face when Mamm showed her the clothes she had brought.

"It was thoughtful of you, but George doesn't want me to be Plain. I'm a town lady, now, and I wear town clothes." Liesbet's chin lifted. Just as stubborn as ever.

"At least take these things I made for the little one. He wouldn't object to these, would he?"

Liesbet reached her hand out to stroke the tiny gown on the top of the bundle on Mamm's lap. "*Ne*, he wouldn't object to this."

"Liesbet, if you ever want to come home . . ."

Liesbet shook her head. "*Ne*. I won't. This is my home now. With George."

"But if something should happen, and you needed us, will you know how to find us?"

"*Ja*, Mamm." Liesbet sighed. Even after all this, she still turned from Mamm's offer. "I'll find you in Indiana. It shouldn't be hard."

Hannah turned from her sister and looked around the

filthy room. She should never have let Mamm come here only to have Liesbet reject her again.

Footsteps pounded on the stairs and Liesbet grabbed the bundle, wrapped it up, and stuffed it under the couch. George stopped in the doorway, blocking the light.

"They're still here? It's time for my dinner."

Liesbet's face turned red and she looked down. "Mamm and Hannah brought us some soup. Would you like that for your dinner?"

Hannah rose and grasped Mamm's hand. "We must be going. Daed is expecting us home."

Liesbet looked at them, her eyes wet. "How is he?"

"He doesn't know we've come."

As Hannah led Mamm out of the room, George was already dipping cold soup out of the bucket. Liesbet would be lucky to get a swallow of that nourishing food.

Liesbet closed the door behind them as Hannah stumbled down the steps, hardly able to see through her tears. They shouldn't have come. Now this would be the memory Mamm would have with her forever, Liesbet living in this squalor.

"Hannah?"

She stopped on the boardwalk as she heard her name called. It sounded like Josef.

"Hannah? Annalise?" Josef pushed through some men in front of the tavern. "What are you doing here?"

Mamm's tears were breaking through, and Hannah had to get her off the boardwalk. She helped her up onto the wagon seat, and then turned to Josef.

"We were visiting Liesbet."

"Liesbet lives here? You told me she was married."

Hannah dared to look into his face. His eyes were questioning, suspicious. What would he say when he learned the whole truth about her sister?

"She is married, but to an outsider. She lives in a room over this tavern."

Josef turned to look up the stairs. George stood at the top, watching them.

Josef took Hannah's arm and lifted her up into the wagon seat next to Annalise and then climbed up after her. This part of Lancaster was no place for two Amish women to be.

And Liesbet? He glanced back at the outside stairway of the tavern as he turned the horses toward the main street. She had joined the man on the landing at the top of the stairs and was watching them drive away. When Hannah had said her sister was married, he assumed it was to another Amish man, someone from their community. This wasn't marriage. That man had ruined a good girl and was now using her for his own benefit.

Josef shook the reins and the horses responded, moving faster through the rutted and muddy streets to the outskirts of town. Once that baby came, the man would abandon the two of them. He had seen the same thing played out before.

Once they were away from the noise of town, Josef pulled the horses to a stop. He rubbed the back of his neck, stiff and sore. His head ached. He turned to Hannah.

"What was going on back there?"

Annalise took Hannah's hand. The two women glanced at each other, and then Hannah said, "We wanted to visit Liesbet. Mamm hadn't seen her since she left home to get married."

"Is she under the *bann*?"

Hannah and Annalise glanced at each other again.

"Is she being shunned? Does the church know about this?"

Hannah shook her head. "*Ne*. She isn't yet baptized, but Daed won't let her come home until she repents."

"But you thought it would be all right to visit her today? Did Christian know about this?"

"Daed knew nothing of our plans." Hannah laid her hand on his sleeve. "Please, say nothing to him. It would upset him so."

Josef swallowed against the thick ball rising in his throat. How did he not know about Liesbet? Why had Hannah, and Christian, hidden it from him? He pressed the heel of one hand against his forehead. The headache that had plagued him all day was only getting worse.

"You know Christian didn't make his decision lightly, *ja*? He had his reasons, and a purpose. How will his decision stand if you take it into your mind to act as if his will doesn't exist?"

Hannah glanced at Mamm. She had never seen Josef so angry. "We just . . . just wanted to see her before we leave."

"So you went against Christian's wishes because you missed her?"

"It isn't like that, Josef Bender." Hannah felt the heat rising in her face. "You saw the way she was living. Shouldn't we show her mercy?"

Josef swung down from the wagon seat and handed the reins to her. "It depends. Is she repentant? Is she sorry for the way she's living and what she has done to the family?"

Hannah took the reins and threaded them between her forefingers and thumbs. They still held the heat from Josef's hands. He was right. Liesbet had shown no repentance. No sorrow. No wish that things could be different. She shook her head, and Josef gave her a quick nod.

"Then she should remain as she is—until she is ready to obey her *vater* and come back to her family, *ja*?"

She nodded as Mamm sobbed into her apron. The reins lost any warmth they had held. Her fingers were chilled, and the cold seeped up her arms and numbed her. She couldn't look at Josef as he paced away from the wagon and then back.

"And what of us, Hannah?" She dared to glance at him. His eyes were stony. "I need to think again about how suitable we are for each other . . . if I should align myself with a family who has a wayward daughter, and another daughter who would think so lightly of her *vater*'s wishes."

He turned on his heel and stalked away, up the Oregon Pike, toward Ephrata, leaving Hannah with a queasy stomach. Was he right? Was her sin as great as Liesbet's?

"We must go, Hannah." Mamm's face was red and blotchy. "I'm sorry I ever suggested we make this trip. We must go home, and I will confess all to your daed."

"*Ja*, we'll go home." Hannah clucked to the horses and shook the reins. She turned them to the right, up Butter Road.

As the team paced through the packed snow, Hannah's misery turned to anger. What right did Josef Bender have, talking to her in that way? They weren't married. They weren't even promised. It was Daed's place to determine if she and Mamm had been right to take the soup and clothes to Liesbet, not Josef's.

If there was anything she needed to convince her to stay on the Conestoga, it was Josef Bender. He could go west without her. She and Mamm together could convince Daed to forget this idea of moving. Liesbet needed them, whether she acknowledged it or not. He had to see that. And they wouldn't be able to help her—wouldn't be able to keep their family together—if they were living in the western wilderness.

She slapped the reins on the horses' backs. If only she knew how to convince Daed.

Regret dogged Josef's footsteps the entire sixteen miles to Ephrata, each step like walking through sludge, his head throbbing. Had he been too harsh with Hannah?

Ne. His feet squeaked in the packed snow. *Ne.* If anything, he wasn't harsh enough. Liesbet had chosen her path in life, and if Christian hoped to bring her back to the family and their faith, Hannah needed to obey his wishes. But from the glimpse he had of Liesbet, she had already taken herself beyond the hope of repentance.

It was too bad. The Yoders were a fine family. At least he had thought so. And to think he thought Hannah would make a good wife . . . He stopped in the road, stepping aside to let a wagon go past him. His head spun.

Hannah.

He looked behind him, down the road toward Lancaster. The sun was disappearing behind the trees, and it was nearly suppertime. She and Annalise would be home by now. Had they told Christian of their trip to Lancaster? What would his reaction be?

In the hours he had spent working with Christian and talking with him, he hadn't seemed like one of the progressives who wanted to eliminate the *bann* from the church. He would apply the same principles in his own family.

"What would a church be without discipline?" had been Christian's words, and Josef had agreed.

He took a step up the road again, and then another, his feet tired and sore. Only a mile or so to go, and then he'd be at the Nafsingers'. They'd let him stay as long as he needed . . . even until they left for Ohio. They wouldn't need to travel with the Yoders and Hertzlers. He wouldn't have to see Hannah again.

And yet . . . He rubbed the back of his neck as a sudden thought came to him. When he and Christian had discussed the *bann*, Liesbet was already married to that outsider. She had left her family. Christian was already praying for Liesbet's return, and as painful as it must have been for him, he supported the *bann*.

So where did Hannah get her rebellion? From her mother? But Annalise seemed to be in complete agreement with her husband on matters of faith.

Josef rubbed his neck again, his hand cold against his hot skin. Something about this situation didn't seem right.

He quickened his pace as the light in the window of the Nafsinger house came into view. Home. Or at least as close to a home as he had ever had here in America. A sick feeling went through his stomach again. He had thought to make a home with Hannah . . . but now that would never be.

Stepping onto the porch of the old log home, Josef knocked on the door as he opened it.

"Hallo? Anyone here?"

Mary Nafsinger turned from the fireplace as he came in. "Josef! My boy, it's so good to see you, and such a surprise."

She grasped his arms and pulled him down to give him a kiss on either cheek. "And you're just in time for supper. Did Daniel know you were coming?"

"I didn't decide to make the trip until this morning. I thought I would stay for a few days, if that is all right with you."

"*Ja, ja, ja.* Your room is just the way you left it, and we'll welcome your company."

Thumps sounded from the front porch, making Josef smile. Daniel stomped his feet on the porch before coming in, whether there was snow or not. Even summer dust got stomped off before he came into the house. It was another sound he had missed while he was away.

"I thought I heard Mary talking to someone," Daniel said. He took off his muffler and coat before taking Josef's hand. "Mama, you have a place set at the table for this boy, *ja?*"

"*Ach, ja.*" Mary bustled around the room, putting food on the table and setting a place for Josef. She was short and round, her skirts swishing as she moved on quick feet, and every time she passed by him, she patted Josef on the arm.

"What brings you this way?" Daniel motioned for him to sit at the table.

"Christian wanted me to discuss some things with you, and I had been wondering how you were both getting along."

"We're doing fine." Mary patted him again as she leaned over to put a plate of ham on the table, and then she took her own seat.

It wasn't until after supper was finished and the evening prayers were said that Daniel settled in his chair at the side of the fireplace and was ready to talk business.

"What is it Christian wanted to discuss?"

344

Josef sat heavily in his usual seat beside Daniel. Why were his legs so tired? Today's walk hadn't been unusual, except for his worry about Hannah.

Mary sat on the other side of Daniel in her rocking chair. She was darning stockings while they talked.

"Elias Hertzler wants to leave a week later than what we had talked about. He hasn't been able to sell all of his stock yet and asked if we could leave the second week of March."

Daniel lit his pipe with a piece of kindling and then threw the stick into the fire. "That shouldn't be a problem. The folks buying this place want to be in before it's time to plant the garden, but they can go ahead and plant the early crops while we're still in the house."

Mary looked up from her darning. "What about that girl of yours? Will you have the wedding before we leave or hasn't that been decided yet?"

Josef felt his face grow hot as he rubbed the back of his neck. "I don't think I'll be courting her any longer. In fact, I think I'll stop in Ohio with you."

"Has something happened?" Daniel leaned forward in his chair. "The last time we talked, you said she was the perfect partner for you."

"I've learned some things about the family since then."

Daniel leaned back in his chair again and drew from his pipe. "Things that prevent you from marrying Hannah?"

Josef's head rang with the dull throbbing of a hammer hitting an anvil. The more he thought about seeing Hannah in Lancaster this morning, the stronger the headache became. He nodded, his throat tight and sore.

"I saw her and her mother this morning in Lancaster, visiting Hannah's sister, who is living there. She's married to an outsider." He rubbed at his forehead, willing the pain away. "I can't marry someone who disregards her *vater's* wishes . . ."

The fire swam in front of his eyes. What was wrong with him? He leaned forward, sounds roaring in his ears, and then he hit the floor and knew no more.

31

Christian turned in his bed once more, trying not to disturb Annalise. Her body, growing larger with the child inside her, was cumbersome. She was uncomfortable most of the time, and while she could sleep, he didn't want to wake her.

But why was sleep eluding him tonight? Most likely because of the same thing that had been preying on his mind ever since Friday, when Annalise and Hannah had come home with their confession of visiting Liesbet.

Liesbetli. His little Liesbetli. Late that night, when the children had gone to bed, Annalise had told him of how Liesbet was living. The dirty room above the tavern, the coarse language of the people around them, her husband's crude ways. And he was helpless. Liesbet had chosen her life among outsiders, and all they could do was to let her go her way.

But why would she choose such a path? Why, when her home was here?

A horse grunted in the yard, and the jangle of chains and

rumble of wagon wheels brought Christian to his feet. He had his trousers on and was pulling on his boots when the pounding came at the door.

"What is it?" Annalise's voice sounded sleepy.

"I'll go see. You stay here."

The pounding sounded again as Christian made his way through the dark kitchen to the door.

"*Ja, ja*, who is it?"

He opened the door to a stranger. An *Englischer*. The man leaned against the doorframe on one hand as if exhausted. His face was drawn, his eyes haunted. He pulled off his cap and gestured to the wagon behind him.

"It's Lizzie. She's in a bad way, she is, and I didn't know where else to take her." He wiped his hand over his face and grabbed at Christian's shirt. "You've got to help her. The baby. It's coming, and it's too early. There's something wrong."

The man's words slowly filtered into Christian's mind. There was a woman in the wagon . . . the man looked familiar.

"George McIvey?" Hannah's voice came from behind him. "What are you doing here? Where is Liesbet?"

The pieces fell into place. This man was Liesbet's husband. So the woman . . . He pushed past George and ran to the wagon. He could see nothing in the dark, but he heard the moans of his daughter.

"Liesbet, are you all right?"

"Daed? Daed, help me. I'm going to die."

"*Ne*, daughter. Don't say that. You're home now. Your mamm will help you."

George helped him pull the pallet of blankets to the edge

of the wagon bed, and they pulled Liesbet to a sitting position. Between them, they carried her into the house. Annalise met them in the kitchen, and they took her into the warm bedroom behind the fireplace.

Annalise lit the lantern, and Hannah lit candles around the room to give more light. His Liesbetli lay on the bed, swollen and distorted. Her face was pale. She clutched at Annalise's hand while Hannah lifted the sleeping William from his bed and took him out of the room.

"Mamm." Liesbet's voice was weak. "Mamm, it hurts so much."

"*Ja, ja, ja.*" Annalise stood and shooed Christian and George out of the room.

Christian caught Annalise's hand. "What is wrong?"

His wife caught her bottom lip between her teeth. "I'm not sure. It could be that the baby is coming, but it's too soon. It's much too soon." Hannah came back downstairs and Annalise pulled her into the bedroom. "Let us take care of this." She glanced back at Liesbet lying on the bed. "And Christian, pray."

She closed the door and he was left alone. *Ne,* not alone. He lit the lamp on the table and saw the man, George, staring at him.

"Will she be all right?"

Christian looked at him, this man who had stolen his daughter. The smell of stale liquor filled the room, and Christian longed to open a window. Even throw the man out of it. But this was Liesbet's husband. The father of his grandchild. He could only shake his head in answer to the man's question.

"It is in God's hands. We will wait and see."

Sounds filtered through the bedroom door. Liesbet's

moans. Annalise's comforting voice. Christian motioned for George to take a seat at the table and then sat down across from him. He tried to pray, but he couldn't take his eyes off the other man's face.

Liesbet's moans became a cry, and George stiffened. At least it seemed he cared for his wife. That was good.

Hannah came out of the room and took a kettle of hot water from over the banked fire.

"Hannah? Is she all right?"

She looked from him to George and laid her hand on his shoulder. "Mamm says she's having the baby, and it will be soon."

Christian squeezed her hand, and then she went into the bedroom, closing the door behind her, leaving him alone with George again. Liesbet's moans grew louder, the cries more frequent.

George rose to his feet at one loud cry, but Christian waved him to his seat again. "My Annalise has given birth nine times. She will do the best she can. We can only pray and wait."

"But what if she . . ." George buried his face in his hands. "I didn't mean for this to happen. I thought she was like other girls . . ."

"What do you mean?"

George rubbed his short beard. "Other girls let you, you know, fool around. If something happens, they take care of it. But Lizzie—"

"Don't call her that. Her name is Liesbet." Christian's own words felt hard and biting in his mouth.

He nodded. "But Liesbet, she got to me. She reminds me of my ma, back in Ireland. I didn't want this to happen to her."

"It's too late now, isn't it? You take a young girl from her home, you have no means to care for her, and you let drink rule your life. What did you expect would happen?"

"But I love her."

Christian held himself in his seat so he wouldn't smash the man's face in. "You love her?" His voice rose in spite of trying to control it. "You love her? This isn't love."

Liesbet's cries grew louder, and George buried his head in his arms. "I can't stand to listen to her."

"You can't stand it? Think how she feels." Christian's voice broke. "Think what my Liesbetli is going through." He rubbed his face, barely keeping himself from crashing the door down and going to Liesbet's side. How could he help her? What could he do?

There was a last scream, and then silence.

George's head snapped up. "What is it? What's happened?"

The silence stretched into seconds. Minutes. And then sobbing. It was Annalise, sobbing as if her heart was breaking. Christian jumped to his feet, knocking over his chair, and ran to the bedroom door.

Hannah still grasped her sister's hand when the bedroom door opened. Daed stumbled in to kneel next to Mamm on the other side of the bed, wrapping his arms around her as she wept.

George stood in the doorway, and then took one step into the room. "Is she all right? What happened?"

Hannah looked at Liesbet's face, distorted in the agony of the pains she had endured, and reached to close the eyelids. She rose and went to George, pulling him out of the room, away from Mamm's sobbing anguish.

"Liesbet is dead."

George ran his hand over his face. He turned to look into the room behind them, and back at Hannah. "She . . . she can't be. She isn't. She's only sleeping . . . you know . . . you know she sleeps so soundly." He crumpled onto the bench at the kitchen table while Hannah righted the chair, setting it in its place.

Liesbet was dead. Her sister, lost to them forever.

"And the . . . the baby?" George whispered the question, as if he didn't want to hear the answer.

"She died before . . . before . . ." Hannah couldn't continue. She dashed away the tears streaming down her cheeks.

George rose, looking around as if he didn't know where he was. "I can't . . . I can't . . ." He stumbled around the table, grabbing his discarded muffler, and then wrenched open the door. He turned to look at Hannah, his face twisted. "Tell your da . . ." He shook his head as if to shake away the events of the night. "Tell your da I'm sorry. I'm sorry."

He left, pulling the door closed behind him. The horse whinnied and the wagon wheels squealed in the frosty air, and then he was gone.

Hannah went to the bedroom door. Daed and Mamm held each other in their weeping while silent tears dripped from her cheeks. She wiped them away and closed the door. The sky outside the kitchen window was turning a pale pink. Morning would be here soon and the children would be hungry.

Numb, she opened the trap door to the cellar and, taking the lamp from the table, went down the ladder to the larder. Mamm had cooked cornmeal yesterday, and the mush was waiting. A solid loaf ready to be sliced for the family's breakfast. Hannah took it and climbed back up the ladder, one rung at a time. The trap door opening loomed above her. Would she ever reach the top of the ladder?

She set the lamp and loaf pan on the table, her hands trembling so that she nearly dropped them. Here, in the kitchen, she could hear Mamm's sobs through the closed door. The tears streamed faster, blurring her vision.

A sudden memory washed over her. Nine-year-old Hannah, huddled in her bed upstairs, alone. Just as she was now. Daed in the cemetery with Jacob. He had taken two shovels for them to dig the graves. And Mamm in her bedroom with Liesbet, kneeling by the bedside.

Hannah had gotten out of her bed, shaky from the fever, and crept down the stairs to the kitchen. She saw Mamm through the bedroom door and Liesbet on the bed, lying so still. She had looked into the parlor, and there, on a platform made of sawhorses and boards, were three small forms. The biggest one was Hansli, then Fanny, and last of all, little Catherine, wrapped in a shawl.

And death. A shadowy presence in the room then and filling the house now. Death. She had been the one to bring it in. And she had to face it alone.

Just like this morning. She couldn't fight death. She could only stand aside and let it have its way. Let it take whomever it wanted.

If only . . . if only Liesbet had listened to her when she told her to leave George McIvey alone. If only she had done something, anything, to keep them apart. If only she had told Daed sooner . . . But she hadn't wanted to believe it could be true that her sister would go with an outsider.

Footsteps sounded on the stairs and Jacob came into the kitchen, rubbing his hands through his hair and yawning.

"What is William doing, sleeping in my bed? I nearly rolled on top of him."

"Shh." Hannah hushed him. "I put him with you. It's the only place I could think of . . ."

Jacob stopped and leaned toward her. He lifted her chin with his finger. "You're crying." He looked toward the bedroom. "What has happened?"

"*Ach*, Jacob . . ." Her tears overcame her. Jacob sat next to her and took her in his arms. He patted her shoulders and rubbed her back as she related the night's events.

"And you're sitting out here alone?"

Hannah nodded.

"And Mamm and Daed, in their room?" She nodded again and he held her close to him. She had never noticed how strong his arms had become. "We can't let this happen again, Hannah."

"What do you mean?"

"When the little ones died, you and I, Liesbet, Mamm and Daed, we all grieved alone. And look what that did to Mamm. Look what it did to you. And look what it did to Liesbet. It tore our family apart." He released her and she drew back, wiping her cheeks again. "I won't let that happen again. We're a family, and we're going to face this together."

Jacob rose and opened the door of the bedroom. He hesitated, and then went in. He lifted Daed up by the arm, and together they helped Mamm to her feet. He led them back to the kitchen, closing the door behind them. Daed took all three of them into his embrace. Hannah could feel Mamm's arms around her, holding her close. Jacob stood behind her, his head leaning on hers. They were together. A family. Together in their sorrow.

32

Josef woke one morning and felt like he had enough energy to move his legs for the first time in days. Mary Nafsinger opened his door, a bowl in her hand.

"Josef, you're awake."

"It feels like I've slept the winter away." He scooted into a sitting position, leaning against the head of the bed, and reached for the bowl of porridge. It smelled wonderful. "How many days have I been sick?"

"You arrived last Friday, and today is Thursday. Nearly a week."

He tasted a spoonful of the porridge. Mary had sweetened it with maple syrup, and suddenly he was starving. He scooped up another spoonful.

"Eat slowly. You don't want to put too much in your stomach at first." Mary straightened his covers and patted his knee. "I'll be in the next room, so don't hesitate to call me if you need anything."

"*Ja*, for sure." Josef took another bite of the porridge, savoring the sweet flavor.

He had been in bed for nearly a week? He remembered Mary and Daniel coming in and out of the room, feeding him meals he didn't want and talking about things he didn't care about. Nothing had interested him. But today the thoughts running through his mind lingered, and he found that he was interested.

One of the thoughts was Hannah. Had she come to visit him, or was that only a dream? He set the half-empty bowl of porridge on the bedside table, suddenly tired again. He got up to use the chamber pot, but by the time he sat back down on the bed, he was exhausted. As he lay down, feeling for the covers with his feet, he pushed away thoughts of Hannah. She was lost to him. He would never see her again.

He closed his eyes, letting sleep take over. At least when he slept, he didn't think of her.

Two days later, Josef felt strong enough to get dressed and join Daniel in the barn. The big old place seemed empty without the pigs Daniel usually kept in the far pen, and no sheep. Even the chickens were fewer, with only a half dozen pecking through the bedding around the horses' stalls.

"It's good to see you up and around." Daniel leaned on his pitchfork as Josef opened the barn door.

"It feels good too." Josef sat down on a stool near Daniel's workbench. The short walk from the house had been tiring. He gazed around the barn, taking in the tools hanging on the walls, harnesses, the old farm wagon, the grain bins . . .

"How much of all this will you be taking to Ohio?"

Daniel followed his gaze. "Only the horses and harnesses. The rest is staying here. We sold nearly everything along with the farm. It will be easier to make new when we get to Ohio, and we won't need most of the farming equipment."

"What will you do without it? How will you work?"

"I'll be working with my oldest son, and he has all the implements we need." Daniel finished cleaning one stall and moved to the next. "Were you serious about coming to Ohio with us instead of Indiana?"

Josef nodded. "*Ja*."

"You're changing all your plans?" Daniel peered at him.

Josef knew the older man was trying to read his expression in the dim light. "Things are over between Hannah and me, and I don't want to live in the same area as her family. You can understand that, *ja*?"

"What I don't understand is what happened to make you change your mind."

Josef dug his heel into the straw-covered dirt. He didn't want to relive that memory again. "Hannah's sister married an outsider."

"*Ja*, you told us that."

"But then Hannah and her mother went to visit Liesbet, against Christian's wishes." He held Daniel's gaze with his own. He was in the right. No Amish minister would disagree with him.

"Did you ask them why?"

"Of course. Hannah said they wanted to see Liesbet one last time before they went west." He dug with his heel in the dirt some more. "They disobeyed her *vater*, which is the same as if they went against the *bann*. I can't marry someone who takes discipline so lightly."

Daniel moved an empty keg nearer to the bench and sat, facing him. "Let me ask you, what is the purpose of the *bann*?"

"To shame the person who has committed a sin and to separate the sin from the church, *ja*?"

"Not exactly. If it was only that, what good would it do?"

Josef couldn't answer. What good could ever come from shunning?

"The purpose of the *bann* is to cause the guilty person to see their own sin as shameful, and then to turn back to the Lord in repentance." Daniel smoothed his beard as he spoke. "It also exists for the protection of the church, that willful sinners within the body would not cause God to censure it. When Christian's daughter married an outsider, she willfully sinned against God, her family, and if she had been baptized, the church."

"Would someone like Liesbet ever come back to the faith? I saw her. There was no sign of repentance in her."

"What did Hannah and Annalise do when they visited her?"

"They took her some food, and some clothes."

"A mission of mercy, then."

Josef shifted on the bench. "*Ja*, I suppose you could call it that."

"Christ commands us to have mercy on our brethren and to help anyone who is in need, even our bitterest enemy. By showing mercy to her sister, Hannah was following our Lord's commands."

"But the *bann* disallows eating with such people or having any dealings with them."

"Was there any evidence that what Hannah and Annalise

did was anything more than a short visit to supply the girl with needed items?"

Josef shook his head.

"And how are we to know that her act of mercy didn't soften her sister's heart? Perhaps the Lord is bringing her back to her family even now."

Josef smoothed the dirt he had been digging at with his foot. "I need to apologize to Hannah."

Daniel laid his hand on Josef's shoulder. "*Ja*, and pray for Liesbet. Pray that she will come to repentance and restoration to the Lord." He rose from his seat. "It is dinnertime. Are you coming in?"

"In a few minutes."

The older man left him alone in the barn. In the dim silence, small sounds became noticeable. The whoosh of a horse's breath, the scratching of the hens, the drip of water from the roof. The weather had turned while he had been in bed. Spring was coming, and along with it, the move west.

He must apologize to Hannah. Would she accept him back?

The dream of the farm in the forests of Indiana with Hannah by his side came rushing back from the place he had tried to hide it. *Ja*, the path was clear. *Ja*, he knew what he wanted, and the future, with Hannah, would be one to look forward to.

But only if Hannah would forgive him.

Hannah sat next to Liesbet's grave, smoothing the mound of newly turned earth. For so many years, she couldn't understand Mamm's obsession with this place, with visiting the little ones' graves, but now she was spellbound by the peaceful quiet. It was a balm to her empty heart. Losing Adam was difficult to bear, but he was pursuing his dreams. Losing Josef—her mouth quivered. She didn't know she would miss him so.

And Liesbet. Poor Liesbet.

Her sister had been buried quietly. The Hertzlers brought dinner, but only Mamm, Daed, and the children had attended the burial. Liesbet had died while unrepentant and living in sin. The congregation's elder had offered comforting words, and their family had been together. Liesbet's death had united them as a family in a way nothing else would have.

She rose from the grass and sat on the low stone wall surrounding the little cemetery. They would be leaving for Indiana in a week. No one would care for Liesbet's grave. Did it matter? Her body was in the grave, but her soul . . . her soul was in God's hands.

A sound behind her made her turn. Josef stood, his hands clasped behind his back. He looked pale and tired.

"Hannah." He nodded to her, then made his way over the low stone wall and sat next to her. He straightened his coat, and then his hat, but didn't look at her. He stared at the new grave.

"Josef." She returned his greeting. She hadn't seen him since he had left her at the side of the road outside Lancaster.

"I stopped by the house. Your *vater* told me what happened."

She had no answer for him.

"I came to tell you . . . to ask for your forgiveness."

"Forgiveness for what?"

He turned to look at her then, and reached over to take her hand. "I ask you to forgive me for being so judgmental. I didn't take the time to ask what you were doing in Lancaster that day, but assumed you were in the wrong."

She nodded, looking at the new grass along the stone wall. Spring had come while she had been in the depths of her grief. Had she and Mamm been wrong to seek out Liesbet that day? If they hadn't, would George have thought to bring her home for her final suffering?

"It has taken you a long time to come home."

"I was ill."

Hannah forgot everything she might have said. "What kind of illness?"

"I made it to the Nafsingers that day when I last saw you, but fell ill that night. Mary Nafsinger called it influenza."

"Influenza? That's a dangerous disease." Hannah leaned forward to search his face for lingering effects. "You will have to be careful and not work too hard. If it comes on you again, it will be worse than before."

Josef smiled. A tired smile on his narrow face. She hadn't noticed how sunken his cheeks were. "I'll be careful." He rubbed the back of her hand with his thumb. "You haven't answered my question. Will you forgive me?"

"Are you sure you're the one who needs to be forgiven? Wasn't I the one who had disobeyed Daed?"

He fixed his gaze on her hand. "I had a talk with Daniel, and he showed me I was wrong in being angry with you. And now I find I was more wrong than I thought. Liesbet needed you and her family. Who knows? Perhaps she did repent before it was too late."

"I think she did. She asked for Mamm to forgive her before she . . . before she died. If she could ask Mamm, she could surely ask our Lord, couldn't she?"

Josef let go of her hand and put his arm around her shoulders, pulling her close to him. "Have you heard anything from her husband?"

Hannah shook her head, and then let it rest on his shoulder. His arm was so comforting. "Not since that night. We don't know where he went, or what he's doing."

"He is in God's hands though, *ja*?"

"*Ja*." She rubbed the edge of his coat between her fingers. A good, broadcloth coat, made to last many seasons, but beginning to wear at the edges. Who would make him a new one when the time came? "The last time I saw you," she sat up, away from his embrace, "you said you didn't think we were suited for one another after all. Have you changed your mind again?"

"I was wrong to say that, Hannah. I was angry . . . and self-righteous . . . and disappointed. I should have trusted you."

She looked across the cemetery to where the Conestoga flowed. Even from here, the sound of its springtime laughter carried on the breeze. Its restlessness pulled at her, tugging at her to follow it to the west. Toward the river, across the mountains, to a future home in the wilderness of Indiana.

"*Ja*, Josef Bender. I forgive you." She turned to smile at him and he took her hand again.

"*Denki*. I hope I never do something so foolish and need your forgiveness again."

"Never is a long time. We will most likely need to forgive each other quite a few times before we reach the end."

"The end of what?"

"The end of our road together."

He put his arm around her and pulled her close, resting his chin on her kapp. "And that is going to be a long, long road."

33

Josef ran his hand over the board he was sanding. Smooth as silk. The ash Christian had chosen for the toolbox was well seasoned and fine grained. Christian had taken it from the stacks of lumber left from the days when his father had a lively wagon-building business years ago.

Across the main room of the barn, Christian and Jacob were installing the wagon bows. They grunted as they wrestled the long oak staves, dripping and hot from being steamed for more than an hour, and turned them into the U-shape needed to hold the wagon cover. Josef ached to help them, but his muscles were still too weak from his illness.

"Take the jobs that require the small tools and the fine work," Christian had said. "We don't want you wearing yourself out. We need your strength on the trail."

So Josef sat, sanding small boards, building the toolbox, the lazy seat, barrels, and other small pieces that would be attached to the wagon at the last minute.

The big wagon was impressive. Josef thrilled to watch the

pieces come together. Sixteen feet long, with a bowed bottom and high sides, the Conestoga wagons were unlike anything Josef had ever seen before. They looked more like ships than the farm wagons he was accustomed to.

As the last bow was set into place, Josef left his work and joined Jacob and Christian to admire the new wagon.

"It's beautiful."

Christian grinned at him as he wiped the sweat off his face with a rag. "She is, isn't she?" He ran his hand along the side with a loving sweep. "My daed and I built many wagons just like this when I was a boy. I never thought I'd make one this big for myself."

Christian walked around the wagon, testing each of the new bows.

"The other wagon," Josef said, walking over to the smaller, green one off to the side, "did you make this one, also?"

"It was the last one Daed made. I helped with a lot of the heavier work, but you can see here—" Christian walked over and pointed underneath the wagon—"his work. He had a unique way of building the undercarriage so the axles always ran smooth and rarely broke. I used the same technique on the new one." He patted the smaller wagon with loving hands. "She's been a good wagon."

"Why didn't you paint both of them the same?"

"I thought about painting it green, to match the smaller one, but Annalise likes the traditional blue. So I painted it to please her." Christian turned to Josef, his eyes moist as they had been lately whenever he spoke of his wife. "We should be getting in. I'm sure supper is ready, and we need to clean up."

Josef nodded his agreement and followed the others to the

house. Pleasing his wife was the perfect way to start a marriage. Whatever she asked, he would give her if he was able.

All through the simple supper, Josef kept staring at her. Hannah kept herself busy with caring for William or Margli, but every time she looked up, Josef's eyes were on her.

She had seen very little of him since their talk in the cemetery. He had spent his days in the barn with Daed and Jacob, working as fast as they could to finish the new wagon before their departure to Indiana next week. She and Mamm had been just as busy, storing linens in boxes, dismantling the loom and getting it ready for travel, preparing food to last them for the journey. And through it all, in spite of the nearness of Liesbet's death, she had felt a curious lightness in her heart, as if she was looking forward to leaving the Conestoga . . .

Ne, not leaving, but an anticipation of her unfolding future. As light and daring as a spring breeze, the far mountains beckoned her. It was an adventure to look forward to.

And then there was Josef. He had said the love grew, but how far? And how fast?

She looked across the table at him and caught him staring again. She smiled as he grinned at her. How far would their road together last? Into the future. Warmth spread through her at the pleasant thought.

After family prayers and the younger children were in bed, Josef leaned close to her as she sat on the bench by the fire, knitting.

"Would you come for a walk with me?"

She looked up from her knitting. "Tonight? In the dark?"

He took her hand. "*Ja*, it's a beautiful night—warm, pleasant—there is no moon, but the stars are bright."

He stood, pulling her up after him. He helped her put on her shawl, and they stepped out into the night.

Hannah let him choose their route. The ground was too wet to try to walk down by the creek in the dark, so he stayed on the farm lane and walked toward the orchard.

"Do you remember the first time we talked?"

"*Ja*. It was here, in the orchard." So long ago, and so much had happened since that day.

"You kept trying to get me to notice your sister."

"And you seemed determined to keep Adam out of my life."

Josef stopped her, turning her toward him. "I think I loved you from the first moment I saw you."

"You didn't even know me."

He cupped her cheek in his hand. "*Ne*, but I started knowing you then. Do you remember what I said?"

She smiled. He had been so serious that day, and his accent had intrigued her. "You said you wanted to court me. That you were looking for a wife."

His thumb stroked her cheek. "I know your heart lies here, Hannah, on this land, along the Conestoga."

She started to shake her head, to protest, but he raised his other hand to hold her face between them. "I want to make you happy, and I want you to be my wife. I think we should settle in Indiana, with your family. You will need them and they will need you. But more than that, I want to marry you. Will you, Hannah? Will you marry me?"

"Mamm told me once that when I married, my heart would lie with my husband." She looked into Josef's eyes, gray in the starlight. "She was right." She laid her hands on his coat, above his heart. "This is where my heart truly lies, with you. We will live wherever you think is right."

"And you will be my wife?"

She smiled, all doubt gone. "*Ja*, Josef Bender. I will be your wife."

He bent down to kiss her, enfolding her in his arms and drawing her close. But he didn't stop with one kiss. He shifted and drew her closer. "This is my promise, Hannah Yoder. I will love you as long as I have breath." He smiled and kissed her nose, her cheeks, and then kissed her lips again.

34

The day of the wedding, the Monday before the families were to leave for the west, was warm and clear. Hannah rose early to help Mamm with the last of the packing before the elder and other church members arrived.

"Hannah," said Mamm as they filled a barrel with bedding, "with all the preparation for the move, we have no time to do anything special for your wedding."

"We don't need to." Hannah rolled a coverlet up and tucked it between a stack of blankets and the side of the barrel. "The ones who are coming won't expect any more than what we usually do for a church service—even less, since they know we are leaving tomorrow."

"But I wanted it to be a special day for you."

"It will be." Hannah smiled as she took the barrel's lid from Mamm. "I'm marrying the most wonderful man in the world, and what could be more special than that?" She laid the lid on the barrel and nailed it down.

Mamm looked around them at the empty parlor. "I think that was the last barrel to pack. The rest are things we'll be using along the way, and we won't need to pack them until this afternoon." She winced as she stretched, leaning back with her hands supporting her back.

"Are you all right?" Hannah eyed Mamm's growing middle. She had said the baby wouldn't come until summer, but could she be wrong?

"It's just the extra work that strains my back. Soon enough, I'll have nothing to keep me busy except riding in the wagon and watching the world go by."

"I'm glad Daed thought to make a place to sit in the wagon. It would have been a long walk to Indiana." Hannah caught sight of movement out the front window. "It's the Hertzlers." She ran out to meet Johanna.

"Are you ready for your wedding?" Johanna's face looked happier than her own.

"For sure I am. There's nothing to get ready for, as long as I have Josef."

Magdalena shooed the girls away. "You two go off and talk and let me help Annalise."

"Come, Johanna." Hannah pulled at her friend's hand. "You can help me pack Margli's things."

They ran up the stairs to Hannah's room. All her things were packed in her chest already, but Margli's new chest, made by Josef after the wagon was finished, stood open and empty. Johanna picked up a coverlet and started folding it.

"Where will you and Josef spend your first night together? Here?"

Hannah felt her face turning red. "*Ne*. If we stayed here, we'd have to sleep in the parlor with Daniel and Mary."

"The Nafsingers? When did they arrive?"

"On Saturday. Josef drove our wagon up to Ephrata to load their things into it and drove them back here to spend the Sabbath and then be here for the wedding."

"I suppose you could just sleep in your own bed, and Josef with the boys, just as you have been doing."

She glanced at her friend just in time to see her face break into a smile.

"You know I'm teasing you. But what do you have planned?"

"Josef and I will start on the road to Indiana right after the wedding. He said we'll go as far as the ferry and cross the Susquehanna, and then find a place to camp for the night. We'll wait there for the rest of you to catch up with us in the morning."

Johanna grabbed her hand and pulled her down to sit on Margli's bed next to her. "What is it like?"

"What do you mean?"

"To be in love. You barely know Josef, and now you're marrying him. Is it wonderful?"

Hannah laced her hands around her knees. "Wonderful? *Ja*, but it's so much more than that." She stared out the window at the blue sky. "You know how in the Good Book it says that when two people marry, they become one flesh?"

Johanna nodded.

She held her hands in front of her, separating the laced fingers, and then joining them again. "It's like this. Once Josef and I were two separate people. But as we learned to know each other and our love grew, we became closer and closer, until today we'll be joined together forever."

"You mean, you didn't fall in love with him all at once?" Johanna's voice sounded disappointed and Hannah laughed.

"*Ne*. At first, I didn't like him very much. I thought he was a little forward, talking about courting the first time we met."

"And there was Adam."

"*Ja*, there was Adam." Hannah had talked to Hilda last Friday. She said Adam had left Philadelphia and gone to Massachusetts where the abolitionist movement was even stronger. Their lives had taken different paths so quickly, and now Adam was gone. She still missed the boy he had been.

"So, what made you fall in love with Josef?"

Hannah lay back on the bed, staring at the ceiling. "It was little things. Bit by bit, our love grew, until I couldn't imagine my life without him in it."

Johanna lay back next to her. "Maybe that's what will happen with Jacob."

"You're still hoping he'll notice you?"

"Don't you think he could learn to love me?"

Hannah sat back up. "I guess. I've never thought of Jacob that way—as a husband to someone."

Mamm called from downstairs. "Hannah! It's nearly time. Are you ready?"

"We need to get Margli's box packed and I need to put my best dress on."

"You get dressed." Johanna stood up and started folding Margli's extra clothes. "I'll do this, and we'll be downstairs in time."

Hannah hurried to put on her blue dress and white apron, folding her brown dress and her everyday black apron in her box. She paused as she lowered the lid. When she opened it again, she would be Josef's wife.

Almost the entire congregation had come to the wedding, even those from the far side of Pequea Creek. Since today was Monday, rather than the Sabbath, families drove their wagons, making the trip easier. Neighbors had been invited to come also, and the Metzlers were there, with a few other Mennonite and Brethren families from along the Conestoga.

There was a festive air, with makeshift tables being set up for the dinner afterward, and people visiting in the warm spring air, but Hannah didn't notice any of it. Josef stood at the side of the yard, talking with Daniel and Jacob, and he was the only person she cared to look at.

Finally the ministers called them all into the house where benches had been set up. Hannah sat between Mamm and Johanna, listening to the sermons exhorting the congregation to take marriage as a sacred trust. She heard again the stories of Isaac and Rebecca, of Ruth and Boaz. She and Josef were entering a stream that had flowed from Adam and Eve until now, and would flow into the future. Two people, marrying in the sight of God, starting a family dedicated to him.

She glanced across the room to Josef and found him watching her. He grinned, and then turned back to the minister. Suddenly, the preaching seemed very long.

But then it was time. She and Josef stood before the congregation and took their vows. They promised to love each other, to bear with each other patiently, to help each other.

After their vows, they returned to their seats and knelt for the final prayer. As she knelt on the hard floor, Hannah's heart seemed like it would burst within her. She and Josef were wed, and they would soon start on their life together. What would the future bring? Her parents had known heartache, his mother had been widowed when he was a young boy. They had no guarantees theirs would be a happy life. But whatever happened, they would face it together.

Soon after the noon meal had been eaten, Josef found her in a crowd of women.

"If we are to make it across the Susquehanna today, we must be going."

Hannah said goodbye to the people of the congregation, but for her best friend and her family, she only needed quick hugs. They would see each other the next day. Josef had already finished loading the wagon and had hitched a four-horse team to it. These were new horses, ones Hannah didn't know, but it wouldn't take long to learn each one's name.

They started walking down the farm lane toward the road, and Hannah stopped, looking back.

Josef stopped and put his arm around her. "What is it?"

"I had forgotten, with the wedding and the busyness of the last week, this is the last time I'll ever see this farm."

"Do you regret leaving?"

Hannah took in the smokehouse, the old cabin, the big limestone house, the chicken coop, the large barn, and off by itself, the cemetery where Liesbet and the little ones lay. She shook her head. "*Ne*, I don't regret it, but . . ."

"But you'll miss this place."

"Not just the place, but the way things were. I miss when Liesbet and Fanny and I used to play together in the orchard. I miss the long afternoons watching the creek flow by. I miss it all." Hannah turned to look at Josef and stroked his cheek. "But those things are of the past, and I'll always have them in my memory. You are my future."

Josef bent to kiss her, a kiss of promise, and then they turned and started down the road toward the west.

Read an excerpt from
Book 2 in the

JOURNEY TO
PLEASANT PRAIRIE

series

COMING FALL 2016

1

"Mattie."

Mattie Schrock ignored Naomi, intent on the flutter of wings she spied through the branches of the tree, pulling her attention from wringing the water out of Daed's shirt. She leaned as far toward the edge of the covered porch as she could, her toes clinging to the worn wooden planks. The bird wouldn't hold still. What kind was it?

"It's your turn to hang the laundry. I have to help *Mamm* get dinner ready." Naomi shoved the basket of wet clothes toward the porch steps with her foot.

Mattie gave up on identifying the bird. Hanging laundry wasn't Mattie's favorite chore, even though it meant she was able to be in the yard instead of in the hot kitchen. She picked up the heavy basket and rested it on her hip as she took the bag of clothes pegs from the hook next to the porch steps. "Your turn is next week, then."

Naomi pulled the stopper from the washtub and let the water drain onto the flower bed in the yard below the porch. "I'd rather hang clothes than work inside today. The weather is so lovely and warm after the days of rain we've had."

Mattie stopped with one foot on the bottom step. "Why did you insist I take my turn, then? You can hang the laundry if you want to."

"*Ne.*" Naomi shook her head and wiped out the empty tub with a rag. "Fair is fair. It's your turn." She gave Mattie a smile. "I know how much you like to be outside."

She hung the washtub on the wall and turned to the rinse tub. Naomi was tall and slender, the opposite of Mattie's own short stockiness. Her hair, which had turned to a soft brown during the winter months, was beginning to lighten to its summer blond where it peeked out from under her *kapp.* Naomi worked with a spare efficiency that wasted no motions. She hung the rinse tub on the wall next to its mate, draped the rag over its hook, and started toward the back door, but stopped when she saw Mattie.

"You haven't even begun yet. What are you doing, standing there? Daydreaming again?"

"You'll be a wonderful wife someday."

Naomi turned her face away. "Are you sure God's plan isn't for me to remain single? A *maidle* caring for *Mamm* and *Daed* in their old age?"

Mattie pulled her bottom lip between her teeth. She shouldn't have said anything. "There is someone for you. Someone wonderful."

"You're kind to say so. But don't worry about me." Naomi

fingered the door latch. "I'll be content, no matter what happens." She slipped inside the door.

Mattie shifted the heavy basket on her hip and crossed the yard to the line strung between the porch roof and the big oak tree. Naomi had never had a beau. The boys who vied for Mattie's attention never noticed Naomi except to eat her pies. They never teased her to join their games or asked her to go for a buggy ride on a spring evening. She never said so, but the slights bothered her. Mattie had heard her crying in the middle of the night when Naomi thought no one would hear, especially after Mattie had been for a buggy ride with Andrew Bontrager or Hiram Mast. There must be someone for Naomi.

Lowering the basket to the ground, Mattie picked up the first shirt, shook it to release the wrinkles, then pegged it to the line.

If the boys ignored her, she wouldn't be as calm as Naomi. At eighteen years old, Naomi should be planning her wedding. She should be filling her wedding chest with quilts and bedding, but Naomi never made anything for herself.

Mattie stopped, a peg halfway onto the line, an apron forgotten in her hands. Why not make something for Naomi's wedding chest herself? Because she could never sit still enough to finish any needlework. Her own quilt was barely started.

She finished hanging the apron and reached for a dress wadded in the basket as an idea swirled through her mind. She could finish that quilt for Naomi. That would show her sister she had faith that there would be a husband for her. That she wouldn't remain a *maidle* forever.

As she hung the last few items of laundry, Mattie tried

to remember where the pieces for her quilt might be. Not in her own chest. She had packed it yesterday for their coming move to Indiana.

At that thought, she looked toward the west. Even though the barn blocked her view, she could see the western mountains in her imagination. Any day now the folks from the Conestoga in Lancaster County would arrive in Brothers Valley, and then they would leave on their journey.

Now she remembered. The quilt had been packed. It was in the barrel, the one with the blue lid, where she had packed her winter shawl and heavy comforter. Daed had already taken it to the barn. If she looked for it now, she could start working on it this afternoon. Naomi needn't know the quilt was for her, she would think Mattie was continuing to sew her own neglected quilt.

Mattie took the basket and bag of clothes pegs back to the porch and hung them in their places. If only she could slip away to the barn before Mamm saw her. With her sister Annie, her husband, and their family coming to share dinner, Mamm would want Mattie's help. But she could find her quilt and be back to help before she was needed.

Mattie ran across the yard to the barn and stopped inside the big open door, catching her breath while she waited for her eyes to adjust to the dim interior. Daed stood on the far side of the center bay, silhouetted against the open door on the other end. Christopher, Annie's husband, stood facing him. Neither of them noticed Mattie.

"We're staying here."

Daed moved to the workbench and dropped a hammer on the wooden surface with a thump. When Mattie saw the expression on his face as he turned back to Christopher, she knew she should make herself scarce. She slid behind some boards standing against the wall next to the door.

"You can't stay here. Our family is going west in a few days. You and my daughter are coming with us."

Mattie peeked out between two of the boards. Eavesdropping was almost as great a sin as . . . as . . . Well, bad enough. She should leave or make her presence known. But she had to find out what was going on. Christopher held himself stiffly. His entire five and a half feet quivered as Daed stepped toward him, a frown on his face as he looked down on his son-in-law.

"We're staying." Christopher squared his shoulders. "I'm not taking my family to the wilderness. It's too dangerous."

"That isn't your only reason though, is it? I saw you talking with Peter Blank last Sunday. You're still in favor of building the meetinghouse."

"I am. I think it's time we let go of the past and move on toward the future. We no longer need to live like our ancestors, afraid of being arrested every time we meet. And hosting the church is too hard for some of the folks. A meetinghouse is the best solution."

"And the Mennonites have meetinghouses." Daed's sarcastic words cut the air.

"I'm not talking about becoming Mennonite. I'm Amish, and that won't change. My family will stay Amish, but we don't need to move to Indiana to do it."

Daed bowed his head. His shoulders sagged. "Annie agrees to this?"

"Of course. I wouldn't make a decision like this unless my wife agreed." Christopher scuffed his foot in the dust on the barn floor. "It isn't easy for either Annie or me, this separation. But we both know you and I would come to an impasse sooner or later. I believe with all my heart that we as Amish need to progress or die. Change is coming, Eli. You need to face that, not run away from it."

Daed's head shot up, his dark eyes lit with fire. "I'm not running. Indiana holds new opportunities for us. For all of us." His expression softened as his voice dropped. "Christopher, come with us. We want you and Annie close. We want to watch your Levi and little Katie grow up."

"Our minds are made up and talking won't change them." Christopher took a step back. "I'll help you load the wagons tomorrow."

"Send us on our way?" Daed turned back to the harness he had been mending, his voice again holding a bitter edge. "We don't need your help. You've made your choice."

Mattie wiped her eyes with the hem of her apron. Christopher hesitated for a few seconds, but when Daed didn't turn from his work, he left the barn.

Wiping her eyes again, Mattie started to follow him, but a sound from the workbench made her turn back. Daed leaned on his elbows, his face buried in his hands, his shoulders shaking as a quiet, sobbing groan escaped. Mattie slipped out the door.

A burning sensation rose in Mattie's breast, constricting her throat. If Annie hadn't married Christopher, this wouldn't be happening. If it wasn't for him, Annie would come west with them. She would walk behind the wagon with her sisters just as they had done when they came to Brothers Valley from the Conestoga ten years ago. They would play games as they walked, and make up stories—

Mattie drove the thoughts away. She couldn't change Christopher's mind, and it was no use blaming him for making a decision he thought was best for his family.

But, oh! If only he had decided to come with them. What did Amish have to do with new ways and meetinghouses anyway?

Mamm was at the table with her back to the door when Mattie walked in. Annie sat on the opposite side, holding little Katie, her baby. Two-year-old Levi was in Mamm's lap. Naomi, sitting next to Annie, looked up as Mattie came near, her eyes red from crying.

Annie had told them the news.

Without a word, Mattie slid onto the bench next to Mamm and handed her a clean handkerchief from the waistband of her apron. Levi looked from Mamm to Annie and back again.

Mattie took a cookie from the jar on the table and handed it to her nephew. "Here, Hansli. Have a cookie."

She set him on her own lap as Mamm sniffed back her tears.

Annie reached across the table toward her mother. "I'm sorry. If there was any way for us to go with you, you know I would. But this is our home."

Mamm nodded, controlling her tears. "*Ja, ja, ja*. I know. But we will miss you." She looked at her oldest daughter then. "Perhaps sometime you might follow us?"

Annie watched their hands, entwined in the table's center. "Who knows what the future holds? Perhaps God will call us to go west someday."

The front door opened. Christopher took one step into the room, his normally pleasant face grim. "Annie, we must go home."

Mamm hiccupped. "You were going to stay . . . it's dinner-time."

Christopher shook his head. "*Ne*, we won't eat here today." He held out one hand. "Levi, come home with Daed."

Mattie lowered the little boy to the floor and he ran to Christopher. Annie slowly let go of Mamm's hand and rose. She didn't look back as Christopher closed the door behind them.

Naomi rose from the table, motioning for Mattie to follow her out the back door.

When they reached the porch, Mattie whispered, "We can't leave Mamm alone, can we?"

Her sister took her hand. "Right now Mamm needs to cry. When she's done, she'll be back to her usual self, but she won't let herself cry while we're in there."

Naomi was right. "How do you know things like that? You always know what someone needs and I never do. I wouldn't have thought that she wants to be alone."

"I saw it on her face. She didn't want to cry in front of us."

She sat on the top step and Mattie sat beside her, leaning her elbows on her knees and resting her chin in her hands. "How long should we wait?"

"For a while. Dinner is in the oven and will be done soon. Mamm should feel better by then."

"I never really thought Annie wouldn't go west with us."

"She needs to stay with her husband."

"Is that what it's like when you get married? Whatever your husband decides, you have to do?"

Naomi brushed some flour off her apron. "Annie said she agreed with Christopher."

"But you saw how miserable she is. And Mamm doesn't

want to go west. She agreed because Daed wants to. If she had her way, she would never leave Brothers Valley."

Naomi scooted down to the next step and leaned back with her elbows propped behind her. "The Bible says that when two people marry, they become one flesh. I suppose married people have to agree on things, or else they'd be torn apart."

"But would you agree with some man if he wanted to do something awful like take you away from your family?"

"First of all, I wouldn't marry 'some man.' If I ever get married, it will be to the man who loves me." Naomi crossed her legs at the knee and bounced one foot in the air. "And second, he would be my family, not you." She bounced her foot again.

Mattie felt a little sick. "You would choose him over me?"

Naomi looked up at her, smiling. "Of course, even though I would hope I will never have to make that choice. But you will do the same thing when you marry Andrew, or whoever wins your heart."

"Never." Mattie shook her head. "If he doesn't do what I want, then I'll head west to Oregon or somewhere without him."

Naomi grinned. "You just wait until you fall in love, like Annie did. Nothing will be as important as being with your husband."

Mattie didn't answer but watched a male robin chase another away from the oak tree. Andrew Bontrager would never win her heart. Only one boy had ever come close to doing that, but when he arrived from the Conestoga, he probably wouldn't even remember her.

Author's Note

Genealogy is a dangerous hobby. You never know where it might lead you!

Several years ago I started searching through records for the story of my father's side of the family. He had done extensive research and had published a book with the tales from our family tree, but there were stories in that book that called me to dig further.

What I found was that my Brethren and Mennonite ancestors had started out in Pennsylvania before they moved to northern Indiana in the 1850s. I found that the route they took from Lancaster County, through western Pennsylvania, Ohio, and ultimately to Indiana, took them through established Amish settlements. I found evidence that showed my Mennonite and Brethren ancestors had descended from some of the first Amish settlers in Lancaster County. They came from Europe in ships named the *Charming Nancy* and the *Francis and Elizabeth* in the 1740s, settling in communities called Northkill and Conestoga.

That's when the questions started: Why did my ancestors move from the Amish faith to the Mennonite and Brethren churches? When did that happen? How did it affect the rest of their families? This book is the story of that journey of discovery.

As I dug into Amish and Mennonite history, armed with some wonderful resources and my ancestors' records, a story developed. The story of a family, facing a changing world and a changing church, who decides to emigrate west to leave chaos behind in search of a promise.

This is a work of fiction, otherwise known as "filling in the gaps." I went beyond the bare facts of several different family lines to tell what *might* have happened. I hope you enjoy this first installment, and join in as the story continues to unfold.

Acknowledgments

No writer works alone.

My poor family. You have been so patient as I spent many, many hours on my computer, scouring bookstores, visiting museums, and reading instead of making supper. Thank you, guys, for stepping around my piles of research books.

I'd like to thank my friends for pretending my imaginary characters were real, and listening politely as I'd tell you what was new in Hannah's life. The Ladies Bible Study of Black Hills Community Church prayed me through my deadlines. Thank you!

I would also like to thank my agent, Sarah Freese of WordServe Literary, for everything she did to make this book a reality.

And without my editor from Revell, Vicki Crumpton, no one would have read Hannah's story. Thank you, Vicki, for all your hard work.

I'm indebted to researchers who went before me to make

the historical facts clear: Steven M. Nolt, Donald B. Kraybill, and David L. Weaver-Zercher—to name a few. I have pored over your works for so long, I feel like we've met over a research table in a quiet library.

Finally, thank you to the staff of the Mennonite Historical Library of Goshen College, Goshen, Indiana. I haven't yet spent as many hours in your facility as I would like, but I appreciate the time and effort you have made to gather such a fascinating collection. It is an invaluable resource. I'll be back for more visits.

Jan Drexler brings a unique understanding of Amish traditions and beliefs to her writing. Her ancestors were among the first Amish, Mennonite, and Brethren immigrants to Pennsylvania in the 1700s. Their experiences are the basis for her stories. Jan lives in South Dakota with her husband, their four adult children, two active dogs, and a cat. When she isn't writing, she enjoys hiking the Black Hills and the Badlands. She is the author of the Love Inspired novels *The Prodigal Son Returns*, *A Mother for His Children*, and *A Home for His Family*.

Meet
Jan Drexler
www.jandrexler.com

Learn about the Amish

Find recipes, sewing, and quilting patterns

And more!